Time and the River

By
Rosetta Khalideen

Published by:
Pine Book Writing
www.PineBookWriting.com
R-10225 Yonge St Suite #250, Richmond Hill, ON L4C 3B2, Canada.
Copyright © 2023 Rosetta Khalideen

ISBN: 979-8-9889621-8-2

All rights reserved.

Time and The River is a work of fiction. Names, characters, businesses, organizations, places, events, and incidents are the product of the author's imagination or are used fictitiously. Any resemblance to actual persons living or dead or locales is entirely coincidental. No part of the content in this book may be replicated or employed for any literary purposes by any means without the permission of the copyright owner and publisher.

For my daughters, Nadira and Subrina - *Love* is life's greatest gift to be treasured.

Acknowledgment

I am grateful to the Team at Pine Book Writing for their assistance in bringing this book to fruition. Sincere thanks to Emerald Anthony for the editorial guidance and advice. Thanks also to my friends Diana Jilwah and Molly Ungar for their helpful feedback. Last but not least, this book would not have been possible without the support and encouragement of my husband. Thank you for believing in me.

Time and the river

Will bring my love to me

If I must, I'll wait forever

By the river that took her to the sea.

- **Nat King Cole**

CHAPTER 1

With figures going around and around in her head, Janet Ramphal, who was deeply engrossed in her budget report, was interrupted by her Assistant, Syd Nichols' half-hearted voice, "I'm sorry to disturb you, Janet. I know you're extremely busy with your report, but there's someone here to see you. I realize it's not the best time to barge in on you right now... Even though he doesn't have an appointment, this gentleman here insists that you wouldn't say no to seeing him... He insists it's really important that he speaks with you."

Syd appeared apologetic, well aware that Janet did not like to be interrupted by unannounced visitors, especially when she was racing against the clock to meet critical budget deadlines. Janet noticed Syd nervously fiddling with her desk nameplate, which read, "*Dr. Janet Ramphal - Director, University Affairs.*" Janet instantly figured out Syd's nervous gesture, which typically indicated that she had taken a course of action that might not sit well with Janet.

Janet looked up from her desk, where a stack of papers threatened to spill over. In a soft voice, she inquired, "If he doesn't have an appointment, as you mentioned, does he at least have a name?" Janet's typically gentle tone still unnerved Syd, who fully knew that during the university's budget season, when Janet was carefully making the yearly financial plans for *University Affairs,* she preferred not to be disturbed. She had once jokingly said to Syd, "During budget time, even if God drops by - and no, I don't mean my husband, I mean the real deal; He would still have to schedule an appointment."

However, the persistent gentleman waiting outside the door declared he had come all the way from Toronto to pay Janet a surprise visit, which is why he hadn't contacted her. He claimed to be an old friend of Janet whom she would certainly want to see. As Syd assessed him, from his salt-and-pepper-grey-black hair to his lilac-colored shirt, brown slacks, and brown loafers, she found him handsome, with a polished, respectable, and classy appearance. Hence, Syd concluded that he was harmless.

"Syd, did you hear me? Does the visitor have a name?" Janet's question, soft and firm, broke into Syd's train of thought.

"Yes, sorry, Janet. He said his name is Abe... Abe Beechan... I think. He said you know him as AB. He seems to be a Guyanese. I can tell by his accent, which is similar to yours."

Janet's pen flew out of her hand and rolled under her desk. Her eyes grew wide with alarm. "What ... what did you say is his name? AB ... are you sure?" she asked in astonishment.

Syd was unaccustomed to seeing Janet so flustered and wondered if she had misjudged the gentleman. "He said he's an old friend, and his name is Abe or AB," Syd repeated.

"He was confident that you would want to see him, but if you can't do so now, I can make an excuse on your behalf and add him to your appointments for later in the week."

"Hmmm... Yes... yes, I think I know who he is. Sorry, Syd, I'm just surprised that he's here." Janet seemed to quickly recover from her initial confusion.

Syd continued, "Well, that's what he wanted... for you to have a pleasant surprise, which is why he didn't contact you prior to his visit. So, will you see him now or a bit later?"

Janet cautiously asked, "Did he mention the reason for his visit?"

"No," replied Syd. "He just pleaded that it was urgent to meet with you."

Before Syd could finish, Janet interrupted her explanation. "Oh, don't bother. Yes... Yes, I'll see him. Give me ten minutes to finish this budget line. Show him to the meeting room and let him know I'll be with him shortly."

Syd was happy to comply. Her hurried retreat allowed Janet to compose herself and control her erratic heartbeat. She wondered what in heaven's name Abe Baichan was doing outside of her office. She had not seen him for the last twenty-eight years. She thought, "This can't be true!" Maybe she was dreaming. Maybe Syd had mistaken his name. But she fully knew that there was no mistake. It had to be AB, whom she never expected to see again, at least not in this lifetime.

Unanswered questions surfaced: Why was Abe here? What did he want? Did his wife finally find out about her relationship with him? Was there a problem that would now challenge her own marriage? She thought of Nat, her husband, who would sometimes unexpectedly seek her out for advice on an urgent issue he might have encountered as a professor in the Social Sciences Faculty. What if he came by, and Syd told him she was meeting with an old friend from Toronto who had unexpectedly come to visit her? What explanation would she offer if asked? She had never ever mentioned Abe to Nat.

"Get a grip on yourself, Janet," she said to herself. She knew the only way to make sense of Abe's unannounced visit was to walk over to the meeting room and find out. She wondered if she would recognize him. What did he look like after all these years? Would he recognize her?

Janet tried to finish the calculation on which she was working. Ten minutes later, she got up and took a quick peek at herself in the mirror, which hung behind her office door. Her navy-blue suit was flattering, and though her fading makeup could not fully conceal the lines around her eyes and mouth, she was undoubtedly an attractive woman. She chided herself for wondering if Abe would still see her as attractive. She straightened her shoulders, composed herself, pasted a smile on her face, and confidently strode across the hallway. The door to the meeting room was closed. Janet took a deep breath, turned the thick brass knob, and braced herself, not knowing what to expect.

Abe was sitting there, an older man of sixty-eight, but he was still AB from the smile that played on his lips and the warm brown eyes that could pierce the depth of her heart. He rose to greet her. She observed his shirt neatly tucked into the waistband of his trousers as his long but now veined hands reached out to take hers. She extended her own hand, her fingers barely brushing his.

"Hello, Janet," Abe greeted her warmly, his voice projecting strength and confidence. "How have you been? My goodness, you haven't aged a day!" he exclaimed, clearly impressed.

"Look, I'm sorry to barge in on you like this, but I really needed to talk with you," Abe continued, his tone apologetic. "I hope you're not upset with me for just showing up. If you're busy and can't talk right now, that's perfectly fine. I can leave and come back at a more convenient time. I didn't mean to put you on the spot," he added, his words tumbling out in a rush.

Janet's mind was racing as she tried to process Abe's sudden appearance. She couldn't help but notice the familiar deep, throaty quality in his voice that had remained unchanged over the years.

"How are you, Abe?" she managed to ask, trying to maintain a sense of composure despite her inner turmoil. "This is quite a shock. But no, I'm not upset," she assured him. "I'm just taken aback, to be honest. It's hard to believe that you're actually here." As she spoke, Janet's hand, not caught in Abe's, reached out to grasp the back of a nearby chair, hoping to steady her nervous frame. Her mind was a whirlwind of questions and emotions, but she knew that she needed to maintain her composure and listen to what Abe had to say.

Abe's gaze locked onto Janet's, his expression earnest. "I can't believe I'm here either," he admitted. "I feel a bit foolish for showing up unannounced like this. I'm sorry if I caught you off guard, but I just had this strong desire to see you. I realize I probably should have let you know, but I acted on impulse," he explained, and his words hinted at regret.

Janet couldn't help but reminisce about Abe's impulsive nature. It was the same trait that had led him to ask her out on their first date when she was just sixteen years old. They had met on San Souci, the island where they both lived, and had taken refuge under the branches of a tall mangrove tree on the beach. They had indulged in stolen mangoes, the juice running down their arms as they furiously ate them. Abe had even attempted to lick the sweet juice off Janet's arms, tickling her sensitive skin and making her burst into uncontrollable laughter. As they huddled together, laughing, and splashing each other with salty seawater, their loud and carefree joy caught the attention of a lone fisherman who was casting his net nearby. Curious, he approached the young couple to see who they were.

The fisherman recognized the girl as the daughter of the school principal, Daniel Ramphal, a well-respected educator and lay preacher known to everyone on the island. Shocked - he couldn't believe that Daniel Ramphal's daughter was out cavorting with a boy, especially one from the Baichan family. Back in the day, it was well-known that teenage girls, especially someone as young as Janet, were not allowed to be with boys unescorted and unsupervised. It was still the 1960s, and San Souci, being an island far removed from the mainland and the city, still held onto the cultural thinking of the 1950s. Unseen, the fisherman made a mental note to inform Mr. Ramphal of Janet's escapade.

Janet was a fourth-generation Indian of East Indian descent. Her ancestors were originally from Bihar and were brought to Guyana as indentured laborers by the British colonizers after the abolition of slavery. Like other East Indians in the country, they brought their language, religion, culture, and traditions with them. They were quite similar to the Africans who came before them, who contributed to shaping the cultural fabric of the new land.

As time passed and generations went by, the culture of the Indian homeland became interwoven with those of the First Peoples, freed slaves, and the colonizers in Guyana. Nevertheless, many of the original values and traditions remained, which were primarily enforced by the elders of the Indian community. Some Indian families, while still adhering to their customs and beliefs, also adopted European or African values into their daily lives and were seen as more progressive. The Ramphals were one such family who respected their traditions while embracing more modern ideas.

As a school principal and educator, Daniel Ramphal had rejected some of the traditional Indian social norms, which he deemed to be outdated and backward, and instead aligned himself with more progressive thinking. He was a political figure in San Souci and hosted regular social gatherings at his home for influential people on the island, with his wife and children in attendance. His wife, Bernice Ramphal, served on the Board of the Anglican church and was actively involved in the Women's Institute. Thanks to her parents' forward-thinking, Janet had access to a complete education. She even participated in extracurricular activities that took her to the city for days or weeks at a time.

Despite his progressive and open-minded approach toward education, there were certain aspects of Indian culture that Daniel Ramphal still adhered to, including conservative attitudes toward dating. Janet, like other East Indian girls, was expected to wait until she was older and had a job before dating because that would give her independence. But even then, her parents would still have a direct say in her choice of life partner. Janet had described this as 'a mixture of the European way and the Indian way' when her mother had explained it to her.

Regardless of people's reluctance to admit it, the social class system that was similar to India still existed in San Souci's cultural fabric. Girls and boys were expected to find partners within their own social standing. However, Janet was not very conscious of her upper-class Western upbringing and the higher social standing of her parents. She never paid attention to whom she befriended, and in fact, she had many friends from low-income families who struggled to get by. Their parents often worked as laborers in the thriving San Souci rice industry while Janet lived in a huge white bungalow facing the ocean with a maid to tend to her needs. Some of her closest friends still lived in mud huts, called *logies*, which were a leftover community from the days of the sugar plantations.

The island of San Souci suffered when sugar fell out of favor, and the rice industry replaced it. Many local San Soucians did not have the means or the inclination to pursue the education necessary to find employment in the civil service. Few who had the finances became rice field owners, the ones with strong arms, laborers in the fields, and the ones with a vision focused their sights on the civil service. Janet's family fell into this last group. Luckily for Janet, her fore-parents had found careers in the teaching profession. Her great-grandfather was a school principal, and so was her grandfather and now her father. Through five generations, the family climbed the social and financial ladder, going from indentured laborers to educators. In San Souci, one's occupation and income determined social class, and Janet's family was part of the upper class due to their successful careers in education.

Abe, on the other hand, came from an economically disadvantaged family. His father passed away when he was only five, and his mother still toiled in the rice fields to provide an education for him and his two brothers. They were not destitute, but they lacked the privileges that Janet enjoyed in her life. When the fisherman told Daniel Ramphal that he had spotted Janet at the beach with Abe and suggested that "something was going on between them," the expected consequences were significant.

"Don't you ever dare try this again, young lady," warned Janet's mother sternly. "While you may be the brightest in your class, if boys become your new interest, you might have to cut short your studies. Abe should know better than to encourage this behavior. You are just a kid, and he is your teacher. How will you face your friends at school? What will they say about your father, who always preaches good values to his students? I expected better from you, and I want you to remember that we will never agree to you being with a boy such as Abe. He does not fit amidst your social class, and his mother is just a laborer. It's time for you to focus on your studies and not get involved in inappropriate relationships."

Janet was insulted and demeaned by her mother's words, which made her feel insignificant. She vowed that no one, including Abe, would make her endure such scolding from her mother again.

Since Abe was a young teacher in training at Janet's school, where her father was the principal, it was no surprise that he was summoned to the principal's office the following day and strongly reprimanded. Daniel Ramphal made it clear that a notation would be placed in Abe's personnel record. As a teacher, he had no business dating a young student. Not only was he violating the school's policy, but he was also defying social norms. Abe had profusely apologized to Daniel Ramphal and was acutely aware that there was now a black mark on his teaching record. In order to keep his job and demonstrate that this was a one-time lapse in judgment, Abe promised that he would not meet with Janet again.

Despite the consequences, Abe never regretted his impulsiveness. A few days after the incident, he confessed to Janet during a quick chat in the lab that he would do it all over again despite promising her father that there wouldn't be a repeat. However, for Janet's sake, he stayed away from her until they coincidentally bumped into each other at the School Track and Field Championship.

Every year, the five schools on San Souci Island participated in a track and field competition to win the prestigious Bruno Benjamin trophy, which the Minister of Education provided. The preparation for this event was a joint effort between the teachers and students, with everyone taking on small and large tasks to ensure their school would win the trophy. Janet, who was the Student President for her Athletic Home, was responsible for securing refreshments for her teams. This involved carrying large platters of fruits, vegetables, and desserts from the caterer to the competition grounds on the day of the event.

As Janet carried the platters of refreshments, she looked up at the clear blue sky and appreciated the beautiful day for the athletics championship. The event was always carefully planned, and everyone worked hard to ensure it was a success. May was typically the chosen month for the championship, as senior high school exams were usually completed by the end of April. Janet had already written her exams and felt confident about her performance. Even though she could have waited until the following year, Janet decided to take her senior high school exams early. Her Dad believed that attempting the exams early would allow her the chance to retake them if needed, which was highly unlikely.

Janet was lost in her thoughts as she made her way toward the Athletics Hall, not realizing that she was nearing Mr. Henry's stable, where several horses were tethered. It was the halfway point of her journey, and she had a tray of fruits in her hands that she was struggling to balance. Suddenly, she noticed Abe in the distance, waving frantically and shouting at her. However, his words were muffled, and she couldn't make out what he was saying, except that it seemed to be about the horse.

As Janet approached the stable, Abe ran towards her, continuing to wave frantically and yelling something about the horse. Without warning, he collided with her, and they both fell to the ground. It turned out that one of the horses didn't like people passing too close and would kick out with its hind legs in protest. Abe had been trying to warn Janet to stay away, but she couldn't hear him. The horse's hoof landed a direct blow to Abe's chest, causing a resounding thud as they both fell onto the soft earth, with Janet caught between the fallen fruits under her and Abe's body on top of her.

Abe tried to shout, "Move… Quickly…" But he was out of breath and writhing in severe pain. Even then, he was prepared to take another kick from the horse if it meant saving Janet. She pulled away and rolled from under him as the horse again raised its legs. This time, Abe was also able to roll out of reach while the angry animal desperately tried to break loose from the straps that secured him to the wooden rails of the stable.

Abe tried to speak again, but his words were muffled by the blood now seeping from his mouth. Janet quickly put her hands under his neck and tried to elevate his head. "Abe, are you okay? You seem to be badly hurt. That horse actually kicked you. Look at me," she pleaded with him, her voice trembling with fear.

Abe weakly opened his eyes and tried to focus. His whisper was almost inaudible, "Get help, Janet." Without a moment's hesitation, Janet tore off the apron she was wearing to transport the food and used it to cushion Abe's head, hoping this would make it easier for him to breathe. She wiped the beads of sweat that were beginning to form on his forehead and put her lips close to his ear, whispering, "Hang in there, Abe. I'll be back with help in seconds."

Janet galloped like a wild horse across the distance, which separated her from the Athletics Hall. At her dramatic, out-of-breath entry, the students and teachers who were helping with the food and beverage distribution stopped and looked at her, the surprise clear on their faces. "It's Abe," she shouted, "He's badly hurt, kicked by that wild horse at Henry's stable … and he's bleeding."

"What!" exclaimed Devin Ghorban, the school's vice-principal. "Where is he?"

"He's next to the stable, lying in the dirt. Please, you must hurry to help him," cried Janet.

"Let's go check on Abe," said Devin to his assistant, who was putting away bottles of coke in a cooler.

"Hurry, please hurry," pleaded Janet. "He's badly hurt."

Devin and his assistant rushed out the door, followed by some of the other students who joined them in running towards the stable. Janet, finally feeling the weight of the situation, broke down in tears. Her friend Chandra, who was on the other side of the room, quickly made her way over and embraced Janet in a warm hug. "I hope he's going to be okay, Janet. What happened?" With an uncontrollable stream of tears and sniffles, Janet recounted what had occurred.

Chandra attempted to comfort her by saying, "I'm so sorry. It's possible that he isn't seriously injured. That horse has kicked so many people in the past, and they've all pulled through." She added, "I'm certain Mr. Ghorban will get him to safety and take him to the hospital."

Abe spent the night at the island's cottage hospital due to severe chest pains, but fortunately, he was going to recover. Medical examinations revealed that he had neither broken ribs nor punctured lungs. Despite the incident, nobody seemed to know what had actually caused the horse to target Abe. He remained tight-lipped, and even the most determined interrogators wouldn't have been able to extract the truth from him. The story that circulated around the island was that Abe was on his way to the caterer to assist with carrying some food trays for the staff, and on his way back, he got too close to the horse and stumbled, causing the sandwich tray that he was carrying to fly into the horse's face. This, in turn, aggravated the animal and led it to attack him.

Once the news of the incident reached Janet's father, he immediately placed the blame on Abe, accusing him of being careless and neglecting important matters. Janet was afraid to disclose the truth to her father because she feared he might not believe her when she said she had not planned the encounter with Abe; then, there would be severe consequences - threats and even more misery.

Janet managed to visit Abe a few days after the incident by pretending to visit her friend Chandra, who had arranged for them to meet. Janet brought a bunch of wildflowers and a cassette recording of their favorite songs. She hugged Abe tightly upon seeing him and expressed gratitude for saving her life. She asked him why he had risked his own safety, pointing out, "You could have been killed. What if the horse had kicked you in the head or the face? Oh, I don't want to even think about it!"

Being his practical self, Abe replied to Janet's concerns by saying, "I'm not dead, Jan. I'm still here. The doctor said I was lucky. Although I have a slight internal injury to my left lung, I sure will be okay."

"I'm relieved to hear that," replied Janet. "I do feel guilty that nobody knows the truth. My father has no idea that you saved his daughter from what could have been a terrible ordeal," said Janet.

"I don't want him to know either, Jan. I don't need his gratitude," Abe responded. "What matters is that you're safe. You don't have to tell your parents a thing about what happened." Janet heeded his advice and never revealed the truth. She carried that secret sewn up within the pocket of her heart.

Abe gazed deep into Janet's eyes and spoke firmly, "If that horse had kicked you, Jan, I would have killed him with my bare hands. I love you and would do anything for you. Try me. Ask me for a piece of my finger, and I'll gladly give it to you."

Janet burst into laughter, rhetorically exclaiming, "Are you out of your mind!"

Undeterred, Abe pulled out his old, fragile switchblade and said, "Nothing to laugh about, Jan. I'm serious right now."

Realizing the gravity of his words, Janet threw herself at him, pleading, "Stop, Abe. I do believe you. I've never doubted you." She hugged him close, feeling every beat of his heart thudding through her cotton shirt, and she finally gazed into his eyes as she added, "I love you, and I'll love you forever."

That was her promise - Forty years had passed since Janet made that promise to Abe. And now, she was married with three grown-up daughters and a husband who was probably not very far away.

CHAPTER 2

Abe expressed his understanding if Janet did not wish to see him, "If you do not want to see me, I'll completely understand your reservations, and I'll respect them. However, I felt it was necessary to take my chance and ask if I could have a few minutes of your time. Right now? Later today or even tomorrow?"

Janet's thoughts were interrupted by the question, and as she was drawn back to the present, she replied, "Of course, I'm willing to talk with you. My assistant mentioned that you came here all the way from Toronto. Are you exclusively here to see me, or do you have other business to attend on Windermere Island?"

"No, I'm here merely to see you. Janet, I genuinely would like to talk with you," Abe's eyes implored her.

Janet's curiosity was piqued, and she couldn't resist asking, "Now if you knew where I work, why didn't you try to contact me through a phone call, email, or find any other means to reach me before coming to meet me in person? Any information about my office is publicly available. I assume that's how you found me, so you could have easily reached out before showing up here. What would you have done if I was not here?"

Abe responded rather sheepishly, "I understand that it was a chance I had to take. I didn't want to make prior contact with you because I was afraid you might say that meeting with me would be impossible. I'm certain you would've provided me with ten good reasons why I shouldn't see you, and I would have wanted to respect your wishes. But here I am, sitting before you, and you have every right in the world to still deny my request and say that spending a few minutes with me is not going to happen."

She tucked a stray lock of hair behind her ear as if to help her think more clearly. "You're here, and I'm willing to talk with you. It's just that I'm shocked and speechless at the moment. I never even wildly imagined that one day, you and I would sit facing each other across a desk in this meeting room. I've conducted countless meetings here, but never one like this!"

Abe smiled once again with that slow, deliberate smile curved on his lips that had charmed her since the first day she crossed paths with him. "Would it possible for us to meet somewhere else, perhaps off-campus, where we could have a quiet conversation, where it's a little more conducive? Maybe a coffee shop would be a good idea?"

"Where are you staying?" Janet asked him politely. "Did you just arrive on the island today, or have you been here for a while?"

"I'm staying at the Fairview," he replied. "I arrived two days ago, and I ended up renting a cottage in Port Whaley for a month through a very good friend whom I've known for almost twenty years. He used to come down here to Windermere Island with his family over the summer vacations. He absolutely loves Canada's west coast. Now, his kids have grown up, and his wife passed away almost three years ago.

As a matter of fact, he barely gets the chance to use the cottage. And so, when I told him I was hoping to be in Windermere for a while, he insisted that I stay at his place in Port Whaley. But as you know, Port Whaley is a bit of a distance from here, so I found it more convenient to stay at the Fairview for a few days until I could finally see and meet you," Abe explained. "Would you be able to have dinner with me this evening, Jan? Can you manage to get free from work by 7:00?" Once again, he looked at her with pleading eyes.

Janet was keenly observing every move he made and every word that came out of his mouth. She noticed that within a few seconds, Abe had gone from suggesting coffee to having dinner together. "No, I can't, Abe. I have another commitment. We have our research awards ceremony at 6:00, and I'll be tied up until 10:00 this evening."

"What about tomorrow?" he countered.

She opened her iPad, which she always carried to meetings for easy access to Syd or to cater to urgent emails. She carefully skimmed through the calendar and checked her schedule to find a suitable time. Abe watched as she scrolled with her eyes fixed on the screen. After a moment, she looked up at him and said, "I'm sorry, Abe, but I can't make it tonight. I have a prior commitment. But I'm free tomorrow afternoon, from 4:00 onwards. Would 6:00 be good for you? I think that gives us more time if needed."

Janet noticed the visible relief on Abe's face as he said with immense gratefulness, "Thanks, Jan. I know it wasn't exactly right to surprise you like this, and I'm sorry about doing so. But thank you for giving me the chance to see you."

***

Janet placed her iPad back in its case, with her finger still trembling out of slight anxiousness. Then, she asked, "So, how are you doing, AB? What have you been up to all this while?"

Abe smiled at Janet's conscious use of his nickname. "I'm doing fine. Both my boys are now married, and you may have heard that Lizzie and I have been separated for the past sixteen years. She's living in the US with her second husband, whom she met a few years ago. He's an Italian American engineer who works with the City of New York. I've visited New York and seen them a few times, and honestly, they both seem very happy."

Janet expressed her surprise upon learning about Abe's separation from his wife, "I didn't know about Lizzie and you being separated. I've hardly been in contact with my old friends from Guyana. I barely find any time for myself. What about you? Did you also find someone eventually?" She could see the tightening of the muscles in his cheeks as he bit down hard on his lips to control the emotion her question seemed to have aroused.

"If you're asking me whether or not I remarried, my answer is no," he replied with a hint of wretchedness in his voice. "There was someone who came into my life for a short while after Lizzie left, but it didn't work out. I guess I wasn't destined to have a partner that lasted *till death do us part*." He subtly attempted to laugh at his own joke, but Janet could see the sorrow brimming in his eyes that contradicted the gesture.

"I'm sorry that you have to go through such a tough time," she whispered.

"Don't be," he said, clenching her fingers, which she had forgotten he was again holding. She tugged her arm to free her fingers from his grip.

"What is not meant to be will not be," Abe continued. "Life is full of surprises, and even the best-laid plans do not always materialize."

Janet nodded in agreement as she said, "Oh yes, I completely agree on that one." She went on, "So, tell me, what have you been up to lately? What are you doing these days, like as of now?"

"I worked as an Insurance Broker in Toronto for the last twenty-two years, and now I'm retired," replied Abe. "The boys continued to stay with me when Lizzie left. They went to school, finished university, and thankfully landed themselves decent jobs. Andy is now an Accountant at KPMG, and Neil is a teacher with the York Board of Education. Andy has a daughter, Kristy, who is five. Meanwhile, Neil has a son, Carl, who is three, and a five-month-old girl, Julia. I have been blessed with two amazing sons and three wonderful grandchildren. I couldn't have asked for more. We are a racially mixed family, with one daughter-in-law, Sandy, who is from Mexico, and the other, Rosalind, who's from Italy. They are beautiful and wonderful women; they are the daughters I always dreamt I would have, and I found that dream in them."

Talking about his family seemed to have stirred a great pride that was evident in Abe's voice. "What about you, Jan? Do you have any grandkids? From what I remember, you have three daughters, and I'm assuming they're all married?"

"Yes, yes… My two elder girls are married. My eldest daughter, who lives in Manitoba, has a five-year-old boy, Jaime. But it's rather unfortunate that I do not see him very often. My other married daughter does not have any children yet, but we're hoping for it to happen in its own due time. As for my youngest, she continues to search for her Mr. Right."

"She will find him when the time is right," said Abe. "Nothing unfolds before its time. Time and tide are elements that we haven't yet mastered control over."

***

Those words of Abe instantly transported Janet back to San Souci. The island, located below sea level, required protection by six-foot-high concrete walls. She remembered sitting on the old seawall with Abe, holding hands and observing the seagulls fight over a fish that whimpered on the sandy beach, waiting for the next wave to wash it back into the ocean and not land itself in the belly of a hungry gull.

As those memories flooded her mind, Janet recalled how, while they were enjoying an afternoon affair on the old seawall, she realized that Abe was leaving in a few days to attend the Teachers' College in the city. He desperately wished to pursue his professional teaching license over the next two years to secure his job. Janet was distraught upon hearing the news. In fact, she had been angry and vocal about how insensitive she considered him to be in deciding to leave her behind.

At the same time, Abe was surprised, or rather taken aback by her outburst. He went on to remind her, "Jan, you and I both knew this was going to happen. I thought we were prepared to face this. I mean, how many times did we not talk about the future? In fact, you agreed that it was fine for me to pursue my dream and enroll in college full-time. You were the one who encouraged me to ensure that I continue my career in teaching so that when I ask you to marry me, I would have the means to take care of you!"

Janet did not want to admit her unfairness. "I know we talked about this, but what will I do now that it's happening? When you leave for College, I'll be all alone. I cannot bear the thought of not seeing you as often."

"Don't say that silly," he said, tweaking her ears. "I will be home at least every two weeks and write you long letters in between. That way, although you won't see me as often, I'll still be here with you, Jan."

It was almost ten months since they first discussed Abe's plans for college, and Janet had tried not to think about what life would be like without his constant presence. Despite her parents forbidding her from having anything to do with him, Janet followed her convictions and continued having secret dates with him. Now that he was leaving in a few days, her heart was breaking. As warm tears cascaded down her cheeks and then his, he hugged her closer, tightening his grip to give her the reassurance she needed. They sat wrapped in each other's arms for a few minutes before he turned her face towards the ocean, where the waves gently lapped along the shoreline.

Abe then explained to her, "See the waves. They come and go. Neither you nor I can control the tide leaving or returning. That's exactly how life is. Time and tide are beyond our control. We will be separated for a short while, but this has to be. However, I will return to you with time, like the tide. I'll always love you, Jan, no matter what, and I'll continue to do so; this is my promise." He then wiped the tears from her cheeks. "Now, look at me... you need to keep that big smile of yours on at all times. That's what I'll take with me. You don't want me to have a picture of a girl with red and puffy eyes and a wet nose."

She smiled weakly and clung to his sleeves, burying her face in the warmth of his chest. He rocked her back and forth, comforting her like a child, until her sobs subsided. They sat there for hours - crying, laughing, and reminiscing until the sun drifted behind the horizon. That's when Janet knew she needed to go. She hugged Abe one last time and ran all the way home without looking back, charged up the stairs to her room, and refused to have dinner, claiming she was infected with the flu. Exhausted, she fell into bed.

***

The painful memories of that day jarred Janet, dragging her back to the present. "Yes, time and the river, how swiftly they go by. I believe the saying is *'time and tide wait for no man'* or woman to be gender sensitive. Time marches on, and the tide's ebb and flow never stops."

"Except for now," said Abe. "You and me sitting here – it sure does feel like time has come to a standstill."

"Has it?" inquired Janet.

He was about to answer when Syd's gentle knock on the door interrupted whatever he was going to say.

Janet quickly got up and opened the door, grateful for Syd's interruption. Syd told her, "I'm sorry for the interruption, Janet. I should remind you that your next meeting will begin in ten minutes. Is there anything else you need besides the file I gave you?"

"Thanks, Syd. I'll be with you in a few minutes, and that is when we can quickly go over your notes. I can't remember if the meeting is in my office?"

"No! You're in Room 2510 at the end of the building."

"Thanks, Syd, I'll see you in five."

As Syd withdrew, Janet turned to Abe. "I've got to go," she said. "But, we'll see each other tomorrow, regardless. So, let's meet tomorrow at 6:00."

"Where?" asked Abe, "We didn't decide on a place."

"Oh yes! Let me think about a few options." She rubbed her fingers across the crinkled ridges of her forehead, a gesture that Abe could not resist noticing. '*God*,' he thought, '*This woman has not changed in all these years.*' "There's a little restaurant called the Silver Platter, about three blocks from the Fairview. It overlooks the water, and someone from the hotel can help you with directions. I think it's easy for you to walk there. Can you do three blocks?"

"Of course, I can. That won't be a problem," Abe affirmed as he smiled at her. "Are you really assuming that I'm too old to walk three blocks?"

"No. No… You're getting me all wrong. I didn't mean that at all. But I do know that it gets a bit cool in the evenings. So, if you're okay with that, I'll see you at the Silver Platter at 6:00."

"Thanks, Jan… I'm sorry about my unannounced visit. I really hope I'm not creating problems for you in the long run. That's the last thing I want to do to you…"

"If you're concerned about my husband," Janet replied as candidly as possible, "He knows nothing about you. I never shared that part of my life with him or anyone else. I'll simply tell him that I'm meeting a friend, which honestly wouldn't be a lie. I have many male friends with whom I socialize. If you would excuse me, I have to get going for my meeting. I don't want to be late. Shall I ask Syd to see you out? Or you'll easily find your way back to the front entrance? Or would you like Syd to call a taxi for you?"

"No. I'm fine. I'll wander around your beautiful campus briefly and then head back to the hotel. I want to take some pictures of the peacocks. They seem to be strutting all over the lawns. I'll see you tomorrow. And genuinely, I'm so looking forward to talking with you."

He stood up awkwardly, wanting to hug her. But instead, he formally reached for the hand she had previously withdrawn. He clasped her fingers and turned her palm upward, bringing it to his lips. Janet felt a whiff of breath caught in her throat, which she felt would choke her. Janet pulled her hand away from him, conscious about the door being open, fearing that Abe's intimate gesture might rouse gossip among her passing colleagues that would certainly spread like wildfire.

Janet almost muttered as she quickly left the room, "See you tomorrow, Abe." She could still feel the warmth of his breath on her palm and was annoyed by the butterflies flitting around in her stomach. "For heaven's sake," she reprimanded herself, "Just breathe for once, will you! You got over Abe long ago, so you must believe that your feelings for him no longer exist. You are no longer sixteen. In fact, you're a considerably grown woman, too far away from being a teenager feeling all those butterflies within. Get a grip on yourself, Janet. You're still clueless about why he's even here."

***

Janet went through the rest of the day completing her tasks as if in a daze, her thoughts preoccupied with Abe. That evening, as she was having supper with Nat at home, he asked, "Are you okay? You seem to have a lot on your mind." Despite feeling that Nat was often not in tune with her feelings, his perceptiveness surprised her at times.

"It's just work," Janet replied, setting down her fork. "As usual, there were too many problems to handle for a single day. I can't believe how many fires we must put out in *University Affairs*. But let's not talk about work. Did you do anything interesting today?" Janet and Nat made a pact to avoid discussing their work problems during their evening meals, which they usually had together, so they tried their best to stick to their promise.

"How did your meeting with Geoff go?" Janet asked. Geoff Baxter was the teenage son of their next-door neighbor, who was in Grade 11 and working on a Social Studies project that studied the economic life of grassroots people in the Caribbean. He had asked to interview Nat to obtain decent and legitimate first-hand data.

"Geoff asked so many questions, too many in fact," Nat responded. "It's surprising how little Canadians know about the Caribbean. For them, it's just a place with vacation hot spots, beaches, music, and happy people dancing. They know nothing of the culture, history, social structure, or the political and economic factors." Janet was well aware of how passionate Nat always was when it came to his birth region. However, there were times when she had to rein him in because he was getting into a heated debate with someone who knew little about Caribbean geography and history. Nothing riled him up more than when someone offered uneducated pronouncements based on a visit they had made to a resort in Jamaica or the Dominican Republic.

Janet tried to calm him down. "Geoff is only a teenager. He'll gain more knowledge as he matures. By the way, the grilled salmon tastes great, as always. Thanks for making supper tonight."

Nat smiled at Janet, seeing through her effort to distract him. "And as usual, you're very welcome," he replied warmly.

As Janet and Nat prepared for bed that night, Janet shared, "I'll be working late tomorrow. Remember I told you about the Chair of the Board meeting with the senior administrators to discuss the next big fundraising event? Well, he's finally decided to do it over dinner. We're meeting at the Grapevine at 6:00 p.m., so I probably won't be home until around 10:00." She knew in her gut that she was providing more details than usual. However, she strongly felt that her little white lie deemed it essential for her to cover up adequately.

"I don't know how you manage to have meetings at the Grapevine!" exclaimed Nat. "You must have to shout at each other to be heard. Couldn't Nick pick a quieter place?"

Janet knew that Nat disliked the Grapevine as it was often crowded with university faculty who met there for drinks after work. The debates and discussions could get quite loud, and the background music was usually too loud for a quiet conversation, making it rather impossible to talk most times. The restaurant had been renamed from the Purple Grape to the Grapevine because of the gossip that often circulated among the professors, who comprised most of its clientele. The name change, in essence, was seen as an appropriate alignment with the restaurant's atmosphere.

Janet added, "It usually gets quieter after 7:00, so we should be fine. I don't expect the discussions to be too serious. Nick has a good sense of humor, and if we're talking about the challenging subject of fundraising, I'm sure he will find ways to try and keep things light. Now, why don't you get some shut eyes? Go to bed."

Janet gently nudged him to his side of the bed, but before she could roll over to hers, he quickly pulled her close and rubbed her ear. "I sense a storm brewing," he said.

"Hmm, you will have to let it pass on its own. At least tonight, that is how it would have to be," Janet chided. "I'm awfully tired and ready to fall asleep."

He pulled her close and hugged her, placing a gentle kiss on her forehead. "Goodnight," he whispered with his breath reassuring and calming her, as a ritual they had maintained for the past forty years.

She nestled in Nat's arms, her head resting on his chest, as she listened to the steady beat of his heart. Knowing well that in a matter of minutes, he would be asleep, she also tried to lull herself to sleep. But after half an hour of tossing and turning amidst the darkness of her room, she realized that her body clock was nowhere close to wanting to sleep.

She gently disentangled her legs from under the grip of Nat's and then headed to the kitchen for a glass of warm milk. She sat at the kitchen counter, slowly sipping from her favorite mug that read, "I love you, Mom," a gift she loved holding close to her heart, given to her by her youngest daughter. Slowly, she traced the embossed words with the tips of her fingers, staring at them as though she saw them for the first time. Meanwhile, she was lost in thought as she replayed her meeting with Abe from earlier that day.

It all felt so unreal - seeing him after decades, and now, all of a sudden, out of nowhere, in the chaotic mix of her life, having plans to meet him again tomorrow. Feelings of apprehension, excitement, and uncertainty churned in her stomach. She couldn't help but wonder - *What did he want from her?*

Chapter 3

Janet sat on a high chair at her kitchen counter, deeply absorbed in thought about how Abe had left or rather abandoned her decades ago. What right did he have to walk back into her life after all these years...

When he left for the Teachers' College, that is precisely when she really wanted him in her life, and she desperately needed him to return. Instead, he deserted her out of his cowardly nature and shattered her heart into a million pieces. She had sworn never to see him again. But of course, that was when she was young, and her heart was fragile and easily damaged. The memories came rushing back—the salty scent of the sea as they sat huddled in their friend's sailboat, finding herself consumed by anger and overwhelmed with tears while he was at a loss for words.

Abe was away at Dartmouth College for the first few months, so his letters arrived like clockwork, at least thrice weekly. She enjoyed immersing herself in his words, repeatedly reading, re-reading, and savoring every declaration of his undying love. There were moments when the poetry he penned touched her heart and soul so deeply that tears streamed down her face, smudging the ink and dampening the pages. She would painstakingly dry the wet letters, unwilling to lose a single page of Abe's heartfelt expressions. Safely hidden among the books in her room, her little treasure box safeguarded these precious love letters. One of his most beautiful poems was dedicated to her seventeenth birthday, titled *Sweet Seventeen*. The words, "Sweet seventeen, you're mine... Mine alone... No one else will ever have a home in my heart..." lingered with her for countless years.

But after eight months, Abe's letters started arriving less frequently at San Souci, and so did Abe himself. Over time, his excuses began to sound trite - too many assignments, field trips that extended into weekends, and a science project that demanded all of his time.... Janet sympathized with him and criticized his lecturers for overworking him. Playfully pulling his hair, she scolded him for complaining about his workload, "Abe, if you want to excel in what you're doing, you'll have to work hard. I understand that we might not be able to see each other as often as we'd like. It pains me to be away from you, and I can't wait for you to graduate so we can be together forever. But I'm making an effort to understand and support you. I'm just happy knowing you think of me and are committed to your studies and end goal."

"Jan..." he whispered, "What will I ever do without you!"

"You never have to do without me," she scolded. "I will always be here for you."

With time, Janet began to sense that something was not right with Abe. He always seemed distracted, and his letters grew shorter and shorter. By the end of the first two semesters, the time between his visits grew intermittently longer. At first, she gently questioned him about the change in his behavior, but later, her inquiries turned into anger. He was adamant that nothing had changed and that he was simply overwhelmed with his studies. However, Janet remained unconvinced by these explanations and grew increasingly alarmed.

On this warm Sunday afternoon, as they sat in the sailboat as they had done countless times before, observing the ebb and flow of the tide and the seagulls bobbing on the waves, Abe finally confessed that there was a significant problem.

"I don't know how to tell you this, Jan," he began. "Something terrible has happened."

Janet's eyes widened with fear as she asked, "What's wrong, Abe? What have you done?"

"It's not really my fault. I don't know what happened. It's just that ... Oh, Janet, what have I done!" he cried.

He tightly gripped her fingers and placed her open palm on his throbbing heart. She could sense his constriction as his breath began coming in gasps. Bringing her face close to his, he gazed deeply into her eyes and said, "Promise me you won't hate me. Jan, I love you despite whatever you may think of me."

She used the hand resting on his chest to gently push him away. "Abe, you're making me nervous. What's happening? If something is wrong, you have to tell me. I'm sure I'll understand, and I want to help you. Trust me..."

"I trust you, Jan. It's me who can't be trusted," he whispered, taking her hands into his.

"Jan, I've betrayed you. I don't know what came over me. You remember I mentioned Mrs. Waishan to you. She's the lady at whose place I'm boarding and lodging. I'm sure I've spoken about her before, and trust me, she's a truly kind woman. She was helping her niece escape from her abusive, alcoholic father, so she brought her to stay at her place. The girl's name is Lizzie, and she seemed deeply troubled.

One day, Mrs. Waishan asked me to give Lizzie a ride on my bike to a friend's party, as the friend couldn't pick her up as arranged. While we were on our way, Lizzie started crying. She expressed how much she appreciated my kindness in taking her to her friend and how rare it was for someone to show her such genuine compassion. She shared how much she missed her home and how sad she felt.

Lizzie also explained that she lived with an abusive father who was both physically and verbally violent and an alcoholic who also abused her mother and her two younger siblings. Overwhelmed by the situation, she quit her job at an insurance company and came to her aunt's place for a few weeks to reflect on her future. She didn't want to return home. She was awfully disturbed and troubled, so much so that she could barely stop crying.

At that moment, I felt so helpless to not be able to make her crying stop. So, when she begged me to accompany her to the party, I agreed, hoping it was the least I could do to comfort her. When we arrived there, I realized that she had many friends who were already there, having a good time. It didn't take long for her to settle and adjust to the party's atmosphere, and Lizzie's mood lifted soon after.

We had a few drinks together. When it got late, she asked if I could take her back to her aunt's house, so I decided to take her back with me, even though I felt uneasy and honestly a bit scared since she seemed quite intoxicated.

We returned to Mrs. Waishan's and quietly crept in, trying not to wake her up. I went to my room, and Lizzie went to hers. A few minutes later, she knocked on my door, muffling her sobs with her pillow. I allowed her into my room and tried to understand what was happening with her.

She sobbed quietly and asked if she could stay with me. I told her it wasn't appropriate and that we would get into trouble with Mrs. Waishan. But she insisted, and before I knew it, she was in my bed, and I just let her spend the night.

Somewhere in the middle of my sleep, I woke up to find her arms around me. She began kissing me and confessed that she had secretly admired me since arriving at her aunt's home and ever since she fell in love with me. She clung to me, asking if I could love her in return. She kissed me again and stirred this passion within me, and the more the kiss prolonged, one thing led to another... and another.

She seemed lost and in need of protection. Mrs. Waishan always asked me to take her place. She even suggested I take her to the movies one day, but I refused. I believe Mrs. Waishan was encouraging an intimate relationship between us..."

"And well, you did get into a relationship with her... Didn't you?" interrupted Janet.

"Jan, I'm deeply sorry. I know I shouldn't have done this. I was confused... I don't understand what came over me. I shouldn't have given in to her. I'm truly sorry for betraying you. I have no excuses, and I won't insult you by making any. I should never have allowed myself to be in that compromising situation."

"You traitor!" Janet yelled, pulling her hands away from him and rising to her feet in such furious anger that she nearly toppled the boat and almost fell into the water.

"Jan, please listen to me," he pleaded. "I never intended for this to happen. It was very foolish of me. I don't know why I wasn't stronger."

"That's because you're selfish. You're a selfish bastard, which is why you're telling me all this. You're a cheater!"

"Well, you didn't let me finish because there's more that I need to tell you about. Things have gotten worse and way out of my hands at this point," he continued. "She's pregnant, Jan. Mrs. Waishan plans to inform her parents. Her mom might disown her, that is, if her dad doesn't kill her first. And to avoid facing all that, she has threatened to take her life. I have to do the right thing here. I'm just as responsible as she is. I can't leave her to face disgrace."

"What are you going to do?" Janet's voice trembled.

"I will have to marry her. I don't have a choice," Abe wept.

"What!? Do you love her?"

"No, no," he cried, "I don't love her, but I can't abandon her, knowing fully well she might end up dead because of me. I won't be able to live with my guilt of having ruined her life and the regret of not fixing it while I could. It might slowly kill me anyway," and as he finished that sentence, tears streamed down his face. "Please, Jan, I never meant to hurt you. I love you and always will…"

By now, Janet had covered her ears to drown out the sound of his voice. In one swift motion, she leaped off the side of the boat and, treading water, made her way towards the shore. Blinded by her tears and the gentle pull of the lapping waves on her legs, she stumbled repeatedly before reaching the warm sands.

Meanwhile, Abe had also jumped into the water, chasing after her. Finally, he managed to grasp her around the waist as he exclaimed, "Jan, listen to me…"

But she turned around towards him and spat the words out, "Take your filthy hands off me! How dare you! Leave me alone! I never want to see you again." She kicked off her wet sandals and squeezed the water out of her soaked skirt that was hindering her escape as she ran along the beach with sheer determination to set herself free from his presence. Abe could hear the echoes of her harsh words carried by the wind, "I hate you... I really do hate you... And you need to make sure that I never see you again."

He stood on the wet sand, watching as her footprints vanished under the incoming wave, only to reappear briefly before being washed away again. An unbearable coldness seeped into his heart with the realization that he had lost Janet forever. The hatred, or perhaps it was the sheer agony in her eyes, made him feel sick. He wished he could throw up, hoping it would somehow alleviate his pain, but nothing could change the harsh reality that he was now bound to Lizzie. The child that Lizzie was carrying was his, and there was only one decision that he needed to make amidst the mess he had created. He was convinced that Janet was a resilient woman, and so he was certain that someday, she would move on and her life would continue like nothing ever mattered. He did, however, think to himself, "Would I ever be able to forget her?" He knew the answer was *never*, but he couldn't allow Lizzie to face the disgrace of being an unwed mother.

Abe had witnessed the consequences that occurred to other young women from his cultural background who became pregnant out of wedlock and were abandoned by their partners to face the repercussions all alone. Many were often disowned by their parents, particularly if their families were of lower economic and social standing. Some resorted to abortion, yet even then, they couldn't escape the lingering social stigma that haunted them for the rest of their lives. Tragically, some girls took their own lives as an unthinkable escape from the wrath of their families or the judgmental society they lived in. This was the legacy of a culture transplanted from the shores of India, shaped by generations of patriarchy, and now deeply entrenched in San Souci.

Abe accepted full responsibility for Lizzie's predicament and could never even closely consider the idea of abandoning her to face the world alone. She had already suffered immensely at the hands of her abusive father. His sense of decency compelled him to give her unborn child his name. If he had a sister facing the same dilemma as Lizzie, he would expect nothing less from the man who contributed to her pregnancy. However, this decision was far from easy, and he felt a profound sense of disgust at the society that had led him to this moment. As the gentle breeze caressed him, he imagined he could still hear Janet's sobs echoing in his mind, remembering how she had meandered her way on the path that led to her house. Sinking into the soft sand, he paid no heed to the rising water around him. For the thousandth time, he questioned how he had allowed himself to fall into a situation that would forever ruin his life.

Replaying the past events in her mind, Janet remained oblivious to Abe's pain ever since she walked out of his life. Abe, known for his honesty, was always ready to do what was right, regardless of the cost. She finished the last sip of her now-cold milk and returned to bed. Lying there, she tried to envision what her meeting with Abe the next day would bring.

Would he dwell on past mistakes? Was he in some kind of trouble and came around seeking her help? Why did he believe he could still rely on her? What favor did he want from her? What did he truly desire? What if... These questions swirled in her mind until, finally, her thoughts faded away as she drifted into sleep.

Abe, on the other hand, was faring no better than Janet. He tossed and turned on the uncomfortable hotel bed, plagued by restlessness. For the umpteenth time since he had made that decision to see Janet, he questioned his course of action. What gave him the right to burden Janet with his troubles, for that was what it was—a burden he had carried for the past two years. He couldn't comprehend why, upon receiving the latest prognosis from the specialist, his thoughts had immediately turned to Janet.

Three years ago, Abe had stumbled upon a picture of Janet on the internet, and it sparked an unexpected curiosity within him. He eagerly delved into researching her current life, finding bits and pieces of information that encouraged him. He discovered that she was now working at a university on Windermere Island in western Canada, and he had access to many of her articles and publications, which showcased her impressive university career.

Desperate for a more recent glimpse of her, he thoroughly searched the university's website, and his heart sang with joy when he found a more recent picture of her. Though she looked much older than what he last remembered of her, her smile remained the same, and her eyes still held their beauty, even with the delicate lines etched around the corners; she had aged gracefully. In that photo of her, she held one of her recently published books, and Abe noticed the lines of age running from her wrists to her fingers.

For the past three years, he continued to gaze at that picture almost every day. He devoured every piece of news he could find about her. He was well informed that she was involved in a Public Health project in Thailand and that she constantly engaged in giving lectures or attended conferences around the world. Her unwavering passion for social justice resonated strongly, and in all honesty, none of her many accomplishments came as a surprise to Abe. He had always known the young Janet as talented, feisty, courageous, ambitious, and brimming with life. He never doubted that she would have a fulfilling career.

Abe massaged his aching left shoulder, attempting to calm his turbulent thoughts and hoping that his sleepless night wouldn't hinder his encounter with Janet the next day. "I will be a wreck by the time I see her again tomorrow," he murmured to himself. Stepping away from the bed, he made his way to the window and pulled back the heavy curtains. From the twenty-fourth floor, he looked down at the illuminated cityscape, observing the steady stream of cars winding along Main Street. He checked the time. Glancing at the clock, he noted that it was 1:10 in the morning, yet there were people on the sidewalk, bundled up in jackets to shield themselves from the chilly April winds, relishing the night hours at the same time.

Windermere Island, located in Canada's far west, enjoyed relatively warmer temperatures compared to other parts of the country. However, being an island, it retained cool nights even during the summer months. It was also known for its continuous downpours, especially in the winter and early spring.

On this particular night, the sky was clear, revealing a multitude of stars. Abe gazed up at the stars in the night sky, contemplating whether he should once again kneel and seek strength from God for his upcoming conversation with Janet. How would he begin? Would he be able to honestly disclose his deteriorating health and the reason behind his desire to meet her? Or would he experience a last-minute change of heart and leave his mission of traveling all the way to Windermere Island unfulfilled? Brimming with determination, he forcefully drew the curtains together, returning to bed. He fluffed the pillows and nestled under the warm duvet, though there were no instant signs of sleep. Eventually, he drifted off, only to awaken abruptly when his eyes flashed open to see the bedside clock displaying 7:28 a.m.

CHAPTER 4

Janet was rushing back and forth between her morning university meetings, yearning for a strong cup of coffee to energize her. She skillfully dodged one of her colleagues who sought her attention and swiftly entered the bustling food court to grab a quick snack. In her head, she often referred to the food court as the students' *jungle*, considering it one of the noisiest places on earth. Despite the clock showing just past eleven, there was already a significant queue of students waiting in line at Tim Hortons. The food court itself was packed, with most tables occupied by groups of boisterous students who were probably arguing some theoretical concept. Others were engrossed in their laptops or books, likely attempting to tackle their overdue assignments.

"Whew," Janet sighed, "I've landed myself in a zoo!" she muttered under her breath. She joined the queue, which during lunchtime could stretch the entire length of the cafeteria and even spill out through the doors, extending down the hallway to the student lounge. Fortunately, at this time of the morning, the line wasn't that long. Janet considered herself lucky, finding herself at number nineteen in the queue. Nevertheless, it was still a pretty long wait for a cup of coffee. Sometimes, she thought that her love for, or rather addiction to, Tim Hortons coffee made her a true-blooded Canadian, even more than her official certificate of citizenship. Canadians truly loved their Tim Hortons coffee, and she couldn't help but notice that in some cities, there seemed to be a Tim Hortons coffee shop within a six-block radius on the busier streets.

Standing in line with nothing else to do, Janet had a few moments to gather her thoughts. Her mind raced ahead to the impending meeting with Abe. *What did he want?* This question had been echoing in her mind ever since she saw him yesterday. "I'll soon find out," she whispered to herself, determined to uncover the purpose behind their meeting.

The student standing in front of her turned around and asked, "Were you saying something to me, Dr. Ramphal?"

"Oh, hi, Jeremy. I did not realize it was you. No, no. I was just talking to myself," Janet replied with a nervous laugh.

Jeremy smiled and commented, "It's one of those days, huh? I hope things aren't as hectic for you as they've been lately."

Jeremy was a third-year student in the Fine Arts program. He was soon going to graduate, but he encountered numerous financial challenges throughout his program, which required multiple interventions from Janet to ensure that he could continue his studies in the same program. Jeremy was immensely grateful for her support and took every opportunity to update her on his progress.

Syd had once jokingly suggested that Janet should adopt him. She had pronounced, "The boy is looking for a mother. I think he believes you can fill that role. He finds joy in spending time with you and clearly enjoys your attention. There's hardly a week that goes by without Jeremy finding an excuse to see you."

"You're exaggerating, Syd. Might you be jealous?" teased Janet.

Janet reassured Jeremy that all was well. "It's busy as usual, but it can't be that bad. I mean, I'm just standing in line with twenty other students to get a cup of coffee. How bad can it be!" she exclaimed.

Jeremy nodded in agreement and then offered to help her get to the front of the line. "My friend Don is third-in-line. I can ask him to switch places with you. I'm sure he wouldn't mind."

"Thanks for the offer," said Janet, "But I wouldn't dream of jumping the queue. I'll wait my turn. Standing here gives me a chance to think, so it's fine."

"I wouldn't bother you, then," replied Jeremy. "I'll let you get on with your thinking."

Janet's mind again wandered back to Abe. It couldn't be a mere coincidence that brought him back to her world. He must have known her whereabouts for years, so why was he choosing to see her only now? She couldn't shake the feeling that he wanted something from her. Men were often driven by their desires. They would crawl to the end of the world and go to great lengths, disregarding consequences if it meant personal gain. Her career had taught her that, working with ambitious men who would do anything to climb the ladder of fame and fortune. She had witnessed the self-centeredness of men through the spouses of her many friends. Life rarely unfolded as people, especially women, anticipated. There are always missing pieces that sometimes take one's lifetime to discover, and even then, many never find what they're searching for.

She compared that search for a fulfilling *whole* kind of life to the process of assembling a three-thousand-piece jigsaw puzzle that once hung on the wall of her family room. Janet, Nat, and the girls had dedicated many weekend hours to finding the missing pieces and putting them together. It felt like a never-ending cycle of fixing one section of the puzzle, only to realize there were still missing pieces in another section. But after months of assembling, disassembling, and reassembling, the highest Indian tepee on Highway 1 between Maple Creek and Medicine Hat in Alberta came to life in her living room. The completed work of art was framed and proudly displayed over the fireplace.

"Maybe, in the end, pieces of life do come together," Janet mused.

"And what can I get you, Ma'am?" the voice of the barista brought her back to reality.

"One medium coffee, with one cream and one sugar."

"Is that all?"

"Yes, that will be all. Thanks a lot!"

"That would be one dolla sixty-five," the server said, pronouncing 'dollar' as '*dolla.*' The server's British accent reminded her of her own British-Caribbean accent, and she could not help but smile at how amusing it sounded in Canada when non-native or foreign speakers did not pronounce their "*r's.*"

Taking her steaming cup of coffee back to the meeting room, Janet delved into the stack of resumes for the Office Manager's position she needed to fill. In the midst of a struggling economy, it wasn't surprising to see a flood of applications from all kinds of individuals, whether they were qualified, unqualified, or even overqualified. Despite clearly stating the required credentials and experience in the job postings, it seemed like many applicants didn't bother to read the details carefully. People were applying for any and every job opportunity without considering the specific requirements. It was no wonder that the stack of resumes consisted of a diverse mix, ranging from cooks to accountants to doctoral candidates, among others.

A few hours later, Janet met with the hiring committee. They engaged in discussions and debates to determine which candidates should be shortlisted for interviews. After much deliberation, they reached a consensus on their top four candidates. Relieved, Janet excused herself from the group. She made her way to the Administration Team Meeting, commonly referred to as ATM meetings, which brought a sense of amusement among the university staff due to the acronym's association with cash vending machines. Today, Janet appeared unusually disengaged from the discussions, which did not go unnoticed by one of her colleagues. Dave, who was the Dean of Student Services, leaned out of concern towards her and asked, "Janet, are you okay? Is something wrong? You seem awfully quiet."

"No, I'm fine," said Janet. "I'm just having a rough day."

"What an understatement!" exclaimed Dave, "In this place, you tell me when a day is not rough!"

"Shhh," she whispered, "Even if I'm not fully here, I still need to hear some of what's going on, so just be quiet."

He playfully made a mock curtsey before leaving her to her thoughts. A few minutes later, Janet's mind shifted to the upcoming meeting with the group of Program Heads that she would need to slip out to attend. A certain program was facing internal conflicts, and she had to find a resolution before the situation escalated. The constant cycle of meetings crossed her mind, and she mused, "Meetings and more meetings. Life as the University Affairs Director is never dull."

Janet arrived at the Program Heads' meeting prepared for a challenging discussion. She had previously organized multiple meetings with the program faculty, urging them to collaborate on the development of a new program they would jointly offer with a community agency. As a last resort, she had given them an ultimatum to either work together on the curriculum or she would involve another department to take over. She tried to be fair to the faculty members. While some of her colleagues called her *patient and long-suffering*, she also understood the importance of setting boundaries when necessary.

"So," she asked at the beginning of the meeting, "have we reached an agreement as to how we intend to move forward?"

Rhonda Keats, the Head responsible for the program under discussion, raised her hand and joined the conversation. "We have discussed potential changes that can ensure inclusivity in the development of the new program. We are open to establishing a task force to define roles and responsibilities," she explained.

Skeptically, Janet questioned, "And when will this task force be formed?" She was well aware of how task forces and committees were sometimes used as delay tactics in academia. While they could be useful in certain situations, she had encountered many instances where they proved to be ineffective and a waste of time.

"Well, no later than the end of this week," Rhonda replied.

Ron Zaber, Head of the Business Department, interjected, "I don't believe a task force is necessary. Why can't individuals decide for themselves how they want to be involved? It's not such a complicated matter."

Others joined the conversation, expressing concerns about workload, lack of faculty expertise in curriculum development, insufficient finances, and various other issues. The majority voiced their support for establishing a task force. As the discussion went on, time slipped away unnoticed, and when Janet glanced at the clock on the wall, it showed 5:00.

Realizing the need to wrap things up, she reluctantly conceded to the task force idea but charged the group with, "I expect to receive a detailed plan outlining the use of the task force on my desk by Friday afternoon. It should clearly identify the individuals involved, their assigned tasks, responsibilities, and timelines. A *Gantt* chart would be helpful, so you should consider that as an option. Also, I'd like to apologize, but I have another appointment to attend to." Making sure that everyone in the room understood her expectations, she swiftly exited the meeting and headed back to her office.

Syd poked her head into the office just as Janet was reviewing her schedule for the following day. "Don't forget you need to leave at 5:45 for your dinner appointment," Syd reminded her.

"Thanks, I've got it covered," replied Janet. "Are you leaving now?" she asked Syd.

"Yes, I am. Is there anything you need before I go?" Syd inquired.

"Nah, I'm good," said Janet. "Have a great evening yourself. See you tomorrow."

Janet was relieved when Syd left. She felt this strong urge to freshen up her makeup and fix her hair before heading out for her dinner meeting with Abe. She questioned herself silently, wondering why she felt the need to look attractive and impress Abe. Normally, she didn't pay much attention to her appearance, often going through an entire day without glancing at herself in the bathroom mirror. She reached into her purse and rummaged around for her lipstick and compact powder.

Standing before the make-up mirror in Syd's now vacant office, she dabbed some powder on her cheeks and refreshed her worn-out lipstick. Her gaze lingered on her dark brown eyes with their long lashes framed by arched brows. Despite just turning sixty-four, she had no visible wrinkles on her oval-shaped face. Only faint lines around her eyes, particularly when she smiled, hinted at her age. Her hair was mostly black, with a few scattered gray hairs beginning to emerge at the edges. Occasionally, she used a bit of color to achieve a more even tone.

***

Her hairdresser had once expressed disbelief when Janet revealed her age. "You're joking, aren't you?" she had exclaimed.

"No, Rachael. I'm honestly not," Janet responded. "I do look exactly my age, my love. You are just flattering me, and I understand that quite well. Trust me, it doesn't mean you'll get a bigger tip!"

Rachael called out to her colleagues for support. "Janet is claiming she's sixty-four. Can you believe it?"

Everyone in the salon shook their heads in disbelief. "Come on, let's forget about my age and get my hair done," Janet chided. "I need to be out of here within the next forty-five minutes."

***

Janet lightly touched the lines around her eyes, secretly wishing she were fifty instead of sixty-four. "Oh, I don't really care!" she lied to herself. "Abe isn't here to judge my appearance. He wouldn't care if I was pretty or not. I'm sure he's here to ask for something." She knew the only way to find out was to get to the Silver Platter.

Quickly grabbing her handbag and the folder containing her meeting notes for the next day, Janet hurried out of her office, down the stairs, and through the parking lot to her beloved little green Volkswagen Beetle. The Beetle had been her dream car since her teenage years, inspired by the movie *Herbie Goes Bananas*. Not being a fan of yellow, she opted for a green Volkswagen instead but insisted on naming the car *Herb*.

Switching on the ignition, she muttered under her breath, "Herb, instead of you going bananas, it seems like I am." With a gentle purr, the Beetle glided out the main gate and through the sparsely populated streets as Janet made her way toward the downtown area. The streets were relatively calm at this time of the afternoon, with most people already at home. Within ten minutes, Janet had reached her destination.

CHAPTER 5

The Silver Platter bustled with an unusual crowd, forcing Janet to navigate carefully around the tables on the patio. Many patrons sought the remaining rays of the afternoon sun. Janet silently hoped she wouldn't encounter anyone she knew, though it wouldn't matter much. She frequently met business colleagues for meals at the Silver Platter, so anyone spotting her with Abe would likely assume it was a business meeting. Her eyes scanned the dimly lit lounge, where the hum of conversations emanated. She followed the trail of artificial hurricane lanterns, leading her into the more spacious dining area.

Seated in one of the booths was Abe, who had exchanged his lilac shirt for a dark blue cardigan, accentuating the bronze tone of his face. As he noticed Janet's arrival, he stood up to greet her. The familiar awkwardness of deciding whether to shake hands, hug, or simply exchange greetings washed over them once again.

"Hi, Abe," Janet exclaimed, catching her breath.

"Hi, good to see you again, Janet. How are you?" Abe inquired.

"I'm fine. Did you arrive early?" Janet noticed the empty coffee mug on the table.

"Not too early. I went for a walk and decided to come in and have my favorite café mocha while waiting for you. Is this table okay? Or do you have a preferred spot?" he asked.

"No... I mean, yes... here is fine," Janet responded. "We have a great view of the ocean."

The space was a bit tight, but Janet managed to squeeze into her seat. She typically avoided booths in this particular restaurant due to their cramped nature. She preferred the open tables, but she guessed Abe had chosen a booth to provide them with a bit of privacy. Abe slid his legs in and settled back into his seat. Two menu cards were lying next to Abe's coffee cup.

Abe handed one to Janet and asked, "Will you have something to drink?"

"I'll have a chamomile tea. I find a nice cup of tea to be most soothing at the end of a tiring workday," Janet replied.

"You don't look tired. Had a hard day?" Abe inquired.

"The usual... a bit of writing, reading reports, problem-solving... and, of course, the many meetings!"

"Meetings! Yes, tell me about it. I know how that goes..."

They were interrupted by the server, who had noticed Janet's arrival. She smiled and said to Abe, "I can see that your friend is here now, and you seem much happier." Turning to Janet, she asked, "Can I get you something to drink?"

Before Janet could respond, Abe interjected, "She would like a pot of chamomile tea, and I'll have a regular coffee."

The server inquired, "No refill on the mocha?"

"Ah... no. Just the regular coffee, for now, will be fine. The mocha was excellent. I finished it so quickly," Abe replied.

The server smiled warmly at him. "Thanks, I'm glad you enjoyed it. Would you like cream and sugar with your coffee?"

"No, plain and black would be fine," Abe answered.

The server turned to Janet and asked, "And what about you? Would you like any milk or sugar?"

Janet politely declined both. The server, taking Abe's empty mug, assured them, "I'll be back shortly with your drinks and to take your order."

"Thank you," replied Abe with a smile. "No rush at all. It seems quite busy here, and you're doing a great job." The server smiled warmly in response.

"Charming Abe," Janet thought to herself, "He's still as charming as ever."

Turning to Janet, Abe said, "Well, finally, we have the chance to sit down and have a real conversation. First, I want to apologize again for catching you by surprise at your office yesterday. I'm truly sorry. It was wrong of me to visit unannounced, and I am so sorry for being rude."

Janet was still feeling nervous. "It's okay. I have to admit I was quite bewildered. I never expected to see you again, especially not at my university. I suppose stranger things have happened, but I was genuinely shocked."

"I understand," he replied. "If someone had told me that one day I'd be here, doing this, I would have thought they were crazy. But I have no doubts about my actions. I've been toying with the idea of seeing you for a long time, but I lacked the courage. Jan, that's what I've been lacking... Courage. I've spent most of my life as a coward, running away from everything. Losing my wife, taking care of my kids, and living a life without a partner have transformed me into a different person. I've engaged in serious introspection, reflecting on who I am, the paths I've chosen, and the decisions I've made. I have many regrets, but one cannot alter the past. We can only seek new ways to face the future."

Janet thought, "Now you're transitioning from charming Abe to philosophical Abe." She wasn't sure which version of him she preferred. Speaking aloud, she said, "We all choose our paths in life and make decisions that, at the time, seem right. I've learned that there's rarely a definitive right or wrong choice. Sometimes, we have to make decisions without being able to weigh all the pros and cons or predict the consequences. We have to be guided by what feels right for us in that particular moment and situation. We rely on our instincts. Sometimes, we have to make decisions on the fly, without much time to analyze the situations we face."

Abe looked directly into her eyes and asked, "Do you hold any resentment towards me for the decision I made over forty years ago? I would completely understand if your answer is yes."

Janet was unprepared for such a direct question but, without hesitation, blurted out the first words that came to her mind. "I never hated you, Abe. I was very disappointed and hurt. Hate is a strong word and a strong emotion which I have tried to avoid."

She paused, her mind drifting back to the moment she had walked away from Abe, a memory that had resurfaced numerous times since she met him yesterday. Janet had continued with her life, embarking on her journey as a Teaching Assistant at the age of eighteen. A year later, she enrolled in the same Dartmouth Teachers' College that Abe had attended, the very institution that had led to their separation.

As she sat in the College's assembly hall or the large lecture theatre, Janet often wondered if she occupied the same seat Abe had once sat in. She would gaze at the walls of certain rooms adorned with the impressive works of past graduates, hoping to stumble upon something that would connect her to him. However, not a single picture, artwork, or essay belonging to Abe could be found. It seemed as though he had vanished completely, and despite her efforts to bring a piece of him back into her life, it proved impossible.

One significant event for Janet was her encounter with Natesh Udahl in those very classrooms and hallways. They had dated, fell in love, and eventually married upon completing their college program. Nat had filled the void in Janet's life, and she was determined to create a fulfilling life for both Nat and the small family they desired. In fact, she was ready to do everything in her power to ensure they lived happily ever after.

However, after just two years of marriage, Janet came to realize that "happily ever after" was nothing more than a fairy tale that rarely manifests in real life. Nat seemed to possess a Jekyll and Hyde personality. At times, he could be the most loving and caring husband, while at other times, he would become indifferent or filled with anger, to the point of making threats. They sought counseling multiple times and received interventions from their pastor in an effort to salvage their relationship, and for the most part, they managed to make things work. They experienced their fair share of ups and downs, though sometimes the downs outweighed the ups. Nonetheless, Janet was determined to keep her family intact.

During the initial years of her marriage, Janet often found herself thinking about Abe, especially when Nat treated her unkindly. She would wonder how her life would have unfolded if she had married Abe instead. She longed for his tenderness and warmth, but she had to constantly remind herself of the cruel and unforgivable blow he had dealt her. As time passed, Janet gradually pushed Abe out of her thoughts, perhaps intentionally avoiding the painful memories associated with him.

But the painful part of her past had unexpectedly resurfaced, seated right in front of her, patiently awaiting her response. With a mix of confusion and concern, she mustered the courage to address the lingering questions in her mind as she expressed, "I'm baffled as to why you're here. Why now? What's going on? Is there something I need to know?"

As Janet spoke, she observed a shadow crossing Abe's face. She sensed his unease. Meanwhile, Abe, seeking a momentary distraction, tightly held onto the menu and suggested, "Can we focus on our orders first? I'm more inclined towards fish rather than steak. I've never been much of a meat person."

Janet smiled, reminiscing about Abe's love of food. "No, you were always a rice lover. I recall your mom piling your plate high with rice, and I would jokingly bet that you wouldn't finish it. But to my amazement, you always did."

"Well, I was a robust young man back then. Now, as a sixty-eight-year-old man, even fish and vegetables can sometimes be too much for me. It's hard to believe you remember how much I enjoyed rice! Do you recall any positive memories of me, Jan?" Abe asked, his voice tinged with curiosity and a hint of vulnerability.

Janet felt a growing irritation and discomfort as Abe continued to delve into the past. "Why are you asking me these questions, Abe? Or, perhaps I should ask, what exactly are you trying to get at?" she responded, her tone sharpening slightly.

"No specific reason," replied Abe. "Just checking." His disarming smile made Janet feel defensive, unsure of his intentions.

"I'm sorry. I didn't mean to be rude. I do remember some good things about you," Janet apologized sincerely. "I remember your sense of humor, your gentleness, and your love of dancing. There was that time when we fooled my mom, pretending I was going to Chandra's birthday party, but instead, I went with you to see Ronald's new jukebox at his café. We played so many records and danced to the heartfelt tunes of Elvis Presley, Cliff Richard, Ricky Nelson, and others. You were an amazing dancer. Do you still dance?" Now, it was Janet's turn to reminisce.

"Of course, I do. Would you like me to show you a step or two?" Abe asked with a playful glimmer in his eyes. Leaning across the table, he gently took Janet's hand. "Madam, may I have this dance with you?"

Janet swiftly withdrew her hand. "Are you crazy? Do you think you're still twenty?" she asked, her tone filled with concern. She felt terrified and alarmingly worried that Abe might do something reckless, and she wouldn't be able to prevent it.

He smiled. "No, I'm not. I was the one who just reminded you that I'm sixty-eight… going on sixty-nine. Let's not dwell on our age."

"You can't escape from that one," she scolded with a hint of sarcasm.

"No, and I won't. Let's take a look at the menu. I can see our waitress coming with our drinks."

***

The waitress greeted them with a smile as she set the napkins and drinks on the table. "Are you ready to place your order?" she asked.

"I am, but I think my friend here needs another minute," Abe replied.

"No, I don't," Janet contradicted. "I'll just have my regular... the frittata with a side salad and a small bowl of soup."

"What kind of salad would you like? We have garden salad, Caesar..."

Janet didn't let her finish. She knew exactly what she wanted. "I'll have the garden salad with raspberry dressing on the side. And for soup, the cream of celery."

Taking note of Janet's order, the waitress turned to Abe. "And what would you like, sir?"

"I'll have the trout with vegetables, and instead of potatoes, can I have the rice pilaf?" Abe winked at Janet.

"Sure, you can have the rice pilaf. Anything else?" the waitress asked.

"No, that's it for now," responded Abe. "I might want to try your desserts later."

"Oh, they're all so good!" the waitress exclaimed. "I can make some suggestions when you're ready."

"That would be wonderful," replied Abe, collecting the two menus and passing them to the waitress.

***

"There he goes again," thought Janet. "I wish he weren't so charming; then sitting here with him wouldn't be so difficult."

Now that the waitress had disappeared, the silence between them became awkward. Abe looked at Janet and asked, "So, how was work today? Was it a tough day?"

"Oh, just the usual," she replied. "Dealing with the same old stuff. Crazy faculty and staff to handle, along with endless and sometimes fruitless meetings."

"Why do you work so hard?" he questioned. "I'm sure you don't have to take on so much if you don't want to. You could have chosen an easier job. I know you're smart and ambitious, but you don't have to exhaust yourself trying to prove it."

Her defenses rose, and her antenna went up quite literally as she exclaimed, "Is that what you believe of me? That I work solely to prove myself? Of course, that's not the reason. This is my chosen career, my true passion. It's what I've always dreamed of doing. Yes, there are challenging days, but I wouldn't trade it for anything in the world."

Abe realized he had struck a sensitive chord. He appeared slightly embarrassed. "I apologize if I came across like your father. I was merely concerned about your stress levels and your well-being. As people age, they often seek simplicity. But here I am, offering advice and discussing simplicity with the most complicated woman I've ever known. Even in your teenage years, Jan, you were never simple. And I can only imagine that over the years, as you've pursued your career path, you have become even more complex... and I mean that as a compliment. You're like fine wine, not growing older but only improving with time." As he finished speaking, Abe appeared to have just delivered the most important speech of his life.

Janet blushed and offered him a shy smile. "No one has ever characterized me as complex. Should I truly interpret that as a compliment or are you suggesting a flaw?" she asked.

Wearing a philosophical expression, he responded, "Well, being complex is neither inherently good nor bad. It all depends on one's perspective. A complex woman is often more intriguing, although some men may find such women to be too challenging."

"Was your wife complicated?" Janet inquired, noticing the slight tightening of his jaw.

Abe reached for his coffee mug, took a sip, and placed it back on the table. Hesitantly, he replied, "Lizzie was a straightforward woman. She knew her desires and pursued them without hesitation. If things worked out, she was content. If they didn't, she was equally fine. She didn't fight for what she wanted, although she had a passive-aggressive side. She didn't say much, but her silence could be quite hurtful."

He paused, his eyes appearing to delve into the depths of his past. Before he could continue, Janet interjected, "I'm sorry. I shouldn't have asked. It's not my place to inquire. You don't have to answer if you don't want to."

"Please," he responded, "you have every right to ask me anything. I show up here after forty-something years and expect there to be no questions. I'm glad to answer anything you want to know. There was a time when I didn't want to talk about my marriage to Lizzie, but it's all in the past now. I've moved on from the pain and tried to forget that chapter of my life. Sometimes, the past isn't worth remembering."

"Really? Can one truly forget the past?" she declared. "Then why are we here?"

"This is different," he answered. "It's not just a past, Jan. It's also a present and, for me, a future. Have you ever completely forgotten the past... our past?"

"I did," she lied, "until you showed up. I was so hurt, Abe. I didn't want to carry that pain with me forever. I had to let it go."

"Completely?" he asked.

"Yes, completely," she lied again.

***

She did not want to confess that, even after her marriage, there were countless nights when she lay awake, consumed by thoughts of him. Whenever she heard one of their songs, her emotions would overwhelm her. She had kept this hidden from Nat when he asked why she played and replayed the song "*All for the Love of a Girl*" on repeat. He wanted to know if the song had something to do with her past.

Each time that question came up, she had adamantly denied any special significance, dismissing his question with, "What past? What are you talking about?"

"I was just checking," he had responded to Janet's denial. "You play that song so often, and I have a feeling that it has nothing to do with me... with us. I'm assuming it's connected to someone else from your past."

"Are you accusing me?" she blazed.

"Why are you getting so upset? I was just curious."

But the truth hurt, and she knew that Nat had noticed her attachment to the song Abe had sung to her so many times. It always struck a chord within her, especially when he emphasized the lines, *"I'm a boy who'd give his life and the joys of this world... all for the love of a girl."*

And when that lyrical stanza came up, Nat would add, "And you're that girl, Jan. Tell me, aren't you?" After she disagreed with Nat, she made a point not to play that song when he was around.

Abe reached for her hand once again, sensing her nervousness. As she fidgeted with the napkin in front of her, he reassured her, "You did the right thing. Painful memories should be left behind." Suddenly, a look of concern washed over his face. "Jan, I'm starting to question whether it was the right decision to come here and see you. We've both moved on and become different people. I thought I had it all figured out in my mind before I arrived, but now I'm having doubts that this visit might be a mistake. The last thing I want is to cause you any pain. I hope you know this. Perhaps I've been too selfish."

Once again, for the third time in two days, Janet gently pulled her hand away from his grasp. However, as she gazed into his eyes and saw the sorrow within them, the weight of those forty years seemed to fade away. Here sat Abe, the only man she had ever truly loved, and despite her prideful instincts urging her to push him away and reprimand him for a past she had yet to fully comprehend, she couldn't deny the surge of anticipation within her. The voice inside her whispered, "This is the day you've longed for all your life. You have the opportunity to confront him, to let him know how much he hurt you."

Defying caution, she threw her reservations to the wind and spoke up, her voice filled with curiosity and vulnerability. "Don't entertain such thoughts, Abe. You're here, and I want to understand why. It must be something of great importance that would bring you to my doorstep. I can imagine it wasn't an easy decision for you, so please, share with me what's happening."

"I don't want to spoil our dinner. Let's eat first and have our conversation afterward," suggested Abe.

"Why? Is what you have to say so unpleasant?" Janet inquired; her curiosity piqued.

"No, no, no!" he shook his head. "I want us to enjoy our meal. It might be the only one we have together. What I have to say is not that extraordinary. It can wait a few more minutes."

Janet's curiosity peaked, but she did not want to push him. Changing the subject, she asked, "So, how is the Fairview? Are you enjoying your stay? I assume this is your first visit to Windermere."

Abe nodded. "Yes, it's my first visit to beautiful British Columbia. I've always wanted to come but never had the chance. From the Fairview, I have a view of the bustling waterfront in the evening. Last night, I was captivated by a talented Scotsman playing Amazing Grace on the bagpipes. He was excellent."

"Yes, I've heard him too," declared Janet. "Every time he plays, I get goosebumps."

"It's his amazing rendition of 'Amazing Grace'!" Abe's laughter resonated deep within his eyes. At that moment, he became a stark reflection of Abe, who was twenty, whose laughter and amusing anecdotes were something that Janet could never get enough of.

However, tonight, she sensed a different aura, a heaviness, and a sense of impending seriousness. But what did she truly know? She thought to herself, "Time changes people, and Abe would surely be no exception."

Chapter 6

Janet sat there, pondering what was truly happening with Abe, when he suddenly posed a question, "Do you still practice your faith? Do you still attend church?"

"Yes, I have never wavered in my faith. It has remained my greatest source of strength and comfort."

Abe wondered whether Janet had required substantial strength and comfort in her marriage. Was she genuinely happy? It was difficult for him to discern. Had she made the right choice for her partner? He was aware of who her husband was, although they had never met. By chance, he had encountered her husband's older brother through a mutual acquaintance at work. The encounter left Abe with the impression that the brother was a gentle and compassionate individual, leading him to assume that Janet's husband possessed similar qualities.

"I hope you've had a good marriage, Jan. You deserve nothing but the best, but I understand that all marriages have their challenges. However, I know that you would confront any challenge with courage. You are an incredibly strong woman!"

"Don't count on that," she responded. "I've faced my fair share of challenges, and there were times when I didn't handle them as well as I should have."

She thought about that time when she should have walked away from Nat, but fear of uncertainty held her back. She craved reassurance through predictability and sought order in her life, longing for a routine to guide her. Despite feeling betrayed, she aligned her moral compass with the belief that marriage was meant to endure, for better or for worse. Thus, she stayed with Nat despite the voices urging her to end their relationship for good.

Nat had met another professor, Theresa Tyndall, at a conference he attended in California. Theresa was a sociologist whose work intersected with Nat's field. They maintained contact and often attended conferences together. Janet assumed their relationship was strictly work-related until Theresa visited Windermere for a meeting of the Western Canadian Sociologists Association. At the end of the first day of the conference, Nat brought Theresa home to visit Janet. Theresa was sweet and charming, and Janet immediately formed a favorable impression of her.

"I'm so glad we've had this chance to meet," Janet declared. "Nat speaks very highly of you and your work. I've read the papers you've co-authored, and dare I say, you keep him motivated."

"I enjoy collaborating with your husband. He has a keen eye for detail and is an excellent researcher. I believe it's the other way around. He's the one who keeps me motivated," Theresa responded.

Nat butted in, "Theresa was mentioning a group of Indigenous people here on the island whom she intends to work with. I suggested that since she's already here, if she can manage to take some time off, she should stay and gather the necessary data for her project."

"Why not?" Janet responded. "How long do you think it will take?"

"After the conference concludes, if I can stay for another week, I should be able to complete my work. It might be sooner if Nat can spare a few hours to assist me," Theresa explained.

"I have a busy schedule at the moment," Nat said, "But I might be able to spare some time in the evenings."

"Well, here's an idea. Why don't you stay with us after the conference?" Janet suggested. "We have a guest room, and that way, you and Nat can work together in the evenings."

"Oh, no, not at all. I wouldn't want to impose on you," Theresa replied. "You're also very busy with your work."

Janet dismissed Theresa's concerns with a wave of her hand. "It's no imposition, Theresa. We'd be happy to have you. I completely understand the nature of this kind of work. I've relied on assistance from colleagues for my own research at times. Let's not argue about it. Nat can bring you after the conference, which you said will be done tomorrow, and then you can stay with us for the week to collect your data. Besides, it would be nice to have someone else in the house to chat with... Not that there's much time for chatting." Janet then turned to Nat and asked, "What do you think, Nat? Are you okay with Theresa staying with us?"

"Well, what can I say? You've already extended the invitation. Do you want to make me the bad guy?" he asked with a chuckle. "I think it's settled. I'll come to get you when your afternoon session is done tomorrow. I have a number of classes to prepare for and teach during the week, but I'll try to help you out in the evenings."

"I would be very grateful, Nat. Sounds like a plan... and thank you so much, both of you, for your kindness. Thank you, Janet."

"Well, now that all of that is settled, why don't you stay for dinner, Theresa?" Janet invited. "Nat is good on the grill, so we'll have some grilled steak and vegetables if that kind of dinner suits you."

"Certainly does," said Theresa.

Janet turned to Nat, "While we're waiting for you to get the grill fired up, how about a nice glass of wine for the ladies?"

"Coming up," said Nat as he went to sift through his liquor cabinet and pour them some cabernet. Knowing that Janet didn't care much for wine, he only poured half a glass for her.

"Is that all you're having?" queried Theresa.

"I'm not big on drinks. My favorite is a large pot of herbal tea."

As women naturally do, Janet and Theresa conversed about almost everything in the world. Janet learned that Theresa's marriage had come to a rocky end five years ago. She didn't have any kids, and the man with whom she had spent nineteen years of her life had finally confessed that he was seeing another man. Theresa shared that she was hurt and angry over her husband's behavior, but she was happy that they had decided to part ways.

After dinner, Janet and Theresa sat around, enjoying mint tea while Nat tidied up the kitchen. As the clock approached eleven, Theresa called a taxi and bade her goodbyes. Although Nat had offered to drive her back to her hotel, she insisted on taking a taxi. "I've already inconvenienced you enough. The hotel is just a short distance away. I'll see you both tomorrow. And Nat, thank you for offering to pick me up after my meeting. I'll be waiting for you at six. Thank you again, both of you." She embraced Janet with such warmth.

Before retiring for the night, Janet expressed her fondness for Theresa to Nat. "I really like Theresa, and I'm sorry I won't have much time to spend with her due to my busy job. But I'm glad you'll be able to assist her with her research. Perhaps you might even gather some new insights for your own article on government land claims."

Nat didn't share the same enthusiasm. "We'll see," he replied. "It's time to hit the bed. I'm utterly exhausted."

Theresa arrived as planned the next day and quickly adjusted to Nat and Janet's routine. Janet didn't have much time to spend with her, but she was relieved that Nat was able to keep her company. On the third day of Theresa's stay, however, things took a turn for the worse. Janet, who was working with the Business Programs Manager on a new project, had forgotten to bring the important *Trillium Tech* file for her meeting with the Executive Director. The meeting was crucial for negotiating a sizable donation to the university's new business incubator. Frustrated with herself, she muttered, "How did I forget the darn file!"

Unsure if Nat was still at home, she attempted to reach him by calling both the home phone and his cell, but she received no response. Feeling she had no other choice, Janet resigned, "I'll have to drive back home myself to get that file."

Janet hurriedly left the office and drove home, aware that she only had an hour before the meeting began. Upon arriving, she was surprised to find Nat's SUV parked in the driveway. Wondering why he hadn't answered the phone, concern crossed her mind. She considered the possibility of him being unwell. As she approached the front door, she noticed it was slightly ajar, heightening her worry. Thoughts of someone breaking into the house and harming Nat raced through her mind. Slowly and cautiously, she pushed the door open and entered. About to call out his name, she heard a woman's giggle that sounded like Theresa's. Then Nat's voice, deep and throaty, followed, saying, "I suppose we couldn't resist. We couldn't stop what was happening..." Intrigued and troubled, Janet silently made her way through the bungalow until she reached the guest room. The door was open, and what she saw left her in disbelief.

There lay Nat on the bed, alongside Theresa, with both of them partially undressed. Janet's angry voice called out, "What on earth is happening here? Nat! Is this what it appears to be?" The stunned expressions on their faces were evident. "How long has this been going on? I can't believe that you, Theresa, would engage in this behavior right under my roof! You both have no shame! Is this what you've been hiding from me all this time? My God, it's unimaginable! Nat, how could you betray me like this? And you," Janet fixed her gaze on Theresa, "I trusted you in my home. Is this how you repay me? Gather your things and leave. I don't want you here." She turned back to Nat, her voice filled with frustration, "What were you thinking, Nat? I can't believe how foolish I've been."

He hurriedly jumped off the bed, pleading, "Wait, Janet. Please, let me explain myself."

She brushed him off, "You'd better not be here when I return." With fury and humiliation consuming her, she stormed off to her home office. She was livid and embarrassed and felt like killing both of them. However, she managed to control her temper, collected the necessary files, and went back to the office for her meeting. To this day, she couldn't fathom how she managed to maintain her composure and continue functioning at work so normally, concealing the personal nightmare she was enduring.

That day was a turning point in her marriage. Nat had left the house, but he continued to call and plead for Janet's forgiveness. He claimed it was a terrible mistake that should never have happened. Janet didn't even want to dwell on the immense grief she experienced. Nights were filled with tears, and days passed in a hazy blur. She felt deeply betrayed, wondering how she could ever face Nat again, let alone hold a conversation with him. At times, anger consumed her, and she contemplated going to the friend's place where Nat was staying to create a scene, even if it meant involving the police.

Throughout this agonizing ordeal, her daughters became her source of strength. Although they were not yet married, the two older ones were studying at the University of Toronto, while the youngest was on a school trip in Europe. The girls believed Janet should give their father a second chance. They accepted his apologies as he maintained close contact with them. Convinced that his infidelity was a one-time mistake, they believed he had learned his lesson and would not stray down that path again.

Janet ultimately made the decision to pursue a divorce from Nat. However, after months of separation and with the support of her daughters and friends, she and Nat managed to reconcile. It was a challenging journey, and Janet struggled to forgive and move forward. One thing she was certain of was that she could never trust Nat again. She questioned why she seemed to always be betrayed by the men who professed to love her, first Abe and now Nat. Despite their reconciliation, remnants of pain lingered in her heart.

"A penny for your thoughts," Abe said, bringing her back to the present.

Janet blushed and asked, "What?"

"I can tell you're lost in your thoughts. You seem distant," Abe replied.

Janet wasn't surprised by his perceptiveness. Abe was someone who lived in the moment, and she could never hide her emotions from him. She remembered times when she felt sad but pretended to be fine, sometimes laughing in a slightly hysterical manner. He would always see through her facade and say, "*You can't fool me, Janet Ramphal.*" Then he would playfully tickle her chin and neck, and her laughter would become genuine, tears of happiness welling up in her eyes.

To Abe's comment, she replied, "I'm just thinking that here we are having dinner together after God knows how many years! Who would believe this? I still can't. It's so incredibly unreal!"

"I know," he whispered. "But isn't it great? I'm so happy to see you, Jan. Did I tell you how good you look?"

She nodded and replied, "And you do, too. You haven't changed a bit, except you're now older."

"I will take that as a compliment," he said.

The smiling waitress arrived with their order and announced. "Fish for the gentleman," as she placed the steaming plate on the table, "And a frittata for the lady. Is there anything else I can get for you?" she inquired.

"Thank you," said Abe. "We're good." Before the waitress could even move away, he picked up the saltshaker and sprinkled some on his fish.

"How do you know it needs more salt?" asked Janet.

"Oh, everything in the restaurant always needs more salt. I'm not supposed to have too much salt, but it's hard to stay disciplined… especially at this time," he replied, giving her another of his winks.

Janet forked a piece of frittata into her mouth, then asked, "At this time? What time are you referring to?"

Abe's expression turned grave for a moment, but he quickly concealed whatever was bothering him. "This unbelievable time I'm having. I won't let a bit of salt get in the way of enjoying my dinner.

Eat up, Jan. How is the frittata? Is it good?" Abe tried to divert her attention.

"I've had this so many times," she told him, "And it always tastes the same. Always good. What about yours?"

"It's delicious," he answered. "Is this your favorite spot?"

"Not really, but it's convenient. The best restaurant for me is the *Greek by the Creek*, but it's a bit too far away, situated on the other end of Windermere, on Creekside Avenue. They serve authentic Greek cuisine."

"And you love Greek food?" he questioned.

"Hmmm. It's the next best thing to Caribbean food. The way they prepare their eggplant is to die for, very similar to the stuffed eggplant we made in Guyana. The Greeks call it moussaka."

"Yes, I've had that, and I love it too. But I still prefer the grilled eggplant we used to make with lots of onions, garlic, and hot peppers. Do you remember that? We called it *choka*."

Of course, Janet remembered. She had never forgotten how to make eggplant *choka,* and although she couldn't find the same flavored hot peppers in Canada, she continued to make it with substitute red bell peppers that her kids loved. One day, when some of her university friends came over to her house for lunch, she served it as a side dish. She had to painstakingly explain that *choka* is a word her fore-parents brought from India to describe a dish of crushed and seasoned vegetables or meat. She went on to tell them about *coconut choka* and how much work it took to make but how special it was for weekend lunches when there was more time available for cooking. Using coconut in this way was beyond her friends' imagination, and their questions kept circling back to the familiar coconut juice they saw in the ethnic section of supermarkets, which had no connection to the making of *choka*. She eventually gave up, realizing that some Canadians were too rooted in their North American culture and culinary preferences.

"If you can believe it, I still make eggplant *choka*," Janet said.

"Do you also make *roti* to go with it?"

"Hmmm," said Janet, "when I have the time. As you know, it's quite a production." Changing the subject, she continued, "Don't you think it's time we talk about why you're here, Abe? I mean, why you're really here? By the time we're done eating, I will have to head out, so we might as well start talking about it now."

Abe took two more mouthfuls and placed his fork on his napkin. Janet followed suit, setting her own fork down.

He gazed at her, a shadow crossing his eyes. "Janet, I've pondered over this endlessly, and I still can't deduce if I'm doing the right thing." He paused, providing Janet a chance to jump in.

"You're here," she stated in her straightforward, practical manner. "Regardless of whether it's right or wrong, I need to understand why you decided to visit me. I don't believe for a moment that it's something trivial."

"Let's continue eating," said Abe, his voice tinged with reluctance. "Although I hate to ruin your meal."

Janet took a few more forkfuls, waiting for Abe to proceed, but he remained silent. "I'm full," she asserted, "So if you don't mind talking while we eat, I'm all ears."

Abe nervously pushed his vegetables around on his plate, a clear sign of his unease. Without any prior warning, he blurted out, "I'm dying, Jan."

"What!" Janet's exclamation was loud enough to draw the attention of a few diners. She consciously made an effort to lower her voice. "What do you mean you're dying? Abe, you look strong and healthy. Are you serious?"

"Do I look like I'm joking, Jan?" He didn't, and this time, when he reached across the table to hold her hand, she allowed him to squeeze her fingers. Painfully, he explained, "I have been battling a chronic form of Lupus for the past two years. Initially, there was hope for recovery, but in the last six months, things have taken a turn for the worse. The disease has targeted my immune system, and more recently, it has begun attacking the tissues of my heart and kidneys. Now, there is inflammation in my mitral valve, which the doctor says is slowly shutting down, and there is no further treatment available. I have undergone various treatments that I could spend the whole night discussing, but I don't want to burden you with those details. At first, I was confident that I would recover after my swollen joints subsided, but now it's not just the joints. My heart and kidneys are affected, and once my heart fails, that will be the end. The doctor has informed me that with the extensive tissue damage I have, I may have only twelve months to live. I'm currently on medication, which allows me to function normally, but I can't be without the pills I'm taking. I also need regular injections at the clinic. Initially, due to my overall strength and good health throughout most of my life, the doctors were optimistic that I could overcome the disease. However, I have been less fortunate, and now I have very little hope of survival."

Janet sat there, speechless, as the words poured out of Abe. Twice, she wanted to interrupt with a comforting comment, but she couldn't find the words.

Abe noticed the raw shock on her face and wanted to ease her burden. He said, "I've had some time to come to terms with my reality. Even before my diagnosis, before falling ill, I wanted to see you one more time, Jan. I simply wanted to talk with you, to hear your voice, and listen to your laughter. Now that I know my time is limited, I couldn't wait any longer, so I took destiny into my own hands. I decided to see you, hoping against hope that you wouldn't turn me away. Now that I've said it all, I feel a bit foolish, but I'm truly grateful that you gave me this chance. You've made me the happiest man alive." He squeezed her fingers again, and she squeezed her eyes shut as if trying to block out the weight of what she had just heard.

It took at least a full minute for Janet to respond. Weakly, she asked, "Are you certain about this?" Her hope was clinging to the faint possibility that he would deny what he had just revealed.

With overwhelming sadness, Abe nodded and responded, "The doctors have exhausted all their efforts. The inevitable is imminent; it's only a matter of time," he stated in the most practical way possible. His words tugged at Janet's heartstrings, causing her chest to tighten and a suffocating feeling to engulf her. She had entertained various reasons for Abe's visit, but nothing had prepared her for the devastating news of his impending death. A solitary tear traced a path down her cheek. How could this be happening to Abe, of all people?

"Have you tried any doctors in the United States?" Janet asked, grasping at any glimmer of hope.

"How will doctors in the US provide a different diagnosis when the specialists in Canada are confident in their prognosis," Abe replied, his tone tinged with resignation.

She pressed on, her voice filled with desperation, "There are renowned treatment centers in the United States. Have you explored that option? And what about non-traditional medicine? I've heard stories of people with various forms of cancer who defied their doctors' prognoses and found healing through alternative treatments. And your faith, Abe? Is your faith in God still as unwavering as it once was? We serve a miracle-working God, capable of healing and restoring us from any ailment. Nothing is impossible for Him." Soon enough, Abe realized that her words were more of a desperate attempt to console herself than to provide true solace to him.

"Believe me, Jan, I've tried everything possible. I did not just sit back and accept that I was going to die. And yes, my faith in God remains steadfast. He is the ultimate Healer, and if it is His will to restore my health, I will embrace it wholeheartedly. I have never ceased praying, and countless others have joined in prayer for me. It would undeniably require a miracle for me to survive." He gently wiped away the tear from her cheek with a tissue he retrieved from his pocket.

"I didn't come here to cause you distress, Jan. Please don't worry about me. I have come to terms with God's decision. I am grateful beyond words that I can see you one last time."

The finality of his words left Janet breathless. Fueled by a mix of anger and pain, she sternly whispered, "So, you just wanted to see me, say what you needed to say, and then walk away, expecting everything to go back to normal? What were you thinking, Abe!" she exclaimed, unable to contain her emotions. Her outburst most certainly took Abe by surprise, and he added, "I'm really sorry, Jan…"

She didn't let him finish. "And I'm sorry too, Abe. Sorry about your illness... Sorry that it's too late... Sorry for so many things... Sorry about the timing..." Her voice trailed off as she quietly sobbed, trying to muffle the sound with her napkin, hoping to avoid drawing attention from other patrons in the restaurant. She couldn't bring herself to say another word or look at Abe. She simply sat there in silence.

"I didn't mean to upset you, Jan. Please believe me when I say that all I wanted was to see you and hear the comfort of your voice one last time before I passed away. It was selfish of me to do so, and I shouldn't have come. The last thing I want is to make you unhappy."

"Really! When have you made me happy, Abe? You are indeed selfish. What were you expecting? That I'd hold your hands and say, 'Thank God you finally took the chance to see me before you die, and I appreciate it.' Tell me, what did you expect?" She looked at him, and he felt the darts from her eyes sting worse than arrows.

He couldn't bear it. Upsetting Janet was never his intention. He had hoped that she would grasp his predicament and understand the depth of love and longing in his heart that had driven him to find her. He didn't seek her sympathy, but he longed for her to comprehend the feelings he had carried for her all these years. He wanted her to know that she had never been forgotten, that she had always been the one he loved throughout his entire life.

However, Janet's reaction left him stunned. He felt a wave of confusion wash over him, but he was prepared to accept whatever outcome their meeting would bring. His primary desire had been fulfilled - he had seen the love of his life again. Although things hadn't unfolded as he had envisioned, he hadn't truly known what to expect. He had braced himself for the possibility of making a mistake and facing disappointment, yet it was still painful to just sit there helplessly and witness the storm raging in Janet's eyes. Abruptly, he stood up, placed a few bills on the table, pushed his chair back, and left the restaurant without casting a single backward glance.

Chapter 7

Janet took a few moments to process the fact that Abe had actually left. Inside, a voice screamed, "No, no, come back. I didn't mean what I said." However, she couldn't find the words to express her thoughts. Years of professional training in controlling her emotions kicked in, and she quickly wiped away her tears, attempting to compose herself.

A swift scan of the room reassured her that no one was paying her any special attention. She sat there for a few more minutes, working to regain her composure, before signaling the waitress. As the waitress approached the table, she noticed Abe's absence and asked, "Where is your kind gentleman friend? I thought he wanted to try the dessert."

Pretending to be engrossed in her cell phone, Janet quickly responded, "I apologize, but an urgent matter has arisen, and we have to leave. He has gone to retrieve the car."

"Oh, that's unfortunate," the waitress sympathized. "But I'm sure I'll see both of you again."

Janet nodded and swiftly handled the bill. Like Abe, she almost sprinted out of the restaurant, anxiously scanning the area outside in the hope of spotting him lingering nearby, giving her a chance to calm her anger. However, he was nowhere to be found. Janet entered her car and, finding solace in the solitude of the parking lot, rested her head on the steering wheel and wept openly. She couldn't comprehend what had compelled her to react in such a manner. Her anger had been unjustified. Abe was undoubtedly experiencing immense pain, and it was unforgivable for her to add to his burden. How foolish she felt! Her weeping grew uncontrollable.

***

Abe, on the other hand, wandered aimlessly through the streets of Windermere, consumed by self-reproach. He berated himself repeatedly for his decision to visit Janet. Now, she was undoubtedly deeply upset with him, and he feared she would never find it in her heart to forgive him for causing her pain once again. *"What were you thinking, Abe?"* he chastised himself. *"Did you believe that the years would simply fade away and Janet would be overjoyed to see you and show interest in your life? How could you have been so naive!"*

He slowed down as he reached the bus stop, where an older woman was seated on the bench, patiently waiting for her bus. Abe took a seat at the other end of the bench, and a sob involuntarily escaped his lips. Startled by his display of emotion, the woman looked up and asked, "Are you okay?"

"Yes, yes... I'm fine," responded Abe, feigning a casual tone. "I think I'm catching a cold." He quickly wiped his soggy nose with a tissue, trying to hide his emotions.

"It's the weather. It can be quite unpredictable out here," said the woman. "The rain cools everything down, then the sun comes out and warms it up, only for the rain to return. Our bodies struggle to adapt to these constant changes."

"Mmmm," Abe murmured in response. He contemplated how the woman would react if he revealed the weighty thoughts occupying his mind. The weather seemed insignificant in comparison, and he had little concern for it, knowing his time on this earth was limited. However, he quickly dismissed the idea of confiding in a stranger. Instead, he sat silently, gazing at the sun descending behind the towering buildings while the first hints of darkness cast shadows over the city.

His mind again drifted to Janet, and he wondered if she had left the restaurant and returned home, leaving their encounter behind. Part of him wished she hadn't, but his deep care for her led him to pray that she would eventually forget their meeting and pretend it never occurred. He believed it would be best for her.

***

As the bus arrived, a couple disembarked while the older woman boarded. The couple, around Abe's age, held hands tightly as they hurried into a small café across from the bus stop, completely engrossed in each other's company. Abe observed their affectionate interaction, evident from the joyous laughter that emanated from the woman. He couldn't help but feel a pang of longing and sadness in his heart. Reflecting on his own life and his marriage to Lizzie, he remembered the initial years filled with happiness. Despite their modest means and the constant struggles that they faced, they had each other and their children - or so it seemed.

When Lizzie gave birth to their first son, Andy, Abe's happiness knew no bounds. Cradling the tiny infant in his arms and gazing into his deep brown eyes, a profound sense of peace washed over him. He now had a family to cherish and protect, and he was determined to work tirelessly to provide for them.

During the initial months after Andy's birth, Lizzie struggled with postpartum depression, which led her to resign from her job as a bank teller. Unfortunately, the private sector in Guyana offered inadequate maternity benefits, leaving them to rely on a single income. This financial strain presented numerous challenges, but Abe did everything within his power to fulfill their financial responsibilities. He remembered sacrificing his own lunches on certain days to save as much money as possible. Despite his demanding full-time teaching job at an inner-city school, he made it a priority to come home early and take care of most of the household chores. His unwavering focus was on nurturing Lizzie back to good health.

Caring for baby Andy brought Abe an immense sense of joy. He treasured every precious moment of bathing, feeding, and strolling with him around the house, soothing him to sleep with tender lullabies. Among these cherished moments, feeding Andy was a heart-warming activity for Abe. He found pure delight in watching Andy eagerly suckle from the bottle, relishing each drop of milk with an angelic smile that warmed Abe's heart.

However, there was one aspect of baby care that Abe approached with a mixture of reluctance and determination: changing Andy's soiled cotton diapers. It was a time-consuming process that involved carefully cleaning off the mess, soaking the diapers in the laundry tub, and diligently washing them before hanging them to dry on the clothesline that extended from the back stairs to the backyard fence. Abe knew that if he didn't secure the diapers tightly with clothespins, they would flutter in the wind like miniature white flags, occasionally landing on the delicate tomato plants in the garden below and causing unintended damage.

At times, Abe had to rewash diapers that had fallen into the dusty garden bed. He couldn't help but yearn for the convenience of disposable diapers like Pampers, yet he understood that such luxuries were not accessible in Guyana during that time. They would only become available years later, long after their children had grown. Nonetheless, Abe recognized that caring for a baby entailed embracing both the joyful moments and the more mundane tasks, knowing that each contributed to the overall well-being of his beloved child.

***

After four months, Lizzie resumed her job, and life seemed to regain its normalcy. She proved to be a devoted mother, showering Andy with constant care and attention. However, there were moments when Abe couldn't help but feel a pang of jealousy. He noticed how Lizzie doted on Andy, seemingly oblivious to his own presence. During a morning break at school, while supervising the children at the playground, Abe confided in his friend Des, who also had a five-month-old daughter. "I sometimes get the feeling that Andy receives all of Lizzie's attention, and she deliberately ignores me," Abe confessed to Des. "Am I losing her interest?"

"Nah," Des consoled him. "Wives feel the need to demonstrate that they are the most attentive mothers, which sometimes means we take a back seat. Mothers see babies as completely dependent and in need of their constant care. We, on the other hand, are grown men who don't require the same level of mothering."

"But I sometimes feel that Lizzie uses Andy as a reason to avoid spending time with me."

"You need to be more understanding, Abe. I know that Nia loves me and cares for me, even though she dedicates a lot of time to taking care of our daughter. If you have confidence in Lizzie's love for you, there's no need to question her intentions or be concerned about the time she spends with your son. It's time you grew up and learned to let go of these worries."

Abe acknowledged that Des had hit the nail on the head. Was he truly confident in Lizzie's love for him, or even his own love for her? Their circumstances had brought them together, and as they planned their wedding, they felt excited discussing the guests, the church, the honeymoon, and all the other arrangements. Although their wedding was relatively small due to the sudden decision, the meticulous planning still consumed much of their attention. After the wedding, their focus shifted to dealing with Lizzie's pregnancy. She experienced severe morning sickness and constant acid reflux issues. As her belly grew larger, she also endured back and leg pains that added to her discomfort.

Despite living together as a couple, their lives seemed somewhat separate. Abe wanted to give Lizzie all the space she needed to be comfortable. There were many aspects of Lizzie's life that Abe was not fully aware of, unlike with Janet, where he could read her every facial expression. He knew what made Janet laugh or cry, her culinary preferences, the books she enjoyed, and even the dynamics of her family relationships. Abe shook his head, wondering why he was thinking about Janet. He had a wife who needed him, and he had vowed to do everything in his power to make their marriage work.

Abe admired Lizzie's practical and straightforward approach to life. Growing up in a family with two other siblings, Lizzie, being the eldest, found herself in a position of responsibility for her younger sisters. Their father, an abusive alcoholic, was someone all the children kept their distance from. Lizzie firmly believed that if her mother had not been financially dependent on him, she would have left him. However, she prioritized the well-being and economic future of her three children. Lizzie excelled at homemaking, ensuring the small house was always immaculately clean. She didn't hesitate to reprimand Abe whenever he left his belongings strewn about. "How many times do I have to tell you to put your dirty laundry in the basket, not on the floor? It's so untidy," she would admonish him.

Sometimes, Abe really wanted to shout that he didn't care about the laundry. He just wanted to be with Lizzie, like they were on their honeymoon at the Roraima ranch. They held each other and watched the moon rise over the water, shining its soft light on everything. They even sang *"Help me make it through the night"* to each other. But Abe tried to be understanding, so he didn't complain and did what Lizzie asked.

***

Three years passed, and not much changed in Abe's relationship with Lizzie until she became pregnant for the second time. Just like before, Lizzie experienced morning sickness and various discomforts that left her exhausted and lacking energy. Abe, being the devoted husband, once again took on the role of caregiver. He showed tenderness and care and did everything in his power to make her feel loved and well-taken care of.

During this period, Abe noticed a significant change in Lizzie's response to the love and care he showed her. She reciprocated his affection with equal measure, and despite the limitations posed by her swollen abdomen, he felt a newfound gentleness and tenderness from her. This made him undeniably happy. He took solace in the fact that Lizzie truly loved him, and he attributed her previous disposition in the past few years to the added responsibilities of being a mother.

Shortly after, Lizzie gave birth to their second son, Neil, and life resumed its familiar routine from when Andy was born. Abe, feeling frustrated, chose not to engage in constant confrontations with Lizzie. Instead, he expressed his dissatisfaction through subtle hints and sarcastic remarks. Unfortunately, these approaches only served to create more distance between them. The situation reached a breaking point when they received an invitation to attend the wedding of Abe's brother on San Souci Island.

A few days after they received the invitation, Lizzie mentioned to Abe during one of their Sunday morning breakfasts, "I can't believe Darsh is getting married. He has grown up so quickly."

As Abe cracked open his egg, he replied, "I'm happy that he's finally finding his place. I need to help Mom with some last-minute wedding preparations, so we'll need to be there a week before the wedding."

"I was actually considering that you should go alone. It might be challenging for me to bring the boys along. I'll join you a day before the wedding, but you can go ahead without us."

"I would not like to show up without you, Lizzie. Mother is also counting on you to be there early. It's hard to believe that you want me to go ahead without you."

"Please, Abe, don't make this into another of your issues. What's wrong with you going to your mother's home without me? I don't understand why you always insist that we put on a face to convince your mother that our marriage is perfect and flawless."

He was getting angrier by the minute, but Abe made a conscious decision not to engage with Lizzie in yet another pointless argument. Instead, he asked, "Are you sure you'll be able to travel on your own with the boys?" Despite his concerns, Lizzie remained adamant, insisting that he go ahead without them.

Reluctantly, Abe embarked on the journey back to the island where he had spent his childhood. It had been five long years since he last visited his family home, ever since he got married. Though his mother and brothers had made occasional short visits, the once-strong bond of closeness among them had been shattered by Lizzie's inability to get along with his mother. Abe's return to San Souci was a bittersweet experience.

***

Even though he was busy preparing for the wedding, Abe found some time to relax. He met up with old friends and took leisurely walks on the beach where he used to spend time with Janet. Sometimes, he thought he heard her voice carried by the wind, reminding him that his feelings for her hadn't completely gone away, even after being married for five years. One day, he unexpectedly met Janet's sister, Jenna. Jenna told him that Janet had continued her studies at the Teachers' College and became a licensed teacher. She was now married and living in the eastern part of the country.

"Is she doing alright?' asked Abe.

"Of course! Janet comes back to visit us during the summer vacation. She loves the small town where she resides and thoroughly enjoys her work at the school. I do not doubt that she will eventually become a principal," Jenna proudly exclaimed.

"Indeed," Abe agreed, nodding. "I have no doubt she will excel. I'm confident in her abilities."

After exchanging some updates about their respective families and lives, Jenna bid him farewell. "Goodbye, Abe. I need to meet Jack now."

"How is he doing?" Abe inquired.

"He's doing well… We're all doing fine. Gotta run…"

Jenna hurried off, leaving Abe alone. He found a large rock near the shoreline and sat down, deep in thought about the void he felt in his own life.

***

Lizzie never made it to the wedding. She called the day before, claiming she had caught a mild case of the flu. She complained of a severe headache and stomach pain that made traveling impossible. Abe's anger flared, and he couldn't help but wonder if Lizzie had never intended to attend the wedding or spend time with his family. He suspected that she purposely kept her distance from them and wanted him to do the same. It was this strained dynamic that had delayed his return to San Souci for so long. Their recurring fights about Lizzie's indifferent behavior towards his brothers only added to his frustration.

Abe found himself making excuses to his mother, brothers, and friends regarding Lizzie's absence from the wedding. He had to graciously explain that Lizzie truly wanted to be there but was unwell and unable to travel. Despite his efforts, he couldn't fool his mother, who, as mothers often do, sensed the strain in Abe and Lizzie's marriage. However, she chose not to reveal her awareness of their troubled relationship. "That's unfortunate," she commented. "I was looking forward to spending time with my grandsons. It's been nearly a year since I last saw them."

"Well, now you'll have to come visit the city again sometime soon so you can see them."

When Abe returned home, he saw that Lizzie was truly sorry and felt remorseful. It seemed that she had been genuinely ill. She sincerely apologized for letting him down and explained, "I didn't mean to make you feel embarrassed, but I couldn't handle being with your family while I was feeling so sick. I didn't want to make things more stressful. I want to be in good health when I visit them."

"Lizzie, they're *OUR* family, both yours and mine. I don't make distinctions between your family and mine. I genuinely care about your family, so why can't you accept mine as well?"

"We've had this discussion countless times, Aberon! Your mother doesn't like me, and I feel the same way about her. I refuse to establish a close relationship with a mother-in-law who consistently shows disdain towards me. She has never fully accepted the circumstances of our marriage, and I'm perfectly content staying away from her."

"You're being unjust. Mother has never treated you unfairly…"

She cut him off before he could finish his sentence, "That's only when you're present. You don't get to witness her body language when you're not around. She doesn't need to verbalize anything. You can simply sense her animosity."

"Let's not continue with this," Abe stated. "I'm exhausted from the constant repetition of negative remarks."

Abe was very tired. The fights they had over the years had made him feel exhausted and emotionally drained. He knew that Lizzie saw their marriage more as a practical decision than a loving relationship. However, he didn't want to separate from her and put their children through the difficulties that come with a broken family. He had seen how other children suffered when their parents separated, and he didn't want that for his sons. So, he decided to stick around with Lizzie, even though he was unhappy, and tried searching for ways to cope with their situation.

***

After fourteen years of marriage, an opportunity arose for Abe and Lizzie to immigrate to Canada. Abe's brother, who had already migrated with his wife, sponsored them, and they moved to Toronto. However, their relationship remained unchanged. If anything, it deteriorated as their sons grew older.

Four years after their relocation, on a winter afternoon, Lizzie returned from her job at the Toronto Dominion Bank and requested a serious conversation with Abe. She revealed that she had met an engineer from New York, and they had been going out for lunches and dinners. Lizzie confessed that she had developed feelings for him, and he, for her. He asked her to marry him, and she wanted to say *yes*. She expressed her desire for a divorce, stating that their sons were now older and capable of coping, and she needed a more fulfilling relationship. Abe couldn't pretend to be heartbroken; in fact, he felt a sense of relief, which he concealed from Lizzie. He took satisfaction in painting her as the one at fault.

After consulting with lawyers and having many conversations with Andy and Neil, Lizzie and Abe were finally divorced. Lizzie was ecstatic to obtain her freedom, although Abe didn't want to admit it, so was he. Their older son, Andy, had started college while their younger son, Neil, was finishing high school. Both boys chose to stay with Abe, and Lizzie was fine with that, suggesting they could visit her in New York. The boys arranged to see Lizzie whenever possible, and the whole family managed to maintain a friendly and civil relationship. Surprisingly, Lizzie's new husband, Robert, grew fond of the boys, and Abe and Robert would occasionally meet for a beer when they were - either in Toronto or New York.

Abe was grateful that things had worked out well for Lizzie, their sons, and himself. He continued with his life as best he could. Janet often crossed his mind, but he had lost all contact with her until five years ago when he accidentally stumbled upon her profile while browsing the internet. He discovered that she was working at a university, and her contact information was publicly available. The temptation to reach out to her arose, but he contemplated the potential complications it might bring.

However, when he fell ill and received the severe Lupus diagnosis, with only a year or so to live, thoughts of Janet consumed his waking moments. A strong desire burned within him; he had this urge to see Janet one last time. It became a haunting item on his bucket list, a chance to reclaim a small part of his life that had been lost for so many years.

Chapter 8

Abe returned to his hotel room and lay on the uncomfortable sofa, his mind consumed with thoughts of what he should do. Janet's reaction at the restaurant had left him feeling hopeless and discouraged. His first instinct was to book the next flight back to Toronto, unable to face her once more. He believed that their brief "relationship" had come to an end.

However, a small voice inside his head called him a coward and urged him to give Janet another chance if he truly believed she was worth it. The voice reminded him that Janet's anger was not directed at him personally but rather stemmed from the frustration of finding him only to potentially lose him again.

He decided to sleep on it, hoping that things would appear better in the morning after a good night's rest. However, sleep evaded him, and he spent another restless night tossing and turning. He played various scenarios in his mind about how he could approach Janet again, but none of them seemed practical.

Eventually, he admitted to himself that he was indeed a coward, and the best course of action would be to retreat to the cottage at Port Whaley, give himself time to heal emotionally, and then return home. Time was running out for him, and there was no need to create further complications for Janet. He had taken his chances of seeing her, and it hadn't worked out. Now, he had to accept his 'normal life' and make plans for his impending death.

***

After having breakfast, Abe checked out of the hotel and hailed a taxi to take him to the ferry terminal. He purchased a ticket for the Whaley River ferry and boarded when it arrived. The day was sunny, with a few wispy clouds drifting across the blue skies. Abe searched for a comfortable seat at the back of the boat, placing his suitcase beside him. He unfolded the newspaper he had bought from the newsstand near the ticket booth. He tried to relax, focusing on an article discussing the ongoing debate about a proposed pipeline from the Alberta oil sands to the Vancouver harbor. The article highlighted the potential economic benefits for Canada as the demand for its crude oil from the Chinese market was growing.

As he recalled his recent flight over Windermere Island, Abe remembered seeing the lumber floating next to cargo ships, some of which had Chinese writing on their hulls. Reflecting on this, he thought to himself, "If they can benefit from Canada's lumber and crude oil, then it's a mutually beneficial arrangement. Their economy appears to be stable."

Curiously, Abe wondered why his mind was occupied with Canada's economy, realizing that he wouldn't be around to witness the outcome of the country's pipeline developments. He reprimanded himself for indulging in thoughts that held little to no significance. The crucial matter at hand was ensuring that Janet was doing well. The question of how to find out about her well-being lingered in his thoughts for a considerable period of time.

***

Little did Abe know that Janet was struggling just as much as he was. After leaving the restaurant, she aimlessly drove around the city center, attempting to make sense of her emotions and actions. She couldn't comprehend why she had reacted so strongly and felt such anger towards Abe. She tried to justify her response by convincing herself that Abe had no right to enter her life and burden her with his problems. They had no familial ties or ongoing connections, and their past relationship was just that - in the past. Therefore, she believed she had no obligation towards him.

Janet reminisced about her second encounter with Abe, which occurred nearly ten years after she had walked out of his life. Having completed her teaching degree, she and Nat were married, and she moved away with him to the town where he lived. Janet became a teacher at an elementary school and found great joy in her work, displaying genuine care and empathy for her students. She actively engaged with her community, involving herself in various organizations such as the Parent Teachers Group, Planned Parenthood, the Athletics Association, the Teachers' Union, and more. The town of Denamstel, where Nat was born and raised, was a small community with a population of less than eighty thousand people. Janet had gained popularity among the parents, to the point that even during her shopping trips when she did not care for company, she would invariably run into someone who wanted to discuss their kid's progress or concerns about their schooling.

Janet found happiness in her small world. Occasionally, her parents, Jenna and Jack, would visit her, and she, Nat, and the children would spend vacations in San Souci. Although Nat wasn't the perfect husband, he showed care in his own way. The arrival of their first daughter, Caitlin, brought immense joy to Janet's life. Three years later, their second daughter, Melina, was born, and Janet felt a sense of completeness. However, unexpected plans unfolded when, two years after Melina's birth, Janet gave birth to their third daughter, Jacinda.

***

The Udahls, as they were often known in the Denamstel community, were well-liked and cherished by their friends and neighbors. When Denamstel High School was searching for a Vice-Principal, Janet received strong encouragement from everyone to take on the role, and she accepted. As the Vice-Principal, Janet realized that furthering her education would be necessary to advance in her career.

Meanwhile, Nat also contemplated a career change beyond the field of education. During a discussion about their future options, Nat proposed the idea of attending university, which would require them to move to the city. Despite the challenges of relocating with their children, Nat believed they could overcome any obstacles with determination.

Janet cautiously expressed, "Nat, moving to the big city will bring about a significant change. Are we confident that we can handle the challenges that come with city life?"

Nat responded, "Look at Raj and his family. They faced numerous challenges, but they persevered and succeeded in their careers. If they can overcome obstacles, why can't we?"

Nat was more of an optimist, and so he firmly believed that everything would fall into place. "Consider Frank and Seema," he said. "They were in a similar situation as us - two kids, limited income. Initially, they were hesitant about moving to Georgetown, but they took the leap, and now they're thriving. They're enjoying their university programs, and their children are excelling in school. We need to have faith and take that leap too."

Persuading Janet to embrace the unknown was not a difficult task for Nat. He knew that she had an adventurous spirit, although, like many women, she desired some level of security. "What's the worst that could happen?" he asked Janet. "If we face financial challenges, I'll take on a second job. I promise to do everything in my power to ensure our daughters are taken care of. I will never let them down."

Janet took a few more days to weigh her options, but ultimately, she realized the importance of securing and advancing their careers. The job market was highly competitive, and it was crucial to focus on their job stability. At the end of summer, they bid farewell to Denamstel and embarked on their new life in the city.

***

Janet adjusted to her new school and university program, forming new connections, and ensuring her children settled into their new surroundings. With her efficient organization skills, she ran her family's routine smoothly. Although the days were demanding and exhausting, Janet remained resolute in making their new life a success - for herself, Nat, and their daughters.

Amidst her challenges, Janet unexpectedly crossed paths with Abe, and the encounter remained vivid in her memory. It was during the long, rainy season in Guyana when heavy downpours were a daily occurrence. The streets were drenched, creating pools in places where the sidewalks had eroded. Taking the bus became an unpleasant experience. Janet would often get soaked while boarding the bus that took her to work.

After drying off in her classroom, the cycle would repeat as she boarded another bus from her school to the university, where she attended afternoon classes for her degree program. On this particular day, tired of being wet and cold, Janet opted to travel by shared taxi to her afternoon university class. The taxi would conveniently pick her up right at her school's doorstep, sparing her the walk to the bus stop. By sharing the taxi, each passenger would contribute a portion of the fare.

The school's secretary arranged a taxi for Janet, and when it arrived, she hurriedly made her way from the door and entered the back seat of the vehicle, closing the door behind her. As she settled in, she struggled to retrieve her handbag from around her shoulder, simultaneously attempting to shift towards the door to create some space between herself and the gentleman seated next to her.

In her maneuvering, the clasp on her bag unexpectedly opened, causing her two textbooks to fall onto the floor of the taxi. She quickly leaned down, attempting to gather her books while apologizing to the other two passengers in the back seat, particularly to the gentleman beside her. "I'm so sorry," she expressed. "It's a bit clumsy carrying this bag filled with so many things."

"Let me help you," the gentleman offered. "The books are within my reach." He leaned down to retrieve the fallen books.

Janet froze in shock. That voice... no, it couldn't be. She took a moment to look at him, and her suspicion was confirmed. Despite appearing a bit older, it was undoubtedly Abe. As he handed her the books, she could see the surprise reflected on his face as well.

"Janet?" he whispered, "My God, I didn't recognize you. This is unbelievable! What a shocking coincidence. Where are you going?"

Now, it was Janet's turn to express her surprise. "Abe, what are you doing here? I haven't seen you in years. I thought you had moved to the United States. How have you been? Where are you going? This is unbelievable!"

The questions and comments poured out, causing Janet to forget the bitter circumstances of their past separation.

"I can't believe it's really you," Abe said, struggling for words. "Are you also enrolled in a program at UG?"

"Yes, I'm pursuing my degree. And I suppose you're attending classes too?" she asked cautiously.

"Yes," confirmed Abe. "I'm enrolled in the Education program. I started three months ago."

"That's exactly what I'm studying too," Janet replied. "It looks like we started our programs at the same time."

Janet exclaimed, "Oh my God, this is incredible. I need someone to pinch me, so I'll know this is real."

Abe playfully pinched her wrist, and she noticed his expression had shifted from shock to amusement. Janet pulled her hand away, clarifying, "I didn't mean for you to actually pinch me." Her tone turned more serious. She could hear the woman sitting next to Abe chuckling. Janet then asked him, "So, what have you been doing? You look well."

"You look well, too, despite being drenched. I heard you're married to someone from Denamstel, and I believe you have two daughters?"

She corrected him, saying, "Actually, I have three daughters. And I assume you're married too and have children, at least one?"

Abe nodded and replied, "Yes, I'm still married to Lizzie. We have two sons. You might remember that Lizzie was pregnant when we got married, so our first son is Andy, and our second son, Neil, is three years younger."

The conversation became slightly awkward, prompting Janet to shift the focus to their degree programs and how they were managing. Abe shared details about the school where he was teaching and the suburb he lived in. Janet reciprocated by talking about her own school, and sharing anecdotes about her students and the unique challenges of living in the big city.

***

As the taxi reached the university campus, Janet and Abe, lost in their conversation, quickly got out of the car along with the other passengers, who went unnoticed. It was still raining heavily, but Abe had an umbrella, and he opened it, pulling Janet closer to keep her dry. He jokingly said, "No need to get wet. Come closer. I won't bite," as he reached into his pocket for the fare. Janet also searched her handbag for her wallet, but Abe swiftly paid for both of them, telling the driver, "That's for both of us."

Janet insisted to the driver, "Here's my fare. Please give him back the change." She turned to Abe, frustration evident in her voice, and said, "Why did you pay for me? I wanted to pay for myself."

The driver, eager to leave, responded amidst the rain, "You two can figure it out," and quickly drove away with screeching tires.

Janet didn't want to make a fuss. Turning to Abe, she said, "Thanks, but don't you ever do that again."

"Do what? Share a taxi with you?" he winked, and Janet recognized his familiar mischievous smile. "Come on, let's go." He pulled her even closer under his umbrella.

Janet felt grateful for the shelter, staying close to him during the short walk to the education building. She could smell his cologne and feel his warmth through the sleeve of his shirt. Memories of walking in the rain with Abe in San Souci flooded back, but she didn't want to show how emotionally unsettling it was to see him again.

As they reached the door, Abe closed his umbrella and shook off the raindrops. Turning to her, he suggested, "My class starts in a few minutes, but if you have some time, we can meet at the cafeteria during the break around 6:00. Jan, I'm really glad to see you. We should catch up."

A nervous Janet replied, "I have a group meeting during the break to work on our project, and I need to go home right after class. It was nice to see you, Abe, and I'm glad to hear that things are going well for you."

Abe sensed that Janet was hesitant to reconnect with him, possibly due to her marital status and the cultural expectations surrounding it. He didn't want to cause her any discomfort or jeopardize her relationship. Understanding her concerns, he reassured her, "That's alright. Since we're both in the same program, we might bump into each other again. Whenever you have the time, we can grab lunch."

"Yeah, sure," she lied. "I should be going, or else I'll be late for my class."

"Goodbye for now," he whispered, more to himself than to her, as he watched her swiftly walk down the long corridor toward the lecture theatre.

Abe walked in the opposite direction. He had twenty minutes before his lecture began, so he entered the classroom, placed his folder on the desk, and sat there, gazing out the window. His mind was in turmoil. He had always believed that he would see Janet again one day, but what had just happened felt unreal. He wondered if anyone would believe him if he shared this chance encounter. They might think he made it up. "Truth is indeed stranger than fiction," he thought, reflecting on the famous line. Whoever wrote that knew what they were talking about.

***

To pass the time before his class began, Abe reviewed his science assignment. He had doubts about whether he had accurately captured the new experiment he conducted on hydrotropism. The experiment involved his Grade Five students at the elementary school where he worked. Since many elementary schools didn't have laboratories, teachers had to be resourceful and creative, conducting basic experiments right in the classroom. In Guyana, at that time, the government provided free education from kindergarten to university, but the economy was struggling, and education funding was limited.

Abe sometimes questioned the idea of free education, as it often meant a compromised quality that hindered students' ability to compete globally. However, his dedication to his students remained strong, and he always sought practical and effective ways to help them learn. He vividly remembered the astonishment on their faces as they observed bean seeds sprouting roots between the blotting paper and the water-filled glass jar. The roots always gravitated towards the water, regardless of the position of the beans. Abe never failed to captivate his students. He hoped that Professor Adjwani would be impressed with the experiment's results and his analysis of the learning process.

Abe greatly enjoyed his classes with Dr. Felix Adjwani, a Nigerian professor temporarily working at the University of Guyana. Today's class with Dr. Adjwani was no exception, and the three hours passed quickly. Saying quick goodbyes to his colleagues, Abe hurried out of the lecture theater to catch a taxi home. It was still raining heavily, and the darkness added to the gloom. He wondered if Janet was also at the taxi stand, but as he looked across the road, he couldn't spot her among the group of students huddled under their colorful umbrellas. He felt a sense of disappointment but reminded himself that seeing her again wouldn't change his life. She was a part of his past, long forgotten.

***

When Abe arrived home, his mind was consumed with family responsibilities that required his attention. He had to take Andy to his cricket tournament the next day, while Neil had a field visit to a sugar factory across the Demerara River. Abe would need to take him to the ferry terminal where his class and teachers would meet. He realized he would have to make arrangements to take time off from work in order to ensure the boys reached their destinations.

As usual, Lizzie was complaining about her job and the additional workload due to a sick colleague. She mentioned how she had to come home and make dinner, emphasizing Abe's limited assistance with household chores due to his heavy involvement in his university program. Abe's thoughts of Janet quickly faded away as he focused on organizing his plans for the following day.

At times, he despised his life. It felt like he was just getting by, day after day, trying to manage a life that he wished was different. However, he had made his choices and now had to accept the consequences. He had already endured nine years and remained optimistic about enduring another twenty. His main desire was to witness his sons' growth, their completion of university, and their attainment of good jobs. Andy seemed inclined towards business, while Neil was still too young to determine his aspirations. Abe held onto the hope that Neil, who shared his passion for science, might pursue a career in that field when he grew older.

***

Life returned to its usual routine for Abe after his first encounter with Janet. He successfully pushed her out of his mind until their second unexpected meeting, which occurred three weeks later. It was during his lunch break in the university cafeteria on a Saturday when he spotted Janet entering with one of her friends. Although there were no regular classes on Saturdays, many students would come to the campus to utilize the library and work on their assignments.

The cafeteria was bustling with people, but when Janet noticed Abe, she felt obligated to greet him. She approached his table with her friend by her side and said, "Hi! Working on a Saturday, I see? I always thought only foolish people sacrifice their Saturdays for studies."

"Well, you can call me a fool," Abe responded, "But if I don't work on my assignments during the weekends, I won't be able to complete them. And it seems like you're in the same boat. Just look around; all of us who teach and study part-time are here. It's the sacrifice we make, giving up our weekends!"

She introduced her friend, saying, "This is Natalia. We're working on a project together. Natalia, this is Aberon Baichan."

Natalia greeted Abe with a nod, and he responded, "Hi, nice to see you, Natalia. I think we've met before. Weren't you at the panel discussion at the students' forum last Friday?"

Natalia recognized him and replied, "Yes, you were the student from the audience who asked me a challenging question about incorporating environmental protection in the Social Studies curriculum."

"Yes, your answer was spot on. I really enjoyed the session, and the panel did a great job. Congratulations!"

Natalia was about to reply when another student approached and tapped her on the shoulder. "Hey, Talia. I was hoping to find you here. Turning to Janet, she asked, "Can I borrow Talia for a few minutes? I need to show her the pictures we took at her friend's wedding. We have a deadline to complete her album."

"Wow! Did you already receive the pictures from Jay?" Natalia asked with excitement. "I really want to see them. We need to choose the best ones for Sally's album." She then turned towards Jan and excused herself, "Can I catch up with you later? You can chat with Aberon until I return. I'll be back in an hour."

"Of course," Janet replied. "Have fun. I'll wait right here for you."

Natalia quickly waved and left. Janet wasn't sure if she wanted to spend time with Abe, but with Natalia gone, she had no choice. Abe pulled back a chair at his table and said, "You're lucky. The cafeteria is crowded, but you can sit here. Have you already ordered lunch?"

She nodded. "I hope the server can find me here." She placed her order tag on the table.

Abe exclaimed, "Fifty, that's my lucky number. Do you remember?"

She thought, *"Don't start,"* but chose to ignore his comment. Instead, she asked, "So, what are you working on?" She attempted to read his notes from the book that was open in front of him.

"I'm researching tropisms," he replied. "I find this subject extremely fascinating. I've had a deep curiosity about nature ever since I was a child."

Janet asked, "Is your specialization in Biology?" She then added, "I've never been particularly strong in the Sciences. I lean more towards Language Arts. The Arts have always been my strong suit."

"You can excel in whatever you choose, Jan. You were always the most intelligent and accomplished in your class, and I'm certain that hasn't changed," he replied.

Janet was uncertain about how to avoid discussions about the past. She made up her mind to skillfully handle any situation that Abe brought up. Her lunch was served - a hot bowl of peas and rice along with a large green salad. "That looks delicious," commented Abe, "Much better than my plain cheese sandwich. Is it beef or chicken?"

"Beef, it would be. I don't like chicken," said Janet.

"I remember," said Abe, "But I still thought it would be better to check with you. Life changes, and one can never know…"

Janet asked, "Are you referring to the food or something else?"

Abe looked straight into her eyes and replied, "Both."

Janet, while devouring her meal, admitted, "Alright, let's talk, Abe. How have things been for you? There have been moments when I've thought about you and wondered how your life was going. I've bumped into your mom a few times, and she mentioned that you were working in the city and seemed to be doing well. We both moved on with our lives. We have our own families now, and although things may not have turned out as we expected, I have no complaints. Life is as good as it can be, I guess."

"Is it?" he asked.

"Is it, what?" she responded.

"Your life… Is it all honky dory? All perfect and smooth sailing?"

Janet responded, "Well, nothing in life is perfect, but overall, my life is good, and I have no regrets. I love my husband, and I adore my kids. So, yes, my life has been good, even great. How about you?"

Abe shared, "I've been doing well. Life has its challenges, but overall, I can't complain. I've made choices, and things have mostly worked out. Lizzie is doing okay, and so are the boys. They bring me immense pride and joy. I often wondered about you, Jan, and how things were going for you. Luckily, I've had a few opportunities to see Jenna, and she would update me on your husband, kids, and work. I had to coax the information out of her, though. I'm sure she still doesn't hold me in high regard. I also crossed paths with your parents a few times, but they greeted me with a chilly hello. I don't think your father ever let go of his dislike for me. I haven't had the chance to meet Jack, but according to Jenna, he's been doing well. Apparently, he's developed a love for motorbikes! Our unexpected lunch together feels like fate. I always believed that, even if it took fifty years, I would see you again. Do you believe in fate, Jan? Well, here we are, having lunch without the fear of being discovered, without you having to face your parents' anger."

"Well, things have changed since then. That was in the past, and now we're in the present. We don't need to revisit those old memories. We've both moved on."

"I've been trying to move on ever since that afternoon I saw you, but it seems like I'm stuck in this place where I yearn to see you again. I want to hear about your life, to witness your laughter, and to know if you still enjoy walking along the beach, inhaling the ocean's salty air. Is there an ocean nearby where you live? Do you still observe the ebb and flow of the tides? Do you see seagulls gracefully descending from the sky...?" He paused, noticing tears welling up in the corners of her eyes.

Janet protested, "Please, Abe, don't do this. If you continue to dwell on the past, we won't be able to have a normal adult friendship where we've moved on from our history. I would like to be your friend if that's possible, but it will only work if you see us as just friends. Whether we can remain friends depends on you. If you desire more than friendship, then it's best for us to part ways now."

Abe raised his hands in surrender. "You're right. I got carried away when I saw you. I promise not to say anything that makes you uncomfortable. Let's be friends, and let's shake on it."

The awkward moment passed, and Janet laughed as she shook his hand. They spent the next hour discussing their respective academic programs. Janet complained about Dr. Barrow, who was a workaholic with high and unreasonable expectations. She mentioned the teaching aids she had to prepare, jokingly saying she might need an actual cart to carry the boxful of materials home after her project meeting was done since she needed them for a demonstration session at her school on Monday. Abe, on the other hand, praised Professor Felix Adjwani, describing him as *open, fair, and generous with his time for students.*

As they neared the end of their conversation and prepared to go to their respective group meetings, Abe suddenly mentioned, "By the way, Felix's son, Noel, will be picking him up at the airport tonight at 6:00. I have some materials that he needs for the lecture he'll be giving at the Police Academy tomorrow morning. I'm going with Noel to the airport to deliver the items and brief him on the outcome of our experiment, which he'll be discussing tomorrow. What time are you planning to leave campus? You can join us for a ride since your home is on our way. I'm sure Noel won't mind."

"Are you sure?" Janet asked, gathering her books to leave. "I need to be home by 5:00."

"I'm sure," he replied. "Now, you don't have to take your box of teaching aids on the bus. It'll be more comfortable to go with Noel in the car."

"Well, thanks," she said. "Taking that box will be helpful. It has been sitting on top of my locker for the past week, and I desperately need it to work on my project and have it ready for Monday. What time and where should I meet you?"

"How about 4:00, right at the front doors of the cafeteria? Will that work for you?" Abe suggested.

She nodded in agreement. "Yes, I'll wait for you at the front doors at 4:00."

Abe then offered, "I can come to your classroom and help you with the box. Will you still be in lecture theatre B?"

"Are you sure?" she asked for the second time. "I don't want to be a bother."

"Yes, I'm sure," he replied with a hint of playful sarcasm. Then, more sincerely, he added, "It's no bother at all, Jan. I'll come to collect you and the box." This time, he had a big grin on his face.

"Sounds good," she said, joining in the laughter. "See you at 4:00. I've got to hurry, or else I'll be late, and that won't go over well with the rest of my group." With that, she quickly left the cafeteria.

Chapter 9

Abe watched as Janet walked away, noticing the changes in her appearance. Her hair was now shorter and framed her face nicely. He also observed how her body had matured in all the right ways. She was no longer a teenager but a woman with a husband and three children. He sensed that she had her own goals, responsibilities, and strong moral principles. Their conversation had been enjoyable, and he appreciated the stories she shared about her staff and the challenges of her role as an administrator. Janet came across as caring yet decisive, with a genuine passion for doing what was best for her students.

Abe couldn't deny the tenderness he felt for her and the realization that he had never truly erased her from his life. However, he knew he had to keep these feelings hidden and locked away, just as he had done for the past ten years. Getting involved in an inappropriate relationship would not benefit either of them; in fact, it would be a disastrous mistake. Gathering his belongings, he made his way towards the science lab.

As Janet engaged in conversation with Abe, conflicting thoughts swirled in her mind. Despite her denial and desire to avoid the past, her heart couldn't help but be drawn to their shared history. The whole situation felt unreal to her. She never thought she would be crossing paths with Abe again, especially not as fellow students in the same university program. Seeing him now with a family of his own, older and more mature, put her into a stream of thoughts, wondering if feelings for someone she once loved ever faded away.

Janet had made a conscious effort to bury her love for Abe deep within her marriage, but she couldn't deny that over the years when her relationship with Nat lacked the passionate love she yearned for, her thoughts would often drift back to the time she spent with Abe. It provided her solace to know that she had once experienced unconditional love, and that was something that could never be taken away from her.

Nonetheless, she was genuine when she expressed to Abe that their relationship would remain purely platonic. She meant every word, and she was determined to keep the true depth of her feelings hidden, never to be revealed.

"Are you ready to share the literature you reviewed? We're ready to listen." Ryan, the leader of the group project, interrupted her train of thought.

"Ahh... Yes, yes, yes. I have prepared handouts summarizing the findings from the studies I reviewed," responded Janet. "Here, I made copies for everyone. She distributed the information sheets and proceeded to explain some of the conclusions drawn regarding curriculum change.

"These findings support my idea of the clarity of learning outcomes," interjected Muriel. "This is awesome work, Janet."

Omar, however, disagreed with the recommendations presented in one of the studies, which proposed giving students the freedom for critical discourse in the classroom. He expressed his dissatisfaction, saying, "This allows too much freedom for students. Teachers should maintain control; otherwise, the classroom will descend into chaos."

"But these high school students are young adults," Janet countered. "You can't exercise control over them and force-feed information for them to simply memorize and reproduce in exams. That approach won't allow genuine and authentic learning."

"Suck it up, Omar," said Jordan. "We have a responsibility to encourage our students to think critically on their own, and so, analyze information. They can't just passively absorb knowledge. They must develop their decision-making skills and become effective leaders. We can't achieve that by exerting control over them all the time. We're not a military organization, Omar. We're educators, and our goal is to facilitate learning in educational institutions."

Soon, the entire group was involved in the debate, and after many compelling arguments, it was time to decide on the next steps.

They agreed to have Jordan summarize the issues that were raised and bring them to the next meeting, where they would develop an action plan. Then, it was time for everyone to head home to enjoy the rest of their Saturday afternoon.

***

It was nearly 4:00, and Janet hurried to her homeroom to retrieve her take-home box. However, the box was placed out of her reach, sitting on top of the storage locker. Determined to get it, she searched for a stool and dragged it over to the locker. Standing on the stool, she reached up to pull the box towards her, but then she felt two strong arms above her head. Abe had quietly entered the room through the side door and noticed her struggle.

"Here, let me help you with that," he offered. "You're a bit short, Jan. You need to grow another five inches." He chuckled as he effortlessly grabbed the box and cradled it in both arms. "Wow, it's quite heavy," he remarked. "You wouldn't have been able to carry it all the way to the bus."

"Sure, I would have," she quickly retorted. "I would have taken out a few items to make it lighter."

"I won't argue," he responded. "Are you ready to go?"

"Yes. Let's go. I just need to lock the door."

Gathering her books, folders, and her bag-pack, she walked with Abe to the parking lot. He introduced her to Noel, who was waiting there, and then placed the box in the trunk of the car.

"Thanks so much for the ride," Janet said to Noel.

"I hope I'm not causing you any extra trouble by asking for a ride home. Abe mentioned that it's on your way."

"Not a problem," said Noel. "I'm happy to help."

As Abe settled into the front passenger seat of the car with Noel, Janet took a seat in the back. She provided Noel with directions to her home. A few minutes into their drive, Abe turned to Janet and asked, "Are you comfortable back there, Janet?"

"I'm fine," she replied. "I have the whole back seat to myself." She winked at Abe's reflection in the rear-view mirror.

Noel engaged in polite conversation, asking Janet questions about her program. "I've heard great things about your Dad," she told him. "My friends say that my program wouldn't be complete without taking one of his classes. I'm planning to enroll next semester."

Noel spoke with pride about his father's numerous accomplishments and shared stories about his dedication to students and willingness to go above and beyond for them.

"That's absolutely true," Abe chimed in. "I have nothing but respect for Dr. Adjwani. He has been an incredible mentor to me."

The conversation continued intermittently as they drove. Janet leaned back and relaxed, enjoying the comforting warmth of the car. The sun was slowly descending on the horizon. In Guyana, located near the equator, darkness fell early in the afternoon, and there were no significant changes in the timing of sunrise and sunset throughout the year due to the absence of distinct seasons. Guyanese people referred to two seasons: the wet season, characterized by relentless rain, and the dry season, when the sun blazed with intense heat and temperatures ranged from thirty to thirty-eight degrees Celsius. Towards the latter part of the year, evenings would become slightly cooler. On this November afternoon, Janet felt the pleasant Atlantic breeze gently flowing through the open car windows.

Suddenly, the car started to go through some jerky motions. Janet, who had almost dozed off, was now wide awake. She asked with concern, "What's happening? Is something wrong?"

The car came to an abrupt halt. Noel said with surprise and worry, "Oh no, we ran out of gas. I forgot to fill up."

"We're quite far from a gas station," Janet remarked. "What will we do now? How will you get the gas?"

"I'll have to call my friend," replied Noel. "I have a jerry can in the trunk. If my friend comes to pick me up, I can fill the jerry can and bring it back to the car."

"How long will it take for your friend to arrive?" Janet asked anxiously. She was worried about being late getting home. "Will you still make it to the airport on time?" She started to doubt her decision to ride with Noel, realizing that things sometimes unexpectedly go wrong. She had been eagerly anticipating a relaxing evening at home, putting up her feet and watching TV with her daughters.

Noel was busy contacting his friend on his cell phone, so he didn't respond immediately. Janet felt relieved when she overheard Noel's conversation, hinting that his friend would arrive soon. After ten minutes, Jonathan arrived in his pickup truck. Noel had already informed Abe that he would stay in the car while he went with Jonathan. Leaving the car unattended on the side of the highway was unsafe and illegal, as there were vandals who would strip it for parts to be sold illegally.

Janet suggested that Noel and Jonathan could drop her off at the nearest bus stop so she could continue her journey instead of waiting for them to return. However, Noel explained that it would be out of their way and would cause further delays. He was also conscious of being late to pick up his father. Janet reluctantly accepted her situation and resigned herself to wait for Noel's return.

"I'm sorry, Jan," apologized Abe as Noel drove off with Jonathan.

"It's okay," lied Janet. "It's not your fault. You were trying to help. We just have to be patient and wait for Noel to come back. I'll keep you company while we keep an eye out for any police or potential car thieves. An unattended car parked on the side of the highway is an easy target for some criminals. I've seen on the news how many cars left on the street get broken into or stolen."

"Yeah," Abe agreed. "We definitely don't want that to happen to Dr. Adjwini's car."

***

As they waited in the fading daylight, they engaged in a conversation about the country's struggling economy and the alarming rise in criminal activities. Abe expressed concern about the kind of future his children would have in such an environment. "No wonder many of my friends are choosing to migrate to North America. If given the chance, it would be the best decision for me," he concluded.

Janet agreed and admitted that she had been contemplating a similar path. Abe leaned over the front seat to continue their conversation, occasionally rubbing his neck. He asked, "Can I come over and join you at the back? It would be easier to talk, and since we're stuck here for at least the next forty-five minutes, we might as well be comfortable."

"Sure," Janet agreed, shifting to the end of the back seat to make room for Abe. Despite the distance between them, she felt that Abe's presence took up a significant portion of the car, making her feel cramped. She made sure not to let her discomfort show and continued their conversation about the financial struggles faced by impoverished families. Abe acknowledged that Janet's delay might disappoint her children, who were likely waiting for her at home. "Will your kids be upset that you're not home on time?" he inquired.

She nodded. "Especially Caitlin. She won't want to have dinner without me. But she will be alright. Their Dad will ensure that they eat."

"Will he be upset that you're late?" Abe asked.

"No, he won't. It's not the first time I've been late. He understands that sometimes classes can run longer, or I get caught up with work in the library, or simply spend a few extra minutes with my friends," Janet replied.

"Do you have any pictures of your kids? Can I see them?" Abe asked.

"Of course, yes. I have a few pictures in my wallet. Let me just grab my bag." Janet reached down to retrieve her backpack from the floor of the car and rummaged through it to find her small wallet. However, as her fingers blindly searched, the wallet slipped from her grasp and fell to the floor with a thud.

"Oops! Let me get that," Abe said, hastily bending down to retrieve the wallet. At the same time, Janet also instinctively bent over, resulting in their heads colliding. Janet let out a shriek of pain, and Abe immediately dropped the wallet to attend to her. Concerned, he placed his hand on the sore spot where they had bumped heads.

"Jan, I'm so sorry. That was so clumsy of me. Let me take a look." Abe apologized, gently removing Janet's hand from the area. In the dim light, he tried to see if there was any visible bruising.

"Ouch," Janet responded. "It really hurts."

Abe reached across the front seat, grabbed his bag, and pulled out his water bottle. He then took out his handkerchief from his pocket, soaked it, and placed it on the bruised area of Janet's head.

"That feels good," said Janet. "Thanks!"

Abe continued to hold the wet handkerchief to Janet's head, expressing his apologies and concern for her pain. After a few minutes, Janet reassured him, saying, "It's alright now. I'm feeling much better. The pain has subsided." However, when she lightly pressed her finger against the sore spot, a sharp pain shot through her.: Ouch!" she exclaimed. "I can't believe this unexpected accident!"

Abe fell silent all of a sudden, and Janet could sense his intense gaze on her. The act of placing the improvised cold pack on her head had brought them close together. She felt her shoulder almost touching him, and his silhouette was more visible than his actual face. Before she could comprehend the situation, Abe pulled her closer, and tenderly, his lips met the spot where the pain was severe. Janet closed her eyes, engulfed in his warmth and gentle touch, feeling a sense of comfort as though she were a child.

Gradually, his kisses moved from her head to her eyes, lavishing them repeatedly until his lips finally found hers. Unconsciously, her arms wrapped around his neck as he drew her even closer, erasing any distance between them. At that moment, she was transported to the ocean at San Souci in their little sailboat that had always been their refuge. The scent of the salty air filled her nostrils, and she could hear the rhythmic swishing of the waves against the boat's sides.

Janet surrendered herself completely to Abe, just as she had in her dreams. She could feel his heart pounding against hers, taste the saltiness of his tears, and sense the overwhelming surge of emotions pulling them deeper into the turbulent ocean. But suddenly, reality struck her like a lightning bolt. What was she doing? This was utter madness. Pushing him away, she cried out, "Stop, Abe! Stop! This is wrong!"

Breathlessly, Abe whispered, "If it's wrong, then I don't want to be right." He attempted to reach for her again. "Jan, you can't deny that you feel the same way I do. Why did I ever let you go? I love you, Jan. I love you," he said, his voice breaking down as he was overwhelmed with emotions.

"Stop!" she exclaimed once more. "We can't do this, Abe. It's not right. What was I thinking? I'm sorry for letting myself get carried away. I should have known that trying to be just friends was a mistake. We can't be anything but two people who fell deeply in love and are still in love. Yes, I admit that I'm still in love with you, and I always will be. But... No! Both you and I have obligations and responsibilities. This is no longer just about us. It's about the other people in our lives, people to whom we're bound by the promises we made, and those promises must be kept. It will be best for both of us to stay away from each other. I don't want to ruin your life or mine. I'll call for a special hire taxi. I know it will cost me a fortune, but I don't mind. You can wait for Noel." With that, she opened the car door and jumped out into the twilight.

Leaning against the closed door, Janet sought support as her knees weakened and her breath felt dry. The cool evening air embraced her as she inhaled deeply, hoping to clear her thoughts. On the other side of the car, Abe stepped out and leaned on his half-open door. He used the wet handkerchief to wipe away his tears, a sight that tugged at Janet's heart.

From across the car's hood, he spoke to her. "I'm sorry, Jan. I shouldn't have done that. I don't know what came over me. You're right. I don't think we should see each other. I'll stay away, not only for my sake but for yours as well. I'll call you a taxi, and I'll cover the cost. This is all my fault. Go sit in the car."

"It's fine. I'll stand here. You go and sit," Janet insisted.

Abe's expression hardened. "Jan, don't make me forcefully put you back in the car," he warned. "Your head hurts. You need to relax."

Reluctantly, Janet climbed back into the car and positioned herself between the seat and the door, using her backpack as a makeshift cushion for her head. Abe also got in and searched for her wallet on the floor. Once he found the small, brown wallet, he placed it next to her, covering it with her fingers. Janet took hold of the wallet and returned it to her backpack. Meanwhile, Abe stepped out of the car and paced along the side of the highway, anxiously waiting for the arrival of the taxi.

***

When Janet stepped out of the car, she noticed that Abe had already spoken to the taxi driver and paid the fare.

"No," Janet said firmly to the driver, "He's not paying for my ride. It's a whole fifty dollars. I'll handle it."

"Please, ma'am, just get in," the driver urged. "I'm already behind schedule. You two can settle the payment later." Impatiently, the driver revved the engine, signaling his eagerness to depart. Reluctantly, Janet complied while Abe swiftly transferred her box of teaching aids from Noel's car into the taxi.

"I'll return the fare," Janet told Abe as he placed the box on the seat next to her.

"Whatever," he replied briskly.

Before Janet could ever try to utter a few words, the taxi suddenly sped away, leaving her unsettled in her seat. In the waning light, Abe failed to notice the large tears streaming down her cheeks.

She felt exhausted both physically and emotionally. The drive back home took another half hour.

***

Janet felt a sense of relief as she arrived at her house and climbed the steps to the front door. The familiar aroma of fried plantains, her favorite side dish, especially on weekends, welcomed her.

Nat greeted Janet warmly as he expressed his surprised concern, "Wow, you're really late tonight. I was assuming you were not going to work after class. Is everything okay? You look more than exhausted. "

"Sorry, Nat. It's a long story. And yes… I am… Really tired. I can tell that you made dinner tonight. But what is it that smells so good?"

Janet's favorite dish, fish with plenty of carrots and tomatoes, filled the air with its enticing aroma. Nat, always observant, remarked, "You must have smelled the plantains from miles away. Why did you take a taxi? Did you miss the bus?"

Trust Nat not to miss anything, Janet thought to herself. "Once again, it's a long story," she replied. "I'll explain later. Where are the girls?"

"They're in the living room watching TV, as usual," he said. As if on cue, Caitlin, Melina, and Jacinda burst out of the living room, eagerly embracing Janet.

"Why are you so late?" queried the older and self-appointed "in-charge" Caitlin. "We were waiting for you to have dinner together, but we got really hungry and ended up eating on our own."

"It's Cate's fault," declared Jacinda. "She was the one who got hungry, so I followed her and Melina."

Janet couldn't help but sympathize as she thought, *Poor Jacinda*. She was always the one to follow her sisters' lead. Janet then hugged them tightly and announced, "Mommy is both hungry and tired. Go ahead and watch your show. I'll join you in a little while." Without looking back, the girls hurried off to the living room.

Janet yearned for solitude, wanting nothing more than to be alone and contemplate how she would handle any future encounters with Abe. She also had a strong desire to repay him the fifty dollars. The university they attended was small, with her faculty and program being even more intimate, making it nearly impossible to avoid crossing paths with him again. After taking a shower, she joined Nat, who was patiently waiting for her at the dinner table.

Steering their conversation towards their plans for the week, Janet managed to avoid any further discussion about her tardy arrival by taxi. The remainder of the evening was spent watching TV with the girls, followed by a movie with Nat. Finally, as Janet settled into bed well past midnight, she renewed her resolve to keep her promise and stay clear of Abe completely.

***

As the days went by, Janet did not encounter Abe. She accidentally ran into one of his friends, Sam, whom she had met in one of her classes. He had come over to chat with her when he heard Professor Keiller call out to her to remind her of their tutorial meeting. Sam had asked, "Are you from San Souci?"

"Why?" she asked inquisitively.

"My good friend Aberon mentioned meeting an old acquaintance from San Souci named Janet. I assumed it was you," he explained.

"Yes, it's me. So, you and Abe are in the same classes?" she inquired.

He revealed that he and Abe were actually both teaching at the same school and had been acquainted for over five years. Janet and Sam had a brief conversation, during which Janet excused herself as she was running late for a group meeting.

Now, spotting Sam in the library, Janet approached him and reached into her purse, retrieving fifty dollars. "Sam," she said, relieved to have found him. "I'm so glad we crossed paths. I need to ask you a favor. Could you please pass these fifty dollars to Abe? Will you see him today?"

"Yes, we have a class together right now. What's the money for?" asked Sam.

"Please, just give it to him. Tell him it's from me. He's expecting it."

Sam nodded silently, accepting the money and promptly stashing it in his pocket. "Thank you," expressed Janet gratefully as she made her way towards the bookshelves to retrieve the psychology textbook she required.

***

Abe made a consistent effort to uphold his end of the deal about not communicating with Janet. During a seminar they both attended featuring a guest speaker, Abe purposely kept his distance. He refrained from even glancing in Janet's direction. Janet couldn't shake off this experience for weeks. She pondered if Abe now harbored hatred towards her. Throughout the presentation and discussions, she discreetly stole glances at him, but he completely avoided making eye contact. "*You can't have it both ways,*" she eventually explained to herself.

The two years of their university program passed swiftly, and on the day of their convocation, Janet secretly hoped to catch a glimpse of Abe adorned in his graduation cap and gown. However, he was conspicuously absent. Janet later learned from a colleague in his science classes that he had been offered a prestigious position as Department Head at a Technical Institute in a different region of the country, making it impossible for him to attend the ceremony.

Janet carried on with her life, never crossing paths with Abe again. They didn't encounter each other at teachers' conventions, celebratory events, or any other occasion. She focused her efforts on nurturing her children and advancing her career, determined to push aside any thoughts of Abe that threatened her peace of mind. And so, it went, until… *She unexpectedly saw him yesterday.*

Janet couldn't just wish Abe away. *"It's the third time in my life I've sent him packing,"* she thought. *"Why did I let myself get so angry?"* The voice of reason, which often spoke to her, urged her to think. *"Think, Janet. Consider what you truly want. You're in control of your life and the decisions you make."* The challenge, however, was that she wasn't quite sure of her own desires. Janet realized she needed some quiet time to think things through.

Her busy work life didn't provide the opportunity to reflect on her personal life. She would often joke about how her job consumed every waking moment, to the point where even getting a manicure felt like a chore. But she wondered if staying busy was just an excuse to avoid facing personal pain. Janet lived for others, and by neglecting self-reflection, was she trying to evade her own emotional struggles and pains?

Chapter 10

After wiping away her tears and pulling herself together, Janet started the car and headed in the direction of the Fairview. It was the first time she felt a genuine sense of owing Abe an apology. She yearned to express her remorse for her foolish outburst and offer her assistance in any way possible. Pulling into the hotel's parking lot, she managed to secure the only remaining spot, which a departing black Subaru had vacated. Hastily exiting the car, she grabbed her purse and hurriedly ascended the four steps leading to the Fairview's lobby. At the front desk, the clerk greeted her with a courteous, "How may I assist you, ma'am?"

Janet, catching her breath, hastily explained, "I'm here to meet a friend. I arrived a bit early. Could you please give him a call to inform him that I'm here? My name is Janet."

The receptionist inquired, "What's the name of your friend? Do you happen to know his room number?"

"Aberon Baichan," Janet replied, "And no, I don't have his room number."

The receptionist focused his gaze on the computer screen, searching through the guest list. After locating Abe's room, he promptly picked up the phone and dialed. Moments later, he turned to Janet and informed her, "He's not answering. It seems like he's not in his room. Perhaps he's on his way down."

"Thank you," Janet replied. "I'll wait over there." She made her way across the lobby, her mind filled with questions about Abe's whereabouts. It seemed that he hadn't returned to the hotel after leaving the restaurant. She couldn't help but wonder if he was wandering the unfamiliar streets. How upset was he? Above all, she hoped he was safe.

"Why am I thinking all of this?" Janet muttered quietly to herself. "Abe is perfectly capable of taking care of himself. I know how strong he is."

With that in mind, Janet decided to go home and allow herself some time to think things through. However, she wasn't certain if she would be able to sleep, given the circumstances. Tomorrow, she planned to reach out to Abe. By then, both of them would have had enough time to calm down and gather their thoughts. It would be a more appropriate moment to have a conversation about his deteriorating health.

***

Fifteen minutes later, Janet arrived home. As she entered, she noticed the lights in the home office were all switched on, and Nat was busy working away on his computer.

"You're home early," he remarked absentmindedly. "I thought the productive fundraising discussions would continue into the late hours. Have you miraculously discovered the secret to raising five million?" he added sarcastically.

"Nope," Janet replied. "People were exhausted tonight. However, we did receive a significant donation from a philanthropist - two million dollars. Nick was thrilled and decided to keep the meeting short. We made some plans that I'll share with you later. I'm glad you're occupied. I have a few tasks to complete before heading to bed. I have an early meeting tomorrow. Goodnight." She gave him a quick peck on the cheek.

"Goodnight," he responded, his eyes remaining fixed on the computer screen. "I need to finish preparing for tomorrow's classes. See you in the morning."

Janet undressed and prepared a warm bath, grateful for Nat's preoccupation. The tub had always been a place where she could think clearly. There was something about the soapy suds and warm water that relaxed her brain cells and enhanced her clarity of thought. She settled into the scented water, taking slow, deep breaths as she had learned in her yoga classes. Inhaling and exhaling, she allowed her mind to wander back to the restaurant and her meeting with Abe.

Outwardly, Abe appeared fine. The disease had not yet taken its final toll on his body, but his eyes reflected a haunting sadness. He seemed to be making a genuine effort to conceal both the physical and emotional pain he was experiencing. Still, Janet could discern the underlying sorrow that flickered in his eyes. She knew how desperately he desired to see her before his condition worsened. Janet realized that once he reached a certain level of illness, he might prefer not to have any visitors, unwilling to be pitied. Deep down, she felt a sense of significance and value, knowing that he had made the effort to see her. She did not doubt that he cherished her. As his first love, their connection was not something he would easily forget. Abe's feelings ran deep, like the stilt roots of the mangrove trees.

Janet painfully resolved that if it were Abe's choice to never see her again, she would respect his decision. There was no point in becoming entangled in a relationship at this stage of their lives and causing each other further pain. In fact, Janet believed she could hurt Abe even more in his current vulnerable state. His declining health and the collapse of his marriage had left him exposed and fragile.

***

Janet was still awake when Nat came to bed at midnight. She closed her eyes tightly and lay perfectly still, hoping he wouldn't realize she hadn't fallen asleep as yet. After about ten minutes, Nat was fast asleep, and Janet observed his rhythmic breathing accompanied by gentle snores. Carefully, Janet gathered her nightdress and quietly slipped out from under the duvet. She made her way to the spare room, deciding it was best not to disturb Nat with her relentless tossing and turning.

In the early hours of the morning, Janet finally drifted into a fitful sleep. In her dream, she found herself seated in a canoe alongside Abe, not far from the shore of Windermere Island. A brewing storm loomed as dark clouds approached from the west. Janet felt an urgency to warn Abe about the impending rain and the need to head back to the safety of the pier. Fearful of being caught in the storm, she desperately tried to reason with him. However, Abe appeared resolute, rowing farther and farther out to sea. His gaze fixed on the distant horizon. He seemed completely oblivious to her presence and her concerns.

Suddenly, the heavens unleashed torrential rain, each heavy drop stinging Janet's upturned face and arms. The once calm ocean grew turbulent, with waves becoming boisterous. Gripping the sides of the canoe, Janet clung on in fear, shouting, "Abe, what are you doing? Let's go back! It's becoming dangerous!" Yet, Abe remained unresponsive, seeming oblivious to her presence. His eyes remained fixed on an unseen and unknown appeal in the distance as if it compelled him to continue moving forward.

Desperate, Janet pleaded once more, "Abe, please turn back!" However, he continued rowing forward, seemingly captivated by whatever lay ahead.

Overwhelmed by fear and desperation, Janet impulsively lashed out, delivering a hard slap across Abe's face. The sudden impact caused the oars to slip from his grasp, sending the boat teetering dangerously, nearly capsizing, and catapulting Janet into the frigid waters below. Gasping for breath, she cried out, "Abe, I'm drowning! Save me!"

At that moment, Abe snapped out of his trance-like state and recognized Janet's peril. Without hesitation, he dove into the water, quickly reaching her as thunder roared over them. Embracing her tightly, he provided a sense of security amidst the relentless bursts of thunder. Janet sought solace by covering her ears, attempting to drown out the deafening noise. Suddenly, her eyes shot open.

Janet soon realized that her hands were indeed pressed against her ears, muting the blaring alarm on her iPad. Glancing at the clock on the bedside table, she saw that it was already 7:00 a.m. Janet wiped her sweaty neck and threw off the covers, glad to have woken up from her bad dream. She turned off the alarm and tiredly got out of bed, yawning, and stretching. She couldn't take her time with yoga and breakfast today because she couldn't be late for her 8:30 meeting with the Provost.

She checked on Nat, who was still fast asleep. Sometimes, she envied his slower-paced life as a professor. In fact, his carefree existence irritated her. He had more control over his schedule, with teaching and meeting with students being his main commitments. He considered other activities like committee meetings as optional. Nat saw his career as having choices and options, which frustrated Janet most times. Once in the past, Janet had compared their workloads over which Nat commented, "If you're trying to make me feel guilty, it won't work. You're the one who will end up disappointed because I don't feel guilty at all. It's about making choices, Janet. You made yours, and I made mine. We want different things in life."

Janet acknowledged the truth in his words. She couldn't hold anyone else responsible for the career path she had chosen. When she accepted the position as Director of University Affairs, she was well aware of the demands it would entail. It was the job she had always aspired to, and she believed it had the potential to make a significant impact in the field of education. However, she also knew that the role could be all-encompassing, leaving less time for personal connections, family, and friendships.

***

Letting out a deep sigh, Janet hurried into the kitchen to prepare her breakfast - a bowl of oatmeal and fruits. She firmly believed in the importance of starting the day with a nourishing meal. It provided her with the energy she needed to tackle whatever challenges awaited her at the office. Janet had learned from experience that she couldn't perform at her best on an empty stomach.

Although she would have to postpone her yoga session, she found solace in the fact that she could still devote time to her morning prayers. She relied on her faith, knowing that she needed God's guidance every minute of every day.

An hour later, Janet was ready for the day. She had taken a shower, gotten dressed, and was now heading to the office. Syd, her assistant, was already organizing her files and greeted her with a cheerful "Good morning."

"Hi, Syd," Janet said. "Looks like it's going to be a busy day. These folders are piling up higher than ever!"

"You got that right," Syd replied. "You have a meeting with James in his office in ten minutes."

"Did he mention the purpose of the meeting? I checked my schedule for today, but I can't remember why we're meeting," Janet asked.

"His assistant scheduled the meeting. She only mentioned that James wants to discuss a new initiative, but she didn't provide any additional details," Syd explained.

"I understand," Janet replied, although she didn't truly understand. Delia, James' assistant, had a habit of withholding information. Janet suspected that Delia enjoyed keeping others in the dark. Well, if that's what she wanted, so be it!

***

Janet entered her office, turned on her computer, and checked her voicemail. Five messages were waiting for her. As her emails started to flood in, she faced a dilemma: should she respond to urgent emails or return the phone calls? Deciding to prioritize her meeting with James, she set aside the emails and calls for later. Grabbing her notebook, she headed towards James' office, which was just a three-minute walk across the green at the opposite end of the campus.

It was a pleasant spring morning, with the sun gradually warming up the sky. The blooming flowers seemed to bask in its gentle light. Despite the temperature being a cool 18 degrees Celsius, students were already lounging on the grass, enjoying the chance to be outdoors and breathe in the fresh air. Janet knew that in a few minutes, they would all be rushing off to their 8:30 classes.

When Janet arrived at James' office, she was greeted by Delia, who wore a forced smile on her face. "Hi Janet, it's such a beautiful day, isn't it? James is currently on the phone, but he shouldn't be much longer. Would you like a coffee?"

"Thanks," Janet replied, "but it's a bit too early for me. I'll have one later."

Although Janet didn't particularly like Delia due to her lack of genuineness, she acknowledged that Delia had always been kind to her. Janet's staff often joked that they needed to be on good terms with Syd, as she seemed to be Janet's gatekeeper, in order to get things done through her office. Janet knew they were right and decided to follow their example. She understood that maintaining a good relationship with Delia would make it easier to access James' office and the resources under his control. She was certain that not all administrators at the university were offered a cup of coffee by Delia.

Janet sank into the comfortable sofa outside James' office. "Is this meeting with James scheduled for only forty-five minutes?" she asked. "I have another meeting at 9:30, so if we go over time, please remind me that I need to leave," Janet requested Delia.

"No problem," Delia reassured her. "James also has a 9:30 appointment, so if he goes beyond 9:20, he will definitely need to be interrupted. You have about forty minutes for your meeting."

"That's alright," replied Janet. "The shorter, the better. I have no idea what this meeting is about, Delia. Any clues?"

"I'm afraid James didn't provide much information. He just mentioned wanting to discuss a new initiative..."

Before Delia could finish her sentence, James suddenly appeared at the door of his office. Despite the early hour of 8:40 in the morning, he looked exhausted, as if he hadn't gone home since the previous day. Janet occasionally felt sympathy for him, understanding the weight of his responsibilities as Provost. Although he had a Vice-Provost to assist him, managing a university with twenty thousand students and over four thousand faculty and staff was undoubtedly a challenging role.

James greeted Janet with a warm smile, one of the things she appreciated most about him. Regardless of the situation, he always had a smile for everyone. "Hi, Janet. Sorry to keep you waiting," he apologized.

"Hi, James," Janet responded. "No problem at all. I understand you're always busy. Delia mentioned that you had an urgent phone call to attend to."

"It wasn't just urgent, it was crucial," James explained. "I was on the phone with the Deputy Minister, and he's requesting that Academic Vice-Presidents from all universities in the province attend a meeting this Friday. The meeting will involve senior government advisors and will focus on the planning of the new education audit. However, I already have a prior commitment on Thursday, as I need to meet with school Superintendents in Port Whaley. Given the circumstances, attending the meeting with the Deputy Minister must take priority. That's where you come in. I'm glad you're here because I need to ask you to fill in for me at the Superintendents' meeting. I believe you would be the most suitable person to represent the university, considering your involvement in the review of the education program, particularly in the area of twenty-first-century learning. It aligns perfectly with your expertise, and I believe you would make valuable contributions to the planning discussion, perhaps even more so than I would."

Janet was taken by surprise and felt unprepared for the upcoming meeting off Windermere Island in just two days. Gathering her courage, she asked, "Is it absolutely necessary for our university to be represented at this meeting? Perhaps you could coordinate with your counterpart at Brooks University and get updated on the discussions."

"No, Janet, it's important for us to have a presence," James insisted. "The optics matter, especially when it comes to our relationship with the school districts in Whaley River. What is preventing you from attending?"

Before Janet could respond, James continued, "I understand that you may have other prior commitments, but you can ask Syd to clear your calendar. She's skilled at managing that. In fact, why don't you take Syd along? She can drive while you catch up on emails and reading. It's imperative that you attend this meeting, Janet."

"Alright, I'll make the necessary arrangements. Please ask Delia to inform the people in Whaley River that I will be your substitute," Janet agreed.

"Thank you, Janet. I'll speak to Delia about it. I'll also have her send you the file and the latest information regarding the meeting so you can have everything before you leave. I truly appreciate your willingness to take on this task. Now, let's remind ourselves why we were meeting," James said, seemingly addressing himself. He then recalled, "Ah, yes! I wanted to discuss with you the opportunity to chair the search committee for the new position of Director of Indigenous Studies. I've already approached two faculty members, one staff member, and the Vice-President of External Relations to join the committee."

Janet interrupted him, seeking clarification. "So, are we going to involve the Herbert and Williams Executive Search Agency for this hire?"

"Yes, that's correct. I've already reached out to them," confirmed James. "Brian, who worked with us on the search for the last Dean, will be our main contact. I've informed him that you will be chairing the committee, so he will be in touch with you soon. I have a file here with the job posting and other relevant information. Delia is in the process of gathering resumes for the committee's review."

James reached into his desk drawer and pulled out a bright blue folder, handing it to Janet. "Once Brian contacts you, you can begin working with him to bring the committee together for an initial briefing and proceed from there. Just keep me updated on the progress. If you need any assistance along the way, don't hesitate to ask."

Janet expressed her enthusiasm for working with Herbert and Williams again. "I had a positive experience with them during the last search, and Brian is excellent at what he does. It should be an enjoyable process, although I can already see that I have a lot on my plate."

"I genuinely appreciate your contributions, Janet. I know I can rely on you. You're a valuable asset to the administrative team," James said with a smile. Janet recognized that he was assigning her additional tasks. Still, she also understood that he entrusted her with these responsibilities because he had confidence in her abilities, and she had consistently delivered results.

Janet humbly responded, "Please, don't flatter me. I'll start the search process, and I'll attend the meeting on Thursday."

"You're truly invaluable. Mount Carmel wouldn't be the same without you!" James exclaimed. He glanced at the clock on the wall. "If there's nothing else, I should move on to my next meeting. I have a report to review, and I need ten minutes."

"I have to go as well," Janet replied. "I'll stay in touch regarding the search and make sure to share my notes from Thursday's meeting." He nodded, but Janet could see his thoughts already moving on to the next thing he had to get done. With a quiet "Bye," she exited his office.

***

Janet's mind was in a whirl as she made her way back to her office. She knew she would need to coordinate with Syd to rearrange her schedule for the upcoming days. Attending the meeting in Port Whaley would require her to stay overnight on Thursday, which meant she would have two days' worth of work left unfinished.

Syd caught up with Janet in the hallway and hurriedly delivered the news, "Meryl has been looking for you. She came by twice, quite concerned. It seems there's a student in her class whose husband, despite having a restraining order, showed up in the classroom. Thankfully, Meryl managed to get him out and lock the door before he could approach his wife. However, the incident has left his wife and the rest of the class fearful ..."

Janet inquired, "Why didn't she call security? That's their responsibility. It's why they are here!"

"She actually did," Syd clarified, "But she wanted to personally inform you. The police have also been notified. Meryl didn't want you to hear about it from someone else."

"I'll speak with her later," Janet responded. "It's unfortunate that the students were frightened. Meryl is usually composed, so I trust she handled the situation effectively."

"She definitely did," Syd affirmed. "You know how much she cares about her students."

Janet changed the topic. "Syd, I need to discuss something urgent with you. Can you come into my office for a few minutes?"

Janet and Syd had separate offices, with Syd occupying the outer office and Janet the inner one. To reach Janet's office, one had to pass through Syd's office. Her staff often referred to Syd as the office cop. Syd understood that Janet's statement was more of an instruction than a question.

"Sure thing. Like, right now?" she confirmed.

"Yes," Janet responded.

Janet stayed seated at her desk while Syd fetched her notebook, which she always kept nearby for their meetings. Syd was careful about taking notes, making sure not to miss any important details or make any mistakes. Perched on the edge of her chair across from Janet, Syd diligently wrote down everything as Janet explained the upcoming meeting in Port Whaley and the need to reschedule tasks. Syd was used to Janet's changing plans; it was a regular part of their work in the academic environment, requiring them to be practical and adaptable.

Janet added, "There's one more thing. How about joining me in Port Whaley? You can drive, and we can work on the Academic Standards Report during the trip and between my meetings."

Syd pondered for a moment and replied, "Hmmm, it could be a nice change of pace for me to get out of the office. Sure, I don't mind going. Should I go ahead and book the hotel for Thursday night?"

"Yes," confirmed Janet. "Book the hotel where James usually stays."

Syd quickly gathered her notepad and hurried off to make the necessary arrangements while Janet focused on her tasks for the day. With Wednesday already underway, she needed to tackle her workload for the day before departing for the meeting on Thursday. Janet also needed to inform Nat about her absence, although she knew he wouldn't complain. He had a good grasp of the demands of her job, and last-minute travel was not uncommon.

As Janet prepared for bed that evening, the events of the day replayed in her mind. Suddenly, in the midst of brushing her teeth, she halted. The thought struck her that if she was going out of town, she should check in with the Fairview to inquire about Abe. Amidst the day's chaos, she had completely forgotten about him. Once she finished brushing, she decided to make a phone call right away.

She walked down to her home office, locked the door, and dialed the Fairview using her cell phone. Janet requested to speak with Aberon Baichan. After a brief pause, the receptionist informed her that there was no guest by that name registered at the hotel.

"But he was there. I spoke with him last evening," Janet insisted. There was a prolonged silence on the other end before the receptionist finally confirmed that Aberon Baichan had indeed checked out earlier that morning.

A wave of heaviness washed over Janet's chest. She was certain that Abe had boarded the next flight to Toronto. The urge to weep and wail overwhelmed her, but the tears refused to fall. Instead, she felt an intense sadness and a deep pain that engulfed her. Speaking to herself, she whispered, *"What did he say? What's meant to be will be. I suppose it wasn't meant for him and me to reunite."*

She spent another night of restlessness, unable to find comfort as she turned and twisted in bed. The next day, she made a firm commitment to focus solely on her work. It had always been her refuge, a remedy for her troubles, and a solution to all challenges. Work demanded only one thing from her: completing tasks. There was no room for foolish emotions. She could make detached decisions because it was all about the job, not her personal life... or at least that's what she believed.

CHAPTER 11

On Thursday morning, Janet and Syd embarked on their journey to Port Whaley, with Syd taking the driver's seat. The island was bathed in sunlight, and a clear blue sky stretched overhead. Janet always cherished springtime on Windermere. Unlike the cooler East Coast, the west coast enjoyed warmer temperatures, allowing flowers to bloom as early as March. The pink and white cherry blossoms had already begun to fade, their fallen petals adding a touch of color to the lush green grass. The air felt crisp, and Janet could swear she could smell the ocean with every breath she took. The April sun gently warmed her skin as it streamed through the large windows of the rented SUV.

"Are we stopping at the first Tim Hortons we spot?" Syd asked.

"Of course," Janet replied. "We both can't function without our Tim's coffee, can we? I had my breakfast, but I still need a coffee fix."

Ten minutes later, Syd pulled up to the window of the small Tim Hortons drive-through on Boulder Road. She placed the order for two coffees and also added a muffin. "Just in case you want something to nibble on," she said to Janet. Once they had their order, they continued on their journey. Syd was a careful driver, so Janet felt at ease and didn't need to keep her eyes on the road. Instead, she delved into the meeting materials that James had given her, highlighting important information and jotting down notes in the margins.

After a ninety-minute drive, they arrived at the ferry terminal, where they would board the ferry to the town of Portsmouth in Port Whaley. Syd joined the line for the crossing while Janet took the opportunity to stretch her legs in the terminal building. She wandered around the gift shop and then joined a small group of travelers who were being entertained by an elderly man playing the banjo. He sang *'You Are My Sunshine,'* and as the song came to an end, he bowed to the small audience, many of whom tossed a few coins into his upturned hat.

As the time to board the *Westcoast Princess* approached, Janet looked around for Syd, who had wandered off on her own. She eventually found her in the gift shop, where she was buying an Oprah magazine.

"I enjoy reading the Dr. Phil column," Syd remarked.

"I do, too," Janet admitted.

"We can share it," Syd suggested. "It looks like it's time for us to head back to the car."

A few minutes later, they rolled into the ferry, and Syd parked the car before they quickly made their way to the upper deck reserved for passengers. They located two comfortable seats by the rail and settled in. Syd became engrossed in reading Dr. Phil while Janet focused on the stack of contracts that needed to be signed and the two new policies that required her review. She became so immersed in her work that she hardly noticed when the ferry arrived at Portsmouth one hour and forty-five minutes later. The drive to the school district's office was brief, taking only fifteen minutes. Janet arrived just in time for her noon meeting.

"What time can I pick you up?' asked Syd.

"According to the agenda, we should be finished by 5:30. Why don't you come back then."

"Alright. I'll be here at 5:30. I'll check in our bags at the hotel, grab some lunch, and work in the business center."

"Make sure to take a break," advised Janet, "You deserve it after all that driving."

"Yes, I'll go for a walk first before I do anything."

***

Janet hurriedly made her way to the meeting room, realizing she was the last one to arrive. A dozen people were already seated around the oval table, each in front of their designated name tags.

Only one seat remained unoccupied, marked with her name tag: *Janet Ramphal.*

"Hi, everyone," Janet greeted the group as she took her seat. "I hope I'm not late."

"No, we're early," reassured Ian Parks, a gentleman from the Ministry, who approached Janet and introduced himself. "Hi Janet, I'm Ian from the Ministry. Thanks for filling in for James. I understand he's been summoned to another meeting with the DM. I'm glad you could make it."

"I'm glad to be here as well. I hope I can contribute to the discussions. James briefed me on some of the ongoing matters, and I also read some of the reports on my way here."

"I'm sure you'll have valuable insights to share," replied Ian.

Ian turned to the others and asked, "Well since we're all here, can we get started?" The members of the group nodded in agreement. "Before we begin, feel free to grab a cup of coffee," Ian suggested.

The meeting commenced with introductions, allowing Janet to get acquainted with her colleagues, who would be collaborating over the next few hours. Ian, an experienced Chair, ensured the meeting flowed smoothly. There were productive discussions about innovative approaches to advancing twenty-first-century learning, but there were also disagreements regarding the government's proposed timeline. Some participants expressed concerns about rushing things, while others embraced the mindset of seizing the opportunity. The discussions occasionally grew passionate, with arguments for and against supporting the government's emphasis on efficiency over thorough deliberation, but everyone maintained a respectful and civil tone.

At 2:00, the meeting broke for lunch, giving Janet the chance to have one-on-one conversations with some attendees. She connected with Bill Weis, a district Superintendent, and Clare Daniels, an elementary school principal. Jim Jardine, a vice-principal in human resources, was the third person she met. Time constraints prevented Janet from speaking with everyone present.

After lunch, the participants were divided into three smaller groups to strategize the implementation of twenty-first-century learning, focusing on Windermere Island and the Whaley River districts. Ian led the groups with determination, pushing for tangible outcomes. Janet thoroughly enjoyed the spirited discussions. When Syd arrived to pick her up at 5:30, Janet found it difficult to bid farewell to her new colleagues. She expressed sincere apologies to Bill, Anna, and Clare for not being able to join them for a drink at the *Roadrunner*. Feeling a bit tired, Janet had planned to continue reviewing policies before bedtime. However, she had also promised to have dinner with Syd. At that moment, all she wanted was to reach her hotel room and rest for a few minutes. Janet instructed Syd, "I'll meet you back here at 7:00 for dinner. What's your room number?"

"570," responded Syd.

"Okay. I'll be there at 7:00," confirmed Janet. She obtained her room key from the front desk and rode the elevator to the seventh floor, where her room was located. Being on the highest floor pleased her as it meant better sleep and less street noise. Syd had learned to always reserve an upper floor for Janet in any hotel she stayed at. Upon entering her room, Janet carelessly dropped her briefcase onto the winged armchair, kicked off her shoes, and removed her blazer before collapsing onto the bed. "*Ah, this feels so good,*" she muttered to herself. Whether it was the substantial lunch or the cheesecake she had during the afternoon coffee break, Janet swiftly drifted into sleep.

***

When Janet woke up, she noticed that dusk was starting to settle. Startled, she quickly sat up, worried that she might be running late for dinner. However, her nap had only lasted for thirty-five minutes, and she still had plenty of time. Despite her rest being short, she felt refreshed. Realizing that she should freshen up, she decided to take a quick shower, brush her teeth, and change into more comfortable clothes - slacks and a cotton shirt that she had brought with her.

Janet proceeded to take a shower and get dressed, but as she reached for her toothbrush in her makeup bag, she realized she had forgotten to pack it. Frustrated, she muttered to herself, "*Darn, what a nuisance. I must have left it on the bathroom counter while I was packing.*" Wanting to resolve the issue, she called the front desk to inquire if they had a spare toothbrush she could use.

Unfortunately, the clerk apologized and informed her that they were currently out of stock, but he could arrange for housekeeping to secure one within the next hour. He explained that the staff was occupied with checking in a basketball team at the moment. Janet thanked him for the information and decided to seek an alternative solution. She dialed Syd's number and explained the situation. "I need to borrow the car," she said. "I forgot to pack my toothbrush. I'm going to get one at the supermarket we passed on our way in. I'll come down and get the keys from you in five minutes."

"I'll get it for you," offered Syd. "You must be tired."

"No need at all. I'm already dressed. It would barely take me ten minutes to be gone and back again. Are you finished dressing?" asked Janet.

"No, not yet," replied Syd.

"So, in that case. It's clear. I'll go, and meanwhile, you can continue getting dressed,"

Janet quickly applied a bit of makeup, grabbed her purse, and headed out the door to retrieve the car keys from Syd. Uncertain about the exact directions, she cautiously pulled out of the hotel's parking lot, unsure whether to turn left or right. The twilight hours made navigating the unfamiliar town a bit challenging, adding to her uncertainty. However, she reminded herself that Portsmouth was a small town, and she could easily find her way around. Unlike Nat, who was hesitant to ask for directions, Janet had no qualms about seeking help if she got lost. She was confident that she could stop and ask someone for directions if needed. From her recollection, the *Food for Less* supermarket was located to the left of the hotel.

Carefully, she proceeded down Wendell Street, which eventually merged into Robinson Street. Janet couldn't help but notice that all the streets in Portsmouth seemed to be named after people, possibly notable figures. As she continued along Robinson Street, she spotted the illuminated sign of the supermarket ahead, slightly to the right. Realizing that she needed to make a right turn onto Perkins Street at the upcoming intersection, she switched lanes and smoothly maneuvered the car into the *Food for Less* parking lot.

With her purse slung over her shoulder, Janet hurriedly entered the store through the automated doors and made her way to the aisle labeled "Personal Grooming." As expected, a wide selection of toothbrushes in different brands, colors, and sizes greeted her. She didn't want to waste too much time choosing a toothbrush out of all things. Reaching up for a Colgate medium from one of the shelves, she was startled by a familiar voice calling her name, "Janet?"

It was hard to determine if it was a question or an exclamation, and the voice… Could it be Abe's? No, it couldn't be. Startled, she dropped the toothbrush and turned around abruptly, nearly losing her balance. To her astonishment, there stood Abe behind her. He reached out his hands to steady her. "Janet, I can't believe it. What are you doing here?" he exclaimed. "I heard you went to the Fairview looking for me. Are you following me?" he added jokingly.

Janet took a moment to collect herself, realizing that if they weren't in a public setting, she would have been tempted to slap Abe and wipe the smile off his face. "What are you even talking about? How would I have known you were here? I came to Portsmouth for a meeting," she retorted, her frustration evident.

Abe could sense that his lightheartedness had upset her. His smile faded, replaced by a look of concern. "I mentioned that I rented a cottage in Port Whaley, so I assumed you came here looking for me. I'm sorry, Jan. I always seem to jump to the wrong conclusions," he admitted, his tone sincere.

His sincerity melted away Janet's anger. She couldn't understand why she always acted so foolishly around Abe. She had believed she had lost him forever, and now fate had brought him right in front of her. "No, Abe, I'm the one who should apologize," she admitted, her voice softening.

Curiosity piqued, Abe asked, "What brought you here? What meeting did you attend?"

Janet quickly explained the purpose of her meeting. "And where are you staying?" he inquired.

"I'm at the Delta Hotel, just ten minutes away. Where is your cottage?" she asked, genuinely interested.

"It's about a thirty-minute drive along the river road," Abe explained, reaching out for Janet's hands. "Jan, we need to talk. I can't let you walk away again. I'm deeply sorry for abruptly leaving you during our dinner. There's no excuse for my behavior, and I truly apologize. I want to make it up to you. Join me for dinner at the cottage. I came to get some spaghetti sauce, and dinner was almost ready. I just need the sauce and twenty minutes. I ran out, and the grocery options in cottage country are limited and pricey."

Janet looked perplexed. "How can I just go with you to your cottage?" she questioned. "My assistant is waiting for me, and I promised to meet her for dinner at 7:00."

"Jan, you can find a way to cancel or reschedule," Abe insisted. "Please don't walk away from me again. I can't believe this is a mere coincidence, us being here at the same time. I don't believe in coincidences. This was meant to happen. We need to have the conversation we never finished. Please, Jan… At least join me for dinner, and we can continue where we left off at the restaurant. Please, do this for me, Jan."

Janet felt torn. She had longed to see Abe again, and now her prayers seemed to have been answered. He was right about Syd; she could find an excuse. Taking out her cell phone, she dialed Syd's number.

Syd answered after three rings. "Hi, Janet. Is everything okay?" she asked.

"Yes, everything's fine," Janet replied. "I'm at the supermarket and ran into the Chair from the meeting. He's having dinner with some government officials and invited me to join them. It's a great opportunity for me to gain a political perspective on twenty-first century learning for James. Their dinner is at 8:00, so I'll browse the bookstore here for a while and then join them. There's a McDonald's across the street where I can use the bathroom and brush my teeth. I'm sorry to cancel on you, Syd, but I think this dinner meeting could be really beneficial. Don't wait up for me. Enjoy your dinner, and as we discussed, we'll sleep in tomorrow and leave for the ferry at 2:00."

"No worries. I'll have dinner at the restaurant here and watch a movie afterward. See you tomorrow at 2:00 in the lobby," replied Syd.

"Sounds good," said Janet. "Goodnight, Syd." Janet put her phone back in its case and looked around for Abe, who had given her some privacy by wandering into the next aisle. "There you are," she said as she approached him.

"So, what's the plan?" Abe asked.

"I don't know. You tell me," she said, throwing caution to the wind.

"I'm taking you to the cottage for dinner, no *ifs* or *buts*. Just follow me, will you?"

"Wait a second, let me pay for my toothbrush first."

***

After checking out at the cashier, they made their way to the parking lot. Abe had also rented a car, but he didn't want Janet to leave her SUV at the supermarket for too long, fearing it might get towed. "Tell you what," he suggested, "I'll drive ahead, and you can follow me. Once we're out of the city, it's a one-lane road with minimal traffic. Just try to stay behind me. If I lose sight of you, I'll stop and wait for you to catch up."

Janet agreed and got into her car while Abe led the way in his rental Honda Civic, driving slowly to allow Janet to follow his signals and stay close to him. The country road was almost dark, and Janet couldn't say she enjoyed the drive. For the last twelve minutes, all she could see were the sparse cottages along the river embankment and the shadowy outline of tall pine trees. Keeping her eyes focused on the Civic's taillights, she stopped her car just behind Abe as he pulled into the short driveway of the cottage. Abe quickly exited his car and ran up the four steps to the front porch, placing his purchase on a wooden chair and turning on the porch lights. He then came to the driver's side of Janet's SUV to ensure she could safely exit in the unfamiliar surroundings. "Watch your step," he said, taking her arm. "The ground here is somewhat uneven."

"Thanks," said Janet, "I can manage."

Abe released her arm and walked ahead to open the front door. The inviting aroma of warm food greeted Janet as she paused at the entrance. "Something does smell really good," she remarked. Abe hurried inside and turned on the lamps, leaving a dim light in the living room.

"Come in, Janet," he warmly invited. "I'm going to start the sauce. Make yourself comfortable. The meatballs are still warm in the oven." His words conveyed a sense of ease, as if entertaining her was a regular occurrence for him.

Janet licked her dry lips. What was she doing? Was this really happening? She and Abe were having dinner at his cottage - it didn't make sense! "Nothing makes sense," thought Janet. "I'm always trying to make sense of things, but not this time. It feels like fate is playing a part in my life." She cleared her mind of other thoughts and focused on the present. She was going to have dinner with Abe and finish their conversation. Tomorrow, she would deal with whatever challenges came her way. "Please, God," she prayed silently, "Let this be right for Abe, and let me be kind to him. It might be my only chance."

Janet cautiously explored the living room, taking in the wicker furniture and the few family pictures adorning the wall. She pointed to a photo and inquired, "Is this your friend with the fishing rod? And is this his wife sitting on the rock?"

"Yes, that's him, and that's his wife," replied Abe from the kitchen. "He mentioned that he'll have to remove those pictures before selling the cottage."

"It's in good shape. It's a shame about his wife's passing. They must have had wonderful moments here," remarked Janet.

"If you knew Gary and Dianne, you'd understand how truly happy they were," Abe remarked, joining Janet by the pictures. Janet couldn't help but remember how much taller he was than her. "I hope Gary finds the strength to rebuild his life. He was a loving husband and a remarkable father."

Janet felt a slight tremor in her body as she sensed Abe's proximity. He seemed to notice and inquired, "Are you cold? There are some clean throws in the bin behind the sofa. You can grab one if you'd like."

Appreciating the opportunity to create some distance, Janet replied, "I'm alright, thank you." The inviting aroma of the sauce wafted into the living room from the kitchen. "Your sauce smells delicious."

Abe extended an invitation, "You can help me set the table if you'd like."

As Abe continued to add various spices to the sauce, creating an enticing aroma while stirring it, Janet rummaged through the cabinets to find plates and cutlery for the table. Meanwhile, Abe glanced into the refrigerator and retrieved a bottle of Okanogan Jackson Estate Shiraz. He turned to Janet and asked, "Would you like to share a glass of wine with me?"

Janet replied with a casual, "Sure, why not?"

"That's my girl," responded Abe with a quirky smile on his face.

As he smiled at Janet, he poured a glass for her and a quarter for himself, explaining, "Only a few sips of wine for me as I'm not allowed alcohol with my medication." Janet couldn't help but marvel at the naturalness of the situation. Here they were, in the kitchen, preparing supper together. Sensing her thoughts, Abe locked eyes with her and asked, "Jan, is this all real? Are you truly here? Are we in a cottage where nobody would ever dream of finding us?"

Janet paused in her task of straightening the table runner, her eyes reflecting the astonishment mirrored in Abe's gaze. With the glasses of wine now on the table, Abe took her hands in his, drawing her closer to him. "Yes, this is not a dream," he reassured her. "I always dreamed of finding you, and now being here with you feels more real than anything I ever imagined." As he held her hands against his cheeks, he tenderly kissed each palm, causing two tears to roll down and meet his lips. Instinctively, Janet released her hand and wiped away the tears, trying to conceal her inner turmoil. "Aren't you forgetting about the sauce?" she asked, attempting to divert his attention. "It's boiling and could spill over the pan."

The awkward moment quickly passed as Abe rushed to the stove to stir the sauce and prevent it from spilling over. He focused on warming the pasta and preparing the meal while Janet pretended that the intense moment hadn't happened. She anticipated that there would be more unexpected moments to come, but she was determined to handle them gracefully. Despite the lingering tension, Janet decided to enjoy the dinner, realizing that she was actually hungry. Abe arranged the bowls on the table and stepped back to admire his efforts. "Well, now that everything's in place, let's dig in," he said, inviting Janet to start the meal.

As they took their seats at opposite ends of the small table, Abe lifted his glass and suggested they make a toast. "We should have a toast," he declared.

"Yes, bon appétit," Janet responded softly, raising her glass. She wished to steer clear of any sentimental remarks.

Their glasses clinked together. "Bon appétit," Abe echoed, and they began their meal.

The meal was simple, yet Janet couldn't deny its deliciousness. After savoring a few bites, she broke the silence. "You're a really talented cook, Abe. The salad is fantastic, and the pasta tastes wonderful. I never knew you had such culinary skills. Back when you lived with your mom, you avoided the kitchen."

"Well, times change," he replied. "For the past sixteen years, especially after Lizzie left, I've had to fend for myself. I either had to learn to cook or go hungry. While I do enjoy eating out occasionally, I prefer not to rely on it too much. So, I had no choice but to learn. With recipes readily available, it's not too difficult. I even find pleasure in experimenting and creating my own concoctions."

"Well, I'm glad I have the opportunity to enjoy your cooking," Janet remarked with a playful wink. "But you better not expect the same from me."

"Never say never," Abe responded, countering her statement. "Did you ever imagine we'd end up like this?"

She shook her head. "If someone had told me this would happen, I would have doubted it. Life can be so unpredictable, don't you think?"

Abe nodded in agreement. "I've learned that anything is possible, whether it's something wonderful or devastating."

They continued to chat casually as he spoke about his family, and she talked about her daughters and the strong connection that she had with them. They enjoyed sipping their wine while conversing and eating. Abe refilled Janet's glass for a second time, and she was surprised that she allowed it. She had let loose a little, going from just half a glass to now having two glasses. The wine flowing through her veins boosted her confidence and allowed her to fully unwind and relax.

Chapter 12

As they finished their dinner, Janet mustered the courage to apologize to Abe for her earlier behavior and opened up about her anger towards him during their previous dinner. She admitted that her anger stemmed from her deep fear of losing him, and just talking about it brought tears to her eyes once again.

"People perceive me as a strong and resilient woman, Abe," Janet confessed. "My colleagues believe nothing can shake me, and everyone relies on me, even in my family. But beneath that facade, I have my fears and anxieties. I put on a brave face for the world, but inside, my heart is tender when it comes to what truly matters to me. Right now, I'm feeling distressed because I don't know how to help you. In my job, I find solutions, face challenges, and bring about change. I'm the one who fixes things and makes them right. But in this situation, I feel powerless to make anything right for you. What do you need from me, Abe?" she sobbed.

Unable to bear seeing Janet in such distress, Abe rose from the table and gently guided her to the couch. "Please, have a seat, Jan," he said, helping her settle among the soft pillows and placing one behind her back. Still holding her hands, he sat down beside her.

"I don't expect anything from you, Jan," Abe reassured her. "I wanted to see you before I departed from this world. I admit I may have asked too much of you, but thoughts of you consumed me day and night. I couldn't shake the desire to meet you one last time. It's not that I believe seeing you will make everything right. I came here out of my selfishness, longing to gaze into your eyes one final time. I had no expectations, but I'm grateful that we did meet, and now, here we are; this is more than I ever hoped for. You don't need to do anything for me, Jan."

"But I do want to help you, Abe. If there's something I can do for you, please let me know. I genuinely want to be helpful," Janet insisted, her voice filled with sincerity.

Abe's eyes locked onto hers, searching for a deeper connection, as he posed his request, "Janet, would you accompany me back to San Souci just for a few days?"

Janet couldn't believe what she was hearing. Was Abe out of his mind? She felt a surge of disbelief and jumped up from the couch. "Abe, how can you just casually ask for the impossible? This is beyond reason! You just said you wanted to see me, and we're here together right now. Why would you expect me to go to San Souci? You know that such a request is entirely out of the question!"

With unwavering intensity, Abe continued to gaze into Janet's eyes as he spoke softly, "Jan, nothing is impossible if you truly desire it. Can you find a way to make this happen? My dying wish is for you to spend some time with me in San Souci. Our family home still stands there, and my nephew takes care of it. My brother and I visit every summer. I don't expect you to stay in the house with me, as I wouldn't want to jeopardize your reputation. However, you can stay at the Guest House on the island. The facilities have improved significantly. Many friends from the island who live abroad choose to stay there when they visit. I know you often return to Guyana to see Jenna and Jack, so perhaps you can plan an earlier visit and include a day on San Souci. Can you at least consider it?"

Taking Abe's request into consideration, Janet's mind was filled with questions. "Yes, I do try to visit Jack and Jenna as often as I can. My last visit was three years ago, and I was thinking of planning another trip by the end of this year. But what do you hope to accomplish with me going to San Souci?"

Abe's eyes gleamed with nostalgia as he replied, "I want to take you back to the place where we first met. I want to relive the most cherished memories of my life. I long to stroll along the old seawall with you, inhale the salty air as we walk side by side. I want to feel the ocean's spray against my face and the soft sand beneath our feet as we run along the water's edge. I yearn to revisit the exact moment when my life changed, the moment you entered it and brought light and joy. Going back to San Souci would be a way to recapture that magic."

Janet could see the earnestness in Abe's eyes, and she realized that he was dead serious about his request. Despite her concern for his suffering, she felt compelled to address her reservations. "Abe, we're treading dangerous ground here. Considering your health condition, I don't want to unintentionally hurt you, but I have to ask: aren't you being a bit selfish? Shouldn't you be asking ME if I would like to go back to San Souci with you?"

Abe's expression softened, reflecting a hint of remorse. "You're right, Janet. I'm fully aware that I'm being selfish. I've pondered this countless times, and now I've finally expressed my true desire." He paused briefly, removing an imaginary hair from her collar, and then he gently lifted her face with his free hand. With sincerity in his voice, he asked, "Jan, would you like to visit San Souci with me, even if it's just for one day?"

Janet frowned, deep in thought, and lowered her gaze. After a moment of contemplation, she responded, "The answer is yes. I would love to go back to San Souci with you. But we must confront the reality that it would cause significant problems within my family. I don't have an answer for how this could happen without repercussions. Are you expecting me to tell my husband about this? Do you think I can simply abandon everything and go on a vacation?"

"No, of course not, Janet. I don't want you to face any problems with your family. But if there's any way for us to spend at least one day together, it's something I desire more than anything else, even more than a cure for my illness. I would rather spend one day with you and then die than live another year without seeing you again after today."

Janet could sense the depth of his desire to be with her on San Souci. Feeling overwhelmed, she sank back onto the couch. Abe wrapped his arms around her, providing comfort. "Jan, I'm torn. I want to be a part of your life, but I don't want you to face any consequences because of me."

"Have you considered the potential problems we may encounter? If your health is not stable, how can you travel? What if your condition worsens in a short period of time?" she asked him softly.

"I'm currently managing my health with medication, and I should be fine for the next six months or so. However, after that, I may end up in the hospital or confined to my home with limited mobility. Time is not on my side. I understand that I'm rushing you into something unexpected. I've had time to think about this, but I've caught you off guard, and I know it's not fair. I don't expect an immediate answer, but I want you to consider it," he explained.

"I would like to go back to San Souci with you, but I need time to figure out how to make it possible without causing any harm to Nat or our daughters. Let me think things through. I have to leave Portsmouth tomorrow, but please give me your telephone number and email address so we can stay in touch. If I can't go to San Souci, maybe we can find another way to spend some time together. I will try to give you two days of my life, but I'm still uncertain about the how and where," Janet explained.

Abe looked at her with a sense of urgency. "I want even a small portion of your time, and it has to be soon," he insisted. "Time is running out for me."

"Yes, I understand," Janet replied. "I'll do my best to explore possibilities within the next two weeks, and I'll contact you either by phone or email." She took out her business card from her purse and handed it to him. "Here's my email address and telephone number. When you send me a message, I'll have your email address as well, so we can continue to correspond."

Abe accepted the card and examined it with a wide smile. "Very impressive," he remarked.

Janet marveled at how quickly Abe could rebound. He took out his wallet and carefully placed the card into one of the slots. "I'll never lose this," he declared.

***

"I need to return to the hotel," Janet reminded him, glancing at her watch. She couldn't believe it was already fifteen minutes past eleven.

"What? Now?" Abe exclaimed. "It's late. You should get some rest. You must be tired after such a long day."

Janet suddenly realized that she was indeed exhausted. It was time for her to go to bed. Was Abe suggesting that she spend the night with him at the cottage? She looked at him questioningly. "Yes, I agree. I need to get some sleep, so I should be on my way."

"Why don't you just stay here?" Abe proposed. "It's already close to midnight." He must have noticed the panic in her expression. "I'm not asking you to sleep with me, Jan. You can have the bed, and I'll sleep on the couch. There's enough clean bedding, and I can assure you that the bed is comfortable."

Janet regarded him suspiciously. "Why should I take your bed and make you uncomfortable? Remember, you're the one who's not well. I can drive to the hotel in less than forty-five minutes."

"You've always been stubborn, Jan." Abe stood up from the couch and made his way to the kitchen to put away the dirty dishes and tidy up. Janet followed him, continuing their discussion. "I don't want my assistant to find out that I spent the night with you. I despise lying and deception."

"How will she find out?" Abe asked. "You'll get some sleep; return to the hotel tomorrow in time to get ready and meet as planned. She's not your bodyguard or your boss. No one will know that you stayed here with me unless you tell them."

Janet felt herself giving in to his persistence. What harm would it do? She did want to stay with him, but she couldn't ignore her desire for propriety. This was typical of her. She always strived to maintain moral and ethical conduct, not wanting to compromise her self-respect. Abe continued persuasively, "You could sleep in one of my shirts. It'll be more comfortable."

"Alright," Janet agreed, "You win. I'll stay, but please set the alarm for 7:00. I can't afford to be late. I have a lot to take care of before breakfast, and I can't miss the ferry back."

"Don't worry," Abe reassured her, "I'll make sure you get back to the hotel on time."

Abe finished washing the last of the dishes and dried his hands on a kitchen towel. He then went into the bedroom to find a sleep shirt for Janet. He also removed the sheets from the bed and took them to the couch. "Just wait here," he instructed, patting the seat on the couch. "I'll find some clean sheets and re-make the bed."

Janet offered to help. She followed him into the bedroom, and after a quick search through the small closet, Abe found a set of sheets and a fuzzy, blue blanket. He sniffed them, reminiscent of how he checked his kids' laundry to ensure the socks were properly washed. "These are clean. They still have the scent of lemon and sea breeze," he remarked. Janet smiled at his peculiar method of checking laundry. He tossed the sheets to her and said, "You work at the foot of the bed, and I'll work at the head."

Janet burst into laughter. "What's so funny?" Abe asked, puzzled.

"Can you imagine us making a bed together for me to sleep in? It's quite amusing!" Janet replied.

Abe giggled, "No, it's more than funny. It's a bit surreal! I can't believe this is actually happening. Maybe I'm delusional."

Janet joined in, still laughing. "Or maybe I'm the one who's dreaming," she added.

"No, you're not dreaming," Abe assured her, closing the distance between them in just a few strides. He held her close, their faces inches apart, and spoke with genuine emotion, "I'm real, Janet, and I've yearned to hold you in my arms for all these years. My God, why did I wait so long?" Resting his chin on her head, he pulled her even closer, their bodies entwined. Janet suppressed her conscience's urge to pull away and allowed herself to be enveloped in the nostalgic warmth of her feelings for Abe, reminiscent of their teenage years. He tenderly caressed her face and then lifted her with great effort, gently placing her on the bed. In his weakened state, she could sense his heavy breathing. She wanted to protest, but she didn't want to ruin the moment. Abe lay beside her on his side, facing her, and whispered, "I could spend the whole night just looking at you with all my love."

"There's nothing much to look at, Abe. I'm becoming just an old woman," Janet murmured, feeling self-conscious. However, she cautiously wrapped her arms around his neck and brought his face closer to hers, planting a light kiss on his lips. He responded with a slow and tender kiss, brushing his lips across her eyelids and cheeks.

"Janet Ramphal," he finally whispered, his voice filled with pain, "Why did I ever let you go!" His words pierced her heart, and she held onto him tightly as quiet sobs escaped her.

"Just hold me, Abe," she whispered softly, and he complied. They lay together, finding solace in each other's embrace.

***

After some time, Abe noticed that Janet's eyes were becoming heavy with fatigue. He gently disentangled himself from her embrace and opened the drawer of the small dresser next to the bed. He pulled out a shirt and playfully tossed it on top of Janet. "Here's what you can sleep in," he said with a smile. "I think you're ready for bed."

Janet slowly stood up. "Yes, I am. I think I'll borrow your toothpaste. Thankfully, I have a toothbrush with me."

"Everything you need is in the bathroom," Abe reassured her. "There are even two new toothbrushes. Just help yourself."

As Janet made her way towards the bathroom, she reminded Abe, "Don't forget to set your alarm for 7:00. We don't want to oversleep, and I'll be late getting back."

Abe chuckled and replied, "That's not going to happen. I might be awake all night. So, no worries about getting you up at 7:00."

Janet hurried into the bathroom, but even in her rush, she couldn't help but notice and appreciate the beautiful lilac flowers adorning the curtain, the soft towels that matched, and even the soap dish with its delicate floral design. As she observed these details, she thought about the woman who had likely arranged everything but was no longer able to enjoy the beauty of the cottage and its surroundings. A feeling of unfairness washed over her, and she muttered quietly to herself, "Life is not fair!"

Quickly, Janet brushed her teeth, washed her face, and changed into the shirt Abe had given her. As she looked at her reflection in the mirror, she felt a sense of detachment. The person she saw didn't seem like herself. It was difficult for her to accept that she was about to spend the night with another man. Meanwhile, her husband slept soundly, completely unaware of the potential betrayal she was contemplating.

Janet felt like an impostor, completely at odds with the person she believed herself to be. If someone had suggested that she would be capable of being unfaithful to Nat, she would have vehemently denied it. The memory of Nat's infidelity lingered in her mind, tempting her to justify her potential betrayal. Yet, she understood that seeking revenge wouldn't make things right. Human emotions could be fickle, and trust could be so easily broken.

She silently argued with herself, desperately trying to convince her inner self that she wasn't truly betraying Nat. After all, she was only fulfilling Abe's final wishes in his dying moments. Nat didn't need to know about tonight or her plans to spend a few days with Abe. Janet was determined to make it clear to Abe that their relationship would remain strictly platonic. She believed that physical intimacy wasn't what Abe truly desired; it was her presence and companionship that meant the world to him.

With her inner conflict seemingly resolved, Janet dried her face with the soft towel and quietly returned to the bedroom, slipping under the warm covers.

***

Abe finished making his bed on the couch, and soon after, he entered the room to check on Janet.

"I'm fine," she assured him. "I don't think I'll be able to sleep either. This whole situation is so surreal... You and me... Being in the same place. I was supposed to be on the seventh floor of the Delta Hotel. What am I doing here? I've never done anything like this before in my entire life!"

Abe sat on the edge of the bed as if it were the most natural thing in the world for him to do. His thoughts seemed different from Janet's. He smoothed out the edge of the covers and said, "I didn't expect this to happen either, but I'm selfish and grateful to have this time with you. Do you want a glass of warm milk?"

Janet shook her head. "I'm still so full. What are your plans?" she asked him.

"Plans?" he repeated.

"Yes. Are you going back to Toronto soon?"

Abe explained that he would stay at the cottage for another week before flying back to Toronto. He had arrangements to make with his kids and wanted to spend time with his grandkids. He had even promised to take the oldest one to Disneyland. Abe planned to leave the house to his two sons, who would later decide what they wanted to do with the property. Janet listened to him as he outlined the details of his fading life. Suddenly, she sat up as he again broached the subject of spending a few days with her.

***

As they continued their conversation, Janet couldn't shake off the thought that going back to San Souci was impractical, and she wasn't sure if reliving a past that happened over four decades ago was the right decision. Suddenly, a thought struck her. She had been contemplating whether she should attend that conference in Cuba, where she had been invited as a speaker. Nat was aware of her impending decision, as she had discussed the conference with him. If Abe could fit the trip into his plans, they might be able to spend some time together in Cuba. The conference would require her presence for three days, but she would have her afternoons and evenings free. Additionally, she could extend her stay by two days and dedicate that time to being with Abe.

Wanting to be transparent with him, she expressed her thoughts, "Abe, it may not be possible for me to go back to Guyana and San Souci. It would be difficult for me to find a justifiable reason for a sudden trip. However, I do have the opportunity to spend five days in Cuba. The University of Holguin has organized a conference, and I have been invited as a speaker. The conference will take place three weeks from now. Can you manage to go on such short notice?"

"I can't believe this. In three weeks!" Abe exclaimed. "Three weeks is sooner than I anticipated. It would be better to go to Cuba than not being together at all. Although San Souci would be ideal because of the memories we shared, we can make new memories in Holguin."

Janet responded, "This is not about making new memories, Abe. We're long past that. You asked me for some of my time, and I'm trying to see how I can give that to you. If you're willing to go with me to Cuba, then we can see how to make it work."

Abe nodded, his expression filled with a mix of nervousness and anticipation. "I understand, Jan… It's not about making memories anymore. I asked for your time, and I appreciate you trying to find a way to give that to me."

They engaged in a lengthy discussion, addressing the various challenges they might encounter. They explored issues such as coordinating flights and accommodations, ensuring Abe had his necessary medication and access to emergency healthcare, obtaining approval from his doctor, and potential issues with travel and health insurance. As they continued to brainstorm and exchange ideas, Janet realized that it was almost 1:00 a.m. and she hadn't slept a wink.

They were still sitting on the bed, facing each other. Janet finally spoke up, "Abe, I think I should go back to my hotel. We've been talking all night, and I'll be completely exhausted tomorrow. I'll email you so we can continue planning our time in Cuba."

Abe's concern was evident on his face. "Janet, you can't be driving back to your hotel at this hour of the night... morning, in fact, I won't let you," he insisted. In response, Janet quickly threw off the blanket covering her.

"Abe, you don't have to let me. I have driven at all hours of the night on my own, whether in Windermere, Panama, or New York. So, there's no need to worry," she reassured him.

Abe remained silent, his gaze fixed on Janet's legs, which were now exposed. Janet felt a surge of self-consciousness and quickly pulled the blanket up to her chin. Abe whispered hoarsely, "You're still so beautiful."

Janet was embarrassed, but Abe insisted, "I'm just stating a fact."

Abe reassured her, "No need to be shy. I would not do anything that you would not want me to."

"Please promise me it will be that way," Janet pleaded.

"I promise, Jan. I cross my heart and hope to die," Abe said, winking. Janet was about to protest about him not taking her seriously when he continued, "I will never do anything to hurt you, Jan. I want you to believe that all I care about is you. I want to see you happy. I want to hear your laughter, watch your eyes, and read your thoughts. I want to take a part of you with me when I leave this world, and I want you to know, to really know how much you're loved." He leaned over and tenderly kissed her eyelids. "I love you, Jan, more than anyone I have ever known."

She choked back the tears that his tenderness evoked and brusquely said, "I'm going to go, Abe. If you're afraid for me to drive alone, then you can follow me back to the hotel." She threw back the cover for the second time and jumped off the bed, heading for the bathroom where she had left her clothes on the two hangers she found on the towel rack. Closing the door, she quickly got dressed.

By the time she came out, Abe was waiting with his light jacket in his hand. He had picked up his car keys and seemed ready to leave. He thrust the jacket towards her. "Here, put this on. It's chilly out there."

"I'm fine, Abe. I don't need a jacket. This shirt is sufficiently warm," Janet explained.

"Are you sure?" he asked, attempting to feel the fabric of her sleeve.

"It's all good. Are you able to drive? You don't have to do this. I'll be safe going alone. I'm not afraid," she reassured him.

"I know you're brave, and you don't need anyone to take care of you, but I'm doing this for my own selfish reassurance. I want to make sure you're safe in your hotel before I go to bed, or else I'll have no sleep," Abe explained, dropping the jacket on the couch.

"I'll call you when I arrive, so you'll know I'm okay."

"No more arguments, Jan," he affirmed rather sternly. He then asked, "Are you ready?"

"I just need to get my bag. You should take the jacket with you in the car, just in case..." Janet suggested.

As Janet went past him to get her purse from the living room table, Abe pulled her close and held her. She buried her face in his warmth, a familiar gesture from their teenage years. Looking up, she gently rubbed his cheeks with her fingers, trying to tickle him under his chin. He smiled and held her even tighter. "My precious, precious Jan., I'm so glad I found you again." He kissed the top of her head and added, "Come on, let's get moving." He playfully slapped her on the rump.

As Janet walked through the front door onto the porch, she wrapped her shirt tighter against the chill that had settled over Port Whaley. The darkness enveloped the surroundings, illuminated only by a few distant stars and the soft glow of the streetlamps. The air carried the sweet scent of lilacs and Russian sage, mingling with the fragrances of roses and honeysuckles. The world around her seemed peaceful and serene, in contrast to the complexity of her inner thoughts.

Just as she was about to get into the driver's seat of her car, Abe approached from behind. He took her hands in his and squeezed her fingers, bringing her hands to his lips and kissing her open palms, reminiscent of their first meeting at her office. "I won't get out of the car when we reach your hotel," he said. "Saying goodbye will be too difficult, so I'm doing it now. Drive carefully and keep your eyes on the road. I'll be right behind you throughout the journey."

She released his hands and swiftly settled into the driver's seat. Turning on the engine and the headlights, she let the car warm up for a minute before pulling out of the driveway and onto the narrow highway. Glancing into the rearview mirror, she could see the headlights of Abe's car following closely behind. The road was unfamiliar to her, so she maintained a slower pace, adhering to the intermittent speed limit signs along the way.

At this early hour, the highway seemed deserted, creating an almost eerie atmosphere. It felt as if it was just Abe and Janet at that moment, navigating the quiet road. As she approached the hotel vicinity, a car passed by in the opposite direction, breaking the solitude of the journey.

"Just Abe and I - and the stars," Janet whispered. Within the next five minutes, she maneuvered her car into the hotel's parking lot. As she came to a stop, she could see Abe's car pulling up a few feet behind hers. Eagerly, she glanced into her rearview mirror, hoping to catch a glimpse of him, but his car remained shrouded in darkness.

Frustrated, she whispered, "Come on, switch the lights on inside," but the car stayed dark, and Janet could barely make out his silhouette through the windshield.

Before she could step out of her car, Abe suddenly accelerated and swiftly drove through the parking lot, his taillights disappearing into the night. "Well, that's Abe keeping his promise," Janet thought to herself.

CHAPTER 13

Janet entered the hotel lobby, feeling completely drained. Exhaustion washed over her, making it difficult to respond coherently to the hotel clerk's greeting. She rode the elevator up to the tenth floor, undressed, set the alarm clock, and climbed into bed. For the first ten minutes, she restlessly adjusted her pillow, pulled the covers up to her chin, tossed them off, and repeated the process before finally falling into a fitful and dreamless sleep.

When the alarm in Janet's hotel room faithfully rang at 9:00, she was ready to start her day. The sun was attempting to filter through the closed drapes, and the faint sounds of traffic could be heard from the street below. Voices and the rolling of suitcases echoed in the hallway, likely belonging to departing guests checking out. Janet yawned, stretched, and reluctantly left the comfort of her bed. She walked over to the small bureau where her iPad sat and noticed that she had received eleven new emails, three of which were marked urgent.

Janet's mind kicked into high gear as she swiftly responded to emails and tackled the urgent matters at hand. Her fingers danced across the keyboard as she delved into her work, fully engaged and alert. It was in these moments that she felt most alive and fulfilled. However, a pang of guilt washed over her as she thought about Nat. He had often expressed his dissatisfaction with her unwavering commitment to her job, feeling neglected and second to her career. "Nat," she exclaimed out loud, realization hitting her. "What am I really doing?"

Janet's mind was consumed with thoughts of her unexpected time with Abe, replaying the surreal experience over and over again. It felt like a dream, something she never could have anticipated when she boarded that ferry to Port Whaley. "Life is truly unpredictable," she mused to herself, contemplating the twists and turns that led her to this moment. Glancing at the clock, she realized that time was slipping away. It was already past 10:00, and she needed to get ready, grab breakfast, and meet Syd.

Janet firmly believed in the importance of breakfast, considering it a saving grace in facing the challenges of a hectic day. Marcia, the Dean of the Faculty of Fine Arts, had once sought Janet's advice on how to navigate a demanding day. Janet's response was simple yet effective: "Say your prayers and make sure you have a hearty breakfast. A full stomach prepares you to tackle the unknowns of the day. Remember, if you're hungry, you're more likely to get angry quickly. They say a hungry woman is an angry woman."

Janet not only dispensed this advice, but she also followed it herself, recognizing the value of taking the time to sit and enjoy her meal rather than rushing through it. She knew she needed to head to the restaurant quickly as breakfast typically ended at 11:00, and she needed time to sit and savor her food rather than rush. That part of the advice she had failed to give Marcia. It was not only having breakfast but taking the time to enjoy it.

Most days, upon arriving at the office, Janet often found herself confronted with a deluge of problems, akin to a tidal wave, requiring her to stay afloat and navigate through the conflicts and organizational politics that threatened to inundate her life. However, after four years of experience, she had become adept at handling her job and no longer allowed these challenges to overpower her. She had developed the resilience and skills necessary to stay above water and maintain control in the face of adversity.

After quickly showering and dressing, Janet patted her still-damp hair into place, grateful for its short length that required minimal styling. She didn't have to spend excessive time curling or crimping like some of her friends did. Glancing at her watch, she realized it was nearing 11:00, prompting her to hasten to the breakfast room before the doors closed for the morning. As she entered, she noticed only one other guest sitting in the far corner - an elderly gentleman engrossed in the front-page news of the *Whaley Times*. He acknowledged her presence with a brief nod.

Janet checked the coffee pot, realizing it must have been sitting there for a few hours. Deciding against it, she opted for instant coffee instead. She poured hot water from the kettle and added a splash of cream from the jug that sat in a bowl of ice cubes. Turning her attention to the food options, she noticed there were still sausages, eggs, biscuits, and scones available, although not piping hot but at least warm. Her stomach growled in anticipation as she sipped her hot coffee, realizing it had been fourteen hours since her last meal. The sausages had fat beginning to congeal around the edges, which didn't appeal to her, so she opted for eggs, biscuits, and a generous serving of fresh fruit, which she topped with plain Greek yogurt. Following her breakfast rule, she focused on protein and kept her carb intake to a minimum.

Janet sat at the opposite end of the room, away from the newspaper reader, and quietly enjoyed her breakfast. Her mind drifted back to Abe. She wondered what he was doing at that moment. Had he returned to bed after she left? Was he now having a late breakfast prepared in the quaint and orderly kitchen of the cottage? She pictured him in his pajamas, making toast and eggs, and sitting at the kitchen table. She imagined him gazing out of the large windows, basking in the morning sunshine and observing the mist gently rising above the river. The cottage's surroundings were idyllically peaceful. Last night, it felt as though the entire world consisted only of her and Abe. Along the river, everything was so serene, and if there were other occupants in the neighboring cottages, they remained unseen and unheard. Janet sighed loudly. She did not hear the approach of the breakfast helper who asked, "Are you okay? Do you need anything else? I'm about to clear away the food."

Janet turned to the breakfast helper, slightly startled by her presence. "Oh, hello. No, thank you. I'm alright. I have everything I need. Do I have to leave soon?"

The breakfast helper smiled kindly. "No rush, ma'am. Take your time. We'll be closing the breakfast service in about half an hour, but you can stay as long as you'd like."

Janet nodded gratefully as she responded, "Thank you. I'll finish up soon, then."

Janet could hear the rustling of newspaper pages coming from the old gentleman's corner. Then she heard the scraping sound of his chair being pushed back. The breakfast helper, Laura, who wore a name tag, spoke up, "No need to rush, ma'am. Feel free to stay as long as you'd like. I'll have to close the door, though, so no one else comes in. Breakfast officially ends at 11:00."

She then turned to address the old gentleman, "And the same goes for you, sir. You're welcome to stay if you'd like."

Janet heard the gentleman say, "Thanks, but I need to get going." His footsteps echoed on the tile as he left the room. Once Laura had cleared away the dishes, Janet was grateful for the solitude that allowed her thoughts to roam freely. She couldn't help but wonder how Abe managed to face his illness with such unwavering positivity. His calmness in the face of adversity impressed her.

Reflecting on her hypothetical situation, she admitted, "*I would have been consumed by worry.*" Janet pondered the idea that in times of great suffering, God grants people the faith and endurance necessary to confront their challenges. Memories of Don, one of her staff members diagnosed with terminal lung cancer, flooded her mind. She vividly remembered the day he tearfully informed her of his long-term disability leave. Janet had tried to console him, offering words of encouragement and hope, but deep down, she harbored doubts about his survival. Their tears had mingled during their embrace, and she sensed that he could discern the emptiness in her assurances.

In the subsequent days and weeks, Don's emotions fluctuated between anger, frustration, and constant anxiety. He sought pity from friends and family, and it was distressing to witness his rapid decline. Instead of extending his life, the chemotherapy and radiation treatments left him depleted and devoid of energy, taking away his remaining ounce of willingness to live. Seven months after his diagnosis, Don passed away. While his death may not have come as a surprise, it dealt a heavy blow to his family.

***

Abe mentioned that his family was handling his health condition well, but Janet couldn't help but feel that his illness was an overwhelming experience for them. She imagined how difficult it must be for his sons to see their father's declining health, especially for his grandkids, who had such a strong affection for him, just as he did for them. The thought of explaining death to young children, like Andy's five-year-old, weighed heavily on her mind. What would Andy and Neil say when the kids started asking about their granddad, who suddenly disappeared from their lives? And as for Abe, what were some of the things he would still want to do before his time ran out, apart from spending time with her?

Life was so complex, Janet pondered. Her life had become somewhat straightforward in recent years. Her two daughters seemed to be happily married and leading fulfilling lives. Jacinda, her youngest, was engrossed in her studies and appeared content. She and Nat had settled into a comfortable routine of work, visiting their daughters, and enjoying well-deserved vacations. Their evenings were often filled with theater outings, book club meetings, formal university dinners, or casual get-togethers with friends. Janet cherished the friendship of two Jamaican women she had serendipitously met at the Farmer's Market. On a rainy Saturday morning, while trying to dodge the raindrops without an umbrella, she accidentally bumped into Claudette. After exchanging apologies, Claudette inquired, "Do I detect a Caribbean accent? Are you from Trinidad?"

"Close," replied Janet. "I'm actually from Guyana." Claudette was thrilled to meet another Caribbean woman, and they exchanged phone numbers, promising to keep in touch.

True to her word, Claudette invited Janet over for tea two weeks later. It was during this visit that Janet met Claudette's friend, Samera, who was also Jamaican. Claudette, who identified as a liberated Caribbean woman of African descent, was known for her outspoken and humorous nature. She proudly shared her story with Janet, explaining that she was an unwed mother who had lived with her son's father for thirteen years. However, due to his laziness and inability to hold down a job, she decided to end the relationship. Later, she was able to migrate to Canada and bring her two sons with her. Both of her sons had completed university, with one working as a banker and the other as a computer programmer. "I'm proud to say that I raised my kids and made a living practically on my own," Claudette declared.

Janet deeply admired the strength and resilience of black Caribbean women. They refused to tolerate any mistreatment from their partners, and if their relationships couldn't work out, they swiftly moved on. These women took charge of their households and worked tirelessly in various jobs to provide for their children. Janet had witnessed some of them engaged in physically demanding labor, such as working in construction, where they would push heavy wheelbarrows filled with sand or tirelessly hammer away on rooftops. She held immense respect and admiration for these remarkable women and their unwavering courage.

Samera, in contrast to Claudette, had an Indian heritage like her. She was married to a Caucasian Canadian named Henry, who hailed from Toronto. Henry held a prestigious position as a senior partner at the renowned law firm MacFaden and Rosario. When the firm expanded to western Canada and established a new branch on Windermere Island five years ago, Henry was chosen to lead the operations. Samera, on the other hand, worked as an elementary school teacher and successfully negotiated a transfer from the York school board to Farley Heights on Windermere. Samera and Henry had been married for twenty-four years but did not have any children.

The first tea at Claudette's house led to more tea and dinner get-togethers. They took turns hosting these social events, which included Nat, Henry, and a fellow named Jason from Barbados, whom Claudette referred to as her "friend." True to their Caribbean nature, their conversations sometimes grew loud and argumentative, especially when the topic turned to politics. The men bantered and teased each other, and Janet particularly enjoyed how easily Henry participated in the heated discussions. Once, he jokingly said to Janet, "I'm only white on the outside. Samera has turned me brown on the inside. I think if I make a few more trips to Jamaica, I'll come back being *irie*. I might even think of wearing dreadlocks!"

Janet had witnessed a similar cultural transition within her own family. Her eldest daughter was married to an Italian, and the middle one to a Caucasian, both of whom had a profound influence on their husbands. They introduced them to their favorite foods, which the men enjoyed, and their favorite dance music became reggae. The girls and their husbands had taken numerous trips to Jamaica, Guyana, and Trinidad and Tobago, and the men were captivated by the people and culture. Henry, although not a fan of dancing, developed a taste for Caribbean cuisine, such as plantains, peas, and rice with okra and salted cod, as well as vegetables cooked in coconut milk. He found the novels by Trinidadian writers V.S. Naipaul and Sam Selvon quite fascinating. He had taken the time to educate himself about Caribbean history, geography, politics, and economics.

Janet was grateful for the friends she had and the life she lived. She had never considered having an affair, not because Nat was the perfect husband, but because she had invested so much time, energy, and effort into building the family she had. She didn't want everything to come crashing down around her. However, there was always a sense of something missing in her life, no matter how content she was with her beautiful home, career advancements, and luxurious gifts from Nat. She questioned whether it was the love she had experienced with Abe, a missing piece that had eventually faded away.

Nat and Abe were two different individuals, and at times, Janet felt that she and Nat had more of a partnership relationship rather than a deeply passionate marriage. She acknowledged that she had to take responsibility for her own decisions regarding Abe and not place blame on Nat. The choice to see Abe again would be solely hers, based on her reasoning. She had a few days to sort out her feelings. For now, she needed to focus on completing her emails and meeting with Syd so they could return home.

***

Janet took the elevator back to her room and focused on her work for the rest of the time. At fifteen minutes to two, she repacked her overnight bag and headed down to the lobby. Syd had already checked out and was engaged in conversation with another hotel guest. Spotting Janet, she waved cheerfully and made her way over.

"Hi Janet, hope you slept well. How was your meeting with the district board members?" Syd greeted.

"Hi Syd. I slept fine, and the meeting was great. I learned a lot," Janet lied. "I arrived late and had an early start dealing with some emails. By the way, I noticed that you were copied on the situation with Yvonne. I asked her to meet with me, so she'll be coming to you to schedule an appointment. I'd like to meet with her as soon as possible to address the issue before it gets out of hand."

Syd exclaimed, "I can't believe how things explode when we're out of the office. Our staff sometimes behave like kids - wait till Mommy is out of the house, then things get torn apart!"

Janet chuckled at Syd's analogy. "I think they take advantage of their Mom. It's time for them to have a Pop now. A male Director would put them in their place."

"I doubt that," contradicted Syd. "They have been kids and will always be kids, no matter who's in charge."

Not wanting to engage in a further debate, Janet handed Syd the car keys and began rolling her suitcase towards the door. "Shall we go? It would be good to get in the ferry line-up early, so we don't have to worry."

Syd followed her, placed the suitcases in the trunk, and took the driver's seat. They drove mostly in silence to the terminal, with Syd humming some old Abba songs and Janet busy on her BlackBerry, dealing with the remaining emails.

The ferry ride was uneventful as Janet tried to read through some of the documents in her "Read Later" folder. However, she couldn't fully focus on the documents as her attention was drawn to the frothy waters left behind by the ferry's propeller in the Straits of Georgia. In the past, she had traveled this route without paying much attention to the ocean. Still, after reconnecting with Abe and revisiting the memories of their past by the ocean, she couldn't help but notice the intricate patterns of the waves, the gentle movement of the clouds in the sky, and the salty scent of ocean water, regardless of its location. Her thoughts also wandered to the plans she needed to make for meeting Abe in Cuba. She realized that she had to work on these plans quickly.

Syd's presence interrupted Janet's focus on her file folder, casting a shadow over it. Syd checked on Janet and asked, "Just thought I'd check on you to see how you're doing."

Janet sighed, "As usual, I'm consumed by all these reports. I've gone through quite a few, but there are still three that I haven't looked at."

Syd nodded understandingly, "Well, we're almost there. Thank God the ferry is on time, and we can get home before it's dark."

Janet smiled gratefully, "I'm so glad you came with me, Syd. Driving requires a lot of concentration and can be tiring. You took a great load off me. Thank you." She meant every word she said, appreciating Syd's presence and assistance. They worked well together, and Janet knew that not all her colleagues had such a positive working relationship with their administrative assistants. She was grateful that she and Syd had hit it off from almost the first day she took the job.

Janet glanced at the time and suggested, "Why don't we get something to drink? We have another forty-five minutes before we land."

Syd agreed, and they made their way to the cafeteria to order tea. Sitting on high stools at the counter, Syd confessed, "I'm feeling a bit tired. Sometimes, it's better when I'm busy. Too much lazing around is not good for me."

Janet chuckled and reassured her, "That won't be for long. I'm sure when you get home, Tony will have made an unholy mess in the kitchen, so there will be lots to do. I know you'll still be tempted to take home some of your work, too, but you shouldn't. Give it a rest this weekend, Syd. We have lots to get through next week, so save some of your energy."

Syd was not one to discuss her private life, but there were times when she had confided in Janet about her husband's lack of tidiness. "Everything's a mess when he's around," she had complained.

Taking another sip of tea, Syd agreed, "You're right. I will take a break this weekend. Some cooking and cleaning, but nothing else."

As they chatted, the ferry finally landed, and they finished their tea before making their way to the car. Syd skillfully navigated off the ramp, and they soon found themselves on the highway, heading home. The clock was nearing six, and the heavy Friday afternoon traffic caused some slow-moving sections. By the time Janet arrived home, all she desired was a shower and her bed. Luckily, Syd was taking care of the rental car.

***

Nat greeted her at the door, holding a glass of red wine. "Glad you're back safe and sound," he said, giving her a peck on the cheek. Janet knew he enjoyed his Friday evening drink after a busy week. "I've made dinner and am waiting for you so we can eat together." He took the bag from her and dropped it on the living room floor.

"What's for dinner?" Janet asked.

"I grilled some lamb and made Greek potatoes," Nat replied.

"Oh great," said Janet. "I'm starving! Let me shower and get changed, and I'll be down as soon as I can."

"Hurry up," responded Nat. "I'm starving, too."

Janet hurried up the stairs and went straight to the bathroom. She quickly undressed and stepped into the shower, letting the warm water relax her tense muscles. Her mind was clouded with thoughts of Abe and the plans that she needed to make to see him. She knew she had to be careful around Nat, ensuring he never sensed that anything was amiss.

Janet and Nat shared a leisurely dinner, and she gradually relaxed. Nat was an excellent cook when he chose to be, and she was grateful to come home to a prepared meal after a long day. They chatted about various topics, and Nat showed genuine interest in Janet's meeting in Portsmouth. Janet eagerly filled him in, glad for the distraction from thoughts of Abe, the cottage, and the reality of Abe's illness.

"I learned a lot," Janet admitted.

"It's always fascinating to see the government's new initiatives and meet dedicated educators. It makes me appreciate the hard work they do, especially compared to some of the wishy-washy faculty I sometimes deal with.

Nat playfully asked, "Does that apply to me, too?" But there was no immediate response from Janet, her mind seemingly elsewhere.

Nat was always genuinely interested in Janet's work, knowing that his teaching could sometimes be mundane in comparison. "I guess James will be happy you took his place," Nat remarked. "You'll have to do some follow-up on the questions; I can see your week ahead being even busier than usual."

Nat's prediction proved true. Janet found herself rushing from one situation to the next as the week progressed. On Tuesday afternoon, in the midst of her busy schedule, she received an email from Abe. It was short and straightforward, and it read as follows:

Hi Janet, I hope you got home safely and all is well. I'm still here, but I will be leaving in the next two days. Let me know how things go with the plans for your conference in Cuba. Will wait to hear from you. Take care of yourself. AB.

Janet expected Abe to be cautious with his words, knowing that their communication could be monitored. However, his message ignited a sense of urgency in her to finalize her plans for the conference in Cuba. She picked up the phone and called Syd, requesting a meeting to discuss the possibilities.

As usual, Syd entered the office prepared with her notebook. "Have you made up your mind about attending the conference in Holguin?" she asked Janet.

"I've been considering it," Janet replied. "I think it's a great opportunity to present my current research and raise the profile of Mount Carmel U. The challenge is finding the right time. The conference is in two and a half weeks. I have all the details in this folder."

She opened her desk drawer and handed Syd a thin red folder, instructing her, "Review the timelines and see if you can free up my schedule for five days. I'll attend the conference for the first three days and take an additional two days to relax before returning. I'll send the acceptance letter today, so if you can work on arranging my flight, accommodation, registration, and other details within the next two days, that would be helpful. Once we have the conference organized, we can focus on the urgent tasks before my departure."

"I'll start working on it tomorrow," said Syd. "By the end of the day, I'm confident I'll have your flight and accommodation booked."

"That's great!" responded Janet. "Please let me know once everything is finalized. I'll also need to coordinate my plans with Nat."

True to her word, the following afternoon, as her workday was coming to a close, Syd entered Janet's office with a smile. "Something good must be happening," Janet greeted her.

"So many good things have indeed happened!" replied Syd, with a playful pause.

"What is it?" Janet asked, intrigued.

Syd enjoyed their relaxed working relationship and the occasional teasing. She knew that Janet appreciated it, too. Syd continued, "Your flights are booked, accommodation is confirmed, registration is completed, and the abstract for your presentation has been sent."

"What? How... How did you get the abstract?" Janet asked in a slightly surprised tone.

"You had given it to me when you first mentioned attending the conference," Syd reminded her. "I had it when I was working on the slides for your presentation."

"Oh, right. I completely forgot about that. Thank you so much, Syd. You're an amazing Admin Assistant. I can't even begin to describe how amazing you are, but I try. I don't know how I could function in this office without you."

"I'm just doing my job," Syd replied modestly.

"And you do it exceptionally well," Janet acknowledged. "Now that I have the dates, I can discuss everything with Nat."

"Everything you need is in the folder," Syd informed Janet, handing it back to her.

Janet placed the folder carefully in her briefcase. She planned to take it home and thoroughly review the details, allowing her to inform Nat about the dates she would be away and any tasks he may need to assist her with during her absence.

***

After dinner, Janet discussed her decision to attend the conference in Cuba with Nat. He wasn't surprised at all and commented that he was actually more surprised it took her so long to make up her mind. He was used to Janet traveling to various educational events, both local and international.

"When are you leaving again?" Nat asked to confirm.

"On May 10th. Thankfully, my flight is in the morning. I'm tired of traveling at night," Janet replied.

Nat then acknowledged his forgetfulness and suggested that Janet should make a list of tasks for him to complete while she was away. Janet was initially hesitant, thinking about the additional work it would create for her, but Nat assured her that he didn't intend to burden her further.

"In fact, on the weekend, when it's quiet, we can sit down and go over the list together. I'll do the writing," Nat proposed.

"Agreed," affirmed Janet, relieved at the compromise reached.

Before going to bed, Janet sent an email to Abe informing him about her travel plans to Cuba. She believed that giving him ample time to make his arrangements would make things easier for both of them. Three days later, she received a response from Abe stating that he had also booked his flight and accommodation. He mentioned that the hotel where she would be staying was fully booked due to the conference, but he had found accommodation at a nearby hotel. Abe provided Janet with all the necessary details. Janet felt a sense of relief knowing that they would not be staying in the same hotel, as it would give them the space they needed.

The days passed quickly for Janet as she tackled numerous tasks and resolved various issues. She sent two brief emails to Abe to inquire about his well-being. However, she sensed that Abe preferred verbal communication over email, so she decided to call him two days before her departure.

As soon as she heard his voice say "*hello*," she momentarily felt foolish and contemplated hanging up the call. But she gathered her courage and continued the conversation, saying, "Hello, Abe. I just wanted to check in and see how you're doing. Are you still feeling up to traveling?"

He chuckled. "I'm fine, Jan. I'm doing well. I'm hanging in there, but I can't do anything without my meds. How about you? Are you keeping busy?"

"I'm alright," replied Janet. "Yes, I'm busy, even busier than usual. You know how it is when you have to leave work for a few days."

"Well, don't overdo it," Abe advised.

"The work will still be there when you get back. If you're too tired, you won't be able to enjoy the conference."

"I understand. I'll slow down a bit and take my time," Janet assured him. "I'm almost ready to pack up and leave."

"And I just want you to know that I'll be thinking of you the whole time. Good luck with your meetings, and take care of yourself, Jan."

After a few more minutes of chatting about random things, such as the weather, and offering advice on self-care, Janet realized she needed to end the conversation. "I've got to go, Abe. Duty calls. I have a meeting with some students in the next ten minutes. I'll email you the evening before my flight leaves. I'm praying that everything goes smoothly. Take care of yourself. I'll see you in the next three days," and with that, Janet hurriedly ended the call and rushed off to her meeting.

Janet walked down the stairs from her office, making her way toward the student lounge, where she would meet with a group of students regarding their upcoming finals. As she walked, her mind wandered to the decision she had made to see Abe again. One part of her conscience affirmed that it was the right thing to do, while another part incessantly accused her of being wrong to indulge in such a meeting.

If she were honest with herself, she would admit that she didn't truly know what was right or wrong in this situation. The die was cast, and she had resolved to follow through. She also had the option to return immediately after her presentation if she felt inclined. For now, she decided to put the internal debate to rest and focus on ensuring that all plans were in place for her departure to Cuba in the next two days.

Chapter 14

Janet arrived at the crowded Windermere Island International Airport at 7:00 in the morning. Her flight was scheduled to depart for Toronto at 9:00, with a connecting flight to Holguin at 6:00 in the evening. Boarding the flight on time, Janet settled into her seat with the ten pages of her conference presentation. She was deeply engrossed in reviewing the topic of qualifications transfer from one university to another when her concentration was disrupted by the passenger sitting next to her.

"University professor, I guess? It looks like you're grading someone's paper," he remarked, nodding towards the pages in Janet's hands, now filled with underlines and red marks.

"Close," replied Janet. "I'm not actually a professor, but I work at the university. I'm going to a conference."

"Oh, in Toronto?" he inquired.

"No, actually, all the way to Cuba."

"Ah, Cuba! Have you been there before?" he asked.

"No, it's my first time. How about you?" Janet responded.

"My wife visited Cuba with a group of friends. She had a wonderful time. She couldn't stop talking about the beautiful white sandy beaches. Although I imagine you won't have much time for that if you're attending a conference. But you should definitely try to take some time to enjoy the sun and the ocean," he suggested.

"I'm sure I will," Janet declared, glancing back at one of the pages of her presentation.

"Well, I should let you get back to your work. Sorry for interrupting," he said.

"No worries," Janet assured him. "We can chat again once I'm finished with these slides."

The passenger nodded, settled back in his seat, and closed his eyes. Janet continued working until the coffee was served. She took a break and engaged in a longer and pleasant conversation with the passenger who had previously spoken with her. The four-hour trip seemed to pass slowly as she alternated between working, chatting, and working again. Finally, the aircraft landed at Pearson International Airport. Janet retrieved her bag and made her way to Terminal 3 for her connecting flight to Holguin. She had an extended wait at the terminal and used the time to work on her laptop, making a couple of calls to Syd to get updates on the assignments she had left her. She also called Nat to let him know that everything was fine so far.

***

The flight to Holguin was uneventful, and Janet found herself deplaning a few minutes after 9:00 at the bustling Frank Pais International Airport. The terminal was filled with passengers as three different flights had arrived almost simultaneously. Janet wasn't surprised, considering that Cuba was a popular sun destination for vacationers from colder regions.

Navigating through the crowded arrival lounge, Janet joined the non-resident line for immigration and passport control. As she waited, she observed some passengers being processed quickly while others faced a barrage of questions from the immigration officer. The delays began to frustrate Janet, who was growing tired and eager to reach her hotel. She scolded herself for her impatience, reminding herself that she had traveled to many places before and should be accustomed to these procedures. Finally, it was her turn at the counter. The officer greeted her with a smile as he took her travel documents. "From Canada, I can see," he remarked. "Toronto?"

Janet was accustomed to the assumption that she was from Toronto whenever someone learned she was from Canada. Toronto, Montreal, and Vancouver were often the cities that came to mind. She shook her head and replied, "No, I'm actually from British Columbia."

"Oh, Vancouver," the officer exclaimed. Janet wanted to explain that she was from a different part of British Columbia, but she decided it would take too much time and effort. Instead, she simply nodded in acknowledgment.

The immigration officer inquired, "Is your visit for business or pleasure?" Sensing Janet's confusion, he added, "Are you here for work or on a vacation?"

"I'm here to attend a conference at the University of Holguin. Would you like to see my documents?" Janet asked.

"Nah," the officer waved off her offer. "How long do you think you'll be here?"

"Just a week," Janet replied. The officer smiled, stamped her passport, and handed her a slip of paper containing her arrival information. "You need to always keep this with you. You will need it when you depart. Enjoy your stay. Adios," he said.

Janet expressed her gratitude to the officer and moved aside to make way for the next passenger in line. She waited patiently for about forty minutes until her suitcase arrived on the conveyor belt. Since she had nothing to declare, she quickly passed through Customs without any issues. Exiting the airport, she was directed towards the waiting coaches that would transport the numerous tourists to their respective resorts.

***

Janet scanned the row of parked vehicles, searching for coach number 70. As she looked around, she felt a firm grip on her arm and someone asking, "Are you Dr. Janet?" Startled, she turned towards the source of the voice.

A tall, elegantly dressed woman stood before her, holding a sign that read "Janet Ramphal." The woman spoke with a heavy Spanish accent as she again asked, "Are you Dr. Janet Ramphal?" Janet nodded and replied, "Yes, I'm Janet."

The woman warmly embraced Janet, planting a kiss on each cheek. "I am Isabelle Ramero. Welcome to Holguin," she greeted her enthusiastically.

Janet let go of her bag and reciprocated the embrace. "It's good to finally meet you, Isabelle. I was wondering if you would recognize me."

Isabelle, the conference organizer, had been in regular correspondence with Janet to keep her updated on the conference arrangements. Isabelle grabbed Janet's hand and shook it vigorously. "I'm so glad to meet you, too. How was your trip?" In Janet's ears, it sounded like "treep" instead of "trip."

"It was fine, a bit long," said Janet. "But uneventful, so that's good."

Isabelle motioned for one of the porters to take Janet's bag to the waiting coach.

"Si, Professor Isabelle, not to worry. It's taken care of," the porter assured in a heavy Spanish accent, even thicker than Isabelle's. He rolled the bag towards coach number 70.

Isabelle continued, "I'll walk you to the bus. I'm so glad you were able to come to Holguin. There are five other Canadians who will be here. You should meet them during registration tomorrow. You can sleep in. The opening ceremony is not until 2:00 in the afternoon, and I hope you will come to the dinner after."

"Yes," confirmed Janet. "I'm so glad I don't have to be up early. And again, Isabelle, thanks so much for inviting me and for all the arrangements. I'm truly grateful. Gracias."

"No problem. No problem. Again, welcome to Holguin. I hope you will thoroughly enjoy your stay and your time at the conference. I shall see you tomorrow. If you need anything, don't hesitate to give me a call. You have my number, so call my cell anytime. The trip to your hotel takes about an hour. I will see you sometime tomorrow. Goodnight. Buenos Noches."

Isabelle hugged Janet and kissed her on both cheeks again. With a wave, she disappeared into the crowd. Janet thought to herself, "I'd better get accustomed to the hugs and kisses." She followed the porter and boarded the coach, which was quickly filling up. Luckily, she managed to secure a window seat. "I guess I'll be seeing Holguin by night," she reassured herself.

As Janet settled into her seat, she couldn't help but notice the intense heat inside the coach. Despite her light jacket and jeans, she could feel herself sweating profusely. The thermostat displayed a scorching 32 degrees Celsius. Janet found it remarkable how her body reacted to hotter climates after living in Canada for so long. She reflected on her time in Guyana, where she had spent a significant portion of her life. The daily temperatures there ranged from 28 to 34 degrees Celsius, but she had never been bothered by the heat back then. It had been the norm.

However, living in Canada had seemingly altered her body's tolerance, and she now felt more sensitive to the heat when visiting the Caribbean, Mexico, or South America. She recalled a particularly challenging experience in Barbados, where the heat had triggered severe headaches, almost making her fear a heat stroke.

As the air conditioning in the coach gradually began to cool the interior, Janet still found herself uncomfortably hot. She had always been sensitive to prolonged sun exposure despite having a darker complexion. Even a short time in the sun would result in sunburn for her. She reminisced about a trip to Aruba, where she had sought refuge in the shade of the divi-divi trees on the beach while her fair-skinned friends coated themselves in layers of sunscreen, aiming to achieve a tan similar to her natural skin tone.

Janet found solace in the darkness of the night and the gentle breeze that rustled through the trees. The fragrance of oleander, frangipani, and night lilies enveloped her, transporting her back to San Souci. Amidst the bustling sounds of the airport's busy parking lot, she could still discern the distant chirping of crickets. She closed her eyes, immersing herself in the symphony of nature's nocturnal melodies, hoping to catch the hoot of an owl in the tranquil night air.

Within minutes, the coach embarked on its journey. Passengers around Janet began shedding their jackets and using them as makeshift pillows, hoping to doze off during the ride. Unlike her fellow travelers, Janet remained wide awake, her eyes fixed on the passing scenery illuminated by occasional lights from nearby homes and businesses. She eagerly absorbed the sights, catching glimpses of the ocean through clusters of trees, its presence confirmed by the salty aroma and the distant crash of waves carried by the wind. As the coach traveled closer to its destination, Janet's gaze lingered on the familiar vegetation, recognizing shrubs and flowers whenever they came into view.

***

Janet's hotel, the Flamingo, was the second-to-last stop on the coach's route. By the time she arrived, the majority of the passengers had already disembarked, leaving the vehicle almost empty. Exhausted from her long journey, Janet was grateful that the check-in process at the front desk was swift, taking only six minutes. Accompanied by a youthful bellboy, she made her way to her room. The bellboy opened the door, switched on the lights, checked the ice bucket, and pointed out the mini bar.

"Thank you so much. Muchas gracias," Janet expressed, extending a generous tip to the attentive young man. Knowing she wouldn't have the energy to unpack at such a late hour, she longed for a refreshing shower, her comfortable pajamas, and a cool bed.

As Janet finished her shower and stepped out, the ringing telephone startled her.

"Jan?" The voice on the other end was familiar - it was Abe. Janet had made plans to meet him at his hotel, Club Amigo, the following morning at 9:00 for breakfast, so she didn't anticipate his call at this late hour.

"Hello, Abe," she greeted him. "I thought you would be asleep. It's one in the morning. What are you doing up?"

"Yes, I know. So, good morning, Jan, and welcome to Holguin. Did you have a good flight?" Abe asked.

"You know I did! I've been texting you all the way!" Janet replied.

"Never mind. I still have to ask," Abe chuckled.

Janet expressed her concern, "Are you okay? I didn't want to bother you when I got in. You need to rest."

"Well, I just wanted to make sure you were fine before I finally fell asleep," Abe explained.

"I'm good. Everything is fine. I'm just a bit tired, so I'm going straight to bed. I'll see you at 9:00 for breakfast. I was told that breakfast at your hotel is served in the Hummingbird restaurant, so I'll meet you there. It can't be too difficult to find," Janet assured him.

"I know where it is," confirmed Abe. "Don't forget I had a day head start over you. Well, not a full day... half a day, so I've had the advantage of checking out the restaurants, the pools, and the beach. I'll see you tomorrow. Sleep well." There was a long pause and then a whispered "Good night" from both of them.

Janet hung up the phone, lost in thought. Instead of fluffing up her pillow and slipping under the thin covers, she sat on the edge of the bed, her chin resting in her hands.

Once again, she found herself questioning her decision to spend this time with Abe. What she was involved in felt like a weighty secret, at times disguised as a noble act, but at others, burdened with the weight of an unforgivable lie. She wished she had found a way to share at least a hint of the truth with Nat, if not the entire truth, so that she could avoid the pitfalls of a deceitful relationship.

Janet harbored a deep resentment towards lies and deceit, fueled by the pain of Nat's betrayal, when she discovered his relationship with Theresa. Their marriage had nearly come to an end as a result.

Now, she found herself questioning her own actions and the potential betrayal of Nat. How was what she was doing any different from Nat's involvement with Theresa? The distinction she made was that Abe was terminally ill. His time was limited, and she saw herself as aiding a dying man in finding peace and fulfillment. Moreover, she believed that Abe cared for her in a way that Nat never could.

The thoughts continued to swirl in Janet's mind, but she was distracted by the whirring sound of the ceiling fan. Determined to find peace and solace, she got up and switched it off. Opening the two large windows, she noticed the presence of holes in the mosquito mesh. Hoping that no insects would intrude through the gaps, she welcomed the cool breeze that brushed against her face and shoulders.

The oppressive heat had dissipated, and Janet knew that the early hours of the morning would bring a significant drop in temperature. "Time for bed," she whispered to herself. "I need to be well-rested for the conference... and for Abe." With that, she surrendered to a deep and dreamless sleep, her exhaustion finally catching up with her.

Janet awoke to the blaring sounds of the Macarena, initially confused by the loud music. As she cleared the sleep from her eyes, she realized it was the alarm clock on the bedside table. After a few attempts, she managed to silence it and saw it was 7:00 a.m. It seemed that a previous guest had set the alarm for their departure; forgetting to check the alarm before bed was a mistake Janet often made. She would have liked to sleep for another hour, but since she was already awake, she decided to start her day early. Despite only having six hours of sleep, she resolved to make the most of it.

Janet rose from her bed and drew back the curtains, revealing a picturesque morning scene. The warm sunlight greeted her, along with the refreshing scent of the nearby ocean and vibrant flowers in the garden below her third-floor window. She admired the yellow buttercups mingling with the golden chalice vines that climbed the brick walls toward the second-floor balcony. The swaying palm fronds danced in harmony with the gentle Caribbean trade winds. The enticing aroma of fried plantains and freshly brewed coffee filled the air, attracting her senses. "Wow, I'm in love with this place," she murmured to herself.

***

Feeling invigorated, Janet decided to take a walk before breakfast to awaken her senses and work up an appetite for the delicious Cuban cuisine she anticipated. She quickly dressed in a comfortable t-shirt, shorts, and running shoes, then headed down the stairs towards the beach.

The beach was already bustling with tourists enjoying the morning sun. Some lounged under colorful beach umbrellas, while others found refuge in cabanas, taking in the breathtaking views. Janet realized she should have brought her hat and sunglasses as the sun's rays were intensifying rapidly. She had forgotten how early and hot the sun rises in this part of the world, being so close to the equator. Glancing at the enormous guitar-shaped thermostat displayed on the eleventh floor of a neighboring hotel, she noted that it had already read 28 degrees Celsius at 7:30 in the morning.

Janet strolled briskly along the beach, her gaze fixed on the horizon where the cloudless blue sky seamlessly met the sparkling sapphire waters of the Caribbean Sea. The gentle breeze caressed her face and stirred up small waves, creating delicate foam caps that eagerly rushed to shore only to dissolve into the pristine white sand. A handful of elegant white cranes gracefully glided on the water's surface while a few sailboats navigated the swells, manned by adventurous tourists seeking thrills. The tranquil and idyllic scene enveloped Janet, offering a sense of peace, relaxation, and picture-perfect beauty.

Leaving the serene beach behind, Janet reluctantly turned back towards the hotel, mindful of not wanting to be late for breakfast with Abe. She quickly organized her clothes, took a refreshing shower, and carefully selected her outfit. Wanting to strike a balance between casual and formal, she opted for khaki capris and a sleeveless blue and white shirt, complemented by a stylish blue sun-hat. With her small handbag slung over her shoulder, she set off towards the neighboring hotel, Club Amigo, where Abe was staying.

***

As Janet made her way to meet Abe, a mix of excitement, anxiety, and trepidation filled her thoughts. She wondered about the topics of conversation they would explore and whether Abe would contribute actively or if she would need to carry on the discussions. There was a lingering question about what they still shared in common after all these years apart. Although they had spent a few hours together in the cottage, the experience had been satisfactory but not particularly revealing.

Their email exchanges had focused mainly on organizing their trip to Cuba, leaving little room for personal discussions. However, Janet realized that their upcoming reunion would involve spending much more time together over the next four days. The long gap of so many years since their last contact made her aware that Abe would likely be a different person from the one she knew in her teenage years. In essence, he was now a stranger to her.

Janet had already made up her mind to limit their time together, intertwining their interactions with her conference activities. She planned to follow a similar pattern as she would with a male colleague at a conference, attending separate sessions and only meeting up for meals. There were plenty of activities to keep Abe occupied, and considering his condition, it was important for him to get adequate rest. Janet had no intention of babysitting him.

Janet stepped into the Hummingbird restaurant and checked her watch. She was ten minutes early. Deciding to take a table, enjoy some coffee, and wait for Abe, she looked around the room. To her surprise, she spotted Abe already seated at a table facing the garden. He noticed her and stood up, waving to catch her attention. Janet waved back and made her way towards him.

"Good morning," he greeted her cheerfully. "How are you on this bright, warm, wonderful day in Holguin?" He stretched out his arms for a hug, and Janet reciprocated, saying breathlessly, "I'm fine. How are you doing? You seem to have slept well. You're so relaxed and chirpy. Did you wake up early?"

"I did. It's a shame not to take advantage of the early morning and go for a long walk. I even went for a swim. The water was a bit cold, but I managed to swim for ten minutes. It's refreshing and has energized me for breakfast... Oh, and look what I found!"

He picked up the pink hibiscus, which Janet noticed was sitting on a small plate next to his book on the table, and handed it to her. "This is for you... a beautiful flower for a beautiful Jan. You look so refreshing," he said with a hint of admiration in his voice.

"Thank you," said Janet, taking the flower from him. "I really appreciate your thoughtfulness."

Before she could react, Abe swiftly took the flower from her hand and instructed her to turn around. With a sense of anticipation, albeit reluctant, she complied, knowing what he intended to do.

As she had anticipated, he attempted to place the flower in her hair right above her ear. However, her hair was too short, and the stem of the flower wouldn't stay in place. "I think you're fighting an almost lost battle," she remarked. "Just give me the flower. I'll keep it in some water in my room."

Disappointed, Abe reluctantly handed her the hibiscus. "I really wanted to see how it would look in your hair. That's what I thought when I got it," he explained.

"You're not supposed to pick flowers from the garden," Janet admonished.

"I didn't. Not that I wouldn't risk getting caught to steal you a flower if I had to," Abe replied indignantly.

With curiosity piqued, Janet asked, "So how did you get it then?"

"As I was returning from my walk, I noticed one of the maids pushing a cart ahead of me. The cart was filled with snacks and had an overflowing vase of flowers. I complimented the maid on her choice of flowers and asked where she was taking them. She explained that there was a meeting with some important politicians in the small ballroom, and the Minister of Finance would be attending. The vase was meant to be a centerpiece for the head table. She was also setting up their mid-morning snack. As the maid pushed the trolley, it hit a bump on the floor, and some of the flowers fell out of the vase. I helped her retrieve them. While she was putting them back in the vase, I asked if I could have the pink hibiscus. I took a chance, assuming that pink was still your favorite color. So, that's how I ended up with the flower," Abe explained with a mischievous smile. He then asked, "Is pink still your favorite color?"

"It is!" Janet burst into laughter. "You are so funny, Abe."

"Well, we're both standing here talking about a hibiscus, which is quite amusing," Abe remarked. "How about we sit down and enjoy our breakfast?"

Abe pulled out a chair for Janet and gestured for her to take a seat. Janet couldn't help but compare Abe's thoughtful actions to Nat's lack of such gestures. Nat would scoff at these "gentlemanly" acts, dismissing them as mere public displays of affection. He often rationalized his behavior, claiming that he didn't need to show chivalry in public displays.

As they settled into their seats, a server approached with fresh coffee and a warm smile. Janet couldn't help but wonder how people with so little could radiate such happiness. She had read about the poverty experienced by many Cubans, but so far, she hadn't encountered a single unhappy person.

"Coffee?" asked the server.

"Please," Janet requested, pointing to both her cup and Abe's. As the server poured the coffee, she gestured towards the buffet spread on one side of the room.

"Gracias," Abe replied, "tenemos mucha hambre y la comida es deliciosa. I'm sure breakfast will also be delicious." The server beamed at him, delighted that he was able to speak their language.

"Where are you from, Senor? Are you and the Senora on vacation?" the server asked in Spanish.

Abe found himself in a bit of a predicament. He didn't fully understand the question and tried to indicate with his fingers that his Spanish was very limited. However, the server continued to smile, bowed, and gestured towards the buffet, indicating the way.

Janet looked at Abe in surprise. "I didn't realize you could speak Spanish," she said.

"I can't," he giggled. "I've only learned a few words to get by. It shows respect when you can speak a bit of the language when you're in a different country. People resent the haughty English-speaking world, thinking everyone should communicate in English. Who do we think we are?"

Janet agreed and felt a newfound respect for Abe. His thoughtfulness towards others remained unchanged. "Shall we get our breakfast?" he urged.

As they walked along the buffet table, selecting from the wide array of food items, Abe leaned towards the more Caribbean dishes. They returned to their table and glanced at each other's plates. Abe had chosen boiled cassava and sweet potatoes, along with a generous serving of callaloo and roasted eggplant accompanied by circular fried bread. Janet had a similar selection, but instead of the eggplant and fried bread, she opted for salted fish with tomatoes.

"No fried bread?" asked Abe. "You used to love floats." (Another name for the fried bread in Guyana).

"That was when I could handle all the oil. Now I have a stomach hernia, so I try to avoid too much fat. But everything looks so good and yummy."

They tried a little piece of each other's food, testing the taste and nodding their approval. "You have to try this eggplant," said Abe. "It's the best thing I've had for a long time." He forked some off his plate and offered it to Janet, playfully feeding her as if she were a child.

"Hmmm... It is good," confessed Janet. "Here, try the salted fish. You can taste the flavorful wiri-wiri peppers." It was her turn to feed him.

They kept sampling from each other's plates as if it were the most natural thing in the world. As they ate, their commentaries on the food were punctuated by laughter as they shared memories of tastes from Guyana.

Finally, when they returned from the "sweet side" of the table with pieces of ripe, juicy mango, Abe reminded Janet of the mangoes they had eaten on their very first "date." He described how he had licked the juice from her lips.

"From my hands," corrected Janet. "Don't let your imagination run away with you!"

"Licking the lips might have been a bit later," teased Abe.

Janet reached across the table and playfully smacked his hand. "Now, you behave yourself, AB. You are not allowed to go back there." But who was she kidding? They were right back where it had all started. She and Abe, the wide blue skies, and the rolling ocean.

Abe was having too much fun to take anything Janet said seriously. Their conversation flowed from food to his job in Toronto and her extensive travels and the diverse cultures she had experienced.

Janet recounted one of her adventures in Bangkok, where she had been followed by a con artist who offered to take her to a small, discreet shopping center to buy jewelry. However, before she could reach the store, she was ambushed by two accomplices and robbed of her cash. Fortunately, she had secured her passport, credit cards, and a larger sum of money in the hotel safe, so she wasn't harmed.

She reported the incident to the store owner, who promptly called the police. Unfortunately, the culprits had vanished into one of the many alleyways that crisscrossed the shopping center. As she finished the story, Abe reached across the table and took her hands in his.

"I'm so glad that nothing worse happened, Jan. If you were my wife, I wouldn't have allowed you to travel to strange places alone."

"Then how would I have done my job? I was always working on various projects in different parts of the world. I find joy in these experiences; they are an integral part of my work and my life. If I were married to you, we would have argued every day. I wouldn't want my husband to deny me my independence. I appreciate feeling protected, not stifled."

"I would have protected you with my life," declared Abe. "And no, I wouldn't have stifled your career, but I would have been consumed with worry about your safety. I can't imagine how I would have coped with the days of waiting for your safe return."

Janet felt her cheeks flush with warmth and attempted to lighten the mood in response to Abe's heartfelt words. "Well, let's just be grateful that you didn't marry me and have to endure all that worry. Otherwise, you would have had a head full of grey hair and looked like an old man by the time you turned fifty. Consider yourself fortunate!"

"Yes, I am lucky. I'm so lucky to be sitting here with you, Jan."

"Let's go for a quick walk," Janet suggested, interrupting Abe's thoughts. "We can take an hour, and then I'll come back to attend to the conference registration matters. I'll bring my presentation on my flash drive to ensure the equipment is functioning properly. I've had some unfortunate experiences with technology in the past. In fact, there was one incident where the power went out in the middle of my talk, and then water started pouring through the ceiling, drenching both myself and the audience. It was quite chaotic as everyone scrambled to find safety."

"Where was this? Was it in one of those third-world countries you were visiting? See, this is what I was just saying about your safety. You take too many risks!" Abe exclaimed.

Janet shook her head vigorously. "No, no, no. I've never had anything even remotely close to that happen to me in Panama, India, Brazil, China, or any of the other distant places I've visited. This incident occurred in your great city of Toronto at a highly prestigious hotel! The silver lining was that they had a very efficient crew who quickly arrived, fixed the issue, and within two hours, everything was back to normal. The room was even fully ready for another conference presenter."

"I can't believe this!" Abe was exasperated.

"Believe it! The worst things sometimes happen in the best places," was Janet's response.

"You're right," agreed Abe. "Sometimes, unexpected and unfortunate incidents can occur even in the most reputable locations. It's a good thing that the situation was resolved quickly and without any serious harm. It's a reminder that we should always be prepared for the unexpected. I don't want to think about this anymore. Let's go for that walk."

As they walked along the street, the heat intensified, and Janet couldn't help but comment on it. "It's so hot," she said, wiping the sweat from her forehead. "Reminds me of San Souci."

"You can say that again," replied Abe, wiping the beads of perspiration from his face with a damp white handkerchief. Janet noticed that he seemed a bit out of breath.

"Are you sure you're going to be able to do this?" asked Janet, expressing her concern about Abe's well-being in the heat.

"I'm okay," he reassured her. "If I can't make it, I'll let you know. I have no problem admitting when my strength is failing... especially to you, Jan. I know you'll understand." Abe's sincerity touched Janet deeply, and she felt a strong urge to embrace him, grateful that he saw her in a way that no other man, particularly Nat, ever had. With total restraint, she kept her hands to her side and plodded on.

They reached a dirt road that led into the village, with the ocean on one side and tall, flamboyant trees on the other. Janet's gaze followed the line of the shore, where she spotted fishing boats anchored in the deeper waters. Some of the fishermen were busy untangling nets, while others were bailing water out of the stern of their boats. Janet could also see jerry cans being loaded onto smaller row boats, which would transport the fishermen back to the shore.

Small cottages flanked the dirt road, their presence partially obscured by the lush shrubs, fruit trees, and multi-colored flowers adorning the yards. Among the greenery, a striking, flamboyant tree stood tall, its vibrant red blooms forming a captivating canopy. Beneath its shade, a group of women had set up two small tables displaying their crafts and jewelry made from beads and sea shells. As Abe and Janet approached, the women eagerly showed them their wares and, in broken English, encouraged them to take a closer look.

"Come and see," one woman said, addressing Abe. "Earrings for the Senora.

Abe graciously halted and examined the coconut shell earrings shaped like a heart. He picked them up and commended the woman, saying, "Good job." Then, with a mischievous grin, he turned to Janet and asked, "Would the Senora like to have my heart?"

Janet couldn't resist chuckling and playing along, responding, "The Senora would prefer to continue our walk. I'm sure we'll encounter more vendors along the way. Come on, let's go."

Abe bid a hasty "hasta la vista" to the woman and obediently followed along. As Janet had predicted, they encountered more women peddling their handiwork. Despite Janet's initial reluctance, she eventually allowed Abe to buy her a butterfly pin made from sea shells. The intricacy of its craftsmanship spoke volumes about the time and effort put into its creation. Janet couldn't help but reflect on the disparity between the value of the pin and the meager price of five dollars. What struck her even more was the dignity of these women.

They weren't seeking handouts or "free money." They were selling their creations, the products of their hard work. When Abe paid for the pin with a ten-dollar bill and told the woman to keep the change, she became visibly upset and thrust the remaining five dollars back into Abe's hand.

Janet didn't understand the woman's words. Still, she could discern from her expressions and body language that Abe had unintentionally offended her by offering charity instead of recognizing her pride and the value of her work. Janet admired the woman's integrity and respected her desire to be seen as a skilled artisan rather than a charity case.

Abe interrupted her thoughts. "Would my Senora allow me to pin this on her blouse?"

Janet smiled and whispered, "I'm not your Senora, but yes, you have the privilege of pinning the brooch on my blouse." She deliberately chose a spot closer to the neck of her blouse, knowing that Abe could easily read her thoughts.

"That's not the spot I would have picked," Abe said playfully, "but I guess I have no say."

"No, you don't. Come on, hurry up. We have to get back," Janet urged, feeling a sense of urgency.

Abe took his time, carefully adjusting the pin next to her collar. "It's fine," said Janet, a hint of impatience in her voice. "Let's go.

***

As they made their way back to the hotel, Janet breathed in the salty sea air, feeling the wind playfully tousle her hair. She took in the scent of the fish market nearby and observed the clouds leisurely drifting across the sky. Memories of her time with Abe at San Souci flooded her mind. She recalled how he would lovingly tuck her wild hair behind her ears as the wind whipped it across her face. She remembered his gentle kisses on her cheeks and eyes and the moments when he held her as if she were a delicate doll, afraid to break her. There were also times when their kisses grew more passionate, his lips pressing against hers with intensity.

However, their relationship had never progressed beyond that. Abe had always promised that they would only have a sexual relationship once they were married. Janet, in her innocence, had once asked him, "And what are we having now? Isn't this sex?"

"Well, sort of, but not really," Abe had responded.

"There is so much I have to teach you, Jan, but now's not the time."

Janet was filled with an overwhelming love for him, trusting him completely to protect her. She believed she could rely on him with her life. Being with Abe brought her immense happiness, simply basking in his affection. She felt loved and cared for in a way she had never experienced with anyone else. Her love for Abe surpassed that of her parents and siblings, as she longed for his presence when they were apart. In hindsight, Janet realized that she was too young to fully comprehend love, but what she felt for Abe was a deep tenderness that resonated with her very soul. It was a love she knew she would never experience again.

She recalled the words of the great poet Rabindranath Tagore, who said, *"One falls in love once, twice, thrice, but one loves wholly and unreservedly only once in a lifetime."*

"I guess he was right," thought Janet. "I have never loved again in the same way that I loved Abe, but I didn't realize it until now. I tried everything to cultivate that tenderness and affection between Nat and me, but there always seemed to be a barrier. Perhaps it was my lingering feelings for Abe, and even though Nat never spoke about his first love, maybe his feelings for her had never truly left him."

Janet recalled the lyrics of a song she had heard, which in part said, *"First love never dies."* She had dismissed it as a cliché, knowing that many others had found happiness with their second or third love encounters in their lives.

She couldn't say that she was unhappy with Nat, but she also couldn't say that their marriage was blissful. Every day, she poured effort, sacrifice, and energy into making things work with Nat, and they did in a practical sense.

She touched the little butterfly brooch for reassurance. "Is your butterfly trying to fly away?" teased Abe.

"No, it's not going anywhere," said Janet. "We're almost back. It's close to noon, so I'll leave you to wander off to the beach or wherever else you have in mind. I'll meet you for dinner at 7:00 in the Riveria dining room at my hotel. Is that okay with you, or do you have another preference?"

"No, I'm fine with the Riveria at 7:00. I think I'll go lay down on the beach for a while," Abe replied, still appearing out of breath and perspiring.

Janet's concern kept growing as she asked, "Abe, are you sure you're not over-exerting yourself? If there's anything I need to know or do for you, please tell me."

"I'm not your baby, Janet. Believe me when I tell you I'm fine. Just go ahead and get your registration done, and I'll see you later. I'm looking forward to dinner."

Chapter 15

The conference registration took longer than Janet had anticipated. The process required her to pay the registration fee in Cuban pesos, which meant she had to go to the National Bank four blocks away to exchange her currency. The queue at the bank was incredibly long, and Janet grew impatient as she kept checking her watch. Each customer took an average of about twenty minutes to be served, a pace that would have caused protests in their Canadian bank.

Finally, it was her turn at the counter. After answering a few questions and providing her passport for identification, the teller counted out the pesos. With a friendly smile, the teller asked, "Are you from Canada? You look like you're from Pakistan."

This comment was nothing new for Janet. Due to her darker skin and black hair, she often received assumptions about her ethnic background during her travels abroad. Although she felt a hint of annoyance, she had learned to brush off such remarks. "Yes, I'm from Canada," Janet confirmed. Now, she anticipated the inevitable follow-up question: Where was she really from?

"Where were you born?" the teller continued. "You don't speak like a Canadian. You don't have the same accent. Canadians are supposed to be white."

While Janet recognized that such a statement would be considered racist in Canada, she understood that cultural differences might shape people's attitudes and expressions in Cuba. Wanting to address the teller's curiosity, Janet decided to share a bit of her background. "I'm actually from the Caribbean, but I migrated to Canada over twenty-five years ago. I consider myself a proud Canadian. Canada is a multicultural country, and if you ever visit, you'll see people of every race and culture. Thank you for your assistance. Have a good day. Adios."

Before the teller could respond, Janet swiftly exited the bank and made her way back to the conference venue. She promptly paid her registration fee, collected her receipt, and set off in search of Room B126, where her session was scheduled. She was determined to ensure that the equipment would function smoothly during her presentation.

As she entered the room, she noticed the neatly arranged chairs in rows, with a small podium at the front. It seemed that around fifty attendees would be present for her session.

A tall, dark young man, who appeared to be a local Cuban, stood in front of the podium, speaking into a small microphone. "Testing, testing, one, two, three..." His words were interrupted by Janet's arrival.

"Oh, hello," he greeted her, stepping forward to meet her. "I'm Juan Carlos, the technician. Are you Dr. Ramphal?" His strong Spanish accent charmed Janet, particularly the way he rolled the 'R' in her last name. She didn't mind whether he addressed her as "Doctor" or simply Janet.

"Si," said Janet.

"So pleased to meet you," continued Juan Carlos. "The microphone is working, and the computer is ready."

"Nice to meet you too," replied Janet, shaking Juan Carlos' hand. "I appreciate your efforts in preparing the room for tomorrow. I'm one of the early presenters after the opening ceremony, so I'm glad to hear that the equipment is functioning. That's a relief. Thank you for your assistance."

"Can I just try my disk to make sure it works?'

"Sure," said Juan Carlos, taking the disk from Janet and inserting it into the laptop's removable disk drive. The screen at the front of the room illuminated, displaying the three files on the drive. Juan Carlos clicked on the one titled "Holguin Presentation" as he spoke to Janet, "I'm assuming that's the file you wanna open."

Janet nodded, but after waiting for thirty seconds with no progress, she grew concerned. "Why is it taking so long to load? Is there something wrong?" she asked Juan Carlos.

"No, it's gonna be okay," reassured Juan Carlos. "The computer is a bit slow, like some of us Cubans." He chuckled at his joke, but Janet didn't find it amusing. She was more concerned about the possibility of technical issues affecting her presentation. However, in the next few seconds, her PowerPoint slides appeared on the screen. "Here we go," said Juan Carlos. "It looks perfecto!" He beamed at Janet.

"I'll review the entire slide show," she stated. "It should only take about fifteen minutes. Do you have any objections to me being in here at the moment?"

"Feel free to take your time," Juan Carlos replied. "No one else will be using the room. I need to check on the other rooms. Would you like to load your slides onto the hard drive?"

"No…thanks. I'm good," responded Janet. She didn't want to take the risk of loading her slides onto the conference computer, considering the number of people using it and the likelihood of the hard drive being infected with a virus. She wanted to ensure her disk remained intact and unaffected. Janet continued, "I have two of these disks, so if one fails, I can rely on the other in case any issues arise. You can go ahead. Thanks for preparing everything."

"No problem," declared Juan Carlos. "Give me a shout if you need anything." He playfully saluted Janet, then grabbed the small toolbox and a roll of what appeared to be extension cords before disappearing through the open door.

Janet swiftly scrolled through her presentation, double-checking for any missing slides. Everything appeared to be in order. Although it would have been more convenient to copy the file to the desktop, she vividly remembered when she had done this at a previous conference she attended in Amsterdam.

A few days after the conference concluded, she was informed by a participant who had attended her session that her presentation was being shared without her consent among individuals beyond the conference. Janet had never authorized the conference organizers to distribute her work. When she confronted them for an explanation, they offered profuse apologies, attributing the incident to a system glitch that allowed public access to their computer system. Having endured enough negative experiences, Janet had concluded that complete trust in today's technology was never guaranteed. It was always wiser to err on the side of caution.

Satisfied that everything was functioning perfectly, Janet retrieved her disk and made her way back to her hotel. It was just a few minutes before two o'clock. Since her meeting with Abe wasn't until 7:00, she figured she could use some rest. A Cuban siesta sounded like a good idea. She was exhausted from the extra hours she had put in at the office, anticipating her absence for the next few days. It was always the same whenever she had to travel abroad - she had to accelerate her work, only to return to a mountain of memos, emails, phone messages, and other tasks awaiting her attention.

Sometimes, she questioned why she bothered going away in the first place. On top of the work, she was also exhausted from the journey. Added to that was the stress of keeping her time with Abe a secret. It troubled her deeply that she couldn't share the burden of her relationship with Abe with anyone. Somewhere in the recesses of her mind, she acknowledged the possibility that Nat might discover the truth and he wouldn't understand her intention to spend a few days with Abe before his impending death.

***

While making her way to her room, Janet noticed a sign advertising a beach barbecue dinner. The idea of dining on the beach seemed much more enjoyable than eating at the restaurant, which was all she and Abe seemed to do lately. Janet wasn't sure if Abe would be open to a change of plans, but she thought it would add some excitement to their evening. After arriving back at her room and slipping off her sandals, she dialed Abe's number. The phone rang without answer, leading Janet to assume he might be taking a walk or lounging by the pool. Deciding to try his cell phone, she patiently waited until he picked up on the third ring. "Jan?" Abe's voice came through.

"Hi Abe, where are you?"

"I'm here at the pool having a latte. Did you call my room? What are you up to?"

"Yes, I called your room, so I figured you might be out. It's nice to know you're enjoying the sunshine," Janet began. "I just saw a notice about a beach barbecue starting at 6:30. I thought it might be a fun change of pace instead of having dinner at the restaurant. I don't want to disrupt our plans, but I thought you might also be interested in dining on the beach."

"I actually saw that information, too," Abe replied. "And to be honest, I was planning to suggest the same thing when I got back to my room. I'm totally up for it, Jan. Having dinner outdoors sounds wonderful. It's amazing how we were both thinking along the same lines.

"Well, I'm glad I reached you. Let's still meet at the restaurant, and then we can go together from there. How about we meet at 6:30?" Janet proposed.

Abe agreed, saying, "Sounds good. I'll see you at 6:30 then. By the way, you didn't mention what you're up to right now."

"I actually have some changes to make in my presentation, so I'll be working on that," Janet fibbed. She didn't want Abe to suggest meeting at the pool or anywhere else, as she wanted to limit her time with him. "You just focus on what you need to do, and I'll see you later." After hanging up the phone, she lay down on the cool sheets. The air conditioning was blasting at full power. Janet closed the blinds, inserted her earplugs, and allowed her mind to relax. Fifteen minutes later, she drifted off into a deep sleep.

Janet suddenly woke up, startled. *Had she heard a knock on her door? Or was it just a dream?* The knock came again, unmistakably real this time. She swiftly got out of bed and approached the door, peering through the peephole to see who was outside. It was a room attendant holding two bottles of water. Janet opened the door, and the attendant explained that she was delivering water for the evening.

"*Dos or tres, bottles?*" the attendant asked.

"*Dos,*" Janet replied. "*Muchas Gracias.*"

"*Denada,*" the girl responded as she handed Janet the two bottles of water and hurried off to the next room.

Janet glanced at the clock and realized it was already 5:30. She had slept for nearly three hours. The sunlight was beginning to fade, and the temperature had noticeably dropped. Her room felt chilly, prompting her to turn off the air conditioning and open the window and blinds. Outside, the coconut fronds swayed in the twilight breeze, and she could witness the sun gradually descending towards the water's edge on the horizon.

Janet decided to check her emails, smooth out her suit for tomorrow's presentation, and then take a shower and get dressed for dinner with Abe. She didn't mind showering multiple times if it helped her stay cool in the warm weather. By 6:20, she was ready, so she headed down to the restaurant to meet Abe.

***

The restaurant was bustling with servers rushing back and forth, skillfully balancing trays filled with hot, steaming dishes. "It amazes me how they never drop those things," Janet pondered. "I definitely wouldn't have the skills." However, she knew that these servers were well-trained professionals who had become proficient in their jobs, just like any other dedicated worker. As Janet stood in the restaurant foyer, a tall server hurried over to greet her. He had short, cropped black hair that he had unsuccessfully attempted to dye brown.

"Hola," he greeted her. "How are you doing this evening?"

"I'm doing well, thank you. I appreciate you asking," replied Janet.

The server introduced himself, saying, "I'm Diego, and I'll be your server tonight. May I seat you?"

"No, thank you. I'm actually waiting for someone. We're meeting here and then heading to the barbecue. We'll be having dinner in the restaurant tomorrow," Janet explained.

"Si, si. Comprendo. Enjoy the barbeque... es very good..." he said, rushing away to attend to another patron who was vying for his attention.

As Janet was about to walk through the door, she nearly collided with Abe.

He stood so close to her that she could catch a whiff of his clean aftershave and feel the warmth of his breath on her face. Abe appeared much more relaxed than he had been earlier in the day. "Hi, Abe," Janet greeted him. "You look well-rested. I must say, that shirt suits you. Blue is definitely your color."

"Well, you'd better like it," he replied with a smile. "I bought this one, especially for our trip."

She gazed at the sailboats and clouds depicted on the blue fabric. The scene resembled the ocean just outside the restaurant's window. "Wait a minute," she said, studying the shirt more intently. "Do those boats actually have names?" Janet pointed to one of the larger sailboats while Abe stood across from her. As she took a closer look, she exclaimed, "Wow! Isn't that something? This one is called Living Doll. I've never heard of a boat with that name before. Usually, you come across names like Queen this or Lady that, but Living Doll sounds rather unusual."

"Strange for a boat, but now I'm going to dinner with a living doll," Abe replied, winking at her with a smile. "So, how did your registration go?"

He extended his arm, gesturing for her to link her arm through his. Janet obliged. "Are you escorting me to the barbecue?" she chuckled.

"Yes, my lady. So, tell me about the registration," Abe requested.

Janet proceeded to update him as they strolled towards the beach. The aroma of seared meat and wood smoke filled the air, accompanied by the melodic sound of steel pans. "I didn't realize there would be entertainment as well," Janet remarked to Abe.

Janet was taken aback to discover that tables were set up on the beach, adorned with white linen tablecloths and napkins, replicating the ambiance of the restaurant. Wine glasses and silverware were carefully arranged, creating an elegant dining experience. The strategically placed lights resembled charming Chinese lanterns, casting a gentle glow over the surroundings. "Wow," Janet exclaimed, "this is absolutely lovely, don't you think?" She turned to Abe, seeking confirmation.

"It's simply perfect," Abe affirmed. "So romantic! I wonder if they knew we would be here?"

Janet playfully slapped his wrist. "Do you always think you're that important? Maybe they set this up because of the conference. Just look at how many people are already here. Do you think we'll be able to find a table for two?" Janet expressed a hint of concern. However, her worries quickly dissipated when a waiter approached them.

"Sir, madam, are you staying for the barbecue?" the waiter asked.

"Si," said Abe.

"This way, please. I have a small table reserved for you." The waiter led them past several tables and guided them to one situated towards the back, closer to the water's edge. "Will this be satisfactory, señor?" the waiter addressed Abe directly.

"Si, perfecto," Abe replied, forming a circle with his thumb and index finger. He seated Janet at the table and handed Abe a menu.

"I suppose in Cuba, men are in control," Janet mockingly remarked. "Or at least they think they are."

Abe didn't respond to her comment but instead exclaimed, "Wow, we even have a menu." He pulled his chair closer to Janet, allowing them to peruse the menu together. "Can you believe the variety of meats they're grilling? There's beef, pork, chicken, fish, and even barbecued crabs," Abe declared. "I'm assuming crabs are still your favorite."

"Mmm," "They definitely are," Janet replied. "Do you remember how your friends used to stick their hands in the holes on the beach in San Souci and pull out those crabs? I can still visualize Ravin tossing one crab after another as he moved from hole to hole. He would flip them onto their backs, causing their shells to crack and preventing them from running away."

"I remember," Abe reminisced. "I also recall you telling me about the crab feasts at your house, where your mom would steam over two dozen crabs in fresh coconut milk in a massive pot. You would eat so much until you felt sick."

"I miss having those blue crabs," mused Janet. "The snow crabs in Canada are good, but they cannot compare with crabs in San Souci."

"So, eat as much as you want. I'm sure the Cuban crabs and Guyana crabs are about the same. Only, please don't get sick."

Janet laughed as Abe called their server over to take their order. Dinner turned out to be one of the most relaxing experiences she had had in a long time. Abe engaged in conversations about a wide range of topics, from the political situation in Guyana, where he expressed concerns about the country's financial management by the current political party, to reminiscing about singers from the 50s like Sam Cooke, Ben E. King, Elvis Presley, and the Drifters, among others.

They chatted, savored their meal, sipped their wine, and found themselves humming and tapping their feet to the lively steelpan music. Everything felt perfect. It was as if Janet and Abe existed in their little world, with nothing else mattering. Janet couldn't help but think that this part of life had been non-existent for her. She had yearned for moments like these with Nat, but they had never materialized. Over time, she had started to believe that this kind of magical connection with someone else would never happen either.

***

The night was so completely dark, and Janet could see the moon rising above the ocean and beaming its light into the black, velvety sky. Although the smell of the food was overpowering, Janet could still distinguish the scent of the night lilies that frequently wafted in on the gentle breeze. "Can you smell that?" she asked Abe, closing her eyes as she inhaled and filled her lungs.

"Smell what?" He looked baffled. "What's bothering you?"

Janet gently intertwined her fingers with his. "Can't you smell the ginger and jasmine of the Cuban orchids? It's reminiscent of the flower gardens in San Souci," she remarked.

Abe clasped her hand, his touch comforting. "My goodness, you're absolutely right. It's quite unbelievable, Janet. Holguin keeps triggering memories of San Souci in so many ways. I feel like we're transported back there, and everything is flooding back. I vividly recall tucking one of those lilies behind your ear. You were wearing a long white dress, standing there, looking like an angel. You were so incredibly beautiful, Jan. You still are, and I love you deeply."

Janet felt as though the air had been sucked out of the atmosphere. She swiftly withdrew her fingers from Abe's grasp. Overwhelmed by a flood of memories, memories she had forcibly buried deep within her. Memories she had vowed never to revisit were now resurfacing. It was unimaginable that she was not only recalling but reliving those memories in this moment. This reunion with Abe would not go well if she delved into the past. She had intended to offer him her friendship as he approached the final stages of his life's journey. She wanted him to feel supported and not alone. However, she was not free to offer anything more than that.

Abe sensed Janet's unease, and he, too, wanted to avoid any conversation that might make her uncomfortable. However, he couldn't hide the love that radiated from his eyes as he gazed at her.

"I'm sorry, Jan. I shouldn't have said anything. Sometimes, I struggle to contain my emotions. I truly don't want to upset you, but I've learned that it's better to express what's in your heart because you never know when that opportunity might be lost."

Dropping her napkin on the table, Janet attempted to shift the focus. "I'm so stuffed. That was certainly enjoyable. It was the best crab feast I've had in ages. Are you finished? All that remains on your plate are the shells."

Abe patted his stomach. "Yes, I'm done and feeling quite stuffed. I think a walk would do us good, help with the digestion."

"Good idea," Janet responded. "Shall we walk for half an hour?" Abe nodded in agreement.

***

They set off along the beach, bathed in the enchanting glow of the moonlight. Other couples could be seen holding hands and strolling along the water's edge. Some more adventurous individuals were still enjoying a swim. The water was yet to reach a temperature cold enough to discourage swimming. For a few minutes, Janet and Abe walked in complete silence, lost in their thoughts, unaware of each other's musings. Breaking the silence, Abe spoke up, "A penny for them…"

"Penny for what?" asked Janet.

"You've been so quiet and lost in thought. It must be something important on your mind. Work, perhaps?" Abe inquired.

"Oh, no. I was just contemplating my presentation for tomorrow. I suddenly thought of two additional slides I could have included," Janet replied, masking her true thoughts.

"Liar, liar," her mind protested. "You were actually thinking about how wonderful it is to be with Abe. Why didn't this happen sooner? Admit it, you love him. You've always loved him. And now, faced with the prospect of losing him forever, how will you ever cope?"

She brushed away a tear that trickled down her cheek, pretending that something had gotten into her eye. "I think a sandfly just flew into my eye," she quickly excused herself.

"Here, let me take a look," Abe offered, attempting to examine Janet's eye.

Janet gently pushed him away. "It's fine. I think I managed to get it out. Look at those bright lights over to your right," she redirected his attention, pointing across the water towards the quay. "Do you think it's a cruise ship?"

"It's quite possible," Abe responded. "I've heard that some of the Caribbean and European cruise lines make stops here."

"Hmmm... I can't recall seeing Cuba listed as a port of call on any of my trips. But then again, each cruise line offers different destinations," Janet pondered.

As they continued their stroll, venturing deeper into a coconut grove, Janet noticed some ripe coconuts scattered on the ground beneath the trees. She pointed towards one that had turned a deep brown. "That coconut reminds me of what I often tell my graduate students about their research. I explain to them that analyzing the data they collect is akin to extracting the milk from the kernel of a coconut."

Abe laughed out loud. "I'm sure that goes over very well!" he exclaimed. "How many Canadians really understand where the coconut milk comes from? In fact, they call it coconut juice. They buy it in a can from the supermarket, and those who have actually seen a coconut on one of their ventures to the Caribbean or the Philippines or Thailand can't decipher between coconut juice and coconut milk or how the milk is derived from the nut."

"Coconut juice?" questioned Janet.

"Yes, which is really what we call the coconut water."

Janet elaborated her focus on the concept of coconut milk. "I emphasize the process of obtaining the coconut milk, which can be quite mysterious to many. I explain how the fibrous husk that protects the dried nut is carefully peeled away, revealing the nut itself. Then, the hard shell of the nut is cracked open, allowing the water inside to be drained out. After that, the white kernel is grated. To extract the milk, water is added to the finely crushed kernel, and it is then squeezed to extract the rich liquid. We ensure that not a single drop of milk is wasted, so the kernel is thoroughly squeezed to ensure every last bit of milk is wrung out."

"Aha, so in research, the data is received, analyzed, reviewed, and analyzed again and again, ensuring that every piece of information is thoroughly examined until you arrive at the essence of the findings," Abe remarked.

"Exactly," Janet concurred.

"What a fitting analogy," Abe concluded.

However, Janet added, "Although, the students don't fully grasp it until I explain the whole process of extracting the milk from the coconut."

"They might grasp the concept better if you explained it in terms of peeling away the layers of an onion," Abe suggested.

"Of course," Janet agreed. "I have also used the metaphor of the onion, but I believe students should learn about concepts beyond their North American boundaries. As an educator, it's part of my role to introduce them to new perspectives."

"I won't argue with that," Abe acknowledged. He glanced up at the sky. "Did you feel those raindrops?"

"Yes," Janet replied. "I think it's going to rain. It's the Caribbean, after all. We should expect sudden downpours."

The wind began to intensify, and the waves crashed more forcefully onto the shore. "I think we should turn back," Janet suggested.

Abe checked his watch. "I agree. I can't believe we've been walking for almost an hour."

They swiftly retraced their steps towards the hotel, but just as they approached the front lobby, a sudden downpour drenched them. They started running, seeking shelter from the pouring rain. Janet struggled to shield her head with a flimsy scarf she hastily removed from around her neck.

"Here, take my hand," Abe offered. "I'll pull you along."

Janet tightly grasped Abe's fingers, and they ran together through the heavy downpour, their vision obstructed by the increasing size of the raindrops. They arrived at the entrance of Abe's hotel, completely drenched and breathless, but their laughter echoed like that of carefree children.

"Look at you," Abe teased, his gaze fixed on Janet.

"Your hair is dripping wet. You resemble a schoolgirl rather than a school Ma'am."

Janet was aware of her disheveled appearance as a small puddle formed on the tiled floor around her feet. Abe's attempt at humor was evident, but she also noticed that he was struggling to catch his breath. The run had exerted him more than anticipated.

"Well, as fun as that was, I think that we both need to get dry before we end up with a cold. You need to go dry off and get some sleep, Abe."

"Yes," Abe agreed. "You should also make sure to get some rest, Jan. Tomorrow will be a long day for you. It's important to have sufficient sleep before your presentation." Janet couldn't help but appreciate Abe's thoughtfulness, always putting her needs first.

"You should also get some rest," Janet replied, only now realizing that their fingers were still intertwined. Abe gently released her hand, using his to brush away a few water droplets that were trickling into his eyes. Janet felt a warmth emanating from within her, much like the water seeping away from the earth after a rainfall. With her hand in his, she felt a deep connection, as if her body and soul were anchored to Abe. In his presence, she found a strength that seemed remarkable coming from a man who was facing the threshold of death.

"I'm feeling a bit tired," Abe admitted. "I'll accompany you to your room and then return to change."

"No, no, no," Janet protested. "I'll be fine. It'll only take me two minutes to get to my hotel. You don't need to be soaked again. You go ahead. Have a good night's sleep, and I'll see you tomorrow. Shall we meet for breakfast at Café Melita at 7:30?"

"Sure," Abe replied. "Are you certain you want to go out in the rain again?"

Janet pretended she didn't understand his implication and didn't even want to entertain the thought. "I'll be fine. Goodnight, Abe." She began to walk away, but on an impulse, she turned back and gave him a quick peck on the cheek. "Sleep well," she whispered, then darted through the door into the pouring rain. Looking up at the sky, she allowed the raindrops to trickle down her face, which had suddenly grown warm from her contact with Abe. She felt relieved to be escaping from him, knowing it was the right decision. "End of day one," she reflected, wondering what day two had in store for her.

Janet was so glad to towel off and get into her pajamas. After a quick check of her email, she grabbed the notes for her presentation and placed them in her tomorrow's folder and then got into bed, pulling the covers around her as if to drown out the splashing raindrops on her window. She plumped up her pillow no less than seven times before she finally fell asleep.

Chapter 16

Janet woke up abruptly, startled by a tapping sound at her window. Her bedside light was still on; she must have forgotten to turn it off before falling asleep. Squinting against the bright glow, she realized her eyelids were just awakening. She quickly untangled herself from the bedding that seemed to wrap around her. "I must have had a nightmare for my bedding to be in this state," she thought.

Quietly tiptoeing to the window, she opened it. The rain had ceased, leaving behind an inky black sky with numerous twinkling stars. On a branch of the tree directly across from her window, there was a sudden movement. Janet could discern the two gold-flecked eyes glowing in the darkness and the silhouette of an owl, which let out a hushed hoot as if acknowledging that it had disturbed her sleep.

"Oh, it's you who woke me up," she said. "Go to sleep. I'm going back to bed." She closed the window and glanced at her watch; it read 2:13 in the morning. Smoothing her sheet, she climbed back into bed, pulling the cover almost over her head, attempting to fall asleep again. It took her a full half-hour of counting sheep and recollecting how she met Nat and fell in love with him before she eventually drifted off to sleep.

Janet woke up to the sound of her alarm at 6:30. The feeling of being refreshed indicated that she must have slept soundly despite the disturbance caused by the owl. She enthusiastically jumped out of bed and opened the balcony door, greeted by the delightful aroma of bacon and coffee filling the room. Alongside these familiar scents, the freshness of the ocean and the sweet fragrance of oleander and morning glory from the balcony below also permeated the air. As much as she wanted to savor the tranquility of the new day on the balcony, she knew she had to hurry, get dressed, join Abe for breakfast, and prepare for the day ahead.

She promptly showed up in the Melita at 7:30 and spotted Abe at one of the patio tables. He waved her in and said a cheerful Buenos to the server. She plopped herself down on the chair which

Abe held out for her. "Good morning," she greeted him, "did you sleep well? You look a bit pale. Are you okay?"

As Abe settled back in his chair, he instinctively raised his hands as if to fend off her words. "Good morning. One question at a time. I'm fine, still a bit tired, but I'll survive. How about you? You look well-rested. That's good. You need to keep your energy up.

"I'm fine. I slept like a log," she declared. "In fact, I feel guilty that I slept so well in a strange bed. I'm getting more accustomed to sleeping away from home. Are you sure you're okay?" she inquired.

Abe did not get a chance to respond as the server came hurrying with his radiant smile and steaming coffee pot. "Coffee?" he asked.

"Please," responded Abe, "for both of us."

"Are you ready to order?" the server continued. "I am Freddy, and I'm pleased to serve you."

"Thanks." Looking at Janet, Abe asked, "Do you know what you want? I will have the special omelet and toast."

"I don't think I want a huge breakfast today. I just feel like I'm eating way too much. In fact, that's all we seem to be doing, Abe," Janet confessed. Addressing the server, she asked, "Can I have the half breakfast?"

"Sure," he replied. "How would you like your egg done?"

"Scrambled."

"What kind of toast and what flavor of yogurt?"

"Brown, and can I have just plain yogurt with some papaya on the side."

"Juice?"

"No, thanks."

"I'll have the guava-pineapple juice," said Abe, "and the big breakfast with brown toast."

The server took their orders and left.

Abe and Janet sat there, seemingly forgetting the thread of their conversation. Janet quickly got back on track, expressing her concern. "Abe, I can't help but be a bit concerned about you. I feel that you're hiding something from me. I'm here to help you if I can, so please ask if you need anything." Her earnest gaze touched him deeply, causing his heart to constrict within his chest. What did she want him to ask for? Was it something she couldn't freely give?

The previous night had been restless for Abe. The sensation of Janet's lips on his cheek had left him paralyzed with a need he didn't believe he had. He stumbled to his room, threw himself on his bed, and wept as he had done when he was twenty-one and Janet had walked out of his life. Uncontrollable tears streamed down his face like rainwater flowing through the gutter along the roof of his balcony. He wept for what he had lost and what he would never have again.

Abe gently covered Janet's hand with his own. "I'm fine, Jan. How many times do you want me to say it? You know that I tire quickly and that I can't help this," his voice conveyed strength and reassurance. "All I want is for you to do well with your presentation and for us to enjoy the sun, the walks, the food, and our time together. It's all good. Let's have our breakfast so that you can take off. I know we're eating a lot. Maybe we should try to take a tour of Holguin tomorrow after your conference stuff is done, but we can talk about that later."

"What will you do after breakfast?" Janet asked.

"Maybe I'll take a walk and read. I'll pull up a chair under one of those cabanas," he said, pointing to the umbrella-like shelters thatched with palm leaves, lining the beach in a long row. "I'll put my feet up, breathe in the salty air, and keep company with John Grisham here," he added, pulling out the novel resting under the table and waving it at Janet.

"*Rogue Lawyer?* I haven't read that one as yet." Janet admitted that she was a John Grisham fan.

"I'll let you have it when I'm done, that is, if you're good and don't ask too many questions," Abe teased.

She playfully slapped his hand, a gesture Abe was becoming familiar with. The smiling waiter arrived with their breakfast. "Here you are. Enjoy," he encouraged as he laid the plates on the table.

"I'm famished," declared Abe. "For a man who's sick, I still have an appetite."

"That's good. It means your body craves energy."

Abe wolfed down his food while Janet toyed with her toast. He looked at her questioningly, "Aren't you going to finish your breakfast? You eat like a bird. You need to have the strength to stand up and deliver your ideas." He launched into a long tirade about why breakfast was the most important meal of the day and how too many people spent too little time attending to it.

Janet interrupted, "I thought I was the one who had to give the lecture."

He smiled contritely and then went on to talk about other Grisham novels he had read. Janet had read some of them, too, so they traded perspectives while discussing some of the characters. Time passed quickly, and it was time for Janet to head out to the conference room. She felt more relaxed and prepared for the day. Janet parted company with Abe, allowing him to stay and slowly finish his coffee. "You're on your own for lunch," she told him. "I'll see you at 4:00. I can get changed and meet you at the beach, or would you prefer we get together for afternoon tea?"

"Tea sounds wonderful. I'll spend all morning on the beach, then take a rest. So, tea at 4:00 would be great. Maybe we can have tea and a swim in the pool."

"Shall we meet here?" she asked.

"There's a mini café near the pool. Why don't we meet there?"

"Fine," said Janet, "see you at 4:00."

As she got up to leave, she was tempted to kiss his cheeks again, but she was afraid that such intimacy might be too emotional. Instead, she walked away with a slight wave.

***

The conference began with an opening speech from the Deputy Minister of Education, a well-spoken woman whom Janet later learned had implemented significant changes to the higher education system through academic reform. She had shifted universities and colleges away from traditional pedagogical practices, emphasizing critical thinking instead. The Minister applauded the conference organizers and the many academics who had come from abroad to share their research and best practices. The audience was visibly impressed, showing their appreciation with loud applause at the end of her remarks. Following her speech, a few other speakers from the organizing committee took the stage, highlighting the conference's importance and its potential impact on educators worldwide. The concurrent sessions were announced, and the audience dispersed to attend in the various break-out rooms.

Janet was thrilled with the thirty-four participants who had come to listen to her presentation. One of the conference volunteers introduced her, and she delved straight into her talk about learning in a twenty-first-century environment. Her discussion covered various aspects, such as teaching and learning, administration, and education leadership. Throughout her presentation, she encouraged questions and engaged in back-and-forth dialogues with the participants, finding it helpful to have their active involvement.

The session sparked healthy discussions, which, at times, turned into feisty debates. Two of her University of Holguin colleagues challenged her perspective, arguing that her analysis seemed skewed towards a Canadian viewpoint and did not fully grasp the difficulties Cuban professors faced, particularly regarding keeping up with technological advances. Janet acknowledged that she might not be fully aware of all the challenges Cuban universities encountered but proposed areas where progress could still be made. Many attendees in the room agreed with her suggestions.

After the two-hour presentation, Janet felt exhausted and decided to relax during lunch, mingling with some of the conference participants. She enjoyed meeting people from different parts of Cuba, as well as those from Australia and Europe. To her surprise, she bumped into a colleague, Bob King, from Waikato University in New Zealand. Janet had previously met Bob while attending a conference at Waikato. They caught up on university news, and Bob inquired whether the New Zealand conference had inspired her to make any changes on her campus.

"Yes, yes," said Janet, "Remember, I was so taken with all the Indigenous names of rooms and buildings you have on your campus, and I thought it was such a great idea to bring more visibility to these people. Well, guess what? I started doing the same on our campus. I got campus facilities to agree to name some of our buildings using the Halq'emeylem language."

"Wonderful," declared Bob. "I'm glad that something worked out."

"Oh, there's so much to still do. It's only the tip of the iceberg."

"Well, keep enjoying the conference," said Bob. "I've got to run. I'm on during the next session. Will catch you later."

Janet contemplated retreating to her room for a few minutes to freshen up before the afternoon sessions began. As she made her way towards the bank of elevators next to the front desk, she was hailed by one of the receptionists, "Dr. Ramphal? Are you Dr. Janet Ramphal?"

"Yes," said Janet.

I have an urgent message for you. I've been trying to reach you for the last hour. Janet went up to the desk. The receptionist rummaged through the stack of notes sitting on her desk. "I wrote it down she said," handing Janet a folded slip of paper. It is from your husband. He said it's very important for you to call him."

"What time did he call?" asked Janet with a sinking feeling in her stomach.

"It's there on the message. I think it was about 11:00."

"Yes, I can see that," said Janet. "Thanks."

"That was almost three hours ago," Janet calculated as she headed to the elevator, her thoughts in a whirl. Various questions flitted in and out of her head. It was unusual for Nat to call when she was at a conference unless something was wrong. What could be wrong? Her initial concern was for her children; did something happen to one of them? Yet, another worry began to creep in—maybe Nat had discovered something about her being with Abe. Despite her efforts to be cautious, Janet knew that clandestine meetings could never be fully covered up. There was always the chance that a tiny detail could lead to discovery, much like a murderer trying to cover their tracks but forgetting a minor detail that eventually gets them caught.

"Murder? What nonsense am I thinking?" Janet scolded herself for such an irrational thought. However, a sense of impending disaster lingered as she opened the door to her suite. "The only way to find out what's wrong is to call Nat," she said to herself.

Tentatively, Janet picked up the phone and dialed the operator, who connected her to the Canada switchboard and then to Nat's number. She could hear the phone ringing at the other end, but there was no answer. It would be close to noon when Nat usually looked at the news or prepped for his classes.

"Come on, Nat, where are you? Pick up the phone," she said to the empty room. She hung up, intending to try again after a few minutes. Five minutes later, she contacted the operator once more, and once again, she heard the phone ringing at Nat's end—one ring, two rings, three rings, four rings, five rings…

She was about to hang up when she finally heard Nat's breathless voice saying, "Hello."

"Hi, Nat. I called before. Where were you? I was told that you called. Is everything alright?" she asked.

"Hi Jan, how are you? I was in the shower when the phone rang, so I rushed out to get it." Nat sounded normal. He didn't seem upset. "Did you get my message?" he asked.

"Yes," said Janet, "this is why I'm calling you. How are you? Are you okay? Is something wrong? Is everything okay?" she asked for the second time.

Nat interrupted her questions. "I'm fine, Jan. I'm okay. Everything is fine here, but I have some bad news for you. Are you standing? Please sit so I can tell you."

"What, what ..., what's wrong?" stammered Janet

"Are you sitting now?" Nat asked.

"Nat, let me hear what you have to say. Yes, I'm sitting." *But my heart is pounding*, she wanted to add.

"It's your brother," Nat began. "I received a call from Jenna. She said that Jack was in a car accident and he was badly injured. He's unconscious and has been admitted to St. Mary's Hospital. Jenna is asking if you can go to Guyana to be with her and Jack. Jack's condition is very critical, and Jenna sounded scared. The doctor doesn't know if he can pull through."

"What! Oh my God!" sobbed Janet. "How did this happen? When? Today? When did Jenna call?"

"She called a few minutes before I called you. Apparently, Jack was on his way to work this morning when a mini-bus, trying to avoid a jaywalking pedestrian, slammed into his car. He was alone in the car. According to the doctor, he suffered some terrible head injuries, and he has been unconscious since. Jenna is terrified, and so are Vandy and the kids. I think you have to go to Guyana, Jan. Jenna needs you, and since you're already in Cuba, you're almost halfway there. Call the University and let them know you've got to take some more time away and see if you can get Syd to arrange a flight for you tomorrow. Don't worry about me. Just go."

Janet was numb with shock. Jack was the baby in the family. When their father passed away almost thirteen years ago, Jack had cried bitterly. Then, just two years later, when their mother followed, they thought Jack would never recover from her death. Janet, Jenna, and Jack - they were the pride and joy of Daniel and Bernice Ramphal, but Jack was special. Their mother loved him in a way that only a kind and caring mother could love her only son.

When their mother became sick with pneumonia and knew the inevitable would happen, she entrusted both Janet and Jenna with the responsibility of watching over Jack. Tearfully, she confessed to Janet, "You know how much I love him. As his older sister, you need to be always there for him, Janet. Promise me you will take care of your brother."

Janet had wanted to tell her mother that Jack was a grown man with a family who could take care of himself, but she understood the pain of not being there for him anymore. Instead, both she and Jenna had promised to keep Jack close. From Canada, Janet stayed in constant touch with Jack and his family, just as she did with Jenna. Despite her best efforts, she couldn't see him as often as she would have liked, as Canada was thousands of miles away from Guyana, and her career kept her busy.

Jenna, living just a few minutes away from Jack, had grown closer to him, but as the eldest sibling, Janet felt responsible for both of them. She would move heaven and earth to be there with Jack in his time of need. How could this have happened to him?

"Janet, are you there?" The sound of Nat's voice brought Janet back to the present. "I'm so sorry. I wish I could be there with you right now. I know this will hit you hard. Things sounded really bad from Jenna, but maybe Jack will be fine."

Janet unconsciously nodded as if Nat was in the room with her. "I know. Don't worry, Nat. I'm okay. I just can't believe this has happened to Jack." She sobbed again.

Nat waited a full ten seconds before he said, "Janet, are you going to be able to go to Guyana on your own? I can come along."

"Don't worry, Nat. As soon as I hang up the phone, I'll call Syd to get me a flight and make arrangements for me to be away. I think I will go for two weeks, and if I need to stay longer, I will work that out."

"Do what you need to do. I feel strongly that I should go with you. We can't fly together, but I can meet you there in two or three days. I can get a sub to take my classes. Getting a flight right away might be difficult, but I'm sure I can be there in a matter of two days or three."

"I'll be fine, Nat. Thanks for wanting to be there with me, but it doesn't necessitate both of us trying to get there in a rush. Why don't I go and see how things are, and then we can make that decision if you need to be there." She wondered if Nat knew what she was thinking. He would definitely need to be there if Jack were to die. No, she wouldn't let that thought take root. Jack would live. She was going to pray her heart out for him. She asked Nat, "How is Jenna holding up? Did she say anything?"

"As you can guess, she is quite distraught. I think she really wants you to be there with her so that you can give her some support. You know Jenna can't think straight when it comes to anything going wrong with Jack. She really needs you, Janet."

"Gosh, Nat, why is this happening? This is a nightmare. I just wish something could pick me up and just drop me off at Jenna's…"

Jack interrupted her, "You've always been strong, Janet. Call Syd right now and get her to find you a flight. Call me back and let me know what arrangements she makes. If she's unable to do this, let me know. I can check the flights for you. I thought of Syd since she makes all your flight reservations and has connections with the university's travel agency."

"Yes, Syd is the best person to do this," Janet agreed. "I'd better get going and try to get Syd. I'll call you back as soon as I know what's the plan."

"Is your conference presentation done? How was it?" asked Nat.

"Yes, thankfully, I just got done with my talk. It was fine. I wouldn't feel bad enough if I had to leave the conference now. At least I did what I came to do. But I should go, Nat. Take care of yourself. Have you told the girls anything?"

"No," "I'll call them later. Don't worry, I'll smooth things over so as not to get them unduly worried."

"I'll call to let you know what's happening as soon as I work things out with Syd. Bye, Nat."

"Love you," he said.

Janet hung up the phone, sat on the bed, and tried to grasp what was happening. Her tears threatened to overflow, but her inner voice told her there was no time to waste. She had to get on a flight as soon as possible and be with Jack. She picked up the phone again to call Syd. Suddenly, she remembered Abe. Her confused thoughts had quite forgotten him. What a mess this trip was turning out to be! "I've got to talk with Abe first before I do anything," she said to herself.

Janet raced out of her room, took the stairs, and almost ran all the way to Abe's hotel next door. She dashed into the waiting elevator and got off on the third floor, her quick steps hammering on the marble tile as she hurried to room 314. The "Do Not Disturb" sign was hanging on the door. Thank God Abe was in his room! She knocked gently, not wanting to disturb the guests in the neighboring suites. She could hear the creak of the bed springs and Abe's weak voice. "I'm resting. Please come back later." He probably thought it was housekeeping.

"Abe," Janet said as loudly as it was polite. "Abe, it's me."

She could barely hear him surprisingly say, "Janet, is that you? Give me a minute."

The door opened in a few seconds, and Abe was standing there in his shorts, still with the sleep in his eyes. He was about to say something funny when he noticed Janet's agitation. "What's wrong?" he queried, his concern creasing the worry lines on his forehead. "Come in, Jan. Is something wrong?"

Janet walked in and took a seat at the edge of the couch while Abe stood over her, waiting for an explanation. He asked again, "What's the matter, Jan? What's going on? Are you alright?"

"Something is terribly wrong, Abe," Janet began, twisting and untwisting her fingers. "Come, sit here." She beckoned him to sit next to her. She could read Abe's thoughts. He was assuming that whatever was wrong had to do with their visit. "No... no. It's not what you're thinking. I just received a call from Nat to tell me that Jack has been involved in a serious accident, and his condition is critical. He's in the hospital unconscious, and I have to go to Guyana. I'm thinking of getting on a flight tonight or tomorrow... whatever can be arranged. But I had to talk with you first. I'm so sorry, Abe. Maybe our coming to Cuba was a mistake. You know how much I love Jack and Jenna. I have to be there with Jenna at this time. She needs me... They both need me." She bit her lip but allowed one tear to trickle down her cheek.

Abe's eyes grew wide with shock. He reached over to Janet and took both her hands in his as he tried to comfort her. "This is shocking, Janet. I'm so sorry. Do you know how the accident happened? When?"

She told him what she had learned from Nat. "You have to get there as soon as possible," was his response. "Have you talked to the hotel about getting a flight?"

She shook her head. "I wanted to talk with you before I did anything. I'm so sorry that I have to change plans. I hope you will understand, Abe." A sob escaped her lips. "Maybe I'm being punished for doing the wrong thing."

"Come on, Jan. You're smarter than that," Abe admonished. "You have nothing to do with Jack's accident!" he said emphatically, pulling her close and gently wiping away her tear with his thumb. "Janet, listen to me. We're going to get through this. Why are you apologizing? You have to go to be with Jack. That is most important, and I'm here at your side to do whatever I can to help. Is Nat going with you?"

"No. I told him to hang in until I could go and see what was happening. No need for both of us to be there right now."

"Then, I'll go with you. Let me get dressed, and we'll go to the front desk to get some help."

"No!" she exclaimed. "Don't cut short your vacation. Stay and enjoy Cuba. You can return to Toronto as planned. I'll be in touch with you after I know what's going on with Jack."

Abe pulled her even closer as if trying to protect her from the pain of the moment. "Hush," he said, placing his finger on her lips. "I'm going with you whether you like it or not."

She saw the tenderness and determination in his eyes. She wanted to burst into uncontrollable tears for the life she had lost with Abe... for his life that was slowly ebbing away... for Jack and the terrible suffering he must be enduring... for Jenna and the intolerable anxiety that must have gripped her. "I will stay away from Jenna and Jack," Abe continued. "I would not want to add to your burden by creating additional problems, but I want to be there for you, Jan, more than anything in the world. You are here for me. It's the least I can do." Janet tried to protest, but Abe continued, "Let's see how quickly we can find a flight." He kissed the top of her head, then released her, going over to the closet to find his shirt.

"I have to call the University to let them know I'll be away," Janet explained. "I also have to call my Assistant. She will get me a flight. To coordinate our travel arrangements, as soon as she gets my flight, we can ask the hotel travel agency to get you on the same flight."

"Okay. You do what you need to. I'll come by and see you within the hour. In the meantime, I'll explore with the front desk here about possibilities."

Janet quickly went back to her room to talk with Syd, who was also shocked by the news. She promised to get back to Janet with arrangements shortly. Janet also called the VP but only got hold of his Assistant, who encouraged her to take the time she needed. "I will help Syd to cancel your meetings and take care of some of your other work. James will totally understand. I'll get him to call you back or email you as soon as he returns from his meeting with the President."

"Thanks, Delia. You're always such a help," said Janet. "We'll keep in touch."

There was not much more that Janet could do but wait to hear from Syd. Luckily, she did not unpack much from her suitcase, so there would not be much re-packing to do should she get a flight within the next few hours. As her mind relaxed a bit, her thoughts went back to Abe. She questioned whether it was right for her to go to Guyana with Abe. She should not do anything to upset Jenna at this time. They were going to be dealing with their own family trauma, so there was no need to add another weight on Jenna's shoulders. Abe had initially asked her to go back to San Souci with him. Cuba was the alternative. Was fate playing a trick on them? Was this God's way of presenting Abe with his wish? No, this was not about Abe and her. This was about Jack, who was fighting for his life.

She was glad to have Abe as a traveling companion. She would not even think beyond that. Whatever fate had in store for her, she would deal with that, moment by moment. She would not anticipate anything. Life was complicated – she loved Abe, but she was married to Nat. She came to Cuba and was blissfully happy in a way she felt she deserved, only now it was all spoiled with the news that her brother may be on the point of death. Abe was supposed to be the one who was slowly dying. She felt like a writer composing a work of fiction and trying hard to find a good ending to the story, except her story was as real as the sun streaming through her window and the shriek of the telephone signaling a response from Syd.

"It's all done," said Syd in response to Janet's question about the progress she had made with getting her a flight. "You are booked on Jamaica Airlines, leaving Holguin tonight at 9:40 for Jamaica. You will be in transit in Kingston for four hours, and then you leave Jamaica on Caribbean Airlines at 5:00 in the morning, arriving in Guyana close to 8:00 in the morning. You will be up all night, but it's the best I could do to get you there early tomorrow. I have emailed you all the information, so you have everything you need to travel. You can print your boarding pass right now, I think."

"That's super," said Janet. "Thanks, Syd. You're the best. Don't worry about me being up. I can handle it."

"I know you can. I thought about the long hours you've spent traveling to Asia. This would be a piece of cake. Just to be doubly sure, I will fax you all the information. I have the hotel's fax number, so check at the front desk in about fifteen minutes. And Janet, you know that my heart goes with you. Take care of yourself."

"Thanks, Syd. I will. We will be in touch by email. You will let me know of any emergencies or any important information."

"You bet." Syd smiled to herself and muttered under her breath, "Really. Do you think I will bother you!" but she loudly said, "Bye Janet."

Janet was thinking that she had to inform the conference about her sudden departure when she heard Abe's knock and opened the door. "Anything yet?" he asked, more business-like than Janet had ever seen him.

"Yes, here's where I'm at." She shared the information that Syd had just given her. "That's exactly what I was told by the hotel's travel agent," Abe exclaimed. "So, if you're all booked, I'll confirm my ticket."

"I'll walk with you," said Janet. "I have to talk with the conference folks to let them know I have to leave. I'm supposed to chair a panel at one of the sessions tomorrow. Also, I have to pick up some faxed information from Syd at the front desk."

As they walked along, Janet said to Abe, "I have a few things I need to get done before we leave for the airport. Can we cancel dinner? I'll work and have something to eat in between. Why don't you make arrangements for a cab to pick us up at 6:30? I'll meet you in the lobby of my hotel then. Leave me a message to confirm."

"Sure. No problem. I can do that. Are you sure you'll be okay? Is there anything else I can do to help?"

"Would you like to write up the briefing notes for my Vice-Chancellor on indigenizing efforts of post-secondary institutions?" she teased.

Abe was so grateful that she seemed somewhat back to her normal self. The pain in her eyes when she talked about her brother had torn his heart. He wanted to hold her and never let her go. He wanted to wrap her in his love and protect her from the rest of the world. How could anyone love someone the way he did? Was such a love possible because he was soon going to lose his own life? He smiled. "No, I'd rather leave that to you. But I'm serious, Jan. If you need anything else, just let me know."

"What about you? Are you going to be fine on your own?"

"I'm fine… very fine… thank you. I'll see you at 6:30."

Chapter 17

The taxi carrying Abe and Janet entered the Frank Pais International Airport's gates precisely at 7:21 p.m. Janet felt relieved to step out and start moving. Despite the driver's friendly demeanor, his English was broken, and Janet struggled to understand about half of what he said. Thankfully, Abe kept up a lively conversation with the enthusiastic fellow, who eagerly provided a historical overview of Cuba during Fidel Castro's rule. He took great pride in his family's cherished possession, a grand Torino. "This car belonged to my father, who acquired it from his friend in 1975," he proudly declared. "It's been in the family ever since."

Janet had observed that most of the taxis in Holguin were vintage cars, which Canadians would consider antiques and would love to purchase. There were Datsun's from the '70s, ancient Chevrolets, and even convertibles that seemed to be from the early days of convertible cars. Janet was intrigued by the choice of these older car models as taxis, especially since she had also seen newer Volvos, Toyotas, and Volkswagens around. Notably absent were any recognizable American-made cars, which she understood the reason for. She had intended to inquire about this unusual phenomenon of taxis with some of the Cubans attending the conference, but the opportunity never arose. "Well," she thought, "I can always find out another time."

Abe and Janet made their way to the Jamaica Airlines counter and joined the waiting queue. The attendants greeted them warmly and displayed remarkable efficiency. In a mere twenty minutes, their check-in process was completed, and they received their boarding passes. "Would you be interested in some coffee?" Abe inquired, gesturing towards a small deli nestled in a corner of the airport.

"No, I'll pass, but feel free to go ahead. You seem like you could use one," she said with a smile. She noticed that Abe's pace had considerably slowed since the morning. Despite his appealing appearance in a floral cotton shirt and linen trousers, Janet could discern a hint of discomfort he was trying to hide. She understood he wouldn't openly admit to it. She contemplated that he could have stayed behind and enjoyed his time in Holguin instead of accompanying her to Guyana. The journey would likely be quite taxing, yet he was determined to do so, and she needed to respect his choices and desires.

Amidst her thoughts, she couldn't help but think of Jack, still unconscious in the hospital. Her prayers were fervent, offered up every few minutes. "Please, God, let him live. Let him be alright. You've promised to answer the prayers of those who persistently seek you. Well, God, I am persistent, so please respond to my plea."

"Are you talking to yourself?" asked Abe, who had snuck up behind her, coffee in hand.

"I'm praying for Jack. He has to survive, Abe. He's far too young to die. What will become of Vandy and the boys... and Jenna... and me...?"

Abe took a seat beside her and gently grasped her hand. "He will pull through, Jan. I'm confident that everyone is offering their prayers. I've been praying ever since I received the news."

She leaned into him, seeking solace. "I thought you might be cynical, saying that you prayed for wellness, and so did others, but the prayers haven't seemed to make a difference."

"How can I be certain the prayers haven't made a difference? It's not about my desires but about God's plan. I'm willing to accept whatever His will is. You see, Jan, there's still a chance for me to be healed. It's what they call a miracle. Do you have faith in miracles?"

"I suppose if you believe in the existence of God, you must also believe in the possibility of miracles occurring. Oh, Abe, I long for a miracle for you and Jack."

"Jack will have his miracle," confirmed Abe.

Almost as if timed perfectly, Janet's cell phone rang. Jenna was on the other end of the line. Amidst tears, sentences that stumbled over each other, and anxious laughter, Jenna managed to convey that Jack had regained consciousness. However, his condition remained extremely critical. Towards the end of their conversation, Jenna offered, "Are you absolutely sure you won't let me pick you up from the airport? I don't mind coming to get you."

Janet declined once again, reassuringly stating, "No, Jenna, you should head to the hospital. I'll meet you there. I'll manage just fine by taking a taxi. I've done it before. No need to worry."

"That was three years ago. You know how things have been changing here. Crime rates are on the rise. You really need to be cautious, Jan. Stick to government-approved taxis; don't go for private hires."

"I'll be fine," assured Janet.

"See you tomorrow."

She put away the phone and tried to stem her unshed tears with a tissue from her purse. Abe looked at her anxiously. "Bad news?"

"Jack has regained consciousness, but his condition is still very critical. It's not good news, but at least it's somewhat better.'

"I told you he will survive this, Jan. Our prayers will be answered." To her surprise, Janet felt absolutely convinced.

They tried to relax in a corner of the airport, making small talk, but ever so often, their conversation kept going back to Jack and Jenna. Two hours later, the loudspeaker abruptly announced the commencement of boarding for their flight to Jamaica. They joined the lengthy queue, and after about fifteen minutes of shuffling forward, they settled into the compact aircraft, which appeared to accommodate roughly two hundred and fifty passengers. The legroom was noticeably restricted, particularly for Abe's long legs. Janet fastened her seatbelt, closed her eyes, and tried to relax. Abe gently squeezed her fingers. "Everything will be alright. Try to get some rest. You'll need to stay awake throughout the night."

"And you too. I imagine this isn't any easier for you. Are you feeling tired?"

"Don't worry about me. I'm alright. I can't sleep on a plane, but I can at least close my eyes and relax. If it helps, you can rest your head on my shoulder."

"Thank you. I'll just lean against the window with my blanket."

The flight took off without any issues, and soon, they were soaring through the extensive expanse of the sky. The surroundings were dark, and Janet's view was limited to the pitch-black night. Her thoughts struggled to anchor themselves to reality. Fragments of memories involving Jack, Jenna, Nat, and herself played in her mind like a medley of tunes.

The experience of being on an aircraft with Abe en route to Guyana felt pretty eerie. She half-expected to awaken any moment and discover that it was all just a dream. The coldness of the coffee and the sandwich, served by a flight attendant with a broad smile, barely registered with her. Meanwhile, Abe was in slumber, and as she nibbled on her food, her mind wandered through the maze of her unexpected and intricate circumstances. She stealthily observed Abe, his eyes closed, his breathing steady, and wondered if his thoughts mirrored her own. Had he ever envisioned that his decision to visit her would lead to a fragment of his dreams coming true? She nudged him gently. "I thought you never slept on planes. You must be really exhausted."

"I wasn't sleeping," he lied, "just resting my eyes."

"Well, you need to eat something. It's already cold. You don't want it to go colder."

Abe unfolded his arms from the blanket, rubbed his eyes, and took a sip of the coffee. "Is this Jamaican coffee?" he exclaimed. "It tastes quite different." He grinned. "But really, why am I complaining? We'll be in Guyana soon, with some delicious food waiting. How's your sandwich?"

"Passable …"

"What grade would you give it? A, B, or a C? Doesn't look like an A."

"It's alright. Just eat up and get some energy."

They continued eating in silence. After a while, Abe turned to her and asked the now familiar, "A penny for them?"

"What?" queried Janet.

"I want to understand what's on your mind," Abe clarified. "I'm truly grateful I can be here by your side during this time. Please don't misunderstand me. I would have never wished for anything to go wrong with Jack." He affectionately patted her hand.

"I know," Janet responded. "I appreciate your presence with me. These are the moments when you want them to be shared, not with just anyone, but with someone who genuinely cares. And I know you do, Abe... even though a part of me wishes you didn't."

"Don't deny me this, Jan. Caring about you is the best thing that has happened to me lately."

"So, what do you think we should do once we reach Guyana?" she inquired. "There's the old Pegasus or the newer Marriott where I could stay. The Marriott would be closer for me to visit Jack. Jenna has offered for me to stay with her, but I don't want to add to her responsibilities."

"I think you should stay with Jenna and support her, Jan. She needs your presence. It would also be wonderful to spend time with her children," advised Abe. "I understand you want to be there for Jack, but he might not be strong enough for visitors."

"You're absolutely right," Janet conceded. "And what about your plans? Where will you be staying? You mentioned that you've chosen the Marriott for your previous visits to Guyana."

"In order to avoid causing any concerns or raising eyebrows, I'll be staying in San Souci at our old house," Abe explained. "As I've often stayed there during my visits, I believe even though I wasn't able to contact my nephew, Hari, right away, he'll make the necessary arrangements for me to stay there. Once we arrive in Georgetown, I'll give him a call. After you've had time with Jack and spent a few days with Jenna, I'm hoping you might consider spending a day with me in San Souci. Would you, Jan?" His eyes bore into hers with earnestness, a plea that Janet found hard to resist.

"Over the years, during a couple of my visits, I stayed with my friend Maria, who still resides in San Souci," she added. "She never married, but she had a daughter with Vincent Charo. Vincent chose not to marry her, and he left the island when their daughter was just three years old. Maria single-handedly raised her daughter. The daughter is now married with two children of her own. While she lives on the West Coast, she frequently visits San Souci to see Maria who lives alone and craves company, so she always welcomes me to spend time at her place. Can you recall Maria... and Vincent?"

"Of course, I remember Maria and Vincent. I've visited with her a few times during my stays on the island," Abe replied.

"Does she know about us?" Janet expressed concern that Maria might feel uneasy if she discovered that Janet's trip to San Souci was specifically to meet with Abe. Maria also had a connection with Jenna. Janet was cautious about any misunderstandings that could potentially create difficulties for Jenna, Jack, and their families. While Janet was living thousands of miles away from San Souci, Jenna and Jack still maintained strong ties to the island. The Ramphals, especially Daniel and Bernice Ramphal, had established a highly regarded moral reputation in San Souci, and Janet and her siblings upheld their legacy. Janet was resolute in not allowing anything to tarnish the Ramphal name.

Abe chuckled, "Know what?" he playfully teased before answering his question. "I think the entire San Souci community knew about my affection for Daniel Ramphal's daughter. But keep in mind that Maria came to the island much later. I doubt she's aware of our love story!" He offered her a broad smile and a wink. "You should be safe, and she'll likely think our visit is just a coincidence."

"Well, that's settled then. You'll stay with your nephew, and I'll stay with Maria. Is your nephew residing in your family home?" Janet inquired.

"No, he looks after our home, but he lives just ten minutes away. He's married and has a ten-year-old son. Hari is my sister's son. His wife is so kind to me. She prepares some truly delicious meals when I'm there. Sometimes, Hari gets a bit jealous and playfully tells her that she cooks better food for Uncle Abe than for him."

Janet smiled. "I can easily picture that. You have a way of charming your way into women's hearts."

"Did I do that with you?" Abe asked with a serious expression, causing Janet to burst into laughter.

"You're quite a character, Abe! You possess the art of charming people. I'm sure there have been many women who've fallen under your spell."

He regarded her with tender eyes. "I don't have any control over who may have fallen for me in the past. I'm not even sure who those women might be. There's only one woman in my life whom I truly wanted to enchant, and she's sitting right here beside me. I hope she's been captivated by my charms. Has she?"

Janet nestled closer to him and grasped his hand. "She has. She truly has. She didn't realize just how deeply until a few days ago."

"I'm overjoyed that she has. I've never felt happier in my entire life," Abe replied, drawing her even closer to him. "I think we both should attempt to catch a bit of sleep." He pulled the blanket up to Janet's chin, and despite her lack of experience with sleeping on an aircraft, she soon dozed off.

An announcement signaled their impending landing in Jamaica. Both Janet and Abe folded away their blankets and began preparing for the descent. "When is our flight to Guyana?" Abe inquired.

"I can't quite recall the exact time," Janet responded, retrieving the information from her briefcase pocket. Her eyes scanned the document for the departure details. "We're departing at 5:00 a.m., so we have about four hours of waiting."

"Yes, I thought we had quite a lengthy layover." Janet sensed the slight quiver in Abe's body as he adjusted his seat for landing.

"Are you still doing okay, Abe?" Janet asked.

He nodded. "My body gets tired so easily. I don't know what's going to happen when I begin to lose my muscles more rapidly. But thank you, I'm fine."

For the second time, Janet gently reminded him that he should have stayed in Holguin and watched the waves come and go.

"With thoughts solely focused on you and the sound of your voice? Wouldn't I have been content!" he stated with a hint of sarcasm.

Janet quickly backtracked. "I apologize, Abe. I don't mean to distress you. I'm just concerned about your health not deteriorating further."

"I'm doing well, Jan. Nothing for you to fret over. I find happiness in each passing day that allows me to be alive and still engage in some of the activities I enjoy."

Janet offered a comforting pat on his leg. As they disembarked at the Norman Manley International Airport in Kingston, she marveled at the bustling activity despite the early hours of the morning. Several excursion flights had seemingly recently landed. Policemen accompanied by drug-sniffing dogs patrolled the arrivals area. Abe kept pace with Janet as they set out to locate their gate and settle down before their flight to Guyana. He carried a small bag containing his medications, but it appeared to be quite heavy for him. Janet pondered about the other items he might have packed in his carry-on. She attempted to take the strap off his shoulder, offering, "Let me help you with this. It'll make walking easier."

"Thanks," he said. "The only reason I'm letting you do this is because I don't want to slow you down."

"Don't worry, silly," said Janet. "I can easily carry this. All I have in my briefcase is a folder of papers and my cell phone. She raised the briefcase to confirm how light it was. "I packed my files in my suitcase."

They navigated their way to Gate 4, where Janet spotted the Caribbean Airlines aircraft already parked. "Looks like our plane has arrived," she mentioned to Abe. "Would you like coffee or some juice?" she asked.

"I'll handle it," offered Abe. "You stay here and rest. Unfortunately, the food spots aren't open yet, so I guess we'll have to make do with options from the vending machine."

"I'd like a passion fruit juice if they have it," Janet requested. "And a bottle of water, too."

Janet aimed to find a seat in a quieter corner among the other waiting passengers, many of whom were attempting to catch some sleep. "Excuse me," she addressed a weary-looking woman, carefully navigating around her outstretched legs. "I'm sorry to disturb you, but I'd prefer not to step over your legs."

"No problem at all. Apologies for being in the way. Oh my, I'm beyond exhausted. I've been traveling for the past thirty hours."

"Where are you coming from?"

"From South Africa."

"Wow, that's a long way from here."

"Yes, I went to visit my sick aunt, so now I'm heading back home."

"Where's home?"

"I live in Guyana, so I'm waiting on the flight out on Caribbean Airlines. And you?" she asked Janet.

"I'm heading there also."

"Are you a resident there?" came the next inquiry. Janet was reminded of how effortlessly people in the Caribbean, including Guyana, could initiate conversations with absolute strangers. She often regarded this part of the world as a place where you could simply be yourself without any pretense. Considering her experiences living in Canada, she couldn't help but find it somewhat impolite to engage in conversations with strangers, particularly those involving personal matters. "No, I don't live there. I used to, but now I'm in Canada. I'm heading back for a visit."

"Do you visit often? You might have noticed all the changes occurring in the country." Janet pondered what the woman's next question might be, but before she could respond, Abe interjected, waving a bottle of water in her direction. "Here's your water. Unfortunately, there's no juice."

"Thank you. The water is perfect. What did you get?" she inquired.

He retrieved a bottle of Sprite from his pocket. "Oh, Abe, you're not supposed to be having a pop, especially at this time of night... or should I say morning?"

"Quit worrying about me," he retorted as he took a seat beside her. "You've always been such a caring individual, Jan. It appears that time hasn't changed you."

"You knew me fifty years ago," Janet responded. "People do change over time. I'm quite certain you're unaware that I've become quite stubborn, set in my ways, and enjoy being in control." She chuckled.

"So, what's changed?" asked Abe with a mischievous smile. Janet playfully gave his leg a light slap. But before she could withdraw her hand, he held it and pressed it to his lips. "My sweet Janet," he whispered. "I wish those fifty years away. Can it really be fifty years? What did I do to deserve sitting here with you?"

Janet held both of his hands. "Abe, we've lost a time that we can never recapture. That's simply life. People often make mistakes and unwise decisions and carry regrets for so many things. Why? It's a question we don't have an answer to. We learn to accept life's ups and downs. We can't turn back time. As countless poets, artists, and writers have expressed, all we possess is this moment. We live in the present and nurture hopes and dreams for the future. I'm here with you now, and we'll exist in the present. What tomorrow unfolds, neither of us can predict, but we'll each confront it when it becomes our present reality."

"Thank you, Jan. Thank you for granting me this time. Even though I can't relive the past, I find happiness in the present, the gift you've bestowed upon me."

She snuggled in closer to him, absorbing the warmth of his body. A sense of tranquility and contentment enveloped her, emotions she seldom experienced. She understood that once this cherished time with Abe concluded, she would have to face the heartache of letting him go once again. The thought of that inevitable parting was something she didn't want to dwell upon. She resolved to tackle that emotional hurdle when it came her way. A tear-filled haze blurred her vision, and an ache surged in her chest. She released a prolonged sigh, and as Abe gently lifted her chin, he detected the threat of tears that lingered beneath her fluttering eyelids.

"No tears for me, Jan," Abe insisted. "Promise me that. I want to always remember your smile."

Janet nodded, her eyes beginning to brim with tears. "I'll do my best, Abe. I'll strive to make only positive memories to hold onto forever," she uttered, her voice slightly hoarse.

They settled into a contented silence, their fingers firmly intertwined. Janet was on the brink of dozing off when the loudspeaker suddenly broke the peacefulness, announcing the boarding of their flight to Georgetown. Janet and Abe made a quick trip to the restroom before joining the boarding queue. The pleasant hostess greeted them as they stepped onto the aircraft, her Guyanese accent discernible. As Janet secured her seatbelt, she remarked to Abe, "The moment you step onto a Caribbean Airlines flight, it's as if you're already at home."

Abe concurred, his excitement evident. "You can almost smell the peas and rice in the air, which I'm assuming will be on the menu. I'm hoping for some fried plantains as well." His eyes lit up with anticipation.

Boarding the flight proceeded at a leisurely pace. Passengers were restless and moving slowly. Eventually, all bags were stowed, and every traveler was accounted for. The aircraft taxied onto the runway, and soon they were airborne. After the meal service, which was essentially breakfast, Janet and Abe spent much of the flight catching up on rest, taking brief naps.

CHAPTER 18

Dawn had just painted the sky with hues of gold and crimson as the Caribbean Airlines flight smoothly taxied on the runway of the Cheddi Jagan International Airport. As Janet and Abe made their way from the tarmac to the airport building, Janet caught a whiff of the fragrant azaleas lining the entrance. Navigating through customs and immigration, Janet and Abe experienced surprising ease without encountering the usual challenges posed by customs officers attempting to extract money or gifts from overseas travelers. "Do you notice the change?" Abe remarked, pointing out, "Government officials are no longer soliciting from passengers."

"It's always so embarrassing," responded Janet. "I'm glad someone has cracked down on this bad behavior."

However, the persistent and undesirable behavior of the taxi "hustlers" continued unabated. They swarmed around Janet and Abe like a flurry of bees, attempting to steer them towards specific taxis in the hope of receiving a generous tip in return. Taking charge of the situation, Abe stepped forward. "We don't need a taxi," he asserted firmly. "We already have someone coming to pick us up, so kindly leave us be." His tone and demeanor seemed to have the desired effect, causing the hustlers to quickly disperse.

Abe and Janet then set out to find a taxi that suited their preferences, as per Jenna's advice, favoring one operated by the government. With the chosen driver, they settled in comfortably, and before long, they were en route. The driver headed straight for the hospital, assuring Abe that afterward, he would take him to the ferry terminal for his journey to San Souci.

Throughout most of the ride, Abe and Janet sat in silence. Both were weary from the tiring flights, and her concern for Jack compounded Janet's weariness. As they approached St. Mary's hospital, Abe spoke, "Well, this is goodbye for now." He embraced her tightly and whispered, "I'll be praying for Jack. Enjoy reuniting with Jenna and the kids. Take care of yourself. I'll be awaiting your call for updates on Jack. Whenever you're ready to come to San Souci, we can figure out the details. There is no need to rush, and if plans change, that's okay, too. Prioritize what you need to do, Jan. Know that I'll be keeping you in my thoughts. Just remember, I love you." He gently kissed her forehead.

Janet reluctantly eased out of his embrace. "I'll call you as soon as I'm able to give you an update. I'll stay in touch with you as much as I can. Don't leave home without your phone. Mine will always be close by. I don't want us to miss each other. Look after yourself, Abe, and do not attempt to do too much. I'm sure Hari will be pleasantly surprised when he hears you're on your way to San Souci. I hope he takes good care of you. I'm sure he will."

Reluctance was apparent in Abe's demeanor as the taxi came to a halt in front of the hospital. Janet alighted from the car while the driver retrieved her suitcase from the trunk. Leaning down to the window, she uttered, "Goodbye, for now, Abe. I'll be seeing you again in a few days." She blew him a kiss as the driver handed over her bag. With a wave, Abe and the taxi gradually receded into the distance along Parade Street.

Janet's thoughts were now entirely focused on Jack. She held hope that there had been some improvement in the hours since her last conversation with Jenna. Swiftly, she entered the reception area of the hospital and inquired about the location of Jack's room. Learning that Janet had flown all the way from Canada to visit her brother, the nurse offered her kind assistance. Guiding her down a lengthy corridor, the nurse led Janet through an atmosphere permeated with the scent of disinfectants and other medicinal odors—characteristic smells unique to hospitals. The polished pine floor exuded a spotless sheen while diagrams and explanations of various bodily structures were hanging against the walls. Yet, what stood out to Janet was the prevailing silence, accentuated by the echo of their footsteps against the wooden floor. It was merely seven-thirty in the morning, and life was gradually returning to the hospital wards.

Due to Jack's critical condition, he was situated in the Intensive Care Unit. The nurse ushered Janet into Jack's room, revealing an array of equipment surrounding his bedside. Amidst the beeping of machines, Jack's form lay still and motionless. He bore an appearance akin to that of one who lay lifeless, his face and head wrapped in bandages. His chest, revealed by the covering extending only to his knees, was similarly bound. Positioned in a chair at the foot of his bed was another nurse. The nurse who had escorted Janet motioned to her colleague by the door and conveyed that they would grant Janet some private time with Jack. Pointing out the emergency summon button for Janet's use in case of necessity, the nurse then left Janet alone, quietly closing the door behind her.

  Janet carefully placed her suitcase in the corner of the room. Approaching the bed, she leaned over Jack's motionless figure, planting a gentle kiss on his forehead while being cautious not to disturb the tubes connected to his mouth and nose. She softly repeated his name in a whisper, her voice an earnest plea. Her fingers brushed against his unruly hair, which peeked out from beneath the bandages. Unlike her restraint in front of Abe, tears flowed freely down her cheeks. Gazing at Jack's battered appearance, she observed the raw bruises marring his arms and face. Gathering her resolve, she lifted the cover, revealing his swollen feet, enlarged to twice their usual size and cradled in a sling-like contraption. His once-handsome face was marked by swelling, and his lips had a pallid gray hue. He bore no resemblance to the vibrant, lively Jack who used to playfully bother her until she was exhausted enough to throw objects at him just to make him stop. How had this fate befallen Jack, who was brimming with life and laughter? Unrestrained sobs overcame Janet as she poured out her heart for the beloved brother she held so dear.

  The door slowly opened, and there was Jenna. She rushed over to hug Janet, and now their sobs and tears mingled together. "I called to see if you had arrived okay, but you never answered your phone," said the sobbing Jenna.

  Janet suddenly realized that she had forgotten to turn on her phone upon disembarking from the aircraft. The guilt welled up within her, recognizing that her preoccupation with Abe had caused her to overlook the fact that Jenna might try to contact her. "I'm sorry, Jen. I forgot to switch on my phone."

Jenna's concern was evident as she continued to study Janet from head to toe. "I was worried that something might have gone wrong. Look at you," Jenna remarked, her gaze lingering on Janet, "you haven't aged a bit since I last saw you." With those words, she embraced Janet once more. "How was your flight? Did everything go smoothly in Jamaica? I didn't expect you to make it here so quickly but thank God you did. Jan, seeing you now is the happiest moment of my life." Jenna's embrace was so tight that Janet felt as though her arms were pinned to her sides.

Janet took both of Jenna's hands in hers, a gesture which, since she was a girl, would bring such comfort to Jenna. Jenna needed her elder sister by her side at this time. Janet told her, "The flight was fine. There were no problems … no mishaps on the way. I'm so glad I could have traveled from Holguin so easily. Gosh, Jen, how did this happen to our Jack!" Fresh tears flowed from both of them.

Jenna shared, "I actually saw Jack the night before the accident. He dropped by with a pizza for Dan and me from that new restaurant down the street. He and Dan had a beer, and then he left. It's just so unbelievable that the next morning, Vandy called me to tell me about the accident and how Jack was in a critical condition at the hospital. I rushed here as fast as I could. But when they told me I couldn't see him, it was almost too much to handle. The doctor wouldn't give a prognosis, only saying they were doing everything they could to save him. His head was seriously injured, so they had to perform a four-hour emergency surgery to relieve the pressure on his brain. They were worried about possible cerebral hypoxia and lasting damage. It's been a nightmare these past twenty-four hours. I left around midnight last night, and thankfully, the doctors confirmed that his condition had stabilized. He's going to make it through, but I can't bear to think about the pain he must be experiencing."

"I know," Janet responded. "Jack has always been a baby when it comes to pain. He's going to need to summon his strength to recover. How can I assist, Jen? This must have been extremely tough for you."

Jenna's voice carried a mixture of relief and calmness. "There's honestly not much to do. I'm just relieved you're here, Jan. I was so afraid we might lose Jack. I even prayed, reaching out to Mom and Dad somewhere up there, hoping they'd ask for divine intervention from God to keep Jack here with us, not to take him away."

Tears welled in Jenna's eyes as she let out a pained sob. Janet instinctively embraced her. "He's going to make it through, Jenna. I'm grateful he's still here with us."

Their moment was disrupted by the entrance of a doctor, who had quietly approached. With a friendly greeting, he asked, "Well, who do we have here visiting my patient so early? Are you the wife?" His inquiry was directed at Jenna.

"No, we're his sisters," Jenna clarified. "I'm Jenna, and this is my sister Janet, who just flew in all the way from Canada."

"Canada, eh?" the doctor chimed in, attempting a Canadian accent. "From where? Toronto?" He lifted Jack's chart from the bed's footrail and glanced over the notes. Maintaining the conversation, he asked, "If not Toronto, then Montreal?"

Janet recognized the common assumption that Canada is often linked to the eastern parts of the country. She replied, "I'm actually from BC - British Columbia. We're more out West."

"Ah, that's where they hosted the Olympics. It's a beautiful place."

While Janet appreciated the sentiment, her primary concern was Jack's condition, not discussing the allure of Canada or the Olympics. She wanted to know about Jack's well-being. Anxiously, turning to the doctor, Janet inquired. "How is he now, Doctor? Will he be able to speak when he wakes up?"

"He will be fine," the doctor assured her. "He's passed the worst of it. Once the effects of the morphine wear off, he should regain consciousness. However, he might not be up for extensive conversation, so I recommend keeping the visits short. His body will be quite exhausted, and rest is crucial for his healing process. Given the significant trauma he's undergone, he'll need a day or two before he can engage in proper conversation. For now, I need to administer his antibiotic injections. If you could step outside briefly, I'll call you back once I'm finished."

In perfect synchronization, a nurse entered the room carrying a covered, sterile tray. Underneath the pristine white cloth, Janet guessed there were needles, pills, and various forms of medication. The nurse offered a warm smile before shutting the door. Janet and Jenna found themselves standing in the corridor.

"I didn't even get a chance to ask about the kids," Janet remarked. "How are they holding up? And Danny? You're looking well, Jenna."

"They're all doing fine. Juanita came by to visit Jack last night. She was really shaken up. You know how she sees Uncle Jack as this invincible figure. Dan was in complete shock. It was hard for him to grasp that, within a matter of hours of seeing Jack, he could be confronted with the news of Jack's accident. He kept saying how short life truly is."

"It's astonishing," Janet agreed. "We're here one moment, but we can never predict what's next. We make plans and try to foresee things, yet life's so unpredictable. Events unfold, and we have no control over them. We don't even understand why things happen; we just have to keep moving forward. We don't know why Jack was in that accident involving the minibus, but I'm so thankful he's still alive. The doctor sounds optimistic, and if he is, then so am I. We should express our gratitude to him for all he's done for Jack."

The doctor emerged shortly after, informing them that they could re-enter the room. "The nurse will keep an eye on him. Make sure you let him rest until he regains consciousness."

"Thank you so much for taking care of him, Doctor…" Janet trailed off, realizing she didn't know his name.

"I'm Dr. Kumar. But it wasn't just me. It was a collective effort. The real credit goes to the Higher Power above. He was looking out for your brother. His survival is nothing short of a miracle. Just stay for about five minutes or so. He'll likely remain asleep for at least another two hours."

Before they could utter another word, the doctor briskly walked away, disappearing around a corner into another patient's room. "We should heed the doctor's advice," Jenna suggested. "You must be tired, too. Let's head home, you can get some rest, and we'll return in the afternoon."

They re-entered Jack's room, once again standing side by side as they gazed down at his motionless figure. The rhythmic rise and fall of his chest, indicative of his steady breathing, was the only reassuring sign that he was still alive. Mindful not to disturb him, Janet and Jenna engaged in hushed conversation. Eventually, Jenna encouraged Janet to bid farewell to Jack. Leaning down, she placed a gentle kiss on his forehead, whispering as if he could hear her, "Goodbye for now, Jack. I'll see you in a couple of hours."

With that, they swiftly left the hospital, heading towards Jenna's, waiting Austin Mini. They found themselves amidst the bustling morning traffic. Despite the activated air conditioning, the intense heat was already palpable. Even as the car's vents released cool air, Janet could still sense the searing heat permeating through the car. Born in Guyana and raised in this tropical climate, she still experienced the discomfort of this sweltering heat each time she returned for a visit. Though she had grown up here, she found the heat and humidity almost unbearable. She often pondered how she had once adapted to living in such conditions, recognizing that her body had acclimatized to the cooler temperatures in Canada. As a result, there was a notable resistance to the tropical heat.

As they sped along Republic Avenue, Janet caught Jenna up on her work, and Jenna, in turn, shared stories about Dan and her daughters. While Jenna's voice filled the car, Janet's gaze was fixed on the rolling expanse of the Atlantic Ocean visible through her closed window. She noted the striking contrast between the chocolate-colored waters of the Atlantic and the dark brown sands of the shore, a far cry from the blue Caribbean Sea and the white sandy beaches of Cuba. Yet, Janet acknowledged that this particular homecoming was the most memorable, encompassing the heat, the muddy water, and all.

Before long, they reached Jenna's cozy bungalow, with its welcoming front garden featuring oleanders, hibiscus, and flame-colored bougainvilleas trailing from the ground up to the roof. The coolness of the living room was a relief to Janet, who gratefully removed her shoes and let her tired feet rest. Her suitcase was casually discarded onto the tiled floor as she sprawled out on the sofa. Jenna, meanwhile, had made her way to the kitchen. Her voice drifted from there, "I'm brewing some fresh coffee, and there are sandwiches and fruits on the sideboard. Feel free to help yourself."

"In a minute," replied Janet. "Let me just relax here for a bit."

"I understand you're worn out. Your bed is all set up in the guest room, so grab a bite to eat, take a shower, and hit the sack. You're familiar with where things are in the house, so feel free to help yourself with whatever you need. If you want to reach me at any time, you have the number. I'll be back from work around three. Dan will finish up around the same time. He'll pick up the girls from UG and bring them home. Later, I'll swing by to pick you up, and together, we'll go visit Jack."

"I'll be alright," Janet reassured her. "You go about your day. I'll figure things out. And yes, a shower and my bed sound heavenly."

Jenna walked over to the couch and planted a gentle kiss on Janet's forehead. "I'm sorry I have to rush off to the office, Sis, but we'll have the whole evening to catch up. There's so much we need to talk about. I wish I could have taken today off, but as I mentioned, we're currently short-staffed at the Bank. I promise I'll make it up to you."

Janet gave her a gentle shove. "Get going. I'll see you when you're back. To be honest, I need this time alone to process all that's happening."

When the sound of Jenna's car faded as it pulled out of the driveway, Janet roused herself from the couch. Carrying her suitcase to the guest room, she sorted through her clothing to find her pajamas. After her shower, she intended to grab some food and then collapse into bed. Jenna had considerately kept the window shades drawn, shutting out the intrusive sunlight. The room was filled with the delicate aroma of roses and lilacs, originating from the bouquet gracing the vase atop the dresser. Jenna had gone out of her way to select the flowers Janet loved. Janet also noted the patterns on the window curtains, intricately woven with vibrant pink flowers - a color she particularly adored.

Slowly, Janet undressed and stepped into the shower. The shock of the cold-water almost made her let out a scream. Each time, she forgot how chilly the tap water could be. In regular Guyanese homes, hot water tanks were uncommon because the average temperature hovered around 35 degrees Celsius year-round. Hot water wasn't a necessity, except perhaps for tourists or visitors hailing from colder regions like North America or the UK.

Nevertheless, the tap water was coldest in the mornings, warming up later in the day as the blazing sun worked its magic on the water lines. For those accustomed to living in Guyana, a brisk cold shower provided relief from the heat. Janet clenched her teeth and let the cold-water cleanse away the grime of travel and travel weariness. However, her shower was notably brief compared to the leisurely baths she was accustomed to at her home on Windermere. She dried herself off, slipped into her short pajamas, and ventured to the pantry. The combination of coffee and fruit-filled her stomach. After tidying up and putting away the used dishes, she pondered, taking a moment to relax rather than immediately crawling into bed with a somewhat full stomach - an action she knew wasn't kind to her delicate digestive system. Yet, her exhaustion quickly overpowered her, and soon, she was nestled under the cool linen sheet, drifting into slumber.

Janet's slumber was interrupted by the buzzing of her cell phone. Blinking away the remnants of sleep, she glanced at the time: 2:00 in the afternoon. She had managed to sleep for nearly four hours. Retrieving her phone from the spot where she had left it on the floor, she noticed the caller was Abe. "Hello," she mumbled, her voice still heavy with drowsiness from her disrupted nap.

"Hi, Janet," Abe sort of whispered, "are you okay? Did I wake you up?"

"Yes … yes … and yes," replied Janet. "Where are you?"

"I just got home on the island. I'm checking to see if things are fine with you."

"All is well here," said Janet. "I was …"

Before she could say anything further, Abe interrupted her. "How is Jack? Have you seen him?"

"Yes, he's still unconscious and heavily medicated," Janet replied, her voice starting to shake off the remnants of sleep. "I'm planning to head back to the hospital shortly. Right now, I'm at Jenna's place. She's going to pick me up in about an hour to take me back to the hospital. I was there for around an hour, but Jack was unconscious, so I decided to leave and try to catch some rest after the exhausting journey. I know you've had a tough time as well."

"I'm relieved that you managed to see Jack, at least. You've been on my mind throughout the journey. If there's anything I can do, please don't hesitate to let me know."

"I'll be alright, Abe. Remember, you need to take care of yourself too. I hope Hari is with you to lend a hand around the house."

"I'm not helpless, Jan. Not yet. Do you have any idea when you might be able to make it here? Scratch that question. I realize you'll come to San Souci when you're ready and able."

"If I can have a reassuring conversation with Jack and know that he's on the mend, I'll try to make it there within the next two days. I'll keep calling you so we can stay connected. I've had my rest, so please make sure you get yours. I'll check in with you later this evening. Take care, Abe."

After ending the call, she powered off her phone and proceeded to the bathroom to freshen up and change her clothes. With Dan's arrival home imminent and Jenna's pick-up time approaching, she wanted to be prepared. Plus, her stomach was voicing its hunger. She needed to locate the sandwiches Jenna had prepared. Within forty-five minutes, she had enjoyed a meal, gotten fully dressed, and was strolling through the garden. Janet noted the thoughtfully designed flower beds and the whimsically adorned painted cans and bottles hanging like lanterns from the sprawling flamboyant tree, which had seemingly chosen to take root in the heart of the garden. As she admired a cluster of vibrant pink sand flowers flourishing at one corner of the garden, the sound of a car horn reached her ears. Clearly, Dan had spotted her amidst the greenery. Dan, Juanita, and Elena arrived with a flourish, the car horn resounding and the girls enthusiastically waving from the open car window.

As soon as the car came to a halt, Juanita and Elena burst out, wasting no time in their eagerness to greet Janet. Juanita hurried towards her with open arms. "Aunty Janet, how are you? When did you arrive?" The moment their embrace met, they held each other tightly.

Elena joined in the warmth of the greeting. "Aunty Janet, I'm thrilled to see you. We didn't expect you to be here now. It's wonderful that you're visiting." Dan soon joined the huddle, attempting to insert himself into the group hug. As the girls released Janet, Dan stepped in. "Hi, Jan. How are you holding up? I'm really glad you made it. How was your flight? Were you able to see Jack? I'm truly sorry about Jack." His questions and expressions of concern flowed rapidly.

They entered the house, Juanita and Elena leading her by the hands. Janet had always held a special affection for Jenna's daughters. Even though they were now grown and university students at the University of Guyana, they retained their childlike enthusiasm whenever she visited. They bombarded her with countless questions, enveloped her in hugs, vied for her attention, and continued to exude care and affection. They settled together on the couch while Dan fetched a cold drink before rejoining them.

Elena inquired, "Did you manage to visit Uncle Jack? How's he holding up? You must have been stunned when you heard about it."

"It was a shock for us here," Juanita added, her voice sympathetic. "I can only imagine how jolting it must have been for you. How's Uncle Nat? Is he planning to come as well?"

"Hey, girls, one question at a time. Let your Aunty Janet catch her breath," Dan interjected with a light chuckle.

Janet reassured them, "It's okay, Dan." She continued, "Yes, it was absolutely shocking to hear about Jack. I spoke to him just a little over a week ago. I'm so relieved he survived. I saw him this morning, and he's in a pretty rough state. But the doctor assured me he's on the path to recovery. It'll take time, but he's past the worst."

Elena contributed, "Mom was so devastated. Having you here means the world to her. You know how inseparable she and Uncle Jack are."

Dan chimed in, "Initially, I was certain he wouldn't make it, but the marvel of modern medicine prevailed. The doctors were incredible. Jenna's feeling better now that he's no longer completely unconscious. She's optimistic that with time, he'll regain his usual self. He definitely gave us all quite a scare."

"Yes, I know," responded Janet. "I'm so thankful that you and Jenna and the girls are here for him."

The conversation flowed on, with Juanita and Elena inquiring about Janet's conference in Cuba. They also delved into discussions about their own studies and the projects they were currently engaged in. Dan quietly sipped his drink, content to mostly listen, aware that he might struggle to get a word in with these lively women engrossed in conversation. He knew, however, that he and Janet would have a chance for a meaningful talk later.

Fifteen minutes later, Jenna made her entrance. She tossed her car keys onto the table and breezed past everyone with a casual "Hi all" as she made her way to the kitchen. Shortly after, she returned with a glass of iced tea and settled into a chair beside Dan. "Phew," she exclaimed, fanning herself with her hand. "It's scorching outside." Shifting her focus to Janet, she inquired, "Are you doing okay? Did you manage to get some rest?" Almost in the same breath, she turned to Juanita and Elena, asking, "What happened today at the university?" Then, addressing Dan, she asked, "How are you, hon?"

Janet laughed. "Well, who's going first? There are a lot of questions to answer!"

Juanita chimed in, breaking the ice, "Mom doesn't necessarily need answers to all her questions. It's her way of saying hi. How about you, Mom? Are you doing okay?"

"Yes, yes. I'm alright. It's just another regular day." Jenna gulped rather than sipped her iced tea.

Dan offered a reassuring smile to Jenna, interjecting, "We'll catch up later. I know you girls need to head to the hospital. Jenna, would you like something to eat?"

"Nah, not hungry," Jenna replied. "I had some coffee and cornbread not too long ago. Come on, Janet, are you ready? Let's go." Addressing her daughters, she added, "I can't stay and chat right now. I don't want to be too late getting to the hospital. But Aunty Jan and I will have more time to talk when we're back."

Both girls nodded in understanding, acknowledging Jenna's schedule.

Janet swiftly collected her purse from her room and followed Jenna to the car. "Goodbye, everyone!" she called out as they departed, and the others waved in response.

As Jenna and Janet drove off, they resumed their earlier conversation. Their dialogue spanned topics like work, their children, and the broader aspects of their lives. "I thought Nat might have joined you," Jenna commented during their discussion. "We haven't seen him for more than five years."

"He did offer to come, but what would have been the point? It would have taken him an additional day to arrange his travel, and it's not like we could have coordinated our trips," Janet explained.

"I understand," Jenna responded. "Now, tell me about Caitlin and your adorable grandson. You mentioned Caitlin got a promotion?"

"Yes," Janet confirmed. "She's doing really well and is now the head of research at her company. Both she and Jonathan are thriving and content. Sometimes, I worry they're too swamped with their commitments to give Jaime the attention he needs. I wish they were living closer to me, and then I could help out more with him."

"Well, look who's talking about her kid being too busy! I think it's like mother… like daughter!"

"Aren't we all just too busy!" Janet exclaimed with a chuckle. "Melina is also swamped with her job. Her Bank recently went through a takeover, so there's even more on her plate. But busy is better than idle, that's for sure."

Shifting her inquiry to Janet's third daughter, Jenna asked, "And how's Jacinda doing? Is she still jet-setting around the globe? I believe she was in New Zealand just last month for a conference?"

Janet nodded. "Yes, she's finally back home now. I really hope she finds someone and settles down. I'm not sure what she's waiting for."

"I thought she was interested in that Ernest guy?"

"So did I, but nothing has come of it. They seem to be good friends, but nothing closer than that."

"Don't worry too much," Jenna reassured. "Things have a way of falling into place when the time is right. As you and I both know, marriage isn't always smooth sailing."

Janet nodded in agreement. The conversation between the sisters flowed naturally. About twenty minutes later, they arrived at the hospital. Janet noticed a few visitors making their way up the imposing concrete stairs leading to the main floor of the building. Jenna found a parking space, and they hurriedly exited the car, making their way up the stairs. As they approached Jack's room, the sounds of voices drifted through the closed door. Janet's steps seemed almost too slow, her urgency to reach the room not fully matched by her feet. She gently turned the doorknob, revealing Vandy, Jack's wife, along with their two sons, Shem and Mel, gathered around Jack's bed. His eyes were open, his face marred by bruises. He looked even more pale than earlier. Connected to numerous machines, he resembled an astronaut in outer space. Despite his condition, his gaze remained focused. Vandy tenderly caressed his swollen fingers while the boys stared at their father, their expressions etched with concern.

Chapter 19

All eyes turned toward Janet and Jenna. Mandy gently laid Jack's hand on the covers as she came over to wrap Janet in an affectionate hug, with the boys following suit. Resting her head on Janet's shoulder, Mandy's tears, warm and unspoken, trickled down onto Janet's face. Janet comfortingly patted her back, a silent understanding drawing them closer. In turn, Janet hugged the boys and gently wiped a small tear from Shem's eye, whispering, "We're in this together. We'll overcome this. Your Dad will be just fine." The boys silently nodded, their expressions mirroring their hope.

Moving over to the bedside alongside Mandy and Jenna, Janet leaned over Jack and placed a tender kiss on his forehead. Initially, he appeared bewildered, but slowly, a glimmer of recognition dawned in his eyes. With an almost triumphant impulse, Janet wanted to exclaim, "He recognizes me! Jack is back! Jack is back!"

The phrase "Jack is back" originated from Jack himself during his teenage years. Whenever he fell ill, his mother would attempt to persuade him to take medicine, but he'd resist by insisting he didn't require any of that "puky stuff." Emphasizing his recovery, he would assert, "Don't worry, I'm fine. Jack is back." Janet noticed a faint smile playing at the corner of his mouth, although she was aware that even mustering a smile caused him considerable discomfort.

Gently, she clasped his fingers and tenderly smoothed the strands of hair peeking out from under the bandages on his head. Whispering into his ear, she reassured him, "It's okay, Jack. You'll be fine. I love you." Her voice quivered, and the tears she had been holding back finally rolled down her cheeks. Mandy, too, shed new tears as she reached for Jack's other hand.

Janet and Jenna shifted to one side of the bed, making space for Mandy on the opposite. Jack, taking in his surroundings, allowed his gaze to wander over all of them before finally fixing on Mandy.

His tears flowed, and Mandy tenderly brushed them away with her lips. His gaze then shifted to Shem and Mel, seeming to convey an unspoken apology for being confined to a hospital bed. As they gathered around him, no words were exchanged, yet the air was filled with profound love, affection, and the unbreakable bond of family.

Jack remained groggy due to the painkillers, causing him to drift in and out of wakefulness. After some time, when they were confident, he had entered a more stable sleep, they made their way to the hospital cafeteria. Here, Janet had the opportunity to catch up with Mandy and the boys, while Jenna kindly offered to stay by Jack's side for a little longer.

Sipping on tea and savoring coconut rolls, Mandy shared the story of the doctors' remarkable efforts to save Jack's life. She remarked, "They truly put their all into it, and I'll forever be grateful to them, to the entire team. I was so frightened, Jan. I've never felt such fear before. The thought of losing him was unimaginable, but as they say, *God is great*."

Janet did her best to provide comfort without burdening Mandy with her worries. Instead, she reassured her, "I met with the doctor this morning, and he confirmed that Jack is on the path to recovery. The prognosis looks promising. I know he'll experience a lot of pain in the coming days, but I'm so grateful that he's still with us. I can't even imagine a world without Jack."

Mandy agreed, saying, "I'm grateful that guardian angels were watching over him. God's mercy has been overwhelming."

Jenna soon joined them, informing them that the nurse had returned to attend to Jack and administer another dose of morphine. The nurse had advised that he would remain asleep until the early hours of the morning, urging them to let him rest. Jenna proposed that they all go back to bid him farewell before departing. Since they didn't want to overcrowd the room, Janet and Jenna took the first opportunity. Janet once again looked upon her peacefully sleeping brother. She held Jenna's hand, and together, they knelt by the bedside, imploring God to continue being Jack's miracle and to accelerate his healing beyond the doctors' expectations. Janet tenderly touched his fingers before leaving the room with Jenna.

Outside, she told Mandy they would wait for her. "Take your time," said Jenna. "Janet and I will hang out. Why don't you come over to my place for supper? Then the three of us can catch up."

"I don't want to give you extra work," Mandy protested.

"No worries," Jenna responded. "I'll order Chinese."

Jenna glanced at Shem and Mel, seeking their agreement. "I need to head home," Shem explained. "I have some urgent work emails that require my attention."

"And I have a date," Mel confessed. "Thanks, Aunt Jenna. We'll pass on the food, but we'll see you again tomorrow."

"Chinese sounds good to me," Mandy said, leading her sons toward Jack's room. When they returned five minutes later, Mandy suggested that Shem take her car to drive himself and Mel home, allowing her to ride with Janet and Jenna.

Staying true to her promise, Jenna ordered several boxes of Chinese food: chowmein, fried rice, chicken chop suey, and barbecued pork. During dinner, the conversation revolved around stories of Jack, the accident, their experiences as parents and working women, and the daily family responsibilities they managed. Dan didn't mind the "women talk." He offered sympathetic comments and eventually excused himself to assist Juanita with washing the dishes. "Don't let me interrupt you," he said. "Keep the conversation flowing." Jenna playfully rolled her eyes, seemingly questioning Daniel's belief in his significance.

While Mandy was engrossed in recounting a tale about Jack's encounter with a grass snake in her rose garden, Janet's cell phone suddenly rang. It was Abe, a presence she had temporarily overlooked amid the day's events.

"I need to take this." Janet excused herself and headed to her room. Once the door was closed, she perched on the edge of the bed, her mind apprehensive about the reason for Abe's call. "Hello," she murmured, almost in a whisper. "Where are you?"

"I'm home," he said. "Can you talk now?"

"Yes. I was just chatting with Jenna and Mandy. We went to visit Jack this afternoon, and he actually opened his eyes. I think he recognized all of us, but he's still in a sort of twilight zone," Janet explained.

"Does that mean he's going to recover?" Abe's tone carried evident concern.

"Yes," Janet affirmed. "The doctor is positive that he'll make a full recovery and be able to return to his normal self."

"I'm relieved to hear that, Jan," he whispered, his relief palpable in his voice.

"Why are you whispering?" Janet inquired. "Is there someone with you?"

"I'm whispering because you're whispering," he responded, a hint of amusement in his words. Their laughter followed.

"I'm whispering because Jenna and Mandy are right outside my bedroom door," Janet revealed in her whisper. "I don't want them to overhear our conversation."

"I thought I should check in with you before I go to bed, just to see how you're doing," Abe continued.

"I'm fine," Janet replied. "It's been a rather long day, but I'm grateful to be here. I don't think I could have continued with my daily life without seeing Jack. How about you, Abe? How are you holding up?" She considered the taxing day he had, coupled with the strain of traveling from Holguin and the toll it might have taken on his delicate health. "You must be exhausted. You should get some rest."

"Yes, it's time for bed," he agreed. "You should rest, too. I imagine you're quite tired. Goodnight, Jan."

"Goodnight, Abe. I hope you have a peaceful sleep. Let's talk tomorrow. By then, I'll have more updates about Jack and might be able to plan a visit to San Souci. Take care," she concluded.

As she resumed her place at the dinner table, Jenna remarked, "I'm pretty sure that was Nat checking in. How is he doing? Why didn't he ask to speak with me?"

"He's exhausted. He returned home not too long ago. He mentioned he'll call back tomorrow. He asked about you and sent his love to both you and Mandy," Janet smoothly delivered the fabricated explanation, amazed by how easily the words flowed.

They lingered for another hour or so, the conversation meandering without any specific topic, relishing the sense of unity that came from women supporting each other during a crisis, a bond that women naturally foster. Eventually, Shem arrived to take Mandy home. She bid her farewells with the assurance of seeing them all at the hospital the next day. "Goodnight," Janet said. "Try to get some rest. Jack is going to recover, and I'm relieved that you'll be there to care for him." She enveloped Mandy in a heartfelt embrace. "See you tomorrow."

Jenna also exchanged goodbyes as Shem guided his mother out the door.

Recognizing that Jenna needed an early start for work the following day, Janet said her goodnight and readied herself for bed. As promised, she called Nat to provide an update on Jack's condition. Nat expressed his contentment with Jack's progress. He mentioned meeting Syd in the afternoon, and she had inquired about Janet's well-being. "You can now tell her that we've spoken and everything is fine. I'll send her an email soon," Janet replied. Nat also mentioned managing household tasks without any issues. They conversed for a while, but Nat, sensing Janet's fatigue, eventually bid her goodnight and ended the call.

Tired, Janet sank into bed, but sleep eluded her. She retrieved some of her reports and read them until the early hours of the morning. The clock had already passed 2:00 a.m. when she finally turned off the lights.

When Janet woke up, the sun was casting a pattern of leaves from the papaya tree onto the window curtains. The first thing she did was check the time; it was past 9:00, and the house was eerily quiet. Outside her window, the sound of birds chirping filled the air. This was a common scene in Guyana – the presence of birds wasn't confined to the woods; they populated the suburbs, nesting under eaves and within the branches of the ubiquitous trees. After washing her face in the bathroom, Janet ventured to the kitchen to see if anyone was up. There, under the teapot, she discovered a note.

Hi Jan,

Take the time to sleep in. Danny and I are off to work, and the girls are at the U. Help yourself to breakfast. I'll be back at noon to pick you up, and we'll go to see Jack.

Love you, Jenna.

Janet eased onto a kitchen stool, rubbing the remnants of sleep from her eyes. The tranquility and solitude of the house were a welcome presence. After yawning, stretching, and a brief internal pep talk, she opened her email, more out of routine than genuine interest in her workplace's affairs. She had to remain attentive to any urgent messages from Syd requiring her prompt response. As she scrolled through her iPad, perusing the roughly three dozen emails, she murmured to herself, "Well, nothing here seems to be a matter of life or death." Following this, she assembled a modest yet nourishing breakfast - oatmeal, yogurt, and fruit from the generous bowl that Jenna had set on the counter.

Janet started by delving into her oatmeal before adding chunks of mango and pineapple to flavor her yogurt. Despite the appearance of ripe mangoes in Canada, they never quite matched the taste of the mangoes in Guyana, especially the Buxton spice variety. Those were bursting with sweet, luscious juice and fiber. As she savored her breakfast, Janet turned on the TV, hoping to catch up on global news from the BBC. She fiddled with the remote control, trying different channels, but struggled to find the right one. Inadvertently, she landed on CNN, where the breaking news centered on the presidential election and the potential victory of Donald Trump. She whispered a prayer, "Please, God, I hope this guy will possess enough wisdom if he wins." Her thoughts were interrupted by her ringing phone. It was Jenna. "Did you sleep well?" Jenna inquired.

"Couldn't be better. I slept like a log," Janet lied. She was becoming such an accomplished liar.

"Did you have breakfast? What have you been up to?" Jenna's questions flowed in rapid succession. "We all slipped out quietly to let you rest. I noticed your light was on pretty late last night. Were you working?"

"Yes," Janet admitted. "I had a few things to finish up, but I'm fine. I didn't hear a sound when you all left. Either everyone was exceptionally quiet, or I must have been in a deep sleep."

"I'm guessing it might have been a bit of both," Jenna speculated. "Are you okay with me picking you up at noon? We can head straight to the hospital from there. Oh, and I have a surprise for you. I called the hospital about half an hour ago, and Jack was awake and responsive. I even had a brief conversation with him for about a minute. The nurse mentioned that he's showing significant improvement today."

Janet's joy was almost overwhelming. "That's fantastic news, Jenna. I'm so relieved. Do you think I can give him a quick call now?"

"I don't think the nurse will allow another phone call. She emphasized that he needed his rest. Noon is just two hours away, so you'll be able to see him soon," Jenna replied.

"Okay," Janet agreed. "I'll get ready and be waiting for you at noon."

Shortly after hanging up the phone, it rang again. This time, it was Abe. He inquired about her well-being and if there were any further updates on Jack.

Janet provided him with the latest information as he listened attentively. Eventually, she asked, "How was your night?"

"Everything's going well. I've already taken my morning walk and had breakfast. My friend Aaron is coming over to visit later. We're planning to go fishing,"

"What!" exclaimed Janet. "Where? I don't think you're in any condition to go fishing …"

He didn't let her complete her sentence. "Take it easy, Jan. In fact, I'll be hitching a ride with Aaron on his tractor to the creek in the back lands. No walking is necessary. I'll simply be lounging beneath a tree with my fishing rod. Aaron's got his net, so I won't need to do much. I'm mainly tagging along for the ride and the sunshine. He's promised to prepare a substantial lunch, and I'm eagerly anticipating his San Souci meatballs."

Janet was relieved. "Can I go fishing too with you and Aaron another day when I get to San Souci?"

"That would be so wonderful, Jan. I'll arrange it with Aaron. When?"

"Let me see how Jack is doing for sure, and I'll call you back this evening. Maybe I might be able to come as early as tomorrow."

"No rush," said Abe. "You promised me one day, and you still have seven days left before you go back to Windermere."

"Well, I'll assess the situation with Jack and then make my decision. Take care, Abe. And watch out when you're with Aaron and the tractor." Janet bid farewell to Abe and ended the call.

After a lengthy and refreshing shower, Janet dressed and strolled onto the patio. She settled beneath the bold blue umbrella, allowing the sun to warm her skin. With the temperature already at 32 degrees Celsius, Janet was well aware she wouldn't be able to endure the heat for an extended period. She typically found herself seeking refuge indoors with air conditioning to escape the sweltering heat. During her previous visits to Jenna and Jack, she always carried a cold-water bottle and a washcloth, which she used to continually wipe away sweat from her neck, face, and arms in an effort to stay cool.

Using her phone, Janet tackled a few of her emails before picking up the newspaper, which lay on the chair, possibly left there by Daniel. She skimmed through some of the headlines but hadn't delved too deeply when Jenna arrived unexpectedly, fifteen minutes ahead of schedule. Dressed comfortably in a linen suit and high-heeled sandals, her sunglasses doubling as a hairband for her loose curls, Jenna greeted Janet with a warm hug. "All ready, big sister?" she inquired. "I see you've been catching up on the news. Anything interesting in there?"

"I've just been passing the time," Janet responded. "I'm sometimes hesitant to read the newspaper. Crime appears to be escalating. I can't fathom why the Government isn't taking a more assertive stance on this issue. When we were kids, there was never a sense of fear that harm could befall us. The trajectory from those days to where we are now is difficult to comprehend. It's disheartening to witness the decline our country is undergoing."

Jenna nodded thoughtfully. "Well, wasn't this the very reason why you and many others left, unable to cope with the lack of safety? The economy isn't improving either. Jobs are scarce, and as you're aware, poverty fosters crime. Nonetheless, you and I can't resolve these larger issues. Shall we get going?"

"Yes, let me get my handbag."

Jenna swiftly downed a tall glass of water and locked the doors before joining Janet in the car. As Jenna navigated the tree-lined Main Street, Janet couldn't contain her eagerness. "I'm really looking forward to seeing Jack. I have so much I want to say to him."

"Our little brother is going to pull through," Jenna reassured. "Did you talk to Nat again?"

"Yes, I called him early this morning," Janet confirmed. "He was genuinely worried about Jack. So, after speaking with you, I phoned him back to share the positive news about Jack's progress. He was greatly relieved to hear the good update."

"Will you go to Sans Souci?" enquired Jenna.

Janet was a bit taken aback by the question. "Why? Is that something I should do?"

"Just making sure. I know you'll never come to Guyana without visiting San Souci. It's always a must," Jenna teased.

"I have to admit. It's been on my mind. If Jack continues to improve, maybe I'll go for a day or two. By the time I return, he might be in a better state for us to spend time together," Janet explained.

"That sounds like a plan. You could take some flowers for Mom and Dad, and perhaps catch up with your friend Maria. Does she know you're here?" Jenna inquired.

"Yes, I gave her a call. She actually suggested that I visit her and stay with her. I told her it all depends on how Jack's condition evolves. I promised to let her know tonight if I decide to make the trip soon."

"Great. How do you like the new hotel?" Jenna switched topics, gesturing towards a building under construction.

"Oh, is that the hotel?" Janet questioned. "I was wondering if they were constructing another Bank of Guyana building. I can't believe another hotel is being erected so close to the Pegasus, but I suppose healthy competition is beneficial."

"The Pegasus is getting older now. People seem to want a new place to stay but still be close to the ocean."

"Is it one of the regular North American chains?"

"You bet," said Jenna. "It's another Mariott."

"Hmmm," Janet pondered. "Many Guyanese from Canada and the US do return for visits, especially when it's cold in those parts of the world. Sustaining business for another hotel shouldn't pose much of a challenge. It would be nice if they could establish a hotel in San Souci; it would certainly make it more convenient for foreign visitors."

"You want to hear the truth, Jan? You're probably among the handful of people who consider a trip to the island a 'must,' given our roots and heritage. Most people prefer to stay closer to the bright lights of the city. Having a hotel in San Souci, that venture would probably fizzle out before it even took off! Look at that! The parking lot is nearly full," Jenna exclaimed, pointing to the hospital's parking lot, which they were approaching.

Jenna smoothly entered through the hospital gates. "There's an available space in the last row," Janet observed. "I hope no one takes it before we reach there."

"Parking here is always a pain," complained Jenna.

"Well, at least it's free," countered Janet. "Come on. We've got more important things to worry about."

Once Jenna had navigated her way between the two SUVs, they swiftly exited the car and bounded up the stairs that led to the hospital's main entrance, much like they had done the day before. They briskly traversed the corridor, making their way to Jack's room. Holding her breath in anticipation, Janet pushed open the door. Jack was propped up by pillows on the bed, positioned halfway between sitting and lying down. One of his legs remained elevated, and two screens surrounded him. His eyes appeared swollen and red, yet they were open, and he was laboring to speak through his swollen lips. Mandy sat in a chair beside the bed, engaged in conversation with him. Janet rushed to his side and attempted to embrace him clumsily. "Jack, Jack, oh Jack, how are you?" she whispered, leaning in toward him. She gently kissed his forehead beneath the gauze and bandages that covered his head. Jack made an effort to nod, though even this small movement seemed painful. However, his eyes conveyed an unmistakable message – he was genuinely glad to see her.

"Jan, Jan … so happy you're here," Jack's croaky voice was barely audible.

"You really gave us a scare, Jack," Janet continued, her voice soft but filled with relief. "But you're going to be just fine. I'm here, little brother, and nothing is going to go wrong. Look at you; you're already improving, much better than yesterday." Janet gently touched Mandy's shoulder in greeting while Jenna positioned herself on the other side of the bed. She gazed at Jack, and tears streamed down her face. A solitary tear also trailed down Jack's cheek.

Attempting to shake his head, Jack winced as the pain from even that slight movement registered. Yet, his message seemed clear: "Please, don't cry." Jenna tenderly placed her hand on the unbruised portion of his face as if to convey that she was there with him, offering comfort and reassurance that he was safe.

For the next three hours, Janet, Jenna, and Mandy maintained their vigilant watch over Jack. He would periodically open his eyes, seemingly to reassure them that he was alright. The women huddled together in his room, engaged in hushed conversations, their attention never wavering from his slumbering form. They didn't even consider taking a break for a drink, fearful that they might miss one of his awakening moments. The nurse was no longer standing guard by his bedside, a positive indication that his condition was improving. Instead, she would check on him every half hour or so, ensuring his well-being.

By four o'clock, Jenna announced that she needed to head home to prepare supper. She kindly informed Janet that if she stayed with Mandy, she would return to the hospital to pick her up later in the evening. Janet was appreciative of the opportunity to spend as much time as possible with Jack. Knowing that she would be returning to Canada not long after, she cherished these moments with her brother.

As Janet and Mandy exchanged stories about Jack, a doctor entered the room. This doctor was different from the one Janet had met the previous day. He exuded a more serious demeanor but remained highly professional, introducing himself as Doctor Perez. Judging from his appearance and accent, Janet sensed that he was of Cuban nationality. Guyana and Cuba maintained a strong partnership in the field of medical training, with many Guyanese students receiving their medical education in Cuba and Cuban medical graduates coming to Guyana to complete their internships.

Dr. Perez reviewed Jack's medical chart, jotting down his observations without uttering a word to Janet or Mandy. Janet couldn't contain her curiosity. "How is he progressing, Doctor?" she inquired, her eagerness evident. "It seems like he's starting to improve."

Dr. Perez nodded in agreement. "He is out of the worst and on the mend. We have to try to manage his pain. The sedatives will help him to rest, and you will see significant improvements each day."

"When will he be able to go home?" enquired Mandy.

"Not for a while yet. I would estimate another ten days, depending on how quickly his body can recover. The trauma he endured was quite severe. We're making every effort to support his healing process," Dr. Perez explained.

"I'm grateful," Mandy replied. "The doctors and nurses have been truly amazing. I can't express my gratitude enough."

Dr. Perez's demeanor softened slightly. "We do our best. Now, it's time for his body to do the healing." He reattached the chart to the foot rail of the bed. "Wishing you a pleasant evening." With that farewell, he swiftly exited the room, presumably headed to tend to his other patients. Janet guessed that Dr. Perez was likely attending to another twenty or so patients in need of his care.

A few minutes later, Janet and Mandy made their way to the cafeteria to grab some coffee and cheese rolls. The pastries were as delicious as ever. Whenever she returned to Guyana, Janet found the baked goods irresistible. She remarked to Mandy, "There's something almost mystical about Guyanese pastries. I don't find these treats in Windermere, but they're available in Toronto. I've brought them back during my visits there, but I can assure you, it's never quite the same. It's like an imitation; that's what you end up with!"

"I bet," said Mandy.

Janet contentedly wiped her fingers and lips with her napkin. As they finished their snack, the evening dusk began to envelop the city. Janet could make out the winking traffic lights. Even the light atop the Lighthouse was gradually becoming visible. "How much longer are you planning to stay?" Janet inquired of Mandy.

"I think I'll wait for another hour or so. The boys will likely arrive by then, and they'll want to spend some time with Jack. I'll head out as soon as one of them gets here."

"Yes, you need to go home and get some rest. Are you still off work tomorrow?"

"No, I took the last three days off. I need to go to the office tomorrow, but I'll come in to check on Jack before I leave. I'll stop by again at lunchtime. If he's feeling up to it, I'll keep him company for a while and skip going back to the office," Mandy explained.

Returning to Jack's room, they found him awake once more. Janet could hear him whisper her name. "Sorry," he croaked, "didn't mean to be a bother," were the words Janet could make out.

Gently shushing him by placing her fingers on his swollen lips, she awkwardly hugged him around his shoulder and whispered, "You're doing fine, Jack. I'm praying for you, as is everyone. You'll recover sooner than you think." She attempted to smooth the hair visible around the bandages on his head. "You need to rest and heal. I'm going to leave now, but Mandy is here with you. I'll come back to see you tomorrow." Jack tried to squeeze her fingers with his swollen ones, though they seemed unable to exert any pressure. Janet felt the faint brush of his fingers and held them tenderly until his eyes closed once more. Wanting to give Mandy the opportunity for her private moment with Jack, Janet mentioned, "I'll call Jenna and take a walk around the hospital to stretch my legs while I wait for her."

Mandy reached out and hugged Janet. "I'll say goodnight to you then. I'll leave when Mel or Shem arrives. See you tomorrow."

Janet gently closed the door behind her as she exited the hospital room. A few minutes later, after calling Jenna for a pickup, she found herself in conversation with a nurse named Sandy. She learned that Sandy's sister was currently teaching at Janet's former school in Denamstel. Eager to catch up on the developments at her old workplace, Janet engaged in what seemed like a Q&A session, with her asking the questions and Sandy providing the answers. "They've added a new wing to your old school, housing the lab. If you could see the improvements that have been made, you wouldn't recognize the building anymore. The school's enrollment has doubled in size. Mr. Das is now the principal. Are you familiar with him?" Sandy shared the updates.

"Prem Das?" Janet inquired. Sandy nodded in confirmation. "We used to attend some of the same meetings when he was just a beginning teacher working on the East Coast. He was a young fellow back then, not too long out of Teachers' College."

Sandy shared the latest news she had gathered from her sister about some of the old staff members familiar to Janet. She talked about how successful the school had become and mentioned some of the major achievements, which she attributed to the astute leadership of Prem Das. Amid their conversation, Janet's cell phone rang. It was Jenna, informing her that she would arrive to pick her up in fifteen minutes. "I know you'll want to check on Jack before we leave," Janet said. "Shall we meet in his room? Mandy is still there."

"I don't think I'll go back to see him. He needs to rest," Jenna replied. "Besides, I have some other things I need to get done before I go to work tomorrow, and Mandy needs some alone time with him. Shall I pick you up at the gate in fifteen minutes?"

"Fine, I'll wait for you there," said Janet, who didn't realize that as she turned her back on Nurse Sandy, she had quietly slipped away. "That was rude of me," Janet confessed to herself. "I should have asked to be excused."

Janet wandered around for another ten minutes, then returned to take a peek at Jack and Mandy. Jack was sleeping peacefully while Mandy lay on the rattan sofa next to the bed, engrossed in a book. She greeted Janet with, "The boys are running late, and I don't want to leave before they get here." She shifted to make room for Janet on the sofa. "Where did you go?" she asked.

"Oh, I just walked around," said Janet. "I ran into a nurse whose sister is working at my old school in Denamstel, so we had a chat."

"By the way," said Mandy, "will you be going to San Souci to see your friend Maria? I know you never come to Guyana without a visit to the island."

"Yes, I would like to go, but I haven't decided when. I'm waiting to see how Jack recovers."

"You don't have much time," said Mandy. "Why don't you go tomorrow? Jack is still not able to say much, but he will come around in a day or two. By then, you can be back to spend some more quality time with him. I know you never miss the opportunity to visit the cemetery, so you shouldn't miss it this time. Jack will be better able to converse with you in another two days for sure. So, why don't you go tomorrow, and then by the time you're back, you and Jack can actually talk to each other. As you can see, he's coming around very slowly, so by the time you get back, he will be in better shape. Just take the time and go look up the old homestead. As I said, you can go tomorrow."

"Tomorrow seems a bit too soon," remarked Janet. "I believe I'll go the day after. Let me ponder it. Jenna will pick me up at the gate, so I'll need to run. See you tomorrow, Mandy."

Janet proceeded to walk over to the bed and gently planted a kiss on Jack's warm forehead. "Goodnight, Jack," she whispered. After bidding farewell to Mandy, she swiftly made her way to the hospital gate to await Jenna. From her vantage point, Janet could perceive the city lights more distinctly. A cool breeze drifted in from the Atlantic, causing the branches of the palm trees that lined the path from the street to the hospital to sway gently. Amidst the dark brown waters of the Atlantic Ocean, she could detect the scent of salt. The once-present traffic had thinned considerably, and the lingering odor of exhaust fume had nearly dissipated. She could also hear the melodic hum of mosquitoes as they drew nearer to her ears. Janet attempted to swat one away, but it landed on her neck. These insects were among the most dreaded nocturnal creatures in Guyana, surpassing even some of the wild animals in the Amazon rainforest, which only posed a threat if provoked. However, mosquitoes could become quite bothersome, particularly during the rainy season when they would breed in the thousands.

Janet felt relieved when Jenna arrived, and during the trip back to Jenna's house, they once again caught up on their respective lives. Janet could sense Jenna's contentment with her small family and her continued satisfaction with her role as the Senior Vice-President at the Bank of Guyana. Before long, they reached home, and following dinner and a brief visit with Danny, Jenna prepared to retire for the night. Meanwhile, the girls were seated in the small study, engrossed in their laptops and their work. They took a moment to exchange words with Janet, inquiring about the condition of their Uncle Jack and whether Janet had managed to communicate with him. Janet provided them with a condensed version of the hospital events, then excused herself and headed to her room to call Abe. He picked up on the second ring as if he had been anticipating her call.

"Hi, Jan, how are you?" he inquired. "How is Jack? I'm hoping for more positive news..."

"Jack is improving," Janet replied. "I've just returned from the hospital. He's been drifting in and out of consciousness, but he recognized me and expressed a desire to talk, though his strength is greatly diminished. It seems we might manage a brief conversation tomorrow. I'm really looking forward to connecting with him. And how about you? Are you still holding up well? Any severe pains?"

"I'm still hanging in there after that fishing trip with Aaron. I'm relieved to hear that Jack's condition is getting better. He'll require ample rest. I truly hope you get the chance to have a substantial conversation with him before you depart for Windermere."

Janet perceived Abe's attempt to steer the conversation away from himself, yet she persisted, saying, "Are you truly alright, Abe? I need to understand how you're holding up."

"I've already told you, Jan. I'm perfectly fine," he replied, his tone slightly agitated. "Quit worrying about me. You've got enough on your plate with Jack."

"Well, my concern extends to both of you. I can't help but worry, Abe."

"It's quite heartwarming to feel cared for from a distance," he teased, and Janet could detect the warmth in his voice.

"Is that a lead-in to the question of when I'll be heading to San Souci?" she inquired. Without waiting for his response, she continued, "I've decided to take the late afternoon ferry to San Souci tomorrow. I'll coordinate the details with Maria." Janet had firmly resolved to travel to San Souci the following day. She had thoroughly pondered Jack's situation, analyzing it thoroughly while participating in the dinner discussions with Jenna's family.

"Are you certain about this, Jan?" he queried. "Perhaps you should consider waiting for another day."

"It's more sensible for me to head to San Souci earlier. That way, when I return, Jack will likely be more prepared to receive visitors. At the moment, he spends most of his time sleeping. There's not much I can do. Frankly, I feel quite ineffectual just sitting by his bedside and reading. So, yes, I'll be there tomorrow."

Janet's tone conveyed her decision clearly, leaving little room for argument from Abe. "Shall I come to pick you up?" he offered. "I can arrange for Hari to drive me to the ferry terminal, and he can bring us back."

"To your house?" she questioned alarmingly.

"Why not? You can join me for dinner, and then Hari can drive you over to Maria's place. Alternatively, you could opt to spend the night if you'd like. Remember, there are three bedrooms here," he added with a chuckle.

Abe sensed her contemplation. When she finally spoke, her tone turned serious. "Without a doubt, I'll be taking the afternoon ferry to San Souci tomorrow, Abe. Kindly ask Hari to pick me up.

Yes, I'll share dinner with you and then head to Maria's. I'll need to fabricate a plausible reason to dissuade Maria from meeting me at the terminal. It seems I'm becoming quite adept at concocting stories," she mused, "so I'll come up with something. Anyway, I'll be seeing you tomorrow."

"Done!" exclaimed Abe. "What would you like to have for dinner?"

"Surprise me," she suggested. "Just remember not to go overboard with the spices. opt for something simple and manageable. Can you ask Monica to lend a hand? I don't want you burdening yourself with extra tasks."

"Your only concern should be getting here, Jan. I'll handle everything else. I've got a dish in mind to prepare. Rest assured, it will be a surprise."

"It's time for me to prepare for bed now, and the same goes for you. See you tomorrow. The ferry is expected around five. I need to give Maria a call to inform her about my plans. Have a peaceful night's rest, Abe. We'll catch up tomorrow."

"I'll be here," he whispered. "Goodnight, Jan."

She hung up the phone, feeling as breathless as ever. Abe's ability to evoke such a reaction from her had persisted since she was fifteen. "I'm just being foolish," she murmured, addressing no one in particular. "I don't even have a clear grasp of what I'm doing!"

Earlier, she had contacted Maria to inform her about her presence in Guyana, her intention to visit Jack, and the likelihood of a short trip to San Souci. "Your room is still here," Maria had warmly assured her. "I hope you'll consider spending a night with me."

"Maybe, who knows, it might turn out to be two," Janet retorted.

"All the better! Even if it ends up being a dozen nights, I would be absolutely delighted to have you here again."

"No need for further discussion. It's settled!" declared Janet. "I'll be in touch again soon."

Janet proceeded to call Maria and explained that she would be arriving the next day but would be getting a ride from the ferry terminal. She had made arrangements to have dinner with another friend, but she would be at Maria's house around nine in the evening. Maria was perfectly fine with Janet being picked up by someone else. In fact, she seemed somewhat relieved, as she had mentioned to Janet that her niece and her children were coming over for a visit, and she would be occupied with her dinner preparations. After a quick shower, Janet prepared for bed. She gave her emails one last check, hoping that there were no urgent matters from the office. Everything appeared to be in order, so Janet crawled under the mosquito net, pulled the covers up to her chin, and eventually drifted off to sleep.

Chapter 20

Janet woke up the following morning and prepared her bag for her trip to San Souci. She intended to spend some time at the hospital with Jack before taking the island ferry. Quietly, Janet entered the kitchen and turned on the coffee maker Jenna had set up the night before, as usual. She chose a mug from the many in the cabinet. The words on it read: *"Life is short. Enjoy your coffee."* Janet thought, "How true!" She poured the hot coffee into the mug and went out to the patio. The sun was beginning to rise over the city's skyline. The weather was warm at this hour, not too hot. It was the perfect time to be outdoors. She noticed a yellow *Kiskadee* flying from its nest on the house's roof to a lamppost by the roadside. The city environment felt so different compared to San Souci. Memories of beautiful sunrises over the Atlantic waters came to her mind. She used to watch the golden sun rising, painting the sky with shades of blue and yellow. The *Kiskadee* seemed to grow bolder in her presence and landed on the table before her. Janet reached out her hand, though empty, as if to say, "I have nothing to offer you, little bird." Her sudden movement startled the bird, and it quickly flew back to the safety of its nest in a nearby tree.

Janet sipped her coffee, taking in moments of serenity. These moments were rare for her, considering her busy life of raising a family and building a career. She often looked back and wondered how she managed to do it all. Life had been challenging, but she had no regrets. Those challenges shaped her character, making her stronger, more courageous, and more empathetic toward others. She was always ready to assist those who were less fortunate.

Jenna, dressed in her pajamas and holding her cup of hot coffee, appeared and interrupted Janet's thoughts. She strolled over to the patio and gave Janet a quick hug. "Good morning, Sis. You're up early. What's the reason? Trouble sleeping?"

"Nah," replied Janet. "I had a good night's sleep, but I woke up and thought I'd enjoy some quiet time before the day gets busy."

"And here I am interrupting," said Jenna.

"Don't be silly. We don't get together often enough. I'm really happy you're here. Come, have a seat." Janet pointed to the empty chair beside her and even moved her own chair closer. Jenna sat down, letting out a long sigh. "Is everything okay?" Janet asked, her concern showing in her eyes. "You look a bit tired, Jen. Maybe you're the one who didn't sleep well."

"I did sleep, but it was a bit on and off, and then I had this strange dream about you."

"What was your dream about?" Janet asked, intrigued.

"I dreamt that you were going back to Canada, but instead of taking a plane, you were on a boat. It wasn't like a big cruise ship, more like a small one, kind of like the San Souci ferry. I was worried that such a tiny boat wouldn't be safe for such a long journey. I called out to you to leave the boat, but you just laughed, waved, and then went to the other side, where I couldn't see you anymore. I felt really scared for you. Then I woke up and realized what a weird dream it was."

"It's just a dream," Janet said, dismissing the idea. "If we took every dream seriously, we'd spend all day trying to figure out what they mean." She chuckled. "Luckily, I've got a plane ticket to go back to Windermere. No boat necessary!"

Jenna joined in the laughter. "I wonder how long it would actually take by boat. Back in the 1800s, people traveled around the world on boats. It must have been quite an adventure."

"What about 1492 when Christopher Columbus discovered the West Indies, including Guyana? He sailed all the way here from Spain. Think about them spending months on those little ships like the Pinta, the Nina, and the Santa Maria, crossing vast open seas. I can't imagine how difficult it must have been. Our world now is so fast-paced. I don't think our generation would have the patience to spend months at sea to travel between places."

"Well, that was a different time. Now is now," Jenna concluded. "I'm grateful for the present. It's always a joy to see you,

Jan. I wish you were still living here so we could spend more time together. I don't usually say how much I miss you, but I do," Jenna admitted. She reached over and held Janet's hand. Janet had been there for her as they grew up. Being seven years older, she was a caring and loving sister to both Jenna and Jack. When Janet, Nat, and their daughters moved to Canada, Jenna cried for days. She felt their absence deeply, but over time, she learned to accept it and became absorbed in her own family.

Janet always made an effort to return for visits whenever possible. Sometimes, she came alone, and sometimes with Nat and the girls. Now that the girls were grown and leading their own lives, Janet mostly visited on her own. Nat's parents had passed away, and his three siblings were living in Birmingham in the UK. Jenna cherished the recent visits when Janet had come to see them, and she and Jack had Janet all to themselves. Three years ago, during Janet's last visit, they all went to San Souci to meet old friends and visit the cemetery by the old church where their parents were laid to rest. They even attended Sunday worship there. Jenna felt the strong presence of their parents, almost as if they were sitting beside her and Jack, just like they used to when the family lived on the island. It was both astonishing and a bit unsettling.

In the city, they revisited familiar restaurants, took trips to the botanical gardens, explored Stabroek and Bourda markets, and even watched a movie at the Metropole Theatre. It was unfortunate that Janet's current visit was under such difficult circumstances, with Jack in a hospital bed.

Janet gently squeezed Jenna's hand. "I miss you too, Jen. I miss you, Jack, living in Guyana and San Souci. I'm hoping that when I retire, Nat and I can come back for longer periods. Maybe we can even consider coming back to live permanently."

"No, you won't," Jenna disagreed. "You'll still want to be close to your daughters, and that's only right. They have their own families and won't leave Canada. Canada is their home now."

Janet nodded, acknowledging that Jenna was correct. Leaving her daughters and grandkids behind would be a tough choice for her.

"We'll have to wait and see what the future brings. It's hard to make solid plans for the distant future,"

She and Jenna chatted about their kids and shared amusing family stories, including some involving their husbands, of course. Jenna's husband, Daniel, was a good partner. They had their disagreements like any couple, but Daniel was affectionate, considerate, and truly cared for Jenna. Around a decade ago, Janet had offered to sponsor Jenna's family to Canada, but Daniel had declined, citing his stable job and content life. Janet felt a bit disheartened but was reassured, knowing that Jenna was well-supported and happy. Janet chose not to tell Jenna about Nat's infidelity and his unpredictable temper. She didn't want Jenna to worry, so she kept the details of her marriage to herself.

Checking her watch, Janet realized that over an hour had passed surprisingly quickly. "Well, I think I'll have to head out if I want to spend some time with Jack and then make my way to San Souci," she said, rising from her seat.

"Who's picking you up from the ferry?" asked Jenna.

"One of Maria's friends, Chris," Janet fibbed. "Don't you remember him? He used to help Dad with his income tax. It turns out Chris needs to pick someone up from the ferry, so Maria arranged for me to catch a ride with him at the same time. Maria's niece is visiting, so she's happy to pass me on to Chris, which is fine."

"That's good. I'm sure Maria will set up some time for you to meet your old friends. I know you'll enjoy the two days, just relaxing and going for long walks. Make sure to have lots of fresh fruits and fish."

"I'm really looking forward to it," Janet acknowledged. "But you know, the most important part of my visits to San Souci is always checking on Mom and Dad. I can't come to Guyana without visiting that cemetery."

"I understand," said Jenna. "But also do other things and try not to worry too much about Jack."

"I'm planning to visit Seth's farm. Maria mentioned he added another acre of fruit trees and a dozen more cows. Do you remember when we were kids how much we loved the fresh milk his dad would bring us? The cream was so thick and delicious. Mom used to make yogurt out of it, and she'd make us eat it, saying it was good for our digestion, even though we hated it."

Jenna wrinkled her nose, recalling the tasteless yogurt that they secretly improved by adding salt, sugar, and even a bit of lime to make it more bearable.

"Seth would be glad to see you," Jenna said. "Say hi to him from my side. I haven't been back to San Souci since your last visit three years ago. I doubt much has changed."

Reluctantly, the two sisters left the comfort of the patio and headed to the kitchen to prepare breakfast. The aroma of eggs and coffee seemed to rouse Daniel and the girls from their beds, drawing them to the dining table. Hugs were exchanged all around – between Daniel and Jenna, Daniel and Janet, Janet and the girls, and Jenna and the girls. "Good morning, good morning," was the cheerful chorus, and Janet couldn't quite tell who was saying it to whom.

Daniel poured his coffee and approached Jenna. "I can handle the toast," he offered, and Jenna accepted his help. Quite different from Nat, Janet thought. On weekends, she would make breakfast so they could eat together. Nat, on the other hand, would come downstairs while she was still finishing up the toast or pancakes. He'd take whatever was ready and go to the table without waiting for her to finish cooking. By the time she joined him, he would be nearly done with his meal, and then he'd leisurely sip his coffee while she ate. She had dropped hints about this habit of Nat's numerous times, but he always brushed it off. Janet had reached the conclusion that he was set in his ways, and she had stopped letting his self-centered actions bother her.

Daniel, Jenna, Janet, and the girls gathered around the kitchen table. They enjoyed their breakfast while chatting, mostly about their plans for the day. One by one, they excused themselves, clearing the table and heading to get dressed and start their day. Jenna let Daniel and the girls leave first as they were on tight schedules, and with only two cars, Jenna's and Daniel's, Daniel was the designated driver for his daughters. Jenna had enough time to get to work and didn't want Janet to feel rushed.

A little later, Janet came out of her room with her overnight bag. "Ready to hit the road?" Jenna asked.

"Yes, if you are. I'm looking forward to giving Jack a lot of my time today."

Together, they walked to Jenna's car, parked in the driveway. They turned onto Lamaha Street and then onto Parade Street, which had earned its name due to its proximity to the army barracks, where parades were a common sight. When they reached the hospital gates, Jenna leaned over to give Janet a quick peck on the cheek. "Give my love to Jack. Let him know I'll come to see him later."

"I will, for sure," Janet promised, getting out of the car and grabbing her bag. With a wave and a "See you soon," Janet bid Jenna farewell.

Janet hurried up the hospital stairs, now familiar to her after three days of visits. The usual scent of antiseptic and disinfectants greeted her as she walked down the corridor. She headed straight to Jack's room, hoping he would be awake. Luckily, he was. "Hello, Jack," she greeted as she hurried over to his bedside. He looked a bit better than the previous day. Despite his swollen lips, a crooked smile appeared on his face. His complexion had regained some color, and his eyes seemed more alert.

"Jan, Jan," he whispered hoarsely. "It's true you're here."

Janet carefully dropped her bag and leaned in to hug him, being mindful not to cause any discomfort. She lightly brushed his forehead with a kiss and tenderly smoothed his hair, speaking in a soothing tone as if he were a child. "Jack, oh my God, Jack, it's so wonderful to see you awake. How are you holding up, *baby boy*?" She used the endearment their mother had always used to make Jack feel especially cherished.

Jack's smile widened, albeit a bit painfully. "I could be better," he admitted in a calm voice, "but I'm grateful to be alive." His words were slurred, requiring Janet to listen closely. She continued to gently smooth his hair. "We're all so thankful you're alive, Jack, even though you're a bit banged up. The good news is that you'll be okay. It'll take time and patience, but you'll be up and moving before you know it. Are you in a lot of pain?"

"My leg hurts a lot, and my head does too," Jack managed to convey, though his speech was difficult to understand. It seemed his leg and head were causing him the most pain.

Janet inquired, "Where is the pain the worst?"

Jack pointed near his left ear, and Janet noticed the gauze covering the wound, stained possibly with blood from the day before. She wanted to touch it, but she hesitated, fearing it might worsen his pain. "Has the doctor come by today?" she asked.

Jack nodded. He tried to speak but seemed drained by the effort. His eyes closed, and Janet reassured him, "Take it easy. I'm here. No need to talk. Just rest." His eyes fluttered open again. "I'm so tired, Jan," he whispered.

"You just relax. Close your eyes. I'm here."

His trembling fingers reached for hers. Struggling to understand his words, Janet heard him asking her to sit and hold his hand, his whispers repeating, "I'm so sorry, Jan. I'm so sorry for the extra trouble."

Though his eyes closed again, Janet continued talking to him, hoping he could still hear her. "You know I had to come to see you, Jack. How could I stay away when I knew you were lying in a hospital bed, wondering if you'd make it? I'll never be okay if anything happens to you or Jenna." She felt the gentle pressure of his thumb against her hand and went on, "Jenna dropped me off and said to let you know she'll come by later, so you'd better be awake and ready to chat with her." Seeing a fleeting smile on his lips, she knew he was still somewhat awake. Janet held onto his hand until she sensed his grip loosen, understanding that he had probably fallen asleep. She felt it was a wise decision to head to San Souci now so that by the time she returned in two days, Jack would be more able to talk and interact with visitors. A couple more days of rest would likely be beneficial for him.

Janet stayed by Jack's side for another hour until he opened his eyes once more. He seemed unaware of the doctor's recent visit. Janet had checked with Dr. Ramirez about Jack's progress earlier and received reassurance that he was making significant improvement and would be able to move a bit in the next couple of days.

As Jack's eyes focused on hers, he suddenly asked, "How was Cuba?" Janet had to listen carefully and even read his lips to understand his words.

"You remember!" she replied. "The conference was fantastic. I met new colleagues, and the people were very friendly. It was almost finished by the time I left," Janet fibbed.

"Tell me more," Jack whispered.

This was classic Jack – always curious about new places and people. Janet shared with him the similarities between the island and San Souci, describing the food, the ocean, the lush vegetation, and the vintage cars she had seen. He managed a slight smile when she mentioned the old pink Crown Victoria that had taken her to the airport, listening intently and occasionally closing his eyes. Janet wasn't sure how much he was able to hear, but that didn't matter to her. She just wanted to keep talking to him. When his eyes remained closed for a solid ten minutes, she figured he had fallen asleep again. And so, they spent the next few hours, Janet talking to Jack and him drifting in and out of sleep.

She took out her phone and tackled some of her emails. Then she settled onto the rattan settee and delved into another lengthy report from the Minister of Advanced Education about new programs introduced by two different universities. Her concentration was broken by the arrival of a nurse who greeted her cheerfully, "Nice to see you back. Your brother is making great progress, as you can see. We're all quite pleased with how he's doing. It's your turn to keep an eye on him today?"

Janet nodded. "He still seems to be in a lot of pain. What about his broken leg? I should've asked the doctor about it."

"It's been reset already. He'll need to keep the cast on for another three months at least. When we discharge him, he'll need to use crutches for a while, but he's going to be alright. I'm sorry, but I'll need a few minutes alone with him to change his dressings and give him a shot. It should take about ten minutes."

"Of course," Janet replied, grabbing her handbag and stepping out into the corridor to wait. Eight minutes later, the nurse emerged. "Heading back to Canada?" she asked Janet, likely noticing her overnight bag.

"No, I'm off for two days. I'm going to San Souci to see some friends."

"Well, enjoy," the nurse commented. "Your brother is doing very well." She then proceeded into the room next door.

Around noon, Jenna and Mandy arrived. Janet decided to find a sandwich to allow them some private time with Jack. She had been by his side for the last three hours. While munching on her fish roll, Jenna joined her and said, "I'm letting Mandy spend some time with Jack."

"Is he awake now?" Janet inquired.

"He was when I left the room. It's heartwarming to see how much better he looks today," Jenna remarked, and Janet agreed. "I briefly spoke to the doctor earlier, and he mentioned he's satisfied with the pace of Jack's recovery. Thank God he's getting better," Janet replied.

"Yes, I'm so thankful," concurred Jenna. Mandy wants to know when he will be going home."

"As the doctor mentioned, it's probably going to be another ten days. I can understand Mandy's worry. She wants to care for him and believes she can nurse him back to health. But right now, the hospital is where he should be. There's no rush to bring him home. If something were to go wrong that Mandy can't handle, he'd be without medical assistance," Janet explained.

"I completely agree," Jenna affirmed.

They continued to chat for a while before Jenna had to return to work. She wished Janet a safe trip to San Souci, advising her to take care and to stay in touch. Janet assured Jenna that everything would be fine. Afterward, she returned to Jack's room and caught up with Mandy. Jack was sound asleep. "Jenna told me you're taking the afternoon ferry to San Souci, just like we had discussed," Mandy mentioned.

Janet confirmed her plans, explaining she would be staying on the island for two days. "I'll spend a few more minutes with Jack, and then I'll call a taxi to take me to the harbor. I should leave around 2:00," Janet said.

"I need to head back now," Mandy said. "I've got to get to the office for a meeting with a client about something unexpected. It's always the way – you try to take time off, but work matters still come up." She let out a long sigh and added, "Doesn't Jack look so much better? I truly believe he's going to be fine."

"He will be," Janet agreed.

Mandy continued, "I'll be back for the longer evening visit. Have a great time on the island. I'll catch up with you when you return." She leaned over and gently kissed Jack's swollen lips before hugging Janet. Then she left the room, closing the door softly behind her.

Janet prepared to leave shortly after. Jack remained still, his chest rising and falling with each breath. Janet called for a taxi and then walked over to the bed, gently squeezing Jack's fingers. He whispered something that sounded like "Mandy?" Janet patted his hand and quietly picked up her bag before leaving. She didn't have to wait long for the taxi, and soon, they were on their way for the hour-long journey to the Lewiston ferry terminal, where she would catch the ferry to San Souci.

Janet requested the driver to turn off the air conditioning so she could roll down her window and enjoy the fresh air. The temperature was around 34 degrees Celsius, and she could feel the heat radiating from the asphalt road as they drove through the city. They passed by the traffic circle near the Bank of Guyana where Jenna worked, then a stately colonial-style building housing the library. Next, they swung by the Victoria Law Courts. The traffic was dense, and the air was filled with dust. The driver honked frequently, and Janet could sense the impatience on the faces of other drivers as they passed by. She decided to close her window and asked the driver to turn the air conditioning back on, which he did without complaint. The streets were narrow, a reminder of an era when there were fewer cars to contend with. However, over the past half-century, globalization brought more of a North American culture to the country, leading to a desire for luxurious cars and large houses.

As they continued, they passed the Brickdam Cathedral, triggering memories of Janet's visits to the city during the early years of her marriage. She would often stop at the Cathedral to offer a quick prayer.

The journey led her along the small West Coast highway. Janet observed the numerous new houses under construction and the nearly finished hospital for infectious diseases. While some of the sugar factories appeared so much older, the strong aroma of raw sugar and molasses lingered in the air, a reminder that the world of sugar cultivation hadn't changed significantly. She could still spot the punts used to transport harvested sugar cane to the factories, resting in the canal that ran alongside the sugar cane fields.

Janet recalled the history that these punts were once pulled by slaves brought from Africa by European slave traders. Today, fortunately, tractors took on the task of hauling the punts, although they were often loaded and unloaded by field laborers. The sugar cane industry in Guyana remained substantial, with sugar being a crucial export for the country. It employed thousands of individuals, although being a "sugar worker" was always demanding labor.

The taxi driver, who had not said much to Janet so far, broke into her thoughts. "Do you live here, Miss?" he asked.

"I used to," replied Janet. "Why?"

"I'm just guessing you're from abroad. The US?"

"No," said Janet. "Canada."

"Visiting?" he continued.

"Yes."

"Are you going to the other Coast?"

"No, to San Souci."

"You don't have to wait for the ferry," he told her. "There are speedboats now that can get you to the island in twenty minutes. It might be a bit more expensive, but it eliminates the waiting time."

Janet inquired, "How many passengers can the boat hold in total?"

"Most of them accommodate about eight or ten people," he replied.

"Can they also transport your luggage?"

"Of course," said the taxi driver confidently. "I know one of the guys who operates those boats. I can arrange for him to take you across if you're interested."

"No, thank you," Janet declined. "I was just curious. I have someone picking me up at the San Souci terminal. Plus, I'm a bit hesitant about the safety of those boats. A friend told me that this boat service started less than a year ago, so I'm not entirely sure about traveling across the rough river in one of those small boats."

"It's quite safe," the driver tried to reassure her. "There haven't been any accidents."

"Not yet," Janet countered. "But I've made up my mind. I'll stick with the ferry."

The journey continued with moments of silence interspersed with the taxi driver pointing out new developments. Janet responded with brief comments or questions to gather more information. After another forty-five minutes, they reached the Lewiston ferry terminal. Janet settled the fare and handed the driver a generous tip, which surprised him. He retrieved her bag and wished her, "Enjoy your time on the island," before moving away, presumably in search of another passenger heading towards the city.

The scent of the ocean, mingled with the aroma of decaying fruits and vegetables, greeted Janet as she walked to the entrance of the terminal. The Lewiston terminal boasted a sizable open market, and the remnants of the vendors' goods were discarded into the brown, murky waters that washed the river's mudflats. Nevertheless, Janet found herself captivated by the market along the pier. It showcased an array of colorful fruits, vegetables, and handicrafts created by women from the numerous islands dotting the river's mouth. The market bustled with activity, and a few schoolchildren had even joined in after classes to help their parents earn an extra income. They called out to the shoppers awaiting transportation to the South Coast or one of the islands.

Janet strolled through the market since she had an hour to spare before the ferry to San Souci departed. She purchased some bananas and pineapple for Maria, then wandered over to the section displaying handicrafts. The creativity on display amazed her – coconut shells transformed into exquisite jewelry, Guyanese woods carved and polished into wall hangings or ornaments. She found amusement in the witty quotes on the "welcome to my home" signs, like "Friends are welcome, family should make reservations," "Thanks for stopping by, please (don't) call again," and "A home filled with family is like a zoo with guerillas." Janet smiled at the last one.

She noticed various pens and desktop items that might be useful in her office. Some of these items were among the souvenirs she had taken back on her previous trips. Above her, she spotted a small triangular wind chime made from bamboo and pieces of glass. The tip of the triangle held everything together and bore the words: "Life – held together by love." Janet found it beautiful and thought,

"I should get this for Abe." She asked to examine the ornament, carefully inspecting it to ensure all the pieces were intact and paid the vendor the marked price of thirty dollars. The vendor seemed surprised that she didn't attempt to negotiate a lower price, but Janet disliked bargaining, recognizing the hours of labor that went into crafting these items. The prices they received rarely reflected the effort and care put into their creation. Janet then found a spot by the side of the pier to relax and wait for the ferry to start boarding.

Chapter 21

Soon, it was time to board the *Lady Althea*, which was about to depart for San Souci. Janet joined the other passengers, mostly women and children, who had traveled to Lewiston for shopping at the bustling terminal market. The river was a bit rough, but the *Lady Althea* courageously rode the waves, slicing through the water with her propeller, and leaving behind a wake of foamy white trails on the surface of the brown Atlantic. A few clouds dotted the sky, and the sun was already beginning to mellow, losing its intense glare. In about an hour, only the comforting warmth of the sun's drowning rays would linger, blending with the gentle Atlantic breezes – It was a soothing sensation Janet had cherished during her time on the island.

The rolling waves wore crowns of foam, and even though the water appeared brown, Janet could spot glimmers of gold within its depth as it caught the rays of the setting sun. She had sailed the Mediterranean, navigated the Pacific waters around Hawaii's islands, crossed the Baltic Sea, and even ventured into the Caribbean waters. Yet, she deemed this boat journey to San Souci as the most cherished. Sometimes, she couldn't help but lament that Guyana couldn't inspire the same kind of tourism that some neighboring Caribbean islands effortlessly attracted to bolster their economies. Tourists sought azure waters and powdery white beaches for their vacations, areas where Guyana couldn't compete with its brown waters and dark, earthy sands.

As the *Lady Althea* began to approach San Souci's shores, Janet positioned herself on the forward deck. Shielding her eyes with her hands, she scanned the small crowd gathered on the pier, hoping to spot Abe among them. It took only moments to distinguish him from the roughly three dozen people who had come to welcome or reunite with their loved ones. Spotting her at the rail of the boat, he enthusiastically waved, and she reciprocated the gesture. Gradually, the *Lady Althea* maneuvered alongside the pier, ready for the hundred or so passengers to disembark.

Without delay, Abe advanced towards her, embracing her in a warm hug. "How are you? How was the journey? You seem weary," he inquired, taking her overnight case from her grip.

Janet could sense his excitement. "I'm well," she responded. "And you? Oh, let me handle the case. It's a bit heavy."

Abe waved off her offer. "No worries. This is Hari. He'll take it to the car." He introduced Janet to a younger man standing just behind him. "Hari, I'd like you to meet Janet, my friend from Canada. Janet, this is my nephew, Hari."

"It's a pleasure to make your acquaintance," Hari greeted politely, extending his hand. "You bear a resemblance to Mr. Jack."

"Do you happen to know Jack?" Janet inquired. "He's my brother."

"Yes, I was much younger during Mr. Jack's time here. I don't personally know you, but I've heard about you. My parents were acquainted with Mr. and Mrs. Ramphal."

A playful wink from Janet toward Abe followed. "It appears you've been busy delving into the family history."

He dismissed her comment and instead remarked, "Hari will be driving us to my place. We've prepared a fantastic San Souci dinner between the two of us, haven't we, Hari?" He turned to Hari, seeking confirmation, and went on, "It's 6:00 now, and we'll have you at Maria's by 9:00. That's the plan." They strolled towards Hari's compact Fiat, parked at the pier's entrance. Abe assisted Janet into the car while Hari tossed her case into the trunk.

"You can take the back seat with Miss Janet, Uncle Abe. I'm fine being your chauffeur for tonight," Hari offered cheerfully.

"That's agreeable with me," Abe said as he settled in next to Janet in the back seat.

The small car felt a bit cramped, and Janet could sense Abe's legs brushing against hers. She also caught a whiff of his subtle after-shave or cologne, a scent that invigorated her senses. Much about Abe felt revitalizing to her - his perspective on savoring Life, his considerate nature, his generosity towards others, and his belief that Life should be relished each day, regardless of circumstances. A memory surfaced of a conversation they had in Holguin, where he had mentioned that too many people fixate on material possessions, disregarding the fact that the most valuable treasures are relationships. And here she was, not thinking much about her material possessions - her job, her status - but simply aiming to be a part of Abe's diminishing journey.

"What are your thoughts on the new and improved cottage hospital?" Abe inquired as they drove past the freshly constructed two-story building, its white paint gleaming in the fading sunlight. The original hospital was small and ill-equipped. Janet felt a surge of satisfaction that the island now had this upgraded facility to cater to its residents, who previously might have had to journey to the city for more serious medical needs.

"I believe it's wonderful that the government recognized the necessity for an upgraded hospital here in San Souci," Janet replied to Abe.

"They've managed to bring in some highly skilled doctors from Cuba, and the staff is well-trained too. It's a significant improvement from our time here," Abe explained.

Janet raised an eyebrow, curious. "Why are Cuban doctors practicing in San Souci? I assumed they would mostly be in the city."

"Many of them actually come here to escape the city's hustle and bustle. They appreciate the peace and tranquility of San Souci. And I must say, they're exceptional doctors," Abe assured her.

"I do not doubt that," Janet agreed. It was common knowledge that among the Caribbean islands, Cuba boasted top-notch medical training and state-of-the-art facilities, including advanced research centers. "Do they rotate frequently?" she inquired.

"Most of them tend to stay for a minimum of two years," Hari added, "and when they do leave, the transitions to the incoming doctors are quite seamless. The system is functioning very effectively. We're content with the medical care, and it's certainly more convenient not having to travel to the city."

Janet turned her attention to Abe. "Have you ever needed medical treatment during any of your visits here?"

Before Abe could respond, Hari jumped in. "Uncle Abe was actually at the hospital just yesterday. He had a blackout while I was with him, and I got really concerned, so…"

"Thank you, Hari," Abe interjected somewhat sternly, "The question was directed at me, not you."

"Oh, my apologies, Uncle Abe. I misspoke," Hari acknowledged.

Abe redirected his focus to Janet, who was giving him a rather pointed look. "It was nothing," he assured her. "I had missed taking my medication and felt tired after being out in the sun for a few hours. I believe I became a bit dehydrated. The doctor checked my blood pressure and heart rate. He reassured me that everything was fine, so there's no need to worry."

"Of course," Janet remarked with a touch of sarcasm. "Abe, you really ought to take better care of yourself. The journey from Cuba to San Souci must have taken a toll on you. I still can't fathom why you were so insistent on making it."

Choosing his words carefully, especially with Hari in earshot, Abe replied, "You understand why I felt it was necessary, Jan."

As the sun began to set, casting elongated shadows, Abe shifted the conversation. "Do you recall the breathtaking San Souci sunsets?" he asked Janet, his hands gently clasping hers, ensuring his gesture remained hidden from the rear-view mirror. A soft caress of her fingers caused Janet's heart rate to quicken as warmth surged through her veins. "I don't think I could ever tire of a San Souci sunset."

"After all my travels," Janet replied, "The lush, untouched beauty of San Souci is still a marvel. Look at those pink oleanders. Their hues always seem more vibrant here than anywhere else. And in the evenings, when the crickets start their symphony, it's a kind of melody I've never encountered elsewhere in my travels."

"This is the reason I find myself returning to San Souci so frequently," Abe admitted. "No other place has the same effect on me as this island does."

Janet detected a tinge of melancholy in his voice. She imagined he must be contemplating how many more visits he would be able to make to his cherished island before his illness ultimately takes its toll. In response, she gave his fingers a gentle squeeze, and he held onto her hand as though he never wanted to let go. Then, he softly patted her arm. "Here we are," he announced as the car pulled up to his family's familiar residence, which Janet remembered so well.

Exiting the vehicle, they waited as Hari went to retrieve her suitcase. "Welcome home," Abe greeted as they stepped into the front yard. A vibrant garden greeted them, brimming with flowers that overflowed from their pots. Large red roses swayed gracefully in the evening breeze, their fragrance enveloping Janet as she took in the scene. Curious, she inquired, "Who tends to all this gardening?"

"Hari arranges for someone to maintain the garden," Abe replied.

"Can you recall old Willie?" Hari inquired from just behind her.

"Do you mean Willie, the caretaker of the school back when my Dad was there?" Janet responded.

"The same Willie," Hari confirmed. "He looks after the yard. Despite his age - he's eighty-three now - he's remarkably skilled with the plants. Gardening is his true passion. He often turns down payment, claiming that being surrounded by his beloved flowers is reward enough."

Janet fondly recalled how diligent Willie had been during the time he worked with her Dad. Even on occasions when her Dad encouraged him to leave early from his role as the school's custodian, Willie would meticulously ensure that every window and door was securely closed and locked.

"He truly is exceptional," Abe chimed in, plucking a large red rose and brushing it under Janet's nose.

"That aroma is exquisite," Janet remarked. Abe handed her the rose.

They ascended the stairs, and Janet observed that the house's fundamental structure remained intact, although significant alterations had been made to the roof and front windows. On her prior visits to the island, she had driven past the house without paying it much heed. Now, however, she took in the intricacies of the new external stairs, the renovated veranda, and the apparent extension of the kitchen. Pausing in the living room, Abe suggested, "Take a moment to relax," indicating the *Berbice* chair with its polished wooden arms and plush maroon cushions.

Janet noted the changes in furniture, the transformation of the wooden flooring into tiles, and the shift in paint color from cream to eggshell blue. The interior of the house bore little resemblance to her memories. She understood that maintaining the house's current state must have required substantial effort. She had witnessed numerous homes on the island succumb to decay and collapse because their owners had moved away. For those who had sold their properties, new owners sometimes razed the old structures to erect more modern dwellings. This fate had befallen their family home as well. Following their parents' passing, Janet, Jenna, and Jack had collectively decided to sell the property to their neighbor, who had replaced it with a contemporary, larger house.

"If you'd like to freshen up before dinner, the bathroom is just down the hallway," Abe offered.

"Thank you. I'd appreciate washing my face. The heat and dust still bother me," Janet replied. She followed the direction Abe had indicated. The cool water was revitalizing. She applied a light touch of new makeup, then gazed at her reflection in the mirror, once again questioning the person staring back at her. But the response remained unchanged – she was undertaking this for Abe, fulfilling the request of a man who was nearing the end of his Life.

A knock on the bathroom door startled her. "Are you alright?" Abe's concerned voice came through.

"Yes, I'm fine. I'll be out in a moment," she reassured him.

"Take your time. I just wanted to ensure you're okay. Hari is waiting to bid you farewell."

Janet hurriedly exited the bathroom, almost colliding with Abe. "Why is Hari leaving?" she inquired with a note of anxiety.

"That was the plan. He needs to return to his family in time for their dinner," Abe explained.

"But how will I get to Maria's? I don't want to be strolling down the street with you in tow, carrying my suitcase. That would surely set tongues wagging!" Janet expressed her concern.

"Just be calm. Hari will come back to fetch you at 9:00. That's in nearly three hours. Is that suitable for you?" Abe reassured her.

"Yes, yes," Janet replied, feeling a touch embarrassed by her outburst. "It's just that I'd rather you not accompany me to Maria's place. I can't predict what she might think, and then the rumors will start flying."

"I understand," Abe acknowledged. "That's precisely why Hari will return."

"Great," Janet said, heading to bid farewell to Hari at the front door. "Once again, thank you for picking me up. I truly appreciate everything you've done and the time you've taken. See you later."

"Ciao," Hari responded. "I'll be back to collect you at 9:00." With a wave, he descended the stairs and vanished from sight.

Alone together now, Abe immediately reached out for Janet, enfolding her in a tight embrace. He was a full head taller than her, and with her shoes off, she nestled just beneath his chin. He inhaled the fragrance of her hair and softly murmured, "Dearest Janet, it still feels surreal to have you here with me, in my home." Drawing her nearer and nearer, she could sense the frailty in his muscles - his arms lacked their former vigor. "Thank you for doing this, Jan. Thank you," he expressed, his voice breaking. As Janet gently extracted herself from his embrace to gaze at his face, she noticed his tears. She attempted to brush them away with her thumb, yet her own floodgates of emotion burst open, mirroring the vulnerability of the man who loved her. Her tears flowed just as freely as his, and as she lifted her face to meet his, their teardrops mingled together – two people who had lost a lifetime of love but who were grateful that fate had reunited them for a few precious hours that they would cherish.

Abe swiftly regained his composure. "Silly of me!" He attempted to wipe away Janet's tears. "No tears, Jan. I can't bear to see you sad. Come on, let's eat. Our dinner might turn cold."

"In this heat!" Janet exclaimed, striving to diffuse the weight of the emotionally charged moment with a touch of humor. "Food doesn't typically get cold on San Souci."

"In any case, I'm sure you must be hungry," Abe concluded. "I hope you'll relish what I've prepared." Taking her hand, he guided her to the table and seated her at the head.

"Is this your usual spot?" Janet inquired.

"Yes, normally I sit here, but tonight, you can be my queen, reigning over the dinner table," Abe responded as he removed the lids from the various serving dishes arranged on the table.

"Mmmm. It smells delicious," Janet remarked, leaning closer to one of the bowls beside her and inhaling its aroma. "What's this?"

"You mentioned in Holguin that *Metemgee* is still one of your favorite dishes, so I've made some for you," Abe explained.

"You didn't!" Janet exclaimed in surprise.

"Yes, I actually did," Abe replied, serving a generous portion onto her plate. "Hari lent a hand quite a bit because, you know, my hands sometimes aren't as steady as they used to be, especially when it comes to peeling and slicing the vegetables."

Metemgee had always been a favorite dish among the people of San Souci. Made from root vegetables, locally referred to as ground provisions, these vegetables were gently boiled in a coconut broth infused with the flavors of abundant onions and other fresh garden herbs. As the vegetables simmered, meat or salted fish were added. Janet cherished the memory of her mother preparing this dish, and during her teenage years, her Mom taught her the art of handling the vegetables and crafting the broth until she could do it independently. Upon migrating to Canada, she occasionally attempted to recreate it for her children. However, sourcing the right vegetables proved difficult, and the canned coconut milk couldn't match the richness of the fresh, hand-squeezed version. Unfortunately, her kids never developed a taste for *Metemgee*, so she eventually stopped making it for their meals.

Yet, the aroma of the dish on her plate was irresistible. "Is this salted beef?" she asked Abe, spooning a bite to savor.

"Yes, indeed," Abe confirmed. "Hari picked it up at the market near the ferry terminal in Lewiston." He dished some of the *Metemgee* onto his own plate. "I'm afraid I can't offer you any wine, though. I don't keep alcohol on hand, as it doesn't quite align with my medications." He chuckled.

"Why do you assume I'd want wine?" Janet questioned.

"In Canada, it's quite common for people to enjoy wine with their dinner, and we did have some at the cottage, remember?" Abe confirmed.

"I'm not much of a drinker, as you well know," Janet replied. "My beverage of choice is tea."

"That I have in abundance," Abe assured her. "I'll brew us a pot once we've finished our meal." He lifted his water glass and proposed a toast, saying, "Cheers!"

"Cheers," Janet responded, raising her own glass. "To the fantastic cook."

"And to the queen of my heart, who reigns supreme," Abe added, gazing at her with eyes that conveyed sentiments beyond mere words.

Janet sampled the vegetables. "This is wonderful, Abe. Thank you for preparing my favorite dish."

"Over here, you'll find some cornmeal dumplings," Abe pointed to another serving bowl within his reach. "Hari brought along some fish cakes, and I've also prepared callaloo with crabs. You won't find that combination in Canada!"

Janet clapped her hands together with childlike delight. "My cherished crabs," she declared, reaching across the table to help herself.

Abe observed the radiant contentment on her face and felt a sense of fulfillment he hadn't experienced in a long while. Here they were, him and Janet, back in San Souci – Life felt immensely gratifying. He felt blessed to have his one cherished dream realized.

They shared their meal and engaged in conversation. Abe opened up further, recounting more tales from his Life. He explained how he had earnestly tried to make things work with Lizzie, but fate had taken a different course. Despite this, Abe held a deep affection for his two sons and their families, and he expressed contentment that their marriages were thriving. Although his future held uncertainty, he harbored no bitterness or resentment. Eventually, he reflected, "Life has bestowed upon me numerous blessings, and I'm grateful for all that I've experienced. There was a time when I dwelled on what I lacked, but that only breeds discontent. It's wiser to tally your blessings and take Life one day at a time. I'm truly fortunate, Jan, to have this time with you."

Shifting the topic, Janet inquired, "So, what's on the agenda for tomorrow?"

"Hari will pick you up around 11:00 or so after breakfast, and we'll head to the beach for a picnic," Abe replied. "I've planned for us to spend the day at the marina. Later in the afternoon, Hari will come back to pick us up. We can do some fishing. We'll sit in the boat just offshore."

"Do you have a boat here?" Janet asked.

Abe chuckled. "Oh, no. I'm not that wealthy, Jan. The boat belongs to my friend Simon. Do you recall him? His father is Vic Shetty, the former road engineer. You might have taught Simon when he was in kindergarten."

"I remember Vic Shetty, but I can't quite recall his children," Janet admitted.

"Don't worry," Abe reassured her. "I used to go ocean fishing with Simon from time to time. His boat is safe, and we won't venture too far from the shore."

"Hmmm," Janet responded, indicating her agreement with Abe's plan.

Abe brought her back to the present. "For dessert, there's a banana pudding, and no, I didn't make it. My culinary skills are decent but not that remarkable. I ordered it from Mamma Nelly."

"Is Mamma Nelly still running her small catering business?" Janet asked in astonishment. "She must be nearing ninety!"

"I believe she's eighty-six," Abe corrected. "Yet, she still bakes for the locals around here. She's introduced three of her granddaughters to the business, so now she's more of a supervisor than the one doing the actual baking."

"Abe, this meal is absolutely delightful. I feel so at ease, more than I have in quite a while. Rarely do I find the time to be completely disconnected, but right now, it's as though I've entered a different realm. It's pure euphoria," Janet declared.

"Cherish it, my dear," Abe advised. "You've only got two days. You should allocate more time for yourself, Jan. Your job isn't worth sacrificing your life for."

Janet shared with him the numerous instances she had contemplated early retirement, but her apprehension stemmed from fearing that without her job, she'd be adrift without purpose. She admitted that while the job itself was stressful, she exacerbated the pressure by striving for perfection. Her desire for flawless execution often drove those around her to their wits' end.

As they savored their meal and conversation, time seemed to stretch pleasantly. After finishing dinner, Abe accepted Janet's offer to assist with washing the dishes. This was the reality of San Souci - dishwashers were not a standard household feature. "Would you like to borrow my apron?" Abe inquired.

"Of course, that would be helpful," Janet replied.

Rummaging in a cabinet drawer, Abe retrieved a dark blue apron. Standing behind her, he meticulously tied the strings around her waist, drawing her close once more. He planted a gentle kiss on her head, and Janet sensed him initiating a gentle waltz, swaying with her in his arms. Gradually, he led her away from the sink. Setting aside the soapy sponge, she allowed him to pivot her around. Without letting go, he moved to the living room and switched on the stereo, an action she suspected he had prepared beforehand. The melodious voice of Engelbert Humperdinck filled the room with the lyrics, *"There's a kind of hush all over the world tonight, all over the world, you can hear the sound of lovers in love...."* As if it were the most natural thing in the world to do, Abe guided her in a dance, seamlessly transitioning from one song to the next. His dancing was fluid and graceful, a far cry from Nat's belief that dancing required no particular skill - just going with the rhythm and one's emotions.

Janet sensed the rhythm of Abe's heartbeat against hers, felt the enveloping warmth of his embrace, and experienced a surge of love that she hadn't felt since that pivotal day on the beach when they had parted ways. Abe held her tenderly, as though every aspect of her being was priceless. She pondered how fortunate she was to have these fleeting moments - a few precious drops of time that could never be erased from her memory.

Although hesitant, Janet finally glanced at the time. Abe appeared disappointed, his voice carrying a note of regret as he uttered, "You're spoiling this, Jan. Don't check the time. Let tonight be one where time doesn't hold sway."

"You've often reminded me, Abe, that time moves inexorably forward. Time and tide wait for no one. It's already so dark out there, and it's only eight," Janet replied.

Continuing to sway to the music, Abe responded, "You still have an hour, Cinderella, before the clock chimes. Let's take a walk outside." He reluctantly let her go, then, with a quick tug of her hand, he brought her back in his embrace and kissed her full on the lips, slowly, lingeringly, as if savouring the moment. Initially hesitant, Janet's resolve crumbled under the insistence of his lips, and she returned the kiss with a fervor and passion she had believed herself incapable of. Abe's lips left her mouth to shower affection on her eyes, hair, and the exposed curve of her neck. Janet felt a jolt of electric emotion, his feelings echoing through every touch. Whispering into her ear, Abe's voice was a hushed promise, "Do you truly understand the depth of my love for you, Jan? Not just for today or tomorrow, but for eternity - forever and always?"

"I know," she whispered in response. Feeling the need to confront her emotions, she continued, "And I have always loved you, Abe. It was hidden deep within my heart, but it has always been there. It's always been you, Abe." With those words, she unburdened herself, free from guilt or shame. Abe held her in silence for a prolonged moment. Time seemed to freeze for them, the cliché of time standing still becoming a reality.

Janet gently pulled away. "Let's take that walk," she suggested. "I believe some fresh air would do us good."

Abe loosened his grip, yet his gaze continued to hold her. They say that the eyes are windows to the soul, and as Janet peered into that window, she glimpsed everything that would hold significance for the rest of her days. The uncertainties of her Life's journey no longer troubled her; she possessed an unwavering certainty that Abe's love would illuminate her path through any challenges.

Hand in hand, they strolled through the quaint garden that stretched from the front of the yard to the back fence. In the center lay a small pond, where several pink water lilies, adorned with their expansive circular leaves, dominated the pond's surface. Amidst the water, Janet could just about discern some drifting pond weeds. With the moon now casting its glow, the darkness of the night seemed to enhance its brilliance. Memories stirred within Janet - the times she resided in San Souci, observing the moon suspended over the ocean, transforming everything into a silvery wonder. She would marvel at the silver-crested ocean waves and the gleaming leaves of trees. Even the rooftops would shimmer beneath the silver moonlight. "What a magnificent night it is!" Abe exclaimed.

"It certainly is," Janet responded. "Abe, I understand why you return to San Souci so frequently. Its beauty is so natural and untarnished. Modernization hasn't made extensive inroads here. While there are better homes and facilities than what we had when we lived here, the essence of the environment has largely remained unchanged. San Souci continues to yield a significant rice harvest, but now tractors, combines, and advanced factories have emerged to process the grains. People still toil diligently, and agriculture remains the cornerstone industry. Despite these signs of progress, substantial parts of San Souci have preserved their authenticity, and that brings me immense joy."

"Yes, and when we head to the beach tomorrow, you'll see the old brick road where we used to stroll as children. Can you recall the particular mangrove tree right at the water's edge?" Abe paused, his gaze fixed on her.

"Eh hmmm," she muttered. She understood he meant the tree where they had shared their first "date." "I remember that tree," she eventually confirmed.

"It's still standing there. Perhaps we could attempt to sit on those stilt roots and see if they're as sturdy as they used to be."

They reached the end of the garden, immersed in the fragrance of the blossoms. Janet drew in the lingering scent of *Frangipani*. While she adored its sweet aroma, it carried a tinge of sadness due to its association with wreaths at both of her parents' funerals. On the island, some referred to them as "dead people's flowers" because they were commonly used in funeral arrangements.

Abe detected her melancholy. "Are you alright?" he inquired.

"It's just that the smell of *Frangipani* makes me feel sad."

"I don't really care for those flowers. Willy believes a garden should be a happy place but also reflective," Abe remarked.

"I prefer the happiness aspect," she continued, "not so much the reflective part. I wish we…" Her words were cut short by a sudden flap of wings and a shadow that swooped just above her head. Reacting swiftly, she turned to her right to avoid whatever it was and accidentally collided with Abe. Then, she recognized the familiar hoot and realized it was an owl. The bird had perched itself on the higher branches of the mango tree that stood guard behind the garden fence. Amid the shadowy leaves of the tree, Janet could have sworn she glimpsed the glistening of its eyes. "It's an owl," she informed Abe. "It certainly gave me a scare." She felt Abe's arms tighten around her and understood that she must have clung to him in her moment of fright. His hand reached her face, tilting it to meet his gaze. Moonlight danced in his eyes, the love within them outshining even the stars that winked in the velvety night sky.

Gradually, he drew his head nearer to hers, his lips softly grazing her eyelids. A shiver rippled through her entire being, and then his lips met hers, kissing her like she had never been kissed before – certainly not by Nat. Janet responded with all the love that brimmed in her heart for the man who had shown her the meaning of genuine love. Her arms wound around his neck, pulling him closer as her fingers entwined in his greying hair.

"Love of my life," Abe whispered. "I'll love you forever." He reluctantly pulled away from her. "Look up at the skies. Before long, I'll become one of those stars gazing down upon you. You'll have to search for me, Jan. I'll be a constant presence, shining for you always and forever."

Janet could hear his breath catching between sobs as he struggled to regain composure. Her fingers traced the contours of his face. "Yes, Abe, I'll keep searching for you. You've captured my heart for all time."

Abe drew her in for a tight embrace and softly hummed, "Let me wrap you in my warm and tender love." He desired to meld their bodies together, but his weakened muscles lacked the strength to achieve such closeness.

Janet shivered slightly. "I think it's time we head indoors," she told Abe, her gaze shifting to her watch. "It's nearly nine, and Hari will be here soon to pick me up. I should help you tidy up the kitchen before I go."

Abe slowly released his grip. "Don't worry about that. I'll handle the cleanup. Tomorrow, my little helper Monica will be here. She'll take care of anything I can't manage. She's always glad to escape her siblings' daily squabbles and find solace at her Uncle Abe's house. She's eager to earn some money; she told me she's saving up to buy that bicycle from Mac's Hardware Store."

"Abe, you're wonderfully kind. It's heartwarming that Monica can contribute to her family's finances. Was this Tilak's idea or yours?" Janet inquired.

"We both came up with it," Abe explained. "I needed the assistance, and Tilak was willing to let his daughter lend me a hand with my tasks and earn a bit of money. However, Monica takes more pride in her work than the earnings she receives."

As they entered the house, Janet ignored Abe's protests and helped clear the dirty dishes. "I can't believe we made such a mess," she remarked to Abe, wiping away a few spots of coconut milk from the tablecloth. "The food was simply delightful. Is that the sound of Hari's car I hear?"

Abe nodded. "Indeed, Hari has arrived. You should gather your things. I wish I could accompany you to Maria, but that wouldn't be wise, of course."

"It's just a short distance away, so it hardly matters. I'll see you tomorrow... at 10:00, was it?" Janet inquired.

"I initially said 11:00. Would 10:00 be more suitable? I thought 11:00 would allow you a leisurely start to the morning, giving you some extra time to unwind. Is that acceptable for you?" Abe clarified.

"Yes, 11:00 works perfectly for me. No need to hurry - we have the entire day. So, I'll see you tomorrow at 11:00. Get some rest," Janet affirmed as she retrieved her bag.

"I certainly will. So, Hari will come to pick you up at 11:00," Abe confirmed.

Right on cue, Hari bounded up the stairs and through the front door. "Hi again, Miss Janet. Hope I'm not running late."

"You're right on time," Abe said, gesturing toward the wall clock. "Janet is all set and ready."

Janet picked up her bag, saying she didn't want Hari to be always carrying it, but Hari grabbed it from her hands, remarking, "This is quite light." He lugged it down the stairs and asked, "Ready?"

"Yes, let's go," Janet responded. "Goodnight, Abe. Thanks again for dinner. I'll see you tomorrow."

"Same here," Hari added. "Should I still bring the picnic supplies?" he inquired of Abe.

"Absolutely, unless you've had a change of heart," Abe replied.

"No worries," Hari assured. "I'll bring everything we discussed. Goodnight."

"Goodnight. Bye to both of you," Abe said to them from the doorway, blowing a kiss to Janet as Hari led her to the waiting car.

CHAPTER 22

In just ten minutes, Hari and Janet arrived at Maria's house. As they pulled up, Maria hurriedly emerged to welcome them. "Hi, Hari! It feels like it's been ages!" she exclaimed as Hari stepped out of the car. Approaching the passenger side, she warmly embraced Janet, who had also just disembarked, in a tight hug.

"Well, my friend, you're finally here! How have you been? You look great since the last time I saw you," Maria remarked.

"It hasn't really been that long," Janet replied with a chuckle, "only three years."

"Three years can feel quite substantial," Maria retorted with a smile, accepting Janet's overnight bag from Hari. "Ciao, Hari. Are you going to pick her up tomorrow?"

"Absolutely, sharp at 11:00. We've got plans," Hari confirmed, and they all shared a burst of laughter as if sharing an inside joke.

"Thanks again, Hari. Please give my regards to your family," Janet conveyed warmly.

"Will do," Hari responded before swiftly returning to the car and driving away. Meanwhile, Maria and Janet made their way indoors.

"Would you like some tea?" Maria offered.

"Thank you, tea would be wonderful," Janet accepted gratefully. Even though she had already had dinner with Abe and was quite full, she didn't want to decline Maria's offer. A cup of tea usually meant a relaxed setting for a good chat between friends. Janet kicked off her shoes and settled onto the sofa. Despite knowing Maria's typical response, she still inquired, "Do you need any help?" Anticipating the response, Janet added, "I know you usually say no."

After preparing the tea and placing thin slices of orange bread on the table, Maria and Janet delved into their conversation, exchanging news about San Souci and Windermere. Janet's curiosity led her to inquire about Maria's niece first. "So, how did your visit with your niece go?"

"We had a wonderful visit. It's been almost a year since I last saw her. She brought her son along, who's an absolute cutie. He just turned three," Maria shared with a smile.

"Is she still living on the East Coast?" Janet inquired.

"Yes, she's still there. She actually came to attend her friend's bridal shower, so she's staying over at her friend's place for the night and will head back home tomorrow," Maria explained.

Changing the topic, Maria mentioned, "By the way, did you hear that Joe Mentis passed away?"

"No, but I can't say I'm surprised. He must have been what... ninety-five?" Janet guessed.

"Ninety-seven and three months, to be precise. He had a severe stroke and passed away within four months. It's really sad. We're going to miss him. I don't know how the caretakers of the cemetery will manage without him. He's been diligently cleaning and maintaining the place for the past thirty-one years."

"I understand," Janet replied. "I assume he had a spot reserved for himself there."

"Yes, indeed. He chose it himself – the best spot under the tamarind tree."

"Kids are actually afraid to pluck tamarinds from that tree. They believe that Joe might wake up and scold them for disturbing the peace," they both chuckled. "So, tell me, what's new on your side? How is Jack doing? I was deeply saddened when I heard about the accident."

Janet's tone turned somber. "He's making progress. It's tough to see him with all those bandages and tubes attached to various parts of his body. But he's starting to recover, and the doctor said he'll be alright."

"Have you had a chance to talk with him?"

Janet nodded as she responded, "He's not able to say much. That's why I decided to visit San Souci now. By the time I return to the hospital, hopefully, he'll be more capable of having a proper conversation," she explained.

"How is Jenna coping with everything?" Maria inquired.

"Surprisingly well. I think she's relieved that I'm here, but she also appreciates having some space for herself. This has truly been an overwhelming ordeal for her," Janet shared.

As they sipped their tea and savored their slices of lemon loaf, they continued exchanging stories about their lives until the clock on the wall struck midnight. "We could go on chatting for another three hours," Maria said with a chuckle, "but you must be exhausted."

"Yes, I realized I forgot to call Jenna. I'll prepare for bed and make sure to call her first thing in the morning. I did send her a text to reassure her that I'm alright," Janet mentioned.

Maria then showed Janet to her room, the same one she had stayed in during her previous visits to San Souci. They bid each other good night, and after a quick shower, Janet changed into her pajamas and slipped under the covers. She spent a long moment in prayer, thinking about Jack, his family, her own family, Nat, and Abe - the thought of him lingered in her mind. She imagined Abe sleeping forever, perhaps in a cemetery in Toronto, and a stream of warm tears trickled down her cheeks. "Crying won't prevent it from happening," she gently scolded herself.

After tossing and turning for another hour, Janet finally drifted into sleep. In her dream, she found herself in a breathtaking garden surrounded by the most exquisite flowers and trees she had ever seen before. The weather was warm and sunny, and the sky radiated an unbelievably bright hue. Beneath a grand, shaded tree, she spotted a marble bench. In her dream, she recalled Abe's words, instructing her to wait there for him. So, she settled onto the bench, captivated by the beauty around her and enveloped in a serene peace. She could feel the warmth of the sun on her cheeks and thought she heard the melodic twittering call of a *Bluesaki*, perhaps conversing with its partner concealed among the foliage.

Gradually, Janet's eyes came into focus. The *Bluesaki* was indeed perched on a branch of the star-fruit tree just beside her bedroom window, and the sun's rays were streaming through the slightly ajar curtains, which she had forgotten to close properly. Glancing at the clock, she saw that it was a little past eight. The sun had been up since six, so her room was pleasantly warm. The aroma of coffee wafted in the air, signaling that Maria must have been busy in the kitchen.

Taking her time, Janet got dressed, and around thirty minutes later, she followed her nose to the kitchen. Inside, Maria was arranging mugs and plates. "Good morning. How did you sleep?" Maria greeted her.

"I had a really restful sleep," Janet replied. "In fact, it was so good that I had a beautiful dream." She proceeded to share the details of her dream with Maria.

"Lucky you!" Claudette chimed in. "My dream wasn't as pleasant. I dreamt I was on my way to Georgetown when the taxi collided with a cyclist and veered into the roadside canal. I felt like I was dying, and then suddenly, my eyes opened."

"That might be because we were discussing Jack's accident before going to bed. It likely lingered in your subconscious," Janet explained.

"It could be. I'm preparing fried salt fish with tomatoes for breakfast," Maria replied.

Janet exclaimed, "Why go through all that trouble! Toast and coffee would have been perfectly fine."

"You can't come to San Souci and settle for plain toast. I know you enjoy the salted fish and sweet potatoes - not the yams you find in Canada, but the genuine Guyanese sweet potatoes. That's what we're having," Maria insisted.

They enjoyed their breakfast on the small deck at the rear of the house, which provided a view of the kitchen garden. "You're still quite skilled at cultivating your vegetables," Janet remarked. "I see the long beans and eggplants. It's such a pleasure to have vegetables fresh from your own garden - certified one hundred percent organic. In Canada, those who can afford it opt for organic foods grown without pesticides or other chemicals. They tend to be quite expensive, and there's always a doubt if they're truly organic."

"Well, we've been consuming organic all our lives!" Maria proclaimed with a chuckle. "I believe everyone in San Souci has their own vegetable and flower garden."

"That's true," Janet agreed. "And I genuinely miss that."

Their conversation shifted back to various aspects of their lives. When 10:30 arrived, Janet informed Maria that she needed to get ready since Hari would be picking her up at 11:00. Maria sounded curious as she asked, "Where are you headed?"

"I'm spending the day with Pat and her family. Did I not mention that I reconnected with her last Christmas? We used to be very close, but then we lost touch for many years. Luckily, another friend helped us reconnect. I promised her that whenever I visit San Souci, I'd make time to see her. I'm actually really excited about spending time with her family. It's been quite a while. She's even planning to take me fishing," Janet explained with enthusiasm.

"That's wonderful. You were friends with Pat, but I just knew her from attending the Women's Institute together. Your visit to the island is short, so you have to schedule your time wisely and see as many people as you are able. Anyway, I'll see you later in the evening when you return." She began to clear away some of the dishes and then continued, "I know you need to get your mind off Jack and see as much of San Souci before you return home, but just be careful, especially with the fishing expedition. Don't take any risks."

"I promise I won't. Thank you so much for the wonderful breakfast," Janet expressed her gratitude. She attempted to help clear the dishes, but Maria playfully waved her away.

"You know I always eagerly await your visits. You've been a true and loyal friend, Janet." Maria embraced her warmly. "Now, off you go. You don't want to keep Hari waiting."

Janet retrieved her sun hat and sandals and applied her makeup, taking extra care to strive for a subtle look. She was careful not to overdo the lipstick, wanting to maintain a casual appearance that wouldn't raise suspicions. Her capris, although relatively new, felt suitable for the river outing. She found herself wondering why her heart seemed so light and why she felt like a sixteen-year-old going on a date with Abe all over again.

Exactly at 11:00, Hari arrived. "I must say, I like your hat. You look like a true San Soucian, Miss Janet," he complimented as she settled into the car.

With the temperature already at around 33 degrees Celsius, even the lightweight pink cotton blouse couldn't prevent Janet from perspiring. "I'd be melting in this heat without the hat," she remarked to Hari. "Every time I return to Guyana, the heat feels more and more intense."

"You're not alone in that sentiment. As much as Uncle Abe enjoys coming back to San Souci, some days, the heat drives him crazy. He's been promising to install an air conditioner in the house every year. Finally, he's agreed to let me arrange for someone to do it next year."

"Really?" Janet's tone held a mix of disbelief and surprise. She noticed Hari's raised eyebrows, prompting her to soften her response. "I'm glad he's open to the idea. It'll be beneficial for him."

Upon arriving at Abe's house, they found him waiting by the gate with a picnic basket in hand. As Hari stepped out of the car, Abe called out, "No need to come in, Hari. I'm all set to go." He approached the car, and Hari opened the rear passenger door for him.

Janet considered suggesting that Abe sit in the front, but before she could voice it, she was pre-empted by Abe himself. "Hello, Janet. I didn't see you back there," he playfully remarked. "I actually prefer sitting in the back for the extra space, but if you don't mind, I'll sit up front with Hari."

Janet understood that Abe was likely aware that always sitting next to her might raise questions for Hari. He settled in beside Hari and then turned to inquire, "How are you doing? Did you sleep well?"

Politely, Janet responded, "I'm doing well, thank you, Abe. I had a good rest. Maria made me a hearty breakfast, so I'm quite full. I hope I don't doze off in the middle of our trip." She chuckled nervously. "And how about you? Are you sure you're up for this? What do you think, Hari? Is Uncle Abe pushing himself too hard?"

Before Hari could respond, Abe interjected, "I'm alright. I've never been more certain about anything in my life."

The three of them conversed for the next half hour as Hari drove down the winding path leading to the beach. "Here we are," Hari announced. "You'll have to walk the last few meters. The path becomes too narrow, and there are too many rocks to navigate. I'll turn the car around from here."

"It's amazing how things haven't changed!" Janet exclaimed as she stepped out of the car. She moved towards the front to assist Abe, but he gently pushed her away, insisting that she should carry the picnic supplies that Hari had prepared. Hari handed her a charming, oval-shaped basket covered with a plaid tea towel. "Can I take a peek under the towel?" she asked Hari.

"Of course. I hope you'll enjoy what's in there. My wife, Della, baked a few items," Hari replied.

"Hmmm... it smells absolutely delicious. Is this lemonade?" Janet asked as she pulled out the tall bottle.

"Yes, freshly made. There's also some fruit, cheese, and bread. I thought of adding a bottle of wine, but I didn't want to tempt Uncle Abe since he can't have alcohol," Hari explained.

"I don't need the alcohol," Abe countered as he slowly emerged from the car. "Life itself is intoxicating. What time will you come back to pick us up?"

"You tell me. I'm at your service," Hari responded.

"It's nearly noon now. How about between 4:00 and 4:30? Just give us a honk when you arrive, and we'll hear you," Abe suggested.

Hari bid them farewell, turned the car around, and departed. Abe and Janet strolled down to the beach, where a small marina hosted a few anchored boats. The water was calm, yet the boats bobbed gently due to the Atlantic trade winds blowing across the water. This portion of the Essequibo River lay right at the mouth of the Atlantic Ocean.

"Which boat belongs to your friend?" Janet inquired.

Abe pointed towards a small white boat with sky-blue accents. "That's the *Lady Rose*," he said. An outboard motor was attached at the rear, although Janet sensed that it had its engine power. Having spent time on the island of San Souci and being familiar with boats, she could even discern the location of the engine room beneath the tiny cabin intended for the captain. The starboard side seemed more spacious, housing two long benches and a small central table. Janet noticed a painting of a beautiful pink rose at the bow of the boat, confirming her assumption about its name, the *Lady Rose*.

Janet glanced at Abe with a questioning look. "How do you expect us to get from the shore to the boat?"

"We'll wade in. The water isn't too deep, and it's warm. I doubt it'll go past your knees," Abe reassured her.

She eyed his vibrant, multi-colored shorts. "I wish you had mentioned this earlier..."

He playfully interrupted, "So that you could have worn short shorts instead of capris?" He winked at her.

"Well, now I'll have to take off my sandals and roll up my capris."

A mischievous grin crossed Abe's face as he offered another suggestion. "There's another option. I can take the baskets first and then come back to carry you."

Janet quickly responded, "Absolutely not. I've lived on this island, and I'm not afraid of the water. I was kidding. I'll wade in after you."

"Just hold the basket a bit higher so it doesn't get splashed. Can you manage that? I can take both baskets," Abe suggested.

"Don't try to be a superhero. I'm perfectly fine. You go ahead," Janet replied.

With his basket on his shoulder, Abe used one hand to hold it steady while he extended his other hand to Janet. They stepped into the water together. The warmth of the thirty-six-degree temperature had heated the edge of the river. With the wind brushing against their faces, they slowly waded toward the *Lady Rose*. Janet noticed the names of the other four boats anchored in the marina – the *Spitfire*, the smallest among them, followed by the *Fair Lady*, *Sea Goddess*, and *Island Woman*.

"Why do most boats have feminine names?" Abe inquired. "It seems that no matter where I go, boats tend to bear names that depict strong and beautiful women."

"That's because a ship is akin to a woman – poised and ready to reach her destination, always on course," Janet explained with a smile.

Abe playfully tugged at her. "If the *Lady Rose* were my boat, you know what I would name her?"

"What?" Janet asked.

"First Love."

"I'm not sure how that would fit in with the other 'Ladies' she'd be surrounded by."

"Then maybe I'd add 'Lady Jan,' first love," Abe mused.

He released her hand and pulled her closer, causing her feet to splash water on both of them in the process. "Hey, be careful!" Janet warned. "My basket might end up in the water, and then we'd be left with nothing to eat."

"Ah, saved by the basket," Abe remarked. "Alright, let's continue. Just a few more steps."

Abe reached the side of the boat and tossed his basket over the rail. "Give me yours, and I'll get on board. Then I'll help you over and in."

"Are you sure you can manage that? Isn't there a ladder or something that can be lowered for me?" Janet inquired. "Maybe I could pull myself up."

With his long legs, Abe effortlessly swung himself over the boat's rail. He then took hold of Janet's outstretched arms and helped her onto the small aft deck. Both of them lay side by side, catching their breath after the effort. "Take your time to recover," Janet advised. "Too much exertion isn't good for you."

As they lay there, Abe turned to look at her. They were stretched out on the deck beneath the azure sky, with the sun casting glimmers of gold into Janet's eyes and illuminating her hair. She looked like an angel, thought Abe. Overwhelmed by his emotions, he drew her closer into the crook of his arm. He gently caressed her cheeks and brushed the wind-disheveled strands of hair away from her face. Janet could sense his trembling emotions.

"Jan," he whispered, "did you ever think this would be possible?"

Overwhelmed by emotion, she couldn't find her voice and shook her head. "My Jan," he continued, "I am nineteen, and you're fifteen, and here we are, back to where it all began on our own island. This is where I first loved you, and it's where I'll always love you. When I pass away, I'll come back to San Souci. My spirit will seek you out. Promise me you'll return to this spot when you visit with Jack and Jenna so that you can feel my presence."

Janet turned onto her stomach, meeting his gaze. "I will come back, Abe. I promise."

He pulled her head to rest against his chest, and they lay there in peace and contentment, listening to the gulls squawking overhead and the gentle lapping of water on the boat's sides. The boat's rhythmic movement was so soothing.

"If I were ever in paradise, this would be it," thought Janet.

They lay in silence for nearly half an hour, absorbing the fresh air and the symphony of their heartbeats. The sun warmed their skin and their thoughts. "Jan," Abe's voice broke the silence, "are we going to spend the rest of the day like this? I would be content to remain still. It's so tranquil."

"I thought we were going to do some fishing," Janet whispered back, her reluctance to move evident in her voice.

Abe pulled her a bit closer, but she suddenly sat upright, smoothing down her blouse, which had ridden up to her belly button. "Come on, let's get up and find those fishing rods before we doze off."

"I wouldn't mind dozing off," Abe groaned.

"Well, you can do that later. Just tell me where the rods are, and I'll fetch them."

Abe gradually sat up and rubbed his eyes. "Even if I tell you, you won't be able to find them. I'll have to get them for you."

"Challenge accepted," argued Janet.

"They're downstairs, well, just two steps really, in the locker to the right. The bait should be in a can on the floor next to the locker – or at least that's where it usually is. But you won't be able to carry everything. I'll come help you."

Janet was already heading toward the door, above which an arrow pointed downward. Abe slowly got up and followed her. Together, they found the fishing rods and brought them back to the small deck. "Before we start, why don't we take a moment to relax and enjoy some coffee? I also brought a small banana loaf for us to share," suggested Abe.

"Sure, why not? I'm not really hungry. I had a substantial breakfast with Maria, but I can sit and savor some coffee while gazing at the ocean. Watching the waves and listening to their rhythm never gets old."

Abe delved into the picnic basket, pulling out a thermos and two tiny mugs. "Here, let me help you," Janet offered.

She placed the thermos and mugs on the table as Abe unwrapped the loaf and pulled out some plastic forks and napkins. She poured the coffee while Abe deftly sliced the loaf.

"Here's your coffee." Janet handed Abe one of the mugs, and he passed her a slice of the loaf. She brought her own coffee cup to her nose, sniffing the fresh brew. "Mmmm … coffee always smells so good."

Abe looked at her questioningly. "Are you addicted?" he asked. "I notice you always sniff your coffee before drinking."

"Maybe I am addicted," she replied. "I like the smell of coffee as much as I like the taste. Nat would say that if he wants to get me out of bed really quickly in the mornings, all he has to do is put on a pot of coffee. That aroma wafting up the stairs to my bedroom sure gets me up." She chuckled.

"I try to have only one cup," said Abe. "The doctor says it's not helpful to my current health. I have settled for herbal teas, but what the heck, I cut myself some slack sometimes!"

As Janet munched on her bread, she said to Abe," This tastes really good. Who did the baking?"

"Monica's Mom, Rohina. She made this especially for me and sent it over early this morning. She knows I love her baking."

"You're so spoiled on San Souci!" declared Janet. "But I'm so glad you have such good friends who take care of you."

"Comes with the territory," said Abe. "They all know that I'm sick."

"Did you tell them about your illness?" Janet was a bit surprised.

"No details, but gosh, Jan, people aren't blind! There was an Abe who came back here every year, sailing, rowing, fishing, and dancing at the disco. Now, there's an Abe who barely makes it through from one day to the next. I have a lot of people feeling sorry for me." He sounded bitter, which was quite unlike him.

"I'm sure that's not the only reason why they do it. San Souci has always had kind and caring people, so different from the people in the city who are busier and self-centered."

"Agree," said Abe. "Look at that." He pointed to a speedboat making its way towards San Souci. "That looks like Sam's boat. He ferries people between Lewiston and San Souci … those people who do not want to wait for the ferry. There is Sam and his friends Dey and Lionel, who pilot the boat. I sometimes take Sam's speedboat when I'm in a rush to get to Lewiston."

"Isn't it dangerous to cross at the mouth of the Atlantic in that small boat? Some people were asking me to take the speedboat when I was coming to San Souci yesterday."

"When the water is rough, it's a bit of a jerky and bumpy ride, but when the water is calm, the ride is smooth."

"What if you fall over? What will they do?" Janet sounded alarmed.

"You can't fall over. There are comfortable seats, and a boat can take about ten passengers. The boats are relatively safe, and they also have life jackets. You must wear a life jacket."

By now, Janet could see the boat plowing through the ocean, its raised bow cutting through the frothy waters.

"Wow! Look at that speed!" she stated.

"That's why it's called a speedboat," laughed Abe. "It takes only twenty minutes to get from here to Lewiston, whereas the ferry takes almost an hour and a half."

Janet could not actually see the faces of the passengers, but their multi-colored clothing was visible in the distance. The boat continued on its course to a landing about a mile away from where the Lady Rose was moored.

"They must have scared away all the fish," declared Janet.

"Nooo… they passed far enough away from the marina."

They sipped their coffee in silence, sometimes commenting on the birds that went by or recalling some funny past incident that would have them breaking out in laughter.

"Do you remember when Jake that fisherman, saw us under the mangrove tree?" asked Abe. "And he went to complain to your dad?"

"Why would I not remember?" asked Janet. "I got the worst scolding from my parents. My Mom threatened to make me quit school. She almost slapped my head off."

"I'm sorry," said Abe, entwining his fingers with hers. "I've caused you so much grief, Jan."

"No need to be sorry. It was what it was then. There was pain, but there was also the happiness I felt when I was with you."

"Do you still feel that now?" he asked, squeezing her fingers tightly.

She turned to look him in the eyes. "What I feel right now is peace and contentment. I've never felt more at peace in my whole life than I do right now. And even though I'm overtaken by guilt every now and again, I have no regrets. This has been the best time in my life for a long, long time."

Abe gave her fingers a gentler squeeze this time. "Thanks for doing this for me, Jan. Thanks for giving me this time." He brought her fingers to his lips.

Janet did not want to continue to pursue this line of conversation, so she changed the subject. "Well, are we going to catch those little suckers now or what?" she asked. "We'd better have something to show Hari."

Abe reluctantly let go of her hand. "Yes, let's bait those lines. I will have you take the boat a little out of the marina. We won't catch anything in here."

Janet jumped to her feet. "What can I help you with?"

"I'll show you how to bait the hooks at the end of the line, so while you're doing that, I'll move the boat."

"Aye, aye, aye, captain, whatever you say." Janet gave him a mock salute.

Abe demonstrated the best way to get the dried fish gut on the hook, and while Janet concentrated on this, he started the engine of the Lady Rose. "You might want to sit," he yelled at Janet from the helm. I have to do a slight turn at which I'm not so good. You may lose your balance. I don't want you falling into the water."

Janet sat flat on the stern deck, planting her bottom firmly on the floor. She watched Abe gently swing the steering wheel, guiding the boat into the open water. It took him less than five minutes to get to the spot he wanted. As he cut off the motor, he weighed anchor. "You can give me a hand with this," he called out to Janet. Together, they let down the weighty anchor using the small winch.

"I thought you had to let the anchor down physically!" exclaimed Janet.

"You mean, lift it and throw it over the rail! No, the *Lady* is more of a newbie." With the anchor weighed, they went to set up their fishing lines. "I'll set mine on this side," said Abe. "You can use the other."

Janet walked her line over to the opposite side and waited for Abe to fix his and then deal with hers. As she watched Abe attaching the line to the rail of the boat, she thought of how much older he was than when she had known him at nineteen. But his features were so much the same – the same long legs, a head full of hair that was now a mixture of silver and black, the same broad shoulders and lean hips. He was still so maturely handsome. He suddenly looked up at her. "Are you admiring me from afar?" he asked, the twinkle in his eyes.

"No," she lied, saying, "I'm just observing how well you're doing so I can learn."

"If you want to learn, you have to come closer," he teased.

She moved nearer, and he took her hands, demonstrating how to attach the line to the rail. "You have to tie the knot tightly; otherwise, if you catch something big, it'll pull the line away."

"Understood," Janet replied, attempting not to be overly aware of his proximity, his masculine scent, or the beads of sweat above his upper lip.

He went to the other side and repeated the process with her lines. They each did two. "Now that the lines are secure," Janet suggested, "should we set out some food, grab the dominoes, and wait for the fish to bite?"

"Sounds like a plan," Abe agreed. Janet found the sandwiches, plates, and napkins. As she was about to arrange them on the table, Abe proposed, "I think you should leave everything in the basket. We can take things out as we need them. I'm not very hungry, but I can nibble on something. Considering the wind, our food might end up flying around the deck. Place the basket next to you, and I'll reach over to help myself. That way, we'll have a clear table for our dominoes."

Janet followed Abe's advice, and soon, they began their domino game, snacking on biscuits and cheese, still sipping their coffee while keeping an eye on the lines. Abe proved to be a competitive player, winning more frequently than Janet. After almost an hour, they both grew disappointed due to the absence of bites on the lines. "I think we're being too noisy and scaring the fish away," Janet concluded, referring to instances when their excitement caused them to slam the dominoes on the table or when

Janet mistook her impending victory, bursting into laughter when he actually held the winning domino.

"I'm tired of the dominoes now," Janet confessed. "Can we try something else?"

Her question's folly became apparent as Abe eagerly exclaimed, "Of course. I'm always up for something new." He wrapped his arms around her waist.

Playfully, Janet pushed him away. "I meant something more constructive!"

"We can do whatever you'd like, Jan," he replied, gazing at her intently.

Avoiding his gaze, she looked across the water towards the shore and noticed the rocky promontory jutting out. Whether it was to divert Abe's attention or not, she said, "Look over there, Abe. Dead Man's Rock doesn't seem so dead after all." She pointed towards the cliff-like structure—an anomaly that, as a child, she had heard numerous strange stories about regarding how it ended up on the shores of San Souci. "Do you remember the greasy pole that used to be there?" she continued. "I recall all those daring men attempting to climb it for the prized bottle of rum at the top. I always thought it was a rather crazy sport. Whenever they slid on the grease and plunged into the water, I worried that someone might drown. I can't see if the pole is still standing from here."

Abe shaded his eyes and peered at the distant rocky formation. "No, the pole's been gone for a while now, and the sport has died out. The younger guys are too caught up with their cell phones, iPads, or watching TV. The greasy pole has become an outdated pastime. I suppose some people, like you, think it's either too foolish or too risky."

Janet reminisced about how every May, on the last day of the month, they would have a greasy pole event. A tall pole, about twenty-four feet high, anchored into the rocky surface, extended into the ocean, its surface coated with engine grease to make it extremely slippery. At the top, a bottle of the finest and most expensive Guyana rum would be placed by a crane. Men would sign up to climb in hopes of claiming the prize. It was a significant event for San Souci residents, drawing crowds to either cheer on their favored competitors or jest at the unsuccessful ones. Vendors sold trinkets and food, and the children played their own games. It was a time of fun for everyone. Janet remembered attending with her friends as a child. Despite the excitement of playing games and releasing balloons across the water, she had always been anxious. As the men slipped and fell into the water, some barely making any progress, she feared that someone might suffer serious injuries from a fall.

"I remember Ben always getting so close to the top and then falling from that height, year after year," she told Abe.

"Ben was a fighter. He never gave up. I suppose he enjoyed the challenge."

"Most years, the winner was Carlton Wade. I don't know how he managed it, but he certainly reached the top often enough."

"Practice," Abe explained.

"What do you mean... practice? Where did he practice?" Janet asked incredulously.

"He had a pole set up in the large pond behind his yard. He and some of the other guys would grease the pole and keep trying to figure out the best way to stay on it."

"How do you know this?"

"My friends and I would sometimes visit his neighbor when they were practicing. Jeet, the neighbor's son, and I were friends. If Jeet heard about a practice session, he would let us know. Of course, Carlton and his friends did this pretty secretly on moonlit nights. Carlton didn't want people to know about his practice, and if you recall, Jeet was his closest neighbor, yet his house was quite a distance from Carlton's. We would go to Jeet's house and secretly watch the practice sessions. We'd hide inside and use Jeet's binoculars to spy on them."

"Goodness me!" Janet exclaimed. "I can't believe you boys did that! More so, I can't believe how important the greasy pole event was to Carlton. Imagine if he found out people were spying on him! What excited us as kids back then is so different from today!"

"Speaking of excitement," Abe interjected, "your line is shaking like a leaf." Janet wondered if Abe was trying to change the topic as he seemed uncomfortable about what he had revealed. Swiftly, she moved over to check her fishing line. It was indeed trembling, so she grasped the reel and began reeling it in. Abe came over to assist, but she insisted, "I've got it. Don't worry."

As the line emerged, she spotted the fish hanging on the hook. "Wow! Looks like you've caught a little sea mullet!" exclaimed Abe. As she reeled in the line toward the boat, Janet observed the silvery fish gasping for air. "Let me get him off the hook," said Abe, taking hold of the line. He gently removed the struggling fish from the hook and placed it on the deck. The fish's scales sparkled in the sunlight, confirming that it was indeed a silver mullet.

"He's a nice one! Appears to be about two pounds," Abe praised. "Great job!"

"What should I do with him?" Janet inquired.

"I'll fetch the small icebox from below. We can give him to Hari. I think there's still some ice left in it."

"Wait," Janet interjected, "let me grab the icebox. You keep an eye on him."

Janet wanted to spare Abe unnecessary effort, but he was resisting like a typical alpha male. "You won't be able to find it, and it's too heavy for you to carry. I'll handle it."

However, Janet had already descended the two steps. The icebox was easily visible on a small overhead shelf. She retrieved it and returned upstairs. Abe was sitting beside the fish and seemed slightly out of breath. That was Abe – always uncomplaining, prioritizing others over himself. Suddenly, Nat came to her mind –

so self-centered and selfish. He consistently placed himself first, sometimes even before the children. Memories of Nat not waking up in the mornings to take Caitlin to school on cold, rainy days when Janet was occupied and he had the time filled her with anger, as these recollections often did. Nat would assert that Caitlin didn't need to be coddled and should take the bus like the other kids. "She needs to learn to handle challenges, not be pampered," he'd say. Janet would argue with him, but he remained steadfast. Caitlin didn't want them to fight on her behalf; it bothered her, especially before an exam. Janet learned to rein in her emotions. "Here's the icebox," she said to Abe. "Are you alright?"

"Of course," he pretended, quickly picking up the fish and placing it inside the small, chilled plastic container. "Most of the ice is gone," he noted, "but there's enough to keep him fresh until we return. So, how does the champion fisherwoman feel?" he teased.

"No different from how she felt five minutes ago!"

"I wonder when there will be some action on my line," Abe declared.

"No need to rush," Janet assured. "Your turn will come."

"I might end up falling asleep before that happens."

"Are we feeling a bit jealous?" Janet teased. "Well then, let's go back to another round of dominoes."

They settled in at the table again. "It would be nice to have a couple of those cheese sandwiches," Janet suggested. "Afterward, we can play dominoes or exchange more stories."

They opted for the latter. Abe once again brought up his marriage to Lizzie, explaining that things were fine at the start but turned sour later on. He proudly shared stories about his two sons and how they brought him happiness and comfort during the challenging times with Lizzie. "Andy had a way of making me smile. When he was around six, he used to tell me, 'You're the best daddy in the world. I'll never ever leave you.' Neil, though younger, was the stronger one. He had a no-nonsense attitude... a real go-getter."

"Just like his dad," Janet interjected.

"Actually, even better than his dad," Abe responded. "He wouldn't give up easily. Sometimes, he got into trouble at school, standing up to bullies. Being the younger one, Lizzie showered him with affection. He didn't always appreciate being smothered by her. He wanted to show his strength. Andy, on the other hand, was gentle and enjoyed being cuddled."

"I wouldn't know how to handle boys. People say they're easier than girls, but I wouldn't know. I've often wondered how I would have fared bringing up a son," Janet admitted.

"They might be easier until they hit their teenage years. I had to keep a firm grip on them during high school, but thankfully, they stayed focused on their studies, and I can't say there were any major issues."

"So, tell me," Janet inquired, "how did you and Lizzie end up separating? How did she meet her new partner?"

"As I mentioned earlier, things weren't going well between us after the baby arrived. Trust me, I gave it my all to salvage the relationship, but she was unhappy, and honestly, I was too. I held onto the hope and prayed that some glimmer of love would remain, but the flames were extinguished before they could be rekindled. Life just seemed to drag on. We moved to Toronto, and the situation remained unchanged. She found a position at the Bank, and that's where she crossed paths with Robert. He was an American consultant from the City of New York and was working on a project with Meridian Financial in Don Mills. Since Lizzie's bank held some of Meridian's funds, he frequented her workplace for business. I think Lizzie was always helpful to him, and one day, he invited her to lunch. From there, lunch turned into regular coffee meetings, then dinners, and one thing led to another... and another. To her credit, when things became serious between her and Robertt, Lizzie actually sat down with me to talk."

"That must have been a difficult conversation for both of you," Janet concluded.

"I was angry initially," Abe admitted. "I thought about the sacrifices I had made for Lizzie. I expected her to be appreciative, to endure the pain in silence as I was doing. But I realized I was being unjust. It was clear that we weren't right for each other. She was brave to step out of a failing marriage. I couldn't prevent her from leaving. My one request was that she leave the boys with me. They were close to finishing high school, and I didn't want their education and lives to be disrupted. She agreed to let me have them, and we arranged how they could spend time with her despite living with me."

"What about the boys? Were they involved in the decision?"

"We spoke openly with them about our lives, our marriage, and Lizzie's decision to get a divorce. Naturally, they were worried about not having their mom around, but understanding that she would be happier with Robert, helped them consider her happiness along with their own. They were firm in not wanting to move to the USA and felt they would be better off with me than with a stepfather. I had always been their primary caregiver, more than Lizzie ever was. In the end, things just fell into place. Jan, I think I told you all of this before, didn't I?"

"No, not everything, and I don't mind hearing it again. Do you have any regrets?" Janet inquired.

"About Lizzie?" Janet nodded.

"No, I believe our separation was unavoidable. I was clinging to a moral stance I had taken, and I believed Lizzie had a duty to honor that choice. But I was completely mistaken. The choice was mine alone. I couldn't hold Lizzie responsible for the love I let go of. It's all on me, Jan. One weak and foolish mistake on my part turned into a lifetime of suffering," his voice broke.

Janet gently placed her finger on his lips. "Hush, it's all in the past now, and we can't change it. I'm sure there were also some good times, and you should hold onto those. Release the guilt and self-judgment. We often dwell on what could have been, but there's no guarantee that you and I would have endured either."

He kissed the tip of her finger. "We would have endured, Jan. We were meant to be together. Love like ours doesn't fade."

Janet shared his sentiment but sought to be rational. "We can't be certain, Abe."

"I am," he countered. "Feel my heartbeat. It beats only for you." He took her hand and placed it over his chest, pulling her close. Gently, he kissed her eyelids. "All the Lizzies in the world could never take your place, Jan. My heart has always belonged to you."

Janet didn't want to prolong her unease, so she inquired, "What should we do now? Hari will be here soon."

He smiled. "We're reminiscing. Reminiscing can be good, don't you think?"

"Yes, but we can't dwell on that forever. Reality awaits."

"What are you afraid of, Jan... that I'll probe into your life?"

She pulled back slightly and looked at him. "My life has been quite mundane and uneventful."

"I still want to know," he insisted.

She hesitated for a moment before starting, "Similar to you, shortly after marrying Nat, I realized that we weren't a good match. He was – well, he still is – selfish and self-centered. My focus was on the girls, and they meant the world to me. Nat pursued a career in social service shortly after we got married. We both attended university..."

"Did you attend the same university? Was he there when I met you?"

She nodded. "Yes, though we were in different departments. We both worked hard during that time. After we moved, he found a position at an immigrant funding agency. Neither of us made much money, so we faced financial struggles. He pursued his Diploma through distance learning and completed his graduate studies at California State University through the same mode. He started additional post-graduate work but didn't see it through. Meanwhile, I sacrificed greatly for my doctorate, and my career flourished. On Windermere Island, he secured a faculty position at the university where I currently work. Our marriage has been challenging; we have differing temperaments. I tend to be the mediator, while he's more reserved and analytical. He's been an acceptable father to the girls, but if I were to assess him, it would be a B at best. I know that sounds harsh, but if he hadn't been good with the kids, I doubt we'd have stayed together for long."

A dry, almost cynical laugh escaped her lips, even sounding that way to herself. Continuing, she added, "He places importance on material possessions, which truly bothers me."

"I can understand why that would be difficult for you," Abe commented.

"Anyway," Janet continued, "I've made efforts to salvage the situation. I've poured my energy into my career, and I feel truly blessed by God. I've been fortunate enough to travel extensively around the world. I've impacted the lives of many people, and my daughters are thriving. The ones who are married have found loving and supportive partners, and that brings me immense joy."

"What about you, Jan? Are you genuinely happy?" Abe inquired.

She pondered his question for a moment. "Perhaps I'm not ecstatically happy, but I've found contentment. I've resolved not to ask for the impossible. I do wish Nat could have loved me as I loved him when we first met. I genuinely cared for him, Abe. My feelings for him were deep, but he shattered my heart. He didn't just break it; he shattered it. It's not just a saying that broken hearts can't be fully mended."

Abe's heart ached for her. He drew her close again. "I'm so sorry, Jan. Why didn't you leave him?"

"I considered leaving many times, but I feared for my daughters. I worried about introducing a stranger into their lives if I were to enter another relationship. Also, I've witnessed the turmoil children experience when their parents separate. Often, it's the children who endure the most pain. I couldn't stand by and let my children go through such a nightmarish situation."

"I understand," he said. "Don't forget, I've also been down that road."

She continued, "As the girls grew up and left home, my focus shifted more to my work, and Nat gradually became a smaller part of my life. We've evolved into mostly good friends now. Yet, I confess that even after realizing things wouldn't work with him, thoughts of you often crossed my mind. I resisted indulging in futile daydreams. Those feelings seemed like distant memories, water under the bridge. I was once a dreamer, but I've grown into a realist. Why waste precious time on things that are beyond reach? You and I being together here..." she paused briefly before continuing, "I never believed this could happen. Sometimes, I feel like I'll wake up and realize that my time with you was just a figment of my imagination. I never anticipated seeing you again."

"Never say never," Abe interjected. "On the contrary, I always held onto the hope that I'd find you one day, though I never imagined it would be like this. I'm profoundly thankful, Jan, for whatever force led me to Windermere Island."

Janet hesitated, reluctant to interrupt his sentiment. These were moments she wanted to etch into her memory forever, yet time was fleeting. She slowly rose from the deck, reluctantly detaching herself from Abe. "I think we should finish up the remaining food and check the fishing lines," she suggested. While moving toward the basket under the table, she spotted Abe's line twitching above the water. "Looks like you've got a bite," she exclaimed to Abe.

He leaped to his feet and reeled in the line, gazing at the small pink and yellow snapper dangling at the end. "Seems like we're even now," he said to Janet, carefully removing the fish from the hook. "I hope I didn't hurt him."

"He's quite small for a snapper," Janet remarked, "he has a lot of growing to do. He's just a little one."

"Should we release him?" Abe inquired.

"Yes. Is he alright? He's not injured, is he?"

"He looks fine to me." Abe turned the small fish over, observing its bright pink gills beneath its pectoral fin. "I'll let him go on the count of three unless you've changed your mind."

Janet acted as if she hadn't heard, allowing him to decide what to do with his catch.

"One, two, three... splash." She leaned over the railing and watched the ripples where the fish had re-entered the water.

Abe wiped his hands on his shorts and joined Janet at the table, where she had begun arranging fruits and slices of banana loaf. "You should wash your hands," Janet instructed. "You were handling the fish."

"My hands are clean. They actually smell quite nice. Nothing beats the scent of fresh fish!" He chuckled and playfully tried to hold his hand under Janet's nose, asking, "Don't you want a whiff?"

Janet lightly swatted his backside with a tea towel. "Stop it! Hurry up and wash your hands so we can finish the meal."

Abe complied silently, and when he returned from the cabin, Janet had set out a spread on the small table. She was already nibbling on a piece of cheese. "Looks like a feast in paradise!" Abe exclaimed as he took a seat across from her. Janet filled up a paper plate with fruits and cheese and handed it to him. They ate in contented silence, the sound of waves lapping against the boat's sides providing a soothing backdrop.

"So, what's your plan once we're back?" Abe asked, knowing he was intruding on their idyllic moment but aware that time was slipping away.

"I'll head back to Maria's. She promised to take me to Mother B's place to get some *Cassareep*. I want to take some back to Canada with me. You can find a version of it at certain supermarkets there, but it's not very authentic. As a result, my pepper pot during Christmas doesn't turn out as well as I'd like. Jack usually brings some for me whenever I visit."

Jack! She had nearly forgotten about Jack while being engrossed with Abe. Jack was the reason she came from Cuba. She needed to make sure she spent more time with him before she left. Jenna had sent her a text, informing her that Jack was awake for longer periods now, and the doctors had confirmed his recovery progress and that he was no longer in danger.

Almost as if he could read her thoughts, Abe inquired, "Are you still planning to leave tomorrow?"

Janet nodded. "Yes, and I'm seriously considering taking one of those speedboats instead of the ferry. You're right, and they're much faster. I won't have to wait around, and I can reach Jenna sooner."

"Are you sure?" Abe questioned. "Those boats still come with their risks."

"But you use them regularly," Janet countered. "I see so many people traveling with them without any issues. I don't see why anything would go wrong for me. Since you're familiar with the operators, could you perhaps arrange for one of the more reliable captains to take me in his boat?"

"Alright. I often use the *Bobby D*. It's a newer boat. My friend Kyle runs that one. I'll speak with him after his final afternoon run. What time would you like to depart?"

"How about 9:00? That should get me to the city well before noon."

"Consider it done," Abe replied with a teasing smile. "Your wish is my command, my lady." However, Janet's thoughts had taken a sudden shift, causing his playful remark not to elicit her usual smile. She was preoccupied with thoughts of Jack and Abe. She wished for Jack's swift recovery and couldn't help but hope that Abe might overcome his medical issues by some miracle. Tomorrow's farewell to Abe might potentially be their final meeting, a realization that stifled the sob that threatened to rise in her throat.

As they finished their meal, Abe checked the time. "We should start heading back. Hari will be arriving soon. He's always punctual."

"I've noticed that" Janet agreed as she began repacking the picnic baskets.

"I'd better stow the rods and other gear properly so Simon can find his equipment when he comes looking," Abe mentioned.

"Do you need help?" Janet offered. "Going up and down into the cabin might not be easy for you."

"Don't worry. I've got it," Abe assured her as he reeled in the line on her fishing rod. Despite noticing the fatigue on his face, she allowed him to uphold his role as the man in charge. After securing all the items as they had found them, Abe started the engine and retrieved the anchor, guiding the boat back toward the marina. As they approached the shoreline where other boats were moored, Abe operated the winch to lower the heavy anchor into the water. It disappeared beneath the receding tide, firmly steadying the boat.

Abe looked at Janet with a touch of concern. "Can you manage wading to shore? Or should I carry you and come back for our belongings?"

"Not on your life, you won't! I'm perfectly capable of making my way to the shore. The tide is out, so the water is still lower than when we arrived. Besides, you appear exhausted, Abe. You should head home and get some much-needed rest."

"I'm fine, and if needed, I could carry a woman twice your size." As usual, Abe was in denial.

"I don't doubt it," conceded Janet. "Are you ready? Let's go." She picked up one of the baskets while Abe took the other.

Chapter 23

Abe observed Janet as she used her eyes to measure the distance from her current position to the small beach. "The shore is a bit far because we had to anchor further out, but I'll assist you," he offered. Allowing him to guide her, they moved through the water with a combination of walking, running, and slashing. Unexpectedly, Janet lost her footing and instinctively reached out to Abe for support. Her hands unintentionally found their way around his waist, prompting him to pull her closer to steady her. For a moment, their proximity lingered as he embraced her, enveloping her in the warmth of his body. In a tender gesture, he bent down and gently kissed the top of her head.

"This is farewell, Jan. Tomorrow when you depart, I won't be able to do this," his voice carried a husky tone. With her free hand, she wiped away a tear that had gathered in the corner of his eye. It wasn't the first time she had witnessed the vulnerability in his tears. Unlike Nat, who never allowed a tear to fall, Abe's emotions flowed freely, defying any notions of weakness. Nat believed that showing tears equated to losing control, a perception he vehemently rejected. Janet paused her thoughts, questioning why she was contemplating Nat at this moment. Soon, she would return to Windermere and would have the opportunity to unravel these complex emotions that had taken root deep within her heart.

"Let's go," Janet said to Abe, her tone determined. "Hari's car is creating quite a dust storm. We shouldn't let him see our pain."

With a basket in hand, Abe and Janet trudged through the seawater. Playfulness returned as Abe lifted the basket and splashed water at her. She retaliated with her own splashes, deftly dodging the drops Abe playfully tossed her way. Amid laughter, their capris were soaked at the knees by the time they reached Hari.

"You two seem to have had a blast," Hari greeted them.

"Yes, take a look at what Jan caught," Abe beamed, opening the picnic basket to reveal the fish. Janet had momentarily forgotten about the fish they had left in the icebox, but Abe had remembered to bring it along.

"Nice catch," Hari remarked. "So, who's going to enjoy it for dinner?"

"Abe should have it," Janet decided. "Hari, you can grill it for him. Remember to season it with sea salt and black pepper."

"Absolutely!" Hari acknowledged. He stowed the baskets in the trunk while Abe and Janet settled into the back seat.

Abe's explanation to Hari was, "I'll sit in the back with Janet. We both got our pants a bit wet. I wouldn't want to soak the seat next to you, just in case you need to take one of the kids somewhere as soon as you get home."

"Not a problem," replied Hari. He handed a sheet of blue plastic to Janet and suggested, "Spread this over the seat. It should help keep it dry."

"Thanks, Hari," Janet said appreciatively as she unfolded the plastic sheet over the seat. "You really do think of everything."

On the journey back, out of Hari's view, Abe and Janet discreetly held hands, their actions concealed from Hari's gaze through the rear-view mirror. Shifting his focus to Janet, Hari inquired, "So, should I take you straight back to Maria's now?"

Before Janet could respond, Abe interjected, "Actually, we'll make a quick stop at home. Remember, you promised Janet to get her some coconut water. How about asking Zade if he can rustle up some coconuts? He's quite the speedy climber and can scale that coconut tree in no time."

"Don't trouble Hari," Janet told Abe.

"It's truly no trouble," Hari assured. "Zade is Abe's neighbor, and he often brings over coconuts. He's like a coconut tree-climbing expert, reaching the top in under five minutes."

"That sounds a bit scary," Janet confessed. "Back when I lived in San Souci, I used to watch boys climbing those towering trees. When the trees swayed in the wind, I'd shut my eyes, half-expecting one of them to fall and be injured."

"Did they ever?" inquired Hari.

"No, I've never witnessed an accident myself, but I've heard stories from others about boys who've fallen and ended up with broken arms or legs from climbing coconut trees. There was even a guy I knew who fell, injured his spine, and couldn't walk again for the rest of his life," Janet recounted.

"It's all part of the journey to manhood," Abe chimed in, gently squeezing her fingers. "But don't worry, Zade is a pro. You can't leave San Souci without experiencing real coconut water. Not the kind you find in Canadian supermarkets, as we've already agreed."

Coconut-related anecdotes and facts took center stage in their conversation for the remainder of the drive to Abe's house. They delved into discussions about the coconut palm's versatility - each part of the tree serving distinct purposes. Abe shared insights about the sturdy trunk being used in bridges and constructing makeshift shelters. The leaves had their uses, too, from thatching shacks to adorning wedding venues or other events, and the rib of the leaves found utility in making brooms. Hari contributed by bringing up the current scientific trend of utilizing the coconut's "meat" for various pharmaceutical products, including skincare items rich in coconut oil. The conversation turned out to be both engaging and educational.

"Have you seen the price of half a liter of coconut oil in Canada? It's unbelievable!" Abe exclaimed. "I still remember my mother making her own coconut oil when I was a kid. That was our only moisturizing lotion. And whenever we had headaches, massaging coconut oil into our scalps would ease the pain."

Janet sat contentedly, soaking in the conversation and reliving memories.

Upon arriving at Abe's place, Hari hurried off to fetch Zade, who would gather a few coconuts from the two trees in the backyard.

Taking advantage of Hari's absence, Abe seized the moment to share some final words with Janet. "Kyle will have everything arranged for your speedboat trip to Lewiston tomorrow at 9:00. I won't come to bid you farewell in person. I'd rather avoid wagging tongues and whispered rumors. You should know that I'll be watching the speedboat landing from my front window, sending you silent kisses as you depart."

Disregarding his last comment, Janet inquired, "Should I confirm the details with you later, just to be sure?"

"No need to worry," Abe reassured her. "Things will be as I've said. If there's any change, I'll give you a call. I sincerely wish you a safe journey back to Canada, and I truly hope your life returns to its normal rhythm. That's what I desire more than anything."

"Well, I hope you'll send me texts every now and then to keep me updated on how you're doing," Janet suggested, avoiding direct eye contact to conceal her teary emotions. She had shed plenty of tears, and now she needed to find the strength to let go. "Just promise me you'll stay in touch whenever possible. You can always call me on my cell. I would like to know how your treatment is progressing. I still believe in miracles, Abe. We serve a God of miracles."

"Absolutely. I'll make an effort to keep you informed," he replied, though he wasn't entirely truthful. Abe had made up his mind that Janet had given him what he asked for, and he didn't want to put her in any more awkward situations. He was content, even if it meant not hearing her voice or seeing her again. He didn't want to exploit her feelings for him any further. There was no need to prolong the pain. "And if you don't hear from me," he added, "just understand that I'm engrossed in my treatment."

Their conversation was interrupted by Hari, who informed them that Zade wasn't at home, so getting coconut water would have to wait for another occasion. "I'm truly sorry," he apologized to Janet. "I wish I had the skill to climb the tree myself, but I don't possess that ability."

"Don't worry," Abe reassured. "There's always another opportunity." He couldn't believe he had told two lies within two minutes. "I've beaten Peter denying Jesus before the rooster crowed three times," he mused silently. "I have some sugar cane juice in the fridge," he directed Janet. "Give it a try. It's not a replacement for coconut water, but it's quite refreshing."

"Oh, yes," chimed in Hari, "I spotted the jug earlier. I considered having some, but I wasn't sure if you were saving it for a specific occasion."

"Well, the occasion is here and now. How about pouring some for us? The weather is warm enough for us to appreciate a cold drink," Abe suggested.

Hari quickly went to fetch the juice. "Is he always this attentive?" Janet inquired. "He seems like such a wonderful person. I'm glad you have him around when you're here."

"Hari takes good care of me. He considers me his favorite uncle," Abe shared.

"Does he know much about your condition?" Janet asked.

"He knows as much as anyone does. He understands that this illness will eventually take its toll on me, but he doesn't grasp how soon. No one does. I believe that's why he wants to do everything he can to support me," Abe explained.

Hari returned with three tall glasses of ice-cold juice on a small tray. He offered a glass to Janet and then to Abe. Pouring himself the remaining glass, he settled into a chair, glanced at his watch, and inquired, "What time should I plan to take Miss Janet back to Maria's?"

"Within the next half hour," Janet replied. "I want to spend some time with her. She promised to take me to see her aunt, B."

"Aunt B hasn't been doing too well," Hari informed. "Her eyesight seems to be fading."

"Well, she's ninety," Abe interjected. "It's not uncommon at that age. Despite that, she's still quite active, though preparing meals has become a challenge. Maria has been helping her out a lot."

Abe turned to Janet and inquired, "Do you remember her cornbread? Aunt B's cornbread is truly one of a kind."

"I do recall her cornbread," Janet smiled. "My mom used to order from her on weekends. We'd sometimes say, *It's cornbread Saturday!*"

"She had orders from so many people. Everyone in San Souci knew that she made the finest cornbread in all of Guyana," Hari added.

The conversation flowed as they discussed Aunt B, Hari's children, and the political scene in Guyana. As the time for Janet to depart drew near, she bid farewell to Abe, hugging him but avoiding his gaze. He adeptly maintained the facade that this was a casual visit from a friend. Turning to Hari, Abe instructed, "Remember, you're picking up Janet and taking her to Park's Landing for the speedboat tomorrow."

"What time?" he inquired.

"The boat departs at 9:00, so you should pick her up around eight-thirty. She doesn't need to be there too early. There's usually not much of a queue," Abe explained.

"Eight thirty works for me," Janet confirmed. "Hari, I feel like I'm burdening you with all this driving. You must think I'm turning you into my personal taxi driver."

"Not at all. It's my pleasure. I'd do anything for Uncle Abe," Hari responded with a wink. "I might even attempt to walk on water for him."

"I might just take you up on that one day, so be careful what you promise," Abe added in a dry tone.

As they walked towards the car, Hari headed to the driver's side while Abe gently squeezed Janet's fingers and whispered, "Goodbye, Jan. We'll talk tomorrow."

Choked up with emotions, Janet could only manage a nod. Abe waved as they drove off, remaining by his driveway until the car disappeared around a bend in the distance. He wished he could vanish too, but instead, he went back inside his house and knelt by the bed, resting his head on the edge. "Lord," he prayed with a heavy heart, "forgive me for loving another man's wife. I'm grateful that you answered my prayer and allowed me time with Janet. I promise not to reach out to her again; I know it's wrong. Give me the strength to stay away. I want her to find happiness with her family. Please watch over her life and shower her with your blessings." Then he wept like a child who had lost his most precious possession.

Abe attempted to eat some dinner, though he struggled to swallow the food down his throat. Despite his efforts, he couldn't find his appetite. He went to bed hoping for a nap, but his mind was restless. Reflecting on his time with Janet, he pondered whether he had been too self-centered. He prayed that these precious moments would remain hidden from her family and that she could seamlessly resume the course of her life.

Janet's state mirrored Abe's. Her visit with Aunt B had been heartening. The older woman shared stories about San Souci that Janet had never heard before. One anecdote that left Janet in awe involved the Police Chief, who had gone to investigate a robbery near the cemetery and ended up being chased by the ghost of Aunt B's husband. "Have you ever heard that story before?" Aunt B inquired. "Perhaps it was after you had left the island. People used to jest with Chief Harlow, advising him to stay clear of the cemetery to avoid encounters with ghosts." Aunt B chuckled wholeheartedly. During the visit, Janet noticed Aunt B's struggle with her eyesight when she attempted to reach for her cane, which was partially concealed behind her chair. She clumsily fell around the seat, trying to locate the cane. Janet placed it in her hand.

"Can you tell that Aunt B is losing her sight?" Aunt B sadly asked Janet.

"It comes with age, but you're still doing remarkably well," Janet reassured her. "You have all your faculties intact. You can still share those beautiful stories, and even with a cane, you're still mobile."

Janet bid her farewell and accompanied Maria on a leisurely stroll through the village. They paused for tea and coconut buns before heading back home. Maria had prepared supper, a spread featuring steamed fish, dumplings, okra, and deep-fried eggplant. "Who's going to eat all of this?" Janet exclaimed in surprise.

"Try to enjoy as much as you can. You won't find this kind of food in Canada," Maria encouraged.

"We do get okra and eggplant. The fish is different, but there are various types available," Janet responded.

"Not like this!" Maria contradicted.

"True, not as fresh," Janet admitted.

Out of consideration for Maria, Janet sampled a bit of everything, though Abe consumed her thoughts. Despite the meal's quality, everything tasted bland as her mind lingered on him. She was relieved when dinner concluded, bidding Maria goodnight before retreating to her room. She repacked her bag and prepared for bed, but sleep evaded her. Her thoughts were fixated on Abe, and tears streamed down her face as she envisioned him lifeless in a morgue. Her desire wasn't necessarily to see him again; she wished for his survival. "God of miracles," she prayed, "nothing is beyond your capability. Please heal him, rescue him, and grant him life."

Throughout the night, restlessness plagued her, and the 7:00 a.m. alarm was accompanied by the sound of rain dripping from the roof. She rose from her bed and peered out the window to a gray, overcast sky and a consistent drizzle. The aroma of coffee reached her senses, an indication that Maria was up despite Janet's request not to fuss. Janet showered, dressed, and made her way downstairs to the kitchen, where Maria had prepared toast and scrambled eggs.

"Good morning," Maria greeted Janet warmly. "Come and have some breakfast. You can't start your journey with an empty stomach."

"I already told you not to worry about breakfast. A cup of coffee would have sufficed," Janet replied.

"Starting the day with a hearty breakfast is unmatched. By the way, did you manage to reach Jenna? How's Jack doing now?" Maria inquired.

It was fortunate that Maria's back was turned to Janet at that moment, as she couldn't see the startled expression on Janet's face nor the coffee that accidentally spilled from her mug. "I haven't received an update from Jenna yet," Janet stammered slightly. "I did call her last night, but she might have been at the hospital late. I'll try again after breakfast. My phone is still charging; the battery's almost drained from all the pictures I took," Janet fabricated. Amid the turmoil of the day's events, she had completely forgotten to check in with Jenna about Jack's well-being.

Janet hurriedly consumed her toast and a portion of the eggs, then hastily retreated to her room to call Jenna. Jenna picked up on the second ring. "Hi Jan, how are you? I tried calling yesterday, but there was no answer. Are you okay? I wanted to reach out to Maria, but I figured you might think I'm being overly concerned. What's going on?"

"I'm just about to leave San Souci. I should be back in the city by 11:00. How's Jack doing? I'll head straight to the hospital once I'm back."

"Jack's improving remarkably. He keeps asking for you. You'll be amazed that his eyes are open now, and he's fully aware of his surroundings. He knows you've been in to see him. He still struggles with conversation; his speech is a bit slurred due to his swollen lips. However, the doctor says he's definitely on the road to recovery."

"That's wonderful news, Jenna. Will you visit the hospital during your lunch break? If so, I'll meet you there."

"Yes, I plan to. Take care and have a safe trip. Make sure you use a reliable taxi when you reach Lewiston."

"I will," Janet reassured. "See you soon." Her thoughts drifted back to Jack. She was eager to see him and relieved to know he was progressing without setbacks. She shared the positive update with Maria.

"I'll be in the city next week, so I'll drop by to see him. Who knows, he might not be in the hospital by then."

"That would be fantastic. Is that Hari's car outside?"

"Yes, he just arrived."

Janet approached the window and waved to Hari, who responded with a thumbs-up, indicating he would wait in the car due to the rain. She collected her overnight bag and bid farewell to Maria. "You've been so kind, Maria. Thank you for having me here. I'm grateful for the time I could spend on San Souci."

"Anytime," Maria said, giving Janet a warm hug. "And thanks for the bottle of Canadian maple syrup. I'm looking forward to enjoying it on my pancakes. Take care, my friend. Give me a call when you're back in Windermere, and pass on my regards to Nat." Maria released her from the hug and handed her an umbrella. "Here's an umbrella. I don't want you getting wet."

"From here to the car? I'll be fine. Besides, how will you get back your umbrella."

"You'll be drenched, my girl. See those raindrops, how they're huge! Leave the umbrella with Hari. He can return it whenever." Maria shoved the umbrella in her hand, and she opened it as she hustled out to the waiting car.

"Dodging the raindrops, Miss Janet," Hari remarked as he swiftly opened the car door. "You must be relieved you brought your umbrella! How was your night?"

"Hi Hari, I'm good," Janet replied in her typical Canadian manner. "And you?"

"Neela was a bit under the weather last night. I think she's coming down with the flu or something. We were up most of the night with her."

"Oh dear, poor girl. I hope she feels better today."

"Kids, you know how they are. They bounce back quickly. I'm sure she'll be fine by the end of the day. The weather isn't too great today. I hope the crossing will be okay for you. Try to find a seat towards the back of the boat so you'll feel less of the rocking."

"I'll manage. I want to reach the city as soon as I can."

"Any updates about Mr. Jack?"

Janet informed Hari about what she had learned from Jenna.

"I'm glad you'll be able to spend the next few days with him."

They arrived at Park's Landing, and Janet noticed eight other people waiting to board the blue and red speedboat, which was gently bobbing at the water's edge. "Well, this is it, Hari," Janet said. "By the way, the umbrella belongs to Maria. Could you return it to her when you have a chance?"

"Of course. Don't worry, Miss Janet. I'll make sure she gets it." Hari assisted her with her overnight bag and called out to Captain Bobby.

Bobby approached, raindrops sliding down his rain jacket. "Are you Janet?" he asked. "Abe spoke to me about taking you across. He even gave me a stern warning that if anything goes wrong with you, he'll raise hell," he joked. Then he inquired, "Do you remember me? My father was James Kawal. Your brother Jack and my father collaborated on a project to establish a fishpond at the other end of the island. I remember you, but I was only about seven when you left San Souci. Jack and my dad became friends."

"I'm delighted to meet you, Bobby," Janet said, extending her hand. "Can your boat handle this weather? The water looks quite rough. I can see the white caps on the rolling waves."

"Not to worry," Bobby reassured her. "This is nothing. We've gone through actual storms. I was going to pilot the *Lady Diana,* but the *Bobby D* has a really powerful motor that's better in this weather."

She pondered why the boat was being referred to as male, yet she knew that "Bobby" was a commonly used name on the island for both males and females. She wondered if it was a coincidence that the boat was named after the captain or if there was another explanation. Why on earth was she pondering this anyway? She needed to get on board.

"Can I take a seat at the back?" Janet asked Bobby.

"Yes, certainly. Abe mentioned that I should reserve that particular seat for you." Bobby held her hands, but before he could assist her into the gently swaying vessel, she turned to Hari and embraced him. "I'm truly glad I had the chance to meet you, Hari. Thank you again for everything you did. I hope you'll continue to take good care of your Uncle Abe. He relies on you. I'm sincerely grateful he has you."

"Don't worry about Uncle Abe. He'll be alright. I'm confident you'll return to visit him again."

Janet released him with a whisper, "Goodbye, Hari. Take care of yourself and your family as well."

With care, Bobby settled her at the rear of the boat and positioned her luggage in a small iron cage at the front. The remaining passengers, consisting of three men and five women, filed into the boat. They greeted her with smiles, gently maneuvering around to find their own seats. In just ten minutes, they were prepared to depart. The ropes that tethered the boat to the dock were untied, and they set off.

Janet felt the wind tousling her hair as the sprays of water from the boat's rear, slicing through the waves, brushed past her face. She wondered if Abe could see her as he had promised. His house was visible through the trees, though she couldn't clearly make out his windows. She hoped he was indeed watching and would notice her departure from the island.

The boat swiftly advanced toward Lewiston. The ocean was misty, with a steady drizzle of rain. Occasionally, visibility became challenging. Through the mist, Janet caught fleeting glimpses of two other speedboats shuttling people between Lewiston and San Souci. The approach of a boat was discernible by the engine's roar and the rhythmic flapping of the boat's underside against the waves. Suddenly, one of the younger men at the boat's front shouted, "Watch out, Bobby! There's a boat up ahead. Its engine seems to have died. It's just floating there. I can see it straight ahead."

Everyone strained their eyes to peer through the mist. "Change course! Move to the right, more to the right!" the man yelled once again. He appeared to be the navigating sailor working with Bobby. Bobby attempted to reduce the engine's speed and veer away from the approaching boat, but his efforts weren't swift enough. Unexpectedly, the *Bobby D* collided with the oncoming boat. The impact caused Bobby *D* to sway and pitch as if it might capsize, but then it swiftly regained its balance with a powerful jolt. This sudden motion threw Janet and the woman beside her into the water through the boat's rear opening. As the *Bobby D* struggled to stabilize itself, Janet plunged into the cold-water face-first. She sensed something striking her head, followed by an intense surge of agony. The water's chill enveloped her, its force attempting to drag her beneath the surface. Janet had never been a proficient swimmer. Desperately, she reached out with both hands, searching for something to grip onto that would enable her to pull herself back up. Regrettably, there was nothing to clutch—only water, an endless expanse of it. Despite her attempts to ascend, she found herself inexorably pulled deeper, as if the ocean's jaws were swallowing her whole.

"Help me! Help me!" her mind screamed, but there were no words and nothing in sight - only the water surrounding her, relentlessly pressing her into unconsciousness. She choked as the water surged into her mouth, filling her nostrils. What was happening? Breathing became impossible. The water seemed to infiltrate every inch of her body, its sting and burn spreading throughout. She coughed, inadvertently admitting more water into her lungs. Despite her struggles, the water's weight bore down on her, an inescapable force. She understood she was drowning, yet powerless to alter the outcome. Her body grew feeble, exhaustion consuming her. She could no longer keep her eyes open. Her senses dulled. Then, an odd lightness enveloped her, a sense of liberation as if she were ascending above the water, higher and higher. Effortlessly, she soared upward, suspended over the *Bobby D*, observing the scene below. Was she a cloud, she wondered. She felt as though she touched the sky, witnessing Bobby and the other sailor plunging into the water frantically. On the boat, the passengers stared, fear etched on their faces, all eyes fixed on Captain Bobby, waiting with a mix of anxiety and anticipation.

Bobby resurfaced once more, and with him, he raised what appeared to be her lifeless body. She lay motionless, her skin taking on an ashen hue. The other woman who had fallen overboard was somehow back on the boat, sprawled on the floor, but her eyes were open. Some individuals gathered around her, trying to make her comfortable, while others let out screams as they witnessed Bobby cradling the limp form, struggling to bring her back onto the boat with the assistance of the men.

Confusion reigned, and additional boats were en route to assist. A fragment of the *Bobby D's* bow had broken off, yet aside from this damage, the boat appeared to have weathered the collision. Drifting far above, Janet observed the scene and grasped that she was no longer intertwined with this earthly existence. She existed in a distinct realm, floating on and on with the wind, a sensation of boundless freedom guiding her onward. She floated ceaselessly, without a destination, accompanied solely by the wind, the sky, and the billowing clouds.

News of the accident reached other passing boats, who then relayed the information to those waiting at Parks Landing. A crowd had amassed, anxious to glean more details. Relatives of *Bobby D's* passengers sought solace in the assurance of no fatalities. Amid the commotion, Abe, drawn by the clamor, seized his umbrella and hurried to the landing. On his way, he encountered Aaron and inquired about the situation. "I'm uncertain," Aaron responded, "But it appears that the *Bobby D* was involved in an accident."

"What? How?" Abe questioned urgently.

"I don't have all the details. Let's talk with some of the individuals over there. My sister was aboard that vessel. I hope she's unharmed."

Abe wished to cry out, "My beloved was on that boat," yet he quickened his pace instead. His footsteps echoed his inner chant, "I hope Jan is safe. She must be safe."

Parks Landing was a scene of pandemonium, myriad voices recounting what they had heard.

"No injuries reported," one account declared.

"Somebody fell overboard but was rescued," offered another version.

Yet another speaker confirmed, "I was told that two people fell overboard. One was rescued, but the other drowned. Her body was recovered, and they're bringing it back."

Abe tried to block out the last comment, praying that it was not true. After approximately twenty minutes of sheer terror and anguish, a voice cried out that *Bobby D* was returning to Parks Landing. Abe's eyes followed the boat's approach, relieved to see it seemingly intact with passengers seated - a positive sign. As the vessel drew nearer, Abe strained to catch a glimpse of Janet. He remembered her attire: a blue shirt and jeans. He had watched her board the *Bobby D*, silently waving as the boat set off. Hari, having heard about the tragic incident, hurried back to Parks Landing, fearing it might involve Captain Bobby. He joined Abe, standing at his side. "Where's Miss Janet?" he inquired, scanning over the heads before them. Abe could only offer a helpless look in response.

As the boat edged closer to the landing, Abe's gaze fixed on a figure sprawled on one of the seats - a blue-shirted, blue-jeaned form. His legs gave way beneath him, his umbrella slipping from his grasp and soaring overhead. He collapsed to the ground. Impossible, his mind screamed. Janet must be unconscious. They needed a doctor. Yet, deep down, his heart conveyed a different truth.

"Uncle Abe, Uncle Abe, are you alright?"

From the depths of his consciousness, Hari's voice reached him. Abe blinked his eyes open, finding Hari attempting to rouse him. He must have blacked out. Several others had gathered, offering first aid. His gaze returned to Hari. "Janet? How is she? Is she …" He couldn't bring himself to say that word.

"I'm so sorry, Uncle Abe. I can't believe this," Hari wept uncontrollably. Abe, still on the ground, observed the crowd moving toward the opposite end of the landing, where the *Bobby D* had now docked. Through the gaps between legs, he discerned Janet's form, appearing as if in slumber on the wooden planks - clad in her blue shirt and blue jeans. Hari extended a hand to help Abe up. "How could this happen? Why did this happen?" Hari's sobs echoed with his questions.

Abe found himself walking toward the crowd, though his feet moved mechanically. He felt as lifeless as the woman lying on the landing. Words floated above him, but none of them truly registered.

"It's Janet Ramphal, Daniel Ramphal's daughter," one spectator uttered.

"She came for a visit from Canada," another added.

"Someone mentioned she was here to see her brother. Remember he had an accident?"

"Who was she staying with here? Who will look after her?"

In response to that last question, Abe's voice broke through. "I will." The crowd parted to make way for him. Abe knelt beside Janet's motionless body, clutching her hands. Tears streamed down his cheeks. At this moment, he cared little for anyone's negative opinions about him or Janet. Hari gently nudged him. "Maria is here."

Maria maneuvered her way through the crowd, kneeling beside Abe. Shock had left her speechless, and she repeated the same questions in a daze, "Oh my God, how did this happen? How will Jenna and Jack cope with this?" Her gaze turned skyward. "Why, God, why?" Trembling, her agitation surpassed the fluttering leaves of the mangrove tree in the wind. Grief engulfed her. Abruptly, her attention returned to Abe. "I didn't know you were on the island. Will you help me? Jenna will need us." As if it were the most natural thing in the world, Maria rested her head on Abe's shoulder. "How could this happen to our Janet? Why? Why?" Several slaps on Abe's chest punctuated her wails of despair.

Abe allowed Maria to express her anger, frustration, and grief, patiently absorbing her emotions. Then he addressed her, "We need to handle this. We can't let Janet down. Let's focus on what needs to be done first." It was a mystery to him how he managed to remain so composed. Rising to his feet, he sought out Bobby, who was also in tears while attempting to recount the incident to concerned listeners. Bobby spotted Abe, approached him, and embraced him, tears flowing anew. "Abe, I'm so sorry. I didn't see that boat until it was too late."

Abe returned the hug. "It was an unfortunate accident, Bobby. Were there any other injuries on the other boat? Whose boat was it?"

"It was Roma's. He was alone. He experienced engine failure, so he was adrift without control. There was no engine noise and no telltale swell that indicated another boat nearby. I'm so sorry, Abe," Bobby repeated, his voice heavy with remorse.

"Have you contacted the police yet?" Abe inquired.

"No. I'm about to do that right now."

"Alright, make the call, and I'll stay here with you. I want to ensure Janet's body is taken to the morgue promptly."

"What about her family? Who will inform them?"

"Don't worry. You handle the police, and I'll take care of the rest."

Abe retraced his steps to find Maria, who remained in a daze beside Janet's lifeless form. He firmly grasped her shoulders and lifted her up. "Maria, we need to take control here. Janet doesn't have anyone else in San Souci. I'll handle the police and the arrangements for the morgue. Your task is to contact Jenna and inform her. I'd prefer not to deal with Janet's family, and I want to keep my role discreet. So, please call Jenna now. Stay in touch with me, and if there's anything you require, don't hesitate to ask. Our priority is being there for Janet."

"I'm aware that you were once in love with her, Abe, and that her family didn't approve. Janet didn't share much with me, but it's clear many people are upset with how the Ramphals treated their daughter."

"You don't have the full story, Maria. Now isn't the time to delve into the past. All I'm requesting is that you maintain close contact with her family. I'll ensure Janet's arrangements are taken care of. I'll keep you informed of every step, and you can let them believe you're taking the lead. Please, do this not just for me but for your friend."

Wiping her tears, Maria nodded, comprehension in her gaze, even as a fresh stream of tears flowed down her cheeks.

With Hari's assistance, Abe efficiently handled all the necessary procedures to cooperate with the police and to have Dr. Fernando, the island's doctor, certify Janet's passing. He completed the payment for the morgue services to transport Janet's body. Abe explained to the morgue staff that Janet was visiting from Canada, and her city-residing siblings would eventually communicate with them to arrange burial details. He anticipated that it might take some time for her family to contact the morgue. In the interim, he provided Maria Stanton's name as the contact for any further arrangements.

Abe marveled at his ability to function, his mind seemingly guiding him through the necessary tasks. Before he knew it, the day had passed, and the sun was beginning to set. Weary, upon returning home, he realized Maria had attempted to reach him five times. He chided himself for forgetting to turn on his phone's ringer. Calling Maria back, he greeted her, "Hello, Maria, it's Abe. How are you holding up?" He could sense her ongoing tears.

"I spoke with Jenna, and she's utterly devastated. She's struggling to inform Jack. She's coming tomorrow morning with her family. She asked me to reserve a room for them at the guest house, which I've done. She's trying to reach Janet's husband to inform him of Janet's passing and to discuss the follow-up arrangements. Oh, Abe, Janet and I shared breakfast this very morning, and now she's gone. I can't believe it!" Maria's voice broke as fresh sobs overtook her. After a pause, she resumed, "Could you come over this evening? I've invited people who know the Ramphals to gather at my house. We'll hold nightly prayers and keep a vigil until the funeral."

"Thank you, Maria, but I believe I'll keep my distance. You know how the Ramphals might react if I'm involved. I don't want to add any complications. I don't want anyone to speak ill of Janet."

"Did she spend yesterday with you, Abe? I don't mean to pry, but for your sake, I hope you were the friend she mentioned she was visiting."

A lengthy silence followed before Maria heard his sobs and his shattered words. "Let the past rest, Maria. If you need my assistance with anything… anything at all, please don't hesitate to ask. Goodbye for now." His voice trembled as he hung up. Abe sat at the edge of his bed, then knelt down. This time, he wasn't making a request of God; he was questioning Him. His questions mingled with anguished groans. "Why, Janet, God? She did nothing wrong. It was me. She was going home to be a better wife... a better person. Why did you punish her for my mistakes? I'm the one who doesn't deserve to live. Why don't you take me now?" His fists pounded the floor, striking the bed, his grief echoing like the crashing of a tidal wave. Drained and weary, he collapsed onto the floor and remained there until dawn heralded a new day.

Chapter 24

It was exactly nine days since Janet had passed. Today marked the occasion of her funeral, and her family had collectively decided against taking her body back to Canada. Instead, they had chosen the serene island of San Souci as her final resting place - where her parents also had been laid to rest. This island held a special place in Janet's heart. The funeral service was held in the small, quaint church that stood adjacent to the cemetery, the very same church that had previously hosted the funeral ceremonies for both of Janet's parents. The church was packed to capacity, with many individuals even gathering outside its walls. Among the attendees were those who may not have known Janet on a personal level, yet they were present to extend their respects to Daniel Ramphal, a man who had left an indelible mark on numerous lives. The Ramphal family still retained a place of affection in the memories of the island's inhabitants.

At the rear of the crowded church stood Abe, making a conscious effort to blend into the background. His primary aim was to evade notice from the Ramphal family members. Particularly, he hoped to avoid catching Jenna's eye, fearing that her interpretation might inaccurately suggest that Janet had spent her time in San Souci with him despite the fact that she had stayed with Maria. Abe couldn't shake the feeling that, even after the passage of numerous years, very little had changed with regard to his relationship with Janet's family. He continued to perceive himself as an unwelcome presence whenever the Ramphals were around. In his various visits from Canada, he had crossed paths with Jack and Jenna on several occasions. However, their interactions never ventured beyond the realm of casual greetings and brief inquiries about his well-being.

All of a sudden, a silence fell over the church, and every gaze turned towards the entrance. Janet's family was making their way in. Leading the group was a tall, unfamiliar figure whom Abe assumed was Janet's husband. Following closely were three graceful women - her daughters. As he watched, his breath caught as he focused on one of the daughters, whom he could tell was the eldest. She bore an uncanny resemblance to Janet herself. Abe couldn't help but imagine this was how Janet might have appeared at the age of forty. He knew the daughter's age since Janet had shared this with him when she had talked about her children with such fondness. The young woman's eyes scanned the crowd at the back of the church. Grief marked the lines of her mouth, yet her eyes, so gentle and keen, mirrored Janet's own. In a fleeting instant, her gaze locked onto Abe, and he felt as though she were peering directly into his soul. Their eyes held each other's for a few heartbeats. At that moment, Abe was bewildered, almost believing that Janet hadn't really passed but was standing here, retracing the steps she had once taken to bid farewell to her parents in this very church. His eyes welled up, and Janet's daughter caught sight of his sorrow-stricken expression and the tears that flowed without restraint. Did he perceive a question in her eyes? Abe couldn't be sure.

The fleeting moment passed as she continued down the aisle, settling beside her father and siblings at the front of the gathering. Following them, Janet's siblings and their families also made their way to the front-row seats in the church. Jenna, accompanied by her husband and two daughters, walked by, her tears absorbed by a crumpled tissue. Then came Jack, confined in a wheelchair, his arms and head still covered with bandages and a cast enveloped his right leg. His face appeared gaunt, bearing signs of considerable weight loss. His wife pushed the wheelchair while their two sons trailed behind. Abe couldn't fathom how Jack had managed this journey. How had he secured medical clearance to travel in his current frail state? The front pews began to fill with not only immediate family but also members of the extended family, all facing the casket containing the earthly remains of Janet. Only her physical form remained - that was all she was now, a vessel of her former self.

"No, no, no," Abe's voice quivered in a hushed murmur. Her fate could not be reduced to a lifeless shell. What had become of the vibrant woman who once stood triumphant in her career? The same woman who had bestowed upon him a precious few days of her existence? Where was the tender Janet, radiating love and care for others, yet tragically denied the same kindness as she met her untimely end within the tumultuous currents of the river?

With a heart heavy and a mind clouded, he fled the church, desperate to escape the oppressive warmth that constricted his lungs. The air, once stifling, now rushed past him in a cathartic release as he stood outside the door. Yet, the aroma of frangipani and island orchids hung in the atmosphere, an almost suffocating reminder of death. Understanding now why Janet had held a sorrowful connection to these blossoms, Abe couldn't imagine ever shaking off their scent. It would always remind him of the day when his world crumbled - a memory that would forever haunt him. This agony, he thought, surpassed even the impending embrace of his death, promising him at least an escape from thought and emotion.

For now, however, he was condemned to exist within the confines of this all-encompassing pain. As though in mourning, the plaintive notes of the church's organ reverberated through the air, a haunting melody that seemed to beckon him. Drawn back toward the congregation, Abe felt himself being summoned to participate in Janet's final rites.

Hymns were sung, and scripture was read, but Abe barely heard a sound. An overwhelming sadness consumed him, preventing him from engaging with the service. His gaze lifted, a wistful expression in his eyes as if he anticipated glimpsing Janet watching from above. He held steadfast to the belief that the soul outlasts the body, persisting beyond death. Resurrection after life's end was a conviction he held dear, and he remained certain that Janet had transformed into an angel - nothing else could be possible. Then, her teary voice reached him from the podium at the altar. He was taken aback, his gaze rising to find her daughter poised to deliver the eulogy. Amid tears and a brave façade, she spoke of her profound love for her mother. Memories flowed - times of joy shared with her sisters under the nurturing embrace of their mother.

The narrative transitioned to Janet's roles as a mother, daughter, sibling, wife, and career woman. The daughter's voice quivered, emotion lacing her words as she recounted her mother's enduring sacrifices. These sacrifices paved the way for their education and the new life they embraced upon migrating to Canada. In this moment, the daughter's heartfelt words revealed a facet of Janet's life unseen by Abe. A life defined by challenges conquered and triumphs achieved, all driven by boundless love. As the daughter's eulogy painted this intricate portrait, Abe's sorrow deepened. He marveled at Janet's multifaceted journey, each role a testament to her unwavering love and selflessness.

Janet's daughter gazed tearfully across the congregation, her eyes once again meeting Abe's, red and moist. She observed him intently, her gaze fixed upon him. Her eyes seemed to deeply search for an understanding of the quiet and uncontrollable sobs that shook his frame. It was as though she sought to unearth the identity of this stranger, so consumed by profound grief for her mother. Afterward, her gaze shifted toward her father, who sat upright, holding the hands of her sisters. Only his fatigued countenance betrayed his feelings. His face appeared pale and worn, though no tears were shed. She had often pondered about the circumstances that might bring him to tears. Now she had her answer - her mother's passing wouldn't. True to his lifelong practice, he maintained his composure, refusing to yield to his emotions. He demonstrated his unwavering mastery over his feelings, a stance he had upheld throughout his life.

She continued, "My mother was a good woman, the best there could ever be. She would do anything to help those she cared about. She was selfless, always placing others ahead of herself. We all loved her dearly." She looked at Abe again, this time with even more directness, before she went on, "But God loved her more, and now He has called her home. We will have to find contentment in that..." Abe wasn't fully attentive to the remainder, lost in his own thoughts: Did this daughter know about him, and if so, how?

The rest of the service passed in a daze for Abe. Then came the time to lower Janet's body into its final resting place. Everyone gathered at the cemetery around the gaping hole in the earth, prepared to receive the casket. Abe stood apart, concealed behind a clump of black sage bushes. A few others joined him, opting to observe the casket's descent from a distance. "Hello, Abe," greeted a woman clad in black, holding a small parasol. "Janet has the best weather today, wouldn't you agree? It couldn't have been a more fitting day for her funeral."

"A funeral was already a bad day. Would the weather make a difference?" Abe pondered. He regarded the woman with a hint of surprise. Could there really be good and bad days for funerals? Nevertheless, he conceded, it was indeed a pleasant, warm day. At three in the afternoon, the sun beamed brightly, the sky was blue with gentle, wispy clouds, and there was no sign of the sudden rain that often drenched the island.

"Do I know you?" Abe inquired of the woman.

"I'm Kathleen ... Kathleen Serwal. You were my teacher. Janet and I were in the same class."

Abe shook her proffered hand, struggling to recollect being Kathleen's teacher. He had taught so many students over the years that it was nearly impossible to remember every individual. Yet, to avoid being offensive, he replied, "Yes, yes, I believe I remember you. Weren't you in my Shakespeare classes?"

Kathleen chuckled. "No, Janet and I were in your science classes. It feels like such a distant past... over forty years, I believe. How you can recall is beyond me! But what I do recall is that you were in love with Janet. I'm not sure why you two didn't marry. She held a deep affection for you as well. Life takes its course, though, and people move forward. I apologize if I've overstepped. I truly have no right to voice what I just did. Please accept my apologies."

"That's okay, it doesn't really matter," replied Abe. "Yes, I wanted to marry Janet, but that was such a long time ago."

"Anyway," continued Kathleen, "I'm glad you're here for her funeral. Were you on the island when the accident happened? I know you live abroad, but you must have been spending some vacation time in San Souci. Do you often come back to the island?"

Abe deliberated over which questions to address. "Yes, I do come back almost every year since I retired. It just so happened I was here when Janet had the accident. What a tragedy!"

"A great tragedy indeed," she concurred. "I'm so sorry for her daughters. They seemed to have had such a close-knit family. I can't imagine what it's like for them to return to San Souci for their mother's funeral. She must have bid them a routine goodbye when she left. Never did they imagine she wouldn't return…"

Abe was reluctant to delve into Janet's family matters with Kathleen, but he struggled to find a way to end the uncomfortable conversation gracefully. As he racked his brain for a suitable response, his thoughts were abruptly interrupted by the piercing wails of an older woman whom, at first, he couldn't place. She bore a resemblance to Bernice Ramphal, Janet's mother. Gradually, Abe realized that she must be Janet's aunt, Bernice's sister. He vaguely remembered seeing her during her visits to the Ramphal family in years gone by. She had relocated to Barbados but would occasionally come to spend time with her sister and the rest of the family. Abe could recall their strolls along the beach and their trips to the local market. Aunt Gloria's anguished display included beating her chest, collapsing to the ground, and uttering incoherent statements. Amid her mourning, Abe managed to catch one fragment: "It's good that Bernice did not live to see this day." The sobbing and lamentation persisted.

"That's Janet's aunt," Kathleen affirmed, indicating the distressed woman with a nod of her head.

As the gathering continued, more individuals sought refuge from the sun beneath the trees. Abe stepped backward to provide more room. His attention was drawn to the slow descent of the casket into the earth. Janet's daughters openly wept, with the younger one unable to contain her grief. She sought solace in her father's embrace, holding him tightly as he tried to console her. Abe grappled with a mixture of emotions, wondering what Janet's husband was feeling. He was certain that having shared the past forty-plus years with Janet, her passing would leave an indelible mark of devastation.

With the casket now lowered completely into the ground, the priest summoned Janet's husband to initiate the process of covering the open grave with earth from a nearby mound. He gently released his daughter and walked over to the mound, scooping up two handfuls of soil, which he then cast onto the casket. Abe could distinctly hear the thud of the earth making contact with the wood. Following suit, the three sisters stepped forward, the younger one supported by the eldest. Subsequently, Jenna, Jack, and their families took their turn. Jenna had brought pink roses, and she and her family scattered them atop the lowered casket.

Abe observed all of this through a lens of indescribable pain. Each thud of earth and petals against the casket felt like a blow to his heart, leaving him gasping for air. The act seemed to extract his breath from his body. Gradually, the grave became covered, and the cemetery workers approached to provide the final touches, smoothing the soil over Janet's resting place. As attendees began to disperse, heading to the family's reception hosted in the church hall a short distance away across the road from the cemetery, Abe, too, took his leave. He navigated through the dispersing crowd, ensuring he maintained a respectful distance from the Ramphal family.

He made his way straight home, ascending the stairs and entering the kitchen in search of the gardening shears that he habitually stored in a locked drawer. Retrieving the shears and his watering can, he ventured into the flower garden, meticulously scouring the rose plants for the finest red roses within reach. With a gentle touch, he snipped them one by one, carefully placing each blossom in the can until he had amassed a generous two dozen. Proceeding with care, he deftly removed excess leaves and trimmed the stems as best he could. He scoured the house to find something suitable with which to tie the roses together. After nearly twenty minutes of sifting through drawers and cupboards, his persistence yielded a length of white ribbon lace. "This is perfect," he murmured to himself. "This is my bouquet for Jan." The process of tying and re-tying the ribbon around the stems of the roses occupied him for a short while until he was content with the result.

In a bid to avoid drawing any unwelcome attention, Abe concealed the bouquet in a shopping bag and retraced his steps back to the cemetery. He surmised that by this point, everyone would have departed for the reception, and his assumption was right. Upon reaching the cemetery, an air of emptiness pervaded. Ensuring utmost caution, he ventured beneath the cover of the black sage bushes, an extra measure to guarantee he remained unseen. He scanned the surroundings, back and forth, to be certain that no lingering observers remained. It was plausible that Janet's husband might have desired a solitary moment after everyone else had departed, yet the cemetery stood now utterly abandoned. Abe had the entire expanse to himself. "Good," he sighed with relief. "Thank heavens there's nobody here."

Approaching the grave, fresh soil recently strewn, he retrieved the bouquet of red roses from its concealed confines within the bag. With a reverent stoop, he tenderly placed the flowers at the head of the grave. Tears flowed anew. "Jan, Jan," he sobbed, his voice a lament, "why did you depart ahead of me? Fate should have claimed me, not you. Why did this tragedy happen? Why? Oh, why?" Although his words emerged as mere whispers, it felt as if even the heavens were attuned to his grief. Kneeling upon the damp earth, he continued, "My dear Jan, I feel so responsible for your death. I feel like this should not have happened if you did not come to see me. What can I ever do to make this right?" The sobs shook his entire frame. He wept openly and unashamedly, and his tears flowed freely.

Suddenly, a shadow fell over Abe's shoulders. He sensed the presence of someone else. He became instantly alert, fearing that it might be Janet's husband or Jenna returning, seeking solitude with her departed sister. He cautiously rose from his kneeling position, pivoting to gaze behind him. To his surprise, it was Janet's daughter, the very one who had regarded him with that knowing look earlier. Her eyes bore the telltale signs of recent tears, a solitary red rose cradled in her hand. She fixed her gaze upon Abe, her voice soft as she spoke, "I held an immense love for her… and I brought her the most exquisite red rose to convey that affection. It seems you held a profound love for her, too." With a tender gesture, she placed her solitary red rose alongside his gathered bunch.

Abe was overcome with emotions, rendered speechless and immobile. The daughter met his gaze once more. "I'm grateful that there existed someone out there who truly loved her … just as much as I did… just as much as anyone could have. She truly deserved that love." Battling back a sob, she turned swiftly and made her way from the cemetery, leaving Abe in a state of profound grief and confusion, his throat tight and his heart heavy.

Abe yearned to call out, to beckon Janet's daughter to return, to inquire about her cryptic words. However, as if struck silent by an invisible force, he stood fixed in place, bereft of speech and motion. It wasn't until he managed to regain his composure that he found his voice again, yet by then, Janet's daughter had vanished from sight. Left alone with his contemplations, Abe wandered back to his dwelling. He poured a glass of water and settled into his hammock on the back porch, though even the water refused to ease his parched throat. Exhausted by his emotional turmoil, he surrendered to sleep.

As the hours slipped away and darkness descended like a drawn curtain, Hari arrived to check on Abe and to invite him over for dinner. "Uncle Abe," Hari's voice resonated, piercing the silence. "Uncle Abe, where are you?"

Abe jolted awake, his senses fully engaged. His muscles throbbed with discomfort, a testament to the intermittent medication he had been relying on over the past several days, merely enough to sustain him. With the compounded weight of Janet's demise - both emotionally and physically - Abe experienced a disturbing sensation of his body's faculties slipping from his grasp. He made a gradual attempt to extricate himself from the hammock, his movements sluggish. The encompassing darkness enveloped him, and his weariness was palpable. Lifting his gaze to the dark expanse of the sky, he was met with a multitude of stars, each one shimmering with its own distant light. Yet, amid the celestial sea, one star shone evidently brighter, standing out from the rest and seeming to wink at him. He wondered if he was really awake or if he was still dreaming. He touched his cheeks and felt his tears mingling with the moist night air, assurance that he was not asleep. The stars up in the sky were real. In a hushed murmur, he asked of the winking star, "Is that you, Jan? Can you see me? Can you hear me?" His voice was barely more than a whisper. "Please wait for me, Jan. I'll be coming to you soon. The river may have taken you away from me, but time will reunite us once more."

Rosetta Khalideen's literary journey has given birth to captivating short stories and poems.

Made in United States
Troutdale, OR
12/08/2023